THE SKELETH

BOOK 2
OF THE NETHERGRIM EPIC

THE SKELETH

BOOK 2
OF THE NETHERGRIM EPIC

MATTHEW JOBIN

PHILOMEL BOOKS

My heartfelt thanks to Timothy King and to Melodie Yen for their invaluable assistance in the creation of the Dhanic language and the other languages in the series.

PHILOMEL BOOKS
an imprint of Penguin Random House LLC
375 Hudson Street, New York, NY 10014

Copyright © 2016 by Matthew Jobin. Map copyright © 2016 by David Elliot.
Penguin supports copyright. Copyright fuels creativity, encourages diverse voices, promotes free speech, and creates a vibrant culture. Thank you for buying an authorized edition of this book and for complying with copyright laws by not reproducing, scanning, or distributing any part of it in any form without permission. You are supporting writers and allowing Penguin to continue to publish books for every reader.

Philomel Books is a registered trademark of Penguin Random House LLC.

Library of Congress Cataloging-in-Publication Data is available upon request.
Printed in the United States of America.
ISBN 978-0-399-15999-2
1 3 5 7 9 10 8 6 4 2
Edited by Michael Green.
Design by Semadar Megged.
Text set in 12.5-point Fiesole Text.

This is a work of fiction. Names, characters, places, and incidents either are the product of the author's imagination or are used fictitiously, and any resemblance to actual persons, living or dead, businesses, companies, events, or locales is entirely coincidental.

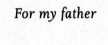

For my father

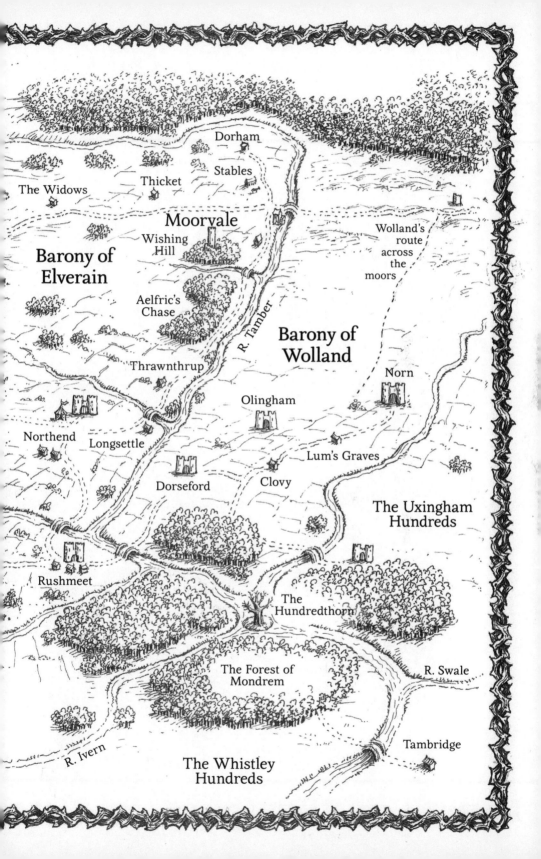

All truly wise thoughts have been thought before;
what is necessary is only to try to think them again.

—Johann Wolfgang von Goethe

Prologue

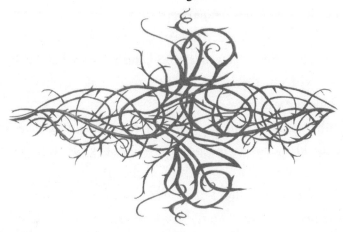

Katherine. Wake up, child."

Katherine opened her eyes. "I'm awake, Papa."

Her father let go of her shoulder. "It's started." He turned and strode from her tiny bedroom.

"Has she broken?" Katherine sat up in the twisted mess of her blankets. Her rag-doll horse tumbled out onto the floor.

"Not yet." Her father leaned over the fire in the hearth, in the room just past her bedroom door. He held out his hands to the warmth—deep orange light traced every line of his palm. "She's down on her side, though. It won't be long."

Katherine reached for her boots and pulled them on over her breeches. "Who was that man, Papa, the one who came by just after dark? I've never seen him before."

Her father made no answer. She watched him through the narrow, crooked doorway of her bedroom. The fire did no more than edge the shadows of the walls around him. He plucked out something from his belt and turned it over on his palm: a worn old silver penny marked with cuts and slashes on both sides.

She got to her feet. "Papa?"

He shut his hand over the coin. "Soot's been up and down three times, child—pawed at the bedding, had her lip back." He turned from the hearth. "She's ready. We shouldn't leave her alone for long."

Katherine rolled up her blankets in a ball and stepped from her bedroom. She turfed down the embers of the fire, then turned to find her father holding out her thickest cloak.

"Every time you stand up, you're taller." He placed the cloak around her shoulders. "You'll pass me before you're done."

"I don't want to get much taller, Papa."

"It's your mother in you. She never minded it." He pushed back the door and she followed him out.

Katherine's back drew in tight against the cold outside. A late frost crunched underfoot. Clouds spindled out in strips beneath the stars. The wind blew sharp from the mountains— it took loose locks of her long dark hair and whipped them in her eyes.

She took a few jogging strides to come level with her father on the path down to the stables. "When did we breed her, Papa?"

"The last full moon before the planting."

"She's early. Especially for a colt."

"I know. You're right again, Katherine—you always are about these things." Her father pulled his cloak around his arms. "Five fillies in a row, child, five new mares for breeding but not a single warhorse. Lord Aelfric will not be pleased."

Katherine stepped into the stable behind him and tucked her wind-thrown hair behind her ears. Pigeons flapped between the rafters above. Two rows of heads poked out over the doors of the stalls along the central passage of the stable—not a single horse slept despite the lateness and the dark. Yarrow whickered, seeking for a pet on the nose. Butterburr looked to want the same, but Katherine knew that she would try to nip. Poor old Clover could not rest with all the stirring; she let out a snort, ears cocked toward the birthing stall at the far end of the stable.

Katherine's father took up the lantern from the door. Its glow picked out the gray from the brown in his beard and showed her a face creased with the sort of look he got when he stared at the wall all night, lost somewhere she could not follow.

Katherine hated it when he got that look. "Papa, what is it?"

"It's a big foal. Very big." He drew back the door to the birthing stall, and there within lay Soot, a horse as black as the gaps between the stars, down on her side in the straw with her legs out and rigid, hooves twitching with every breath.

Katherine dropped to her knees in the straw of the stall, her stomach sinking. She had started helping her father with the foalings when she was seven and had come to know a hard one when she saw it. Soot jerked her head up and back in time with her grunts. Her coat had taken on a sheen of sweat—the stall smelled of it, smelled of fear. The swelling in her belly looked all wrong.

Katherine's father hung up the lantern and plunged his hands into the bucket of water in the corner; it made Katherine shiver just to see it. He crouched down by Soot's hindquarters. Soot twitched—her next grunt was a groan.

"Hush. Hush now, all is well." Katherine put a hand to Soot's cheek. "Papa, she's hurting."

Her father sat back. He put his clean hand to his forehead.

"Papa?"

He looked up at her. "It's a breech. The foal's backward."

Katherine cradled Soot's head. "Is it alive?"

"Tried to bite me, just now."

"Can you turn it, Papa? Can you get it out?"

"I don't know," said her father. "Biggest foal I've ever felt in a mare her size, and it's an awful tangle in there. I can't work out where to start."

Soot's back bunched, the whole of her pulsed in an effort to push out the foal. She strained and contracted, strained again, then released. Katherine's father tensed and tried to turn the foal, set his shoulders and tried again. He breathed out a snort through his nose; so did Soot. He let go.

"Papa, her water's broken." Katherine felt along Soot's flank—a big foal, huge, kicking and struggling; helpless, all wrong. "We've got to birth the foal soon or we'll lose it. We might lose them both."

"Curse me for the worst of fools," said her father. "I knew we shouldn't have bred her to Break-spear for her first—but Lord Aelfric wants his great warhorses, wants his new blood. Curse me for a fool and him for a knave."

Katherine ran a hand through the mare's sodden mane. "You can do it, Soot. You can. Please don't give up."

"Yes, come, girl. Come, Soot. We'll do it together." Her father got up on his knees and strained with careful effort for a long, long time, pulling, shifting and pulling again. The other horses whickered and stamped. One of the barn cats paced by the stall, looked in on the proceedings, then kept on with his nightly rounds.

Soot let out another groan, softer than before. Her contractions slowed and weakened. She sank exhausted in the straw, her gaze withdrawn from the world.

"Please keep trying." Katherine rubbed under Soot's chin. "You can do it, keep trying. Please."

"Katherine." Her father kept his head low. "Please go and get the slaughter mallet."

Katherine's belly gave a lurch. "Papa, no!"

"We can't let this go on, child. We cannot let them suffer." Her father sucked in a breath and tried again, but his voice spoke defeat.

"Please, Papa!"

"Get the mallet, Katherine. You don't have to stay."

"No!" Katherine got up and ran from the stable. The wind greeted her face with a slap. She sank down on an old stump by the wall and wrapped her arms around her middle.

Clouds slid hissing through the sky. Night proceeded in its fall toward the moment of its deepest chill. The moon rose in a slow arc at the horizon, the first crescent of spring.

Katherine's father stepped out into the cold. Blood traced in runnels down his hands, dripping from the ends of his fingers. "Come inside, child."

"No, Papa, please. I can't."

"Come." He led her inside and down the passage. It felt like some appointed cruelty, some hard lesson about hope, about death. He opened the door to the birthing stall.

The foal raised its head, its ears pricked up high, slick with the fluids of its birth.

"Papa!" Katherine seized her father's hand, bloody though it was. "Papa, you did it!"

"They did it." Her father leaned against the door. "I don't even know if I helped. All of a sudden, it just happened."

Soot stood up, snapping the cord between her belly and the foal. She turned and bent her head to lick its dark fur.

"You were wrong, Katherine." There was a note of teasing triumph in her father's voice. "A colt, a boy—and a big, strong one. He's bound to be a warhorse of the first rank or I'm the Duke of Westry. Lord Aelfric will be pleased with us after all."

Soot licked her foal clean with careful vigor, then she lowered her head and gave him a nudge with her nose. The foal let out an indignant snort, but his mother persisted, so after a few more pushes he made an attempt to stand. He cranked his untested muscles and propped up his rump on his gangly hind legs—then looked at a loss for what to do next. He scrabbled his forelegs through the straw and tried to lever himself to all fours, but succeeded only in collapsing the lean-to he had made for his rear end and crashing back to the ground. Katherine laughed—her father laughed.

The foal shook his head, blew hard through his nose, and got his hind legs raised again with such speed that the motion seemed powered by embarrassment. Then, with his mother supporting him, he stood up on all four of his tiny hooves. His mother turned around, and with sure swiftness he found a teat and began to feed.

"I'll never get tired of seeing that," said Katherine's father. "Not if I see it a thousand times."

The foal tottered over to Katherine with his mother close behind. The lantern wavered, deepening the coaly darkness of his coat, gray falling to black through a shadowed hint of blue. He looked up at Katherine, tiny and frail—and bold, springing upon the world as though a blast of trumpets had announced him. She felt a shiver; from the ground, from her feet to her eyes.

She reached out her hand. "Your name is Indigo."

Chapter 1

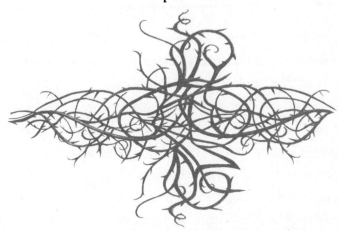

L et the light of the stars descend." Edmund Bale held
forth his hand, indicating the place where the spell
should begin. "Stars, attend me. Surround me. Let your
light descend."

Nothing happened. Edmund sighed and turned to light a
torch.

**How can you know what light is, if you do not know
what darkness is?**

Edmund startled and dropped the torch in the moorspike
grass. "How many times do I have to tell you?" He reached out,
scratching his hands against the toothy leaves, and retrieved
it only just before he set the land around him ablaze. "I'm not
listening. Go away."

He drove the torch upright into the earth beside him and
sat down on the spread of blankets he had used to make his
seat. He found his place in the book he had brought with
him, turning the parchment page to catch the torchlight, and

started reading the passage he had marked the night before: *The Nethergrim has taken many shapes and guises through the ages of the world. Ever and again does it rise to—*

Edmund. The Voice came without sound, like a thought that Edmund could not recognize as his own. **I am right here. Why search a book to learn about me?**

"Because you lie." Edmund could not work out why the Voice sometimes came to him as words, sometimes the fleeting ghosts of unfamiliar feelings, and sometimes merely a hanging presence, the sense that something was watching him from just over his shoulder. He had gathered all the books he could find to help him learn and understand, but that did not amount to much. He was, after all, just a fourteen-year-old boy, the son of peasant innkeepers, and the village where he lived stood at the crossroads of nothing and nowhere.

Ever and again does it rise to throw down the works of men. The letters scribed upon the parchment page seemed to float in the orange flicker. *Slay one form, and it takes another. Defend against its claws, and fall victim to its honeyed smile. I lacked the power to halt this eternal cycle, but I could slow it long enough that others might one day do what I could not. If destroying the body of the Nethergrim could do it no lasting harm, then I would trap it in a sleep of centuries. I—*

How I have longed to hear the sweet music of your thoughts once again. The Voice felt the same as it had beneath the mountain, amongst the swirling smoke before the seven-pointed star. **Wayward though you are, still you find your way back to me. I can only think that this means you care.**

Edmund plugged his ears, even though he knew it was useless. "Go away. Just go away."

But I have missed you, child. Have you not missed me?

"No!"

Edmund. The Voice seemed somehow both near and far, inside his thoughts while at the same time feeling as though it had come from between the distant stars above. Do you truly wish to learn the art of magic?

"Not from you." Edmund shut the book, then shut his eyes. Sometimes, if he concentrated, he could make the Voice recede and tease out his own thoughts from the thoughts it tried to worm into his mind.

It is a simple thing, at heart, said the Voice. Consider again, child—can you know what light is, if you do not know what darkness is?

Edmund started to make a retort, but the idea the Voice had planted took root within him.

It might help you to imagine that you were born blind, and that everyone you knew was also blind. How then would you know that what you saw was darkness?

"I suppose I wouldn't know." Edmund shook his head. "Does that make me stupid?"

Not for one of your kind. Open your eyes, Edmund.

Edmund did so. He half expected to see the form the Nethergrim had taken in its chamber in the mountains—coils twisting within coils, mouths and eyes bubbling forth from a roll of smoke. Instead he saw only his burning torch, his book and blankets, and beyond that the moonlight touching gray upon the rises of the dead and empty moors.

Take up your cup, Edmund. Fill it with water. Hold it to the light.

Edmund reached for the stoppered jug he had taken from home and poured out some water into an earthen mug. All the while, something in him told him to stop, to disobey the Voice, but at the same time something else told him to listen and learn.

Touch the water, spoke the Voice. Watch the waves.

Edmund touched a fingertip to the surface. The waves spread in ripples around it, stuttering in the torchlight.

What do you call a wave that has a crest, but not a trough? A top, but no bottom?

Edmund considered. "Nothing. There is no such thing."

Then what is a wave?

Edmund sat watching the waves dissipate, dying to a glassy flatness. He tried to find the words—he could not, but he could find the thought. A feeling of certainty grew in him, a tingle on his neck that was more than the icy touch of the wind.

Douse the torch, Edmund.

Edmund poured out the water over the torch, then ground it in the dirt, frightened all the while by his obedience. "Why are you telling me all this? Why are you trying to teach me?"

Look to your right.

Edmund faced south, so turning to his right meant looking west. In that direction he saw his home, the village of Moorvale. It was as much memory as sight that shaped its familiar outline in the dark, its thatch-and-timber houses huddled in by the bridge at the bend of the great river Tamber. Everyone in the village had long gone to bed, exhausted from their labors gathering in the last of the harvest. Not even his own home, his parents' inn where he lived and worked, showed a glimmer of flame—but that was no surprise, for he had only been able to slip out once all the guests had left the tavern and his father had closed up for the night.

Now consider, Edmund. When you looked to your right, what did you also do?

Edmund ignored the Voice. He gazed up past his shadowed village, westward to Wishing Hill and to the ruined keep where his whole life had changed two weeks before. Beyond that stood the starlit peaks of the Girth, the mountains where he had fought against the Nethergrim and won. He had found a way to break a spell devised between the world's most celebrated wizard and the Nethergrim herself. If he could do that, he wondered, then why could he not call down light?

Edmund.

"I heard you," said Edmund. "I understand what you are asking me. If I look to my right, I look away from my left. If I face to the west, I turn away from the east."

Thus speak the masters of *Dhrakal*, the wizards whose works you so adore. All things have their needful opposites. Light needs darkness. The dawn carries with it certain knowledge of the dusk. You can have what you want, but you must always pay for it. Now—understand, and try again.

Edmund found the balance in his mind. He reached forth to tip it. "LET THE LIGHT OF THE STARS DESCEND. I GRIP THE SLEEVE OF NIGHT. STARS, ATTEND ME." He lowered his hand, indicating the place. "DESCEND."

The sky above him warped, and the stars turned their faces, casting their cool and indifferent glow upon the little heathered hollow where he sat. It was not much, just enough for reading. The night beyond grew just a little blacker, a little deeper—a simple cost for a simple spell, straight across the Wheel from Light to Darkness.

There, said the Voice. **Not so very hard, after all.**

"Now get lost." Edmund took up his book and spread it out across his lap. "I'm trying to find a way to kill you."

Edmund. You never looked east.

"Why should I?" Edmund turned his head, even as he spoke. "There's nothing that way except—"

What Edmund had meant to say next was that there was nothing to his east except for empty moors. What he had meant to say next was that eastward, from where he sat, there were but barren rolls of ground choked with weeds and moorspike, with hardly a tree to break up the monotony all the way to the horizon. What he had meant to say was that there was nothing to see in that direction, for no one had gone three rises east of the Moorvale Bridge from time out of memory. Instead he said nothing, because he saw something he did not expect.

Edmund leapt to his feet. "Is that torchlight?" He peered eastward—another torch appeared behind the first, and then they both began slowly to descend, as though their carriers had crested a rise on the great West Road, and now followed its path down into the hollow.

Your book speaks truth, Edmund. The tone of the Voice changed, seeming to taunt him. **I have indeed taken many**

forms in this world. It is also true that I have many ways of working my will upon it.

"Who is that?" Edmund forgot that he was speaking with the Nethergrim, the being that had stolen away the lives of two children before his eyes. "No one takes the West Road in from the moors. No one comes from that way—not ever."

You know that I was not destroyed, there within the mountain. You know, in the deepest part of yourself, that I cannot be destroyed.

Edmund let the light of his spell go out, the better to see the lights upon the moors. The glow of the torches lit what looked like men on horseback, and even in the deep of night their garments marked them out as men of noble rank, coats of arms laid over mail armor, woad blue and madder crimson, the glint of steel and cloth of gold.

"What is it that you want?" Edmund spoke as though the Nethergrim stood beside him. "What is it that you are trying to do?"

This much is certain, Edmund Bale. If you carry on against me, I will be your death.

Edmund clenched his fists. "I will find a way to stop you. This I swear."

No reply came, save for the wind.

"Do you hear me?" Edmund did not know why he looked upward at the stars, since he was not at all sure where the Nethergrim was, if it could in truth be said to be anywhere at all. "I will fight you and I will beat you!"

Into the answering silence crept a sound, a rustle in the

moorspike from the dark along the road. Edmund tensed. "Who's there?" He drew his knife—a work knife, short and single-edged, made for whittling and carving more than fighting.

The rustling sound shifted, seeming to come from behind him. He whirled about with his knife raised high, but even as he did so, hands flashed forth from the gloom, and words rained down upon him: "I GRANT THE CURSE OF PEACE."

With a clear, high pinging sound, the blade of Edmund's knife snapped in half, the point falling to drop amongst the grass. A figure emerged from the shadows, a girl of perhaps fifteen, in a dove-gray dress and dark hair bound up beneath a hood. "I'm sorry about the spell. Are you Edmund Bale? The Wizard of Moorvale?"

Edmund scrabbled backward and tripped in the moorspike. "What's it to you?"

The girl approached. She looked around her. "Who were you talking to?"

Edmund stared up at the girl. She was not quite what he would call pretty, but he could not help looking long at her, not least because each of her two large eyes was a completely different color—one brown, the other a glimmering blue.

"I saw your light." The girl's voice had a sweetness to it, with just the trace of a rolling accent. "Were you waiting for me? Is that why you're out here—did you know I was coming?"

Edmund got to his feet. "Who are you?"

The girl drew back her hood. "My name is Elísalon, but folk in the north just call me Ellí." Long, straight hair slipped free to hang in tresses as black as the surrounding sky. "Is it true,

Edmund? Did you truly fight the Nethergrim? Did you see it, did you face it down?"

That forced a laugh from Edmund, though the sound died lonely on the moors. "I wouldn't call it facing her down, exactly—but, yes, I saw her, and I fought her as best I could."

"Help me." The girl drew near, hands clasped and held out as though to beg. "Please. I'm trying to fight it, too, but if they find out what I'm trying to do, they will . . ." She trembled.

Edmund watched the girl in silence. No matter how long he looked at her, he could see nothing but her fear.

The girl turned to look east, toward the torches and the riders on the distant rise of moor. "Please, I'm scared. I'm all alone."

"I will help you." To Edmund's ears, his own voice had never sounded so deep, so measured and assured. "Tell me how."

Chapter 2

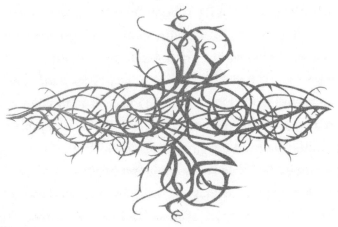

T he page boy looked Katherine up and down—but mostly up. He poked his head through the door behind him. "My lord? It's Katherine." He waited. "Katherine, my lord—the marshal's daughter."

At a muttered reply, he made a sweeping bow. He turned back to Katherine. "Go on in, then." He drew the door wide. "But you'd best not anger him."

Katherine picked up the skirts of her good blue dress. She limped across the threshold with her weight on her uninjured leg. "My lord, I am here at your summons."

Her lord did not answer, and neither did anyone else in the room. Tapestries graced every inch of wall, trapping the heat of the well-tended fire in the hearth. Scribes and clerks stared up at Katherine from their seats around a table strewn with ledger books, inkwells, piles of coin and a set of fine brass scales. Servants stood ready to attend the table with ewers of wine and a plate of sweetmeats, but no one looked hungry.

"You sent for me, my lord?" Katherine made a slow curtsy with her bandaged leg held carefully straight in front of her.

No answer came. The scribes kept to their work. Katherine flicked a glance at the table, stunned by the glint of more silver and gold than she had seen in the whole of her life.

"My lord." One of Lord Aelfric's household guards leaned out from where he stood beside the wall. He put one hand to the back of the largest chair. "John Marshal's daughter—she's here."

Lord Aelfric of Elverain sat hunched over the vellum scroll that he held in wrinkled hands adorned with silver rings. He did not turn to Katherine, nor speak, so she stood up straight again, and composed herself in the best dignity she could muster.

One of the younger clerks spoke under his breath. "Didn't someone say that this girl was supposed to be pretty?" His fellows took up snickering, until the chamberlain glared them all back to silence.

Katherine shifted her weight onto her good leg and felt at the lump of the bandage under the skirts of her dress. She had feared that the slash that crossed her thigh would never heal right, but Tom had tended it so well on their way home from the mountains that it only ached when she climbed stairs or stood in one place for too long. All in all, it could have been much worse.

"Has Squire Harold not yet returned?" Katherine took a look around her, as though the one person she had hoped would be in the room had somehow escaped her notice. She tried and failed to get Lord Aelfric's attention. "Your son, my lord, is he still not back from the south?"

The castle guard shot her a narrow look and answered in the place of his lord. "What business is it of yours?"

Lord Aelfric chewed his lip, his gaze fixed upon the scroll before him. He had a long, sharp face, little softened by his beard. White hairs grew in tufts from his ears, while above his eyes his straggled brows preserved what little brown he still possessed. Light from the arrow-slit window shone through the scroll from behind and showed Katherine that the words written upon it were handsomely scribed, though few in number.

Katherine waited for as long as she could stand it. She raised her voice just a little. "My lord, I ask you to take some thought for your horses."

Lord Aelfric cast a chilly glance up at her.

"The horses, my lord—the breeding mares from the farm my father keeps for you." Katherine waited for a reply, but when none came, she could not stop herself from going on. "They are not well tended, here at the castle, and neither are their young. If the yearlings and foals are not turned out onto open ground soon, they will not thrive. They will not grow into horses fit for war."

Lord Aelfric returned to the scroll, as though nothing had been said. He seemed to be reading it over and over again.

"Mind your place, girl." The castle guard spoke through clenched teeth. "You'll speak when you're spoken to, and not else!"

After a time Lord Aelfric seemed to rouse himself. He fixed a look on Katherine. "Sit." He gestured to the chair directly across from his own. The young scribe seated there gathered up his books and stood.

"Leave me. All of you." Aelfric waved a hand and the rest followed suit, pushing their parchments into piles and laying tasseled bookmarks in the ledgers before snapping them shut. The chamberlain poured handfuls of coins into velvet bags and stacked them tightly in a wooden coffer. Katherine lowered herself into the chair and let her head droop in a pose of deference.

"My lord." The guard bowed as he followed the clerks from the chamber. He closed the door behind him.

Silence fell thick between Katherine and her lord. She looked down into the polished brass of the scales and winced at what she saw. The reflected light brought out the weary circles under her eyes. She had put on her only good dress for her summons to the castle, but her hair was a knotted tangle that looked as though it had been arranged in the dark. Too many nights filled with too many nightmares—too many terrors that shook her from sleep.

"When your father left Elverain, where was he bound?" Lord Aelfric's sudden question made Katherine jump.

"To Lord Tristan, to his castle at Harthingdale." Katherine set her elbows on the table, leaning closer on the hope: "Have you any news of him, my lord? Any at all?"

"You were summoned here to answer, not to ask," said Lord Aelfric. "For what purpose did John Marshal make this journey?"

Katherine sat back in confusion. "I thought you knew, my lord. Papa left because of Vithric, because of the Nethergrim."

Lord Aelfric stroked his beard, deep in shadowed thought.

He glanced out the window, then over at the shelves where sat his store of musty old books. "Vithric is dead. He died many years ago."

"He is not," said Katherine. "I saw him. My papa saw him."

"You are sure it was Vithric that you saw?" Old age had robbed Lord Aelfric's voice of much of its power, but none of its tone of unyielding authority. "Think carefully."

Katherine's confusion began to turn into alarm. "He was my papa's old friend. Why would Papa lie about it?"

"Indeed." Lord Aelfric picked up the scroll again. He glanced over the words. "What cause could your father ever have to lie?"

Katherine recoiled and held herself back from a retort with some effort. She could never have imagined allowing such an insult to her father to pass unchallenged, but she had been taught all her life to honor and respect her rightful lord— indeed, it was her father who had taught her so.

"My lord, I still don't understand exactly what it was that I saw beneath that mountain." Katherine met Aelfric's searching and unfriendly gaze. "But I know that Vithric is not dead, and neither is the Nethergrim. I don't even know if a thing like the Nethergrim can truly die—I only know that it was there, that it was somehow forming anew."

Lord Aelfric fiddled with the silver chain that hung around his creased old neck. He stared out the window at the dying sun. Katherine did not know what she disliked more, the stony look he struggled to keep upon his face, or how easily and often it cracked.

"Why Tristan?" Lord Aelfric muttered the words. "Why Tristan, and why now?"

Katherine chose to answer, though she was not sure if she had in truth been asked. "I think he went to Tristan to tell him that they had failed, that everything they had suffered through thirty years ago was in vain, and that their old friend Vithric had betrayed them." She had no trouble recalling Vithric's face, a vicious man who had stolen seven children, she among them, and dragged them all before the Nethergrim to die. "If you wanted to understand what happened in the mountains, my lord, you should have summoned Edmund."

Lord Aelfric blinked. "Who?"

"Edmund. Edmund Bale, from my village." Bookish little Edmund—the son of innkeepers, and no one's idea of a hero— had come through suffering and despair, tracking Vithric and his captives through the passes of the Girth to the deep and ancient lair of the Nethergrim. Katherine warmed to think of it. "Did no one tell you, my lord? Edmund broke the spell. He saved my life, me and all the children but two." Edmund had stormed with Papa to the rescue and stepped up into Vithric's face, right up under the thrumming presence of the Nether-grim itself, and ended the spell before it could claim all its victims. If that could not be fairly called a miracle, then too much was being asked of the word.

Lord Aelfric flicked his hand. "When was the last time your father had contact with Tristan?"

Katherine searched her memory. "I don't know, my lord. Years ago."

Lord Aelfric held her in a fishy stare. "We have only your father's word that the man he saw was Vithric."

Katherine stood up flaring. "You doubt my father's word?"

Lord Aelfric set his fleshless lips. He turned pointedly away from Katherine and flicked a look toward the door. "Eustace?"

The door drew back, and the page boy looked in. "My lord?"

"Send for my lady wife." Lord Aelfric turned back to Katherine. "Girl, your father left my castle in no good grace. I judge that when he did so, he also left my service. He is marshal of my stables no longer."

Katherine tried to speak over the lump in her throat. "But, my lord—"

"The lady Isabeau." Eustace drew back the door with another officious bow. Lady Isabeau swept within, veiled in purple satin and girdled in gold. She was not young, but her husband would have been a man full grown on the day that she was born.

Lord Aelfric stretched a finger to point at Katherine. "When this girl's father was here last, he extracted a promise from me, my word of honor made in haste. I told him that, whatever happened, I would see to the care of his only child. Find her a place within the castle."

Lady Isabeau eyed Katherine in displeasure. "I do not wish it, my lord. I find her ill to look upon."

The many rings on Lord Aelfric's hands clacked and clinked when he closed his hand. "My lady, you are not called here to tell me what you wish."

Lady and lord stared long at each other. Katherine spent the silent moments of their struggle thinking that if she could get no better than such looks from a husband, she would much rather be alone all her life.

Lady Isabeau broke first. She turned on Katherine. "Can you cook?"

Katherine bobbed her head. "Somewhat, my lady."

"Can you mend and embroider? Weave at the loom?"

Katherine smoothed down her dress. "Not well, my lady." She had let it out twice as she had grown—it was still the only thing she could wear in good company, but she knew that she had nearly ruined it.

Lady Isabeau pursed her lips. "What was your father about, letting you grow so wayward? Have you any talents at all?"

Katherine turned back to Aelfric. "My lord, you know what I can do, and you know I do it well. I can train horses. It is all I have ever done."

"And did you imagine you would continue in that place forever?" Lady Isabeau clicked her tongue. "Did you think you would remain Katherine Marshal all your life? Your second name will change—indeed, it is already erased and awaits its replacement."

Katherine hid her hands up the sleeves of her dress so that her lord and lady could not see that they were clenched into fists.

"Your father is no longer here to speak for you, Katherine." Lord Aelfric crooked his finger at Eustace the page boy, drawing him back into the room. "This promise was his wish, and so it rules you."

Katherine searched his face. "My lord, you speak as though my father will not come back for me."

Lord Aelfric returned to contemplation of the vellum scroll

before him. Lady Isabeau fussed with her fine silk veil, shooting Katherine cutting looks from the corner of her eye. Katherine thought of running, fleeing from the castle to wander the roads, but could not think of what good it would do.

"My lord?" Eustace glided across the stone floor with a smooth gravity that looked thoroughly out of place on a ten-year-old boy. "What is your will?"

"Have my chamberlain enter this girl into the castle rolls." Lord Aelfric waved a hand. "My lady wife will see to her placement."

"I will find her a place here, my lord, something that will teach her better grace." Lady Isabeau favored Katherine with a smile doubly veiled. "I have always said that she needs some shaping."

Katherine curtsied and turned to go, hot to the tips of her ears. She could not stop herself from looking back at the threshold. "My lord, what is written on that scroll?"

Lord Aelfric rolled it up. "Nothing that it would befit a girl to know. Get you gone from my sight." He nodded to the page, who closed the door.

Chapter 3

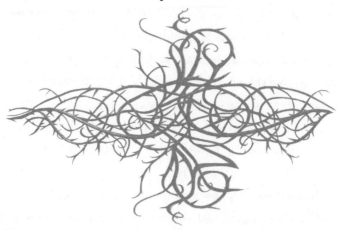

Tom reached out to grasp the black-and-white muzzle. "Quiet, Jumble! No barking."

Jumble sat back on his haunches. He beat his ragged tail in the mud. Tom let go; Jumble's mouth stayed shut.

John Marshal slid down to join them at the edge of the moat. "Well done, Tom." He turned to look up the steep banks, to the drawbridge where they had stood but a moment before. Hoofbeats clopped past on the planks above, thumping and thunking right over their heads. "We got out of sight just in time. You have fine ears."

"Jumble's ears are better still." Tom reached down to scratch them—one black, the other mostly white. The drawbridge obscured half the sky above, and with it the moon, leaving all else he could see lined in its reflected glow. "Master Marshal, what is happening?"

John Marshal waved out an arm. "Watch from the other side, Tom. Tell me what you see."

Tom grabbed for one of the iron rings that dangled from the lowered drawbridge and used it to steady himself while he peered out from beneath its expanse. A damp cold had descended with the death of the day. Curls of steam rose from the reed-choked moat below. He had not known what to expect when he arrived at the castle of Lord Tristan, the greatest knight and hero he had ever heard about, but whatever he might have guessed, it would not have been what he saw just then.

"Aldred!" The rider who had passed by above dismounted in the tunnel that ran through the gatehouse of the castle, and thundered an armored fist on the narrow door recessed into one side. "Aldred Shakesby, I say! It is Wulfric of Olingham—you will open this door at once!" He wore thick mail armor under a deep blue surcoat, emblazoned with the image of the head of a ram. He bore two swords, one in his hand and another, larger one hanging from the saddle of his horse.

A roar resounded from farther down the tunnel, dozens of men shouting all together in the courtyard of the castle. "On three, boys! One, and, two, and—" A splintering boom drowned out the "three."

John Marshal craned forth from cover, then ducked back to whisper. "Tom, my heart misgives me. I had hoped to bring you to a place of safety, somewhere far from the reach of your old master where you could begin your life anew. Instead, I might have led you into the gathering action of a war."

The beginnings of a growl rose in Jumble's throat. Tom shot him a look of command; he licked his chops and fell quiet again.

MATTHEW JOBIN

"Good dog." Tom returned to his watch on the castle just before him. "I see a rider, Master Marshal, a knight in blue."

"Sir Wulfric of Olingham." John Marshal knit his graying brows. "The only son of Edgar, the baron of Wolland."

"Is he a friend of Lord Tristan's?"

John Marshal shook his head. "He is not."

"Aldred!" The young knight beat the pommel of his sword against the door. "It is Wulfric! Open, I say!"

"Aye, sir knight, aye, we hear you." The side door drew wide to reveal an old man, bald-pated and with a scar that cut from eye to chin. A younger, taller man with a braided beard leaned out from behind him, covering the tunnel with a loaded crossbow.

"What news, Aldred?" The young knight looped the reins of his horse over the posts of a broken-down cart in the tunnel beside him. "Quickly, man—tell me how we fare."

"Tristan's villagers are all down in the courtyard, sir knight, the whole stinking pack of 'em." The old man spoke in a guttering slash, as though every word were a curse. "They've got a battering ram cobbled together, and they've started taking runs at the tower door. We've been picking 'em off with crossbows from the battlements to slow 'em down a bit."

"You will cease your fire at once." Wulfric shouldered his way inside. "We have these men just where we want them. So long as they remain in the courtyard, you will not shoot without my orders. Now come, and show me about the battlements. We must make sure that their numbers match our needs."

The scarred old man peered out, looking inward down the tunnel, then outward, forcing Tom and John to duck back into the shadows under the drawbridge. "Never heard of such a fool caper in all my born days." He slammed the side door shut.

"Just where we want them, he says." John Marshal rubbed his beard, deep in thought. "Their numbers match our needs—how to read such a riddle?"

"I don't understand." Tom stroked a hand through Jumble's burr-infested coat. "Tristan is the greatest of all heroes. He once led an army against the Nethergrim, a creature that threatened all the world. Why would such a man have enemies?"

"It is a sad truth of life, Tom—you do not have to earn your enemies." John squinted at the darkening scene before him. "This is how I read it. A force of Wollanders has taken Tristan's castle by surprise or by trick, and now the men from Tristan's village have come to take it back."

Tom knew nothing of war, and so was not sure whether his question would have an obvious answer. "Then why is the drawbridge down?"

John nodded once. "You have the problem exactly, Tom. Why indeed? What attacker would be so foolish as to seize a castle, but then leave the gates open so that a relieving force could seize it right back?" His hood slipped back from his grizzled hair—he did not resemble his daughter, Katherine, so much in the shape of his features as the expressions that crossed them. Folk often said that Edmund thought a great deal, and Katherine had once told Tom that he thought deeply, but both Katherine and her father thought fast.

"It's a trick, Tom. A trap." John's eyes flashed dark. "That's why Tristan's enemies left the gates up—they wanted the men of Tristan's village to storm right into the courtyard."

"But why?" said Tom. "What sort of trick is it?"

"That I do not know, though I fear . . ." John shook his head, as though unwilling to utter his guess aloud. "There's nothing for it, though—we must warn them of their danger."

A wind gusted up to crackle the leafless branches of the forest that ringed the castle. It brought a sound—shouts and cries from somewhere down the castle hill, higher in pitch than those that arose from within the courtyard, and speaking more of terror than of rage.

"That's coming from the village just south of here, where most of Tristan's people live," said John in answer to Tom's look. "Women and children."

Tom felt his stomach give a lurch.

John Marshal braced his knee against the slope to give Tom a step upward. "I wish there was somewhere safe that I could send you, but I have no idea where safety might be found tonight. Stay close at my side."

Tom seized hold of the chains of the drawbridge to help him scrabble onto level ground. A feeling of exposure gripped him as soon as he got up out of the moat, for the crossbowman walked the parapets above and not a bush grew within bowshot of the walls. "Master Marshal, do you see him?"

"Stay low, Tom. We are well within his range." John took Tom's offered arm and tried to hoist himself up out of the moat with his right hand—the bandaged hand. He hissed in pain, let go, and changed to his left. Once up onto the green, he pushed Tom in behind one of the two stones that marked the place where the lip of the drawbridge came down to touch the road, then sank against the other.

Tom reached into his belt and produced a quid of leaves—bruisewort and glorypith—snipped and bound at moonrise. He held it out.

"Thank you." John took the leaves and put them in his mouth. He unwound the bandage to inspect the stump of his missing finger—the little finger, but it was his right hand, his sword hand.

Tom grabbed Jumble in his turn, pulling him up onto the grass by the scruff of his neck. "That knight, the one you called Wulfric—he didn't look much older than I am."

John wrapped the bandage tight again. "Wulfric's only seventeen, if I recall correctly, but already a veteran of a battle or two away south."

Tom hid himself behind the other stone; Jumble snuffled close and huddled in between his feet. "There was blood on his sword."

"I know," said John. "I saw."

Another roar erupted from the castle courtyard, the sound of dozens of men shouting all at once. Fire awoke in the arrow slits of the gatehouse above the entrance tunnel, yellow crosses in the gloom.

"Run with your head low, quick but quiet." John got up into a crouch. "If I tell you to retreat, do it at once, and do not stop until you reach the trees."

Tom followed John to the lip of the drawbridge, then looked back. "Jumble. Jumble, come."

Jumble would not budge. He huddled by the verge of the road, his hackles aquiver, a nervous whine rising at the end of every breath. His eyes flashed yellow, reflecting torch and full moon.

Tom tapped the chilly ground. "Here. Jumble, come here."

Jumble turned his head, looking off into the distance. He looked at Tom again, then backed away from the castle with his tail dropped low.

Tom crept over to scratch Jumble's head. "What is it, Jumble? What's the matter?"

Jumble licked Tom's hand, quaking with fear. Travel, strange smells, the frightful noises from the castle—any of these might make a dog unhappy, fearful and unsure of the world. Tom could not quite figure why, but he felt sure that there was something else, something he very much wished Jumble could tell him. He stopped scratching, and let him go where he would.

Jumble crept away at once, retreating from the castle and out onto the green. He turned at the edge of view, staring at Tom, his face a question, or a warning.

"We've no time, Tom. We'll have to trust that he can find us again." John Marshal started onto the drawbridge, and after a moment's reluctance, Tom went after him, still glancing back in hopes of beckoning Jumble along. Tom felt the pain of separation, but could only hope that Jumble would be safer alone outside than in the midst of battle. He soon lost sight of Jumble's receding form in the shadows and had to turn his attention to his own feet, to make sure he padded as silently as he could along the wooden span of the drawbridge so as not to draw the attention of the crossbowman on the walls just above.

Piles of sacks lay heaped along the walls of the gatehouse

tunnel, some opened to reveal their contents—a few bushels of apples going fast to rot. Rushes lay stacked in bundles on two carts, one of which looked in very poor repair. Tom pointed upward, at the line of holes cut into the high arched ceiling. "Master Marshal, what are those for?"

"Dropping things on people." John pulled Tom aside, keeping to the wall of the tunnel. "They're called murder holes— stay clear of them."

Wulfric's horse snorted and tossed his head, still standing tied to the cart where his rider had left him—an enormous beast, the kind of grand stamping charger Tom had often seen in training at John Marshal's farm back in Elverain. John approached the horse, one hand held forth in a calming gesture. "Steady, lad. Steady, now—you'll get no trouble from me." He reached out, and in one swift motion drew the sword from its scabbard on the saddle. "Young Wulfric might live to regret leaving his great sword-of-war unguarded. Then again, he might *not* live to regret it."

Tom stared at him.

"This is war, Tom, and Wulfric is in it by his own choosing." John leaned by the side door through which Wulfric had passed. He readied the sword, preparing to swing at anyone who opened it, then nodded for Tom to pass on by.

A crash and a clang sounded from above. Tom craned back to look. He saw nothing but torchlight through the murder holes, but voices floated down from the gatehouse: "Drop the gates, drop the gates! Her eminence is almost ready!"

Tom exchanged a look with John—*her eminence?*

The voice of Aldred Shakesby rasped out in command. "To the winch, boys, and jump to it! Move, I said! Tanchus— Tanchus, you dung-for-brains, put that down! There's time for counting spoils later."

"Spoils, my eye!" A third voice spoke—male, like the others, but whiny and high-pitched. "Look at this hovel—I'd get better plunder sacking a poorhouse!"

"Shut your noise, you ugly rat." Aldred barked the complaints down to silence. "Now come on, boys, move it, move!"

John seized Tom by the arm. "Onward, Tom—run!" They pelted down the tunnel together, bursting out into the courtyard just in time. An iron portcullis banged down across the inner mouth of the tunnel behind them, missing John by a matter of inches.

"This way!" John dodged to the left, leading Tom into the shadows under the wooden outbuildings that ringed the castle walls. He peered out at the battlements above. "Keep to the shadows, and watch for that crossbowman."

Tom glanced back at the gatehouse. "But aren't we trapped?"

"There is a postern gate, a back way that leads from the courtyard down to the river that flows behind the castle." John crept onward, under the eaves of what looked like an abandoned smithy. "We must get a warning to Tristan and his men, and then get clear of the castle. From there we can decide our next move all together."

"What about Jumble?"

"We'll look for him as soon as we can, I promise you." John beckoned him in between a pair of wooden buildings by the wall. "Many of the older men of Tristan's village will know me on sight, and the younger ones should at least know me by name. Stay near."

Tom ducked and dodged after John through courtyard grass that seemed surprisingly long and poorly tended. Piles of debris lay strewn all about—old tools, rotted wood, a plowshare gone to rust. A tower loomed at the opposite end of the courtyard, taller by far than anything else in the castle. Torches swarmed and swirled at its foot, racing back and forth as the village men plied the ram to the door.

"The postern gate is over there, Tom, right behind the great hall." John gestured out across the courtyard. "If we get separated, go through it and down the tunnel to the river. The village is downstream—follow the banks."

Tom took a momentary pause to get his bearings in the moonlight. The buildings—a smithy and perhaps a stable—looked in very poor repair, half bald of thatching on the roofs and full of holes in the wattle of the walls. The great watchtower leaned well out of straight, joined to the rest of the walls with too much mortar and precious little skill. Even amidst his terror, it still came as a shock; the more he saw of Tristan's castle, the shabbier and more run-down it looked.

John peered around the back of the long, low stables. "Now come, we've got to reach the men and persuade them to retreat. Their lives depend on it."

Tom darted out behind him, watching the battlements for any sign of the crossbowman. He saw no one on the walls, though he thought he caught a flash of movement atop the watchtower, someone looking briefly down at the attackers below before withdrawing from view.

"Men of Harthingdale!" John raised his voice as they reached the crowd of torches by the foot of the tower. "It is John Marshal. Listen and heed me, you have walked into a trap!"

An old man stepped out of the torchlight. "Well, I'll be a bolgug's grandmother!" He leaned on a spear whose shaft was almost as twisted as his back. "Now, there's some luck—lads, this here is John Marshal himself! Here, John, we've got the northern battlements and we're almost through the door, so give us the word on how to fight once we're in."

John Marshal took his introduction for all it was worth. "All of you men—all of you, listen!" He stepped out into the light. "As you value your lives, you must leave now. The gates are shut, so take the postern tunnel. Hurry, with me!"

The men at the battering ram paused in their count, looking back in confusion. "But we're almost through. We've almost got them!"

Tom shot a look up the steps to the door. They really were almost through—the door was half off its hinges, staved in at the middle and ready to give way. Men held up boards to shield the battering crew, but no one fired or dropped anything from the tower or surrounding walls.

"You must trust me," said John. "You have walked into a trap! We have no time to discuss the matter!"

The village elder stretched out an arm at the walls around him. "If these brigands keep this castle, there won't be anywhere safe in this valley, as well you know, John Marshal.

They could ride out at us whenever they like, and our lives wouldn't be worth living."

"We don't have time to argue!" John lost his temper. "We must retreat! Where is Tristan? He will heed me. Where is your lord?"

"Why retreat when we can attack?" The men took up their battering ram. "Let's batter through, and whoever's in that tower, let them look to running while they can!"

Tom's stomach clenched in. He felt exposed, surrounded by the high curtain walls from which an attack might come at any instant. He kept to the shadows, scanning the western corner of the castle before him. Doors opened out onto the battlements from each side of the watchtower, and it looked like a fight had taken place atop the northern wall, for men lay collapsed and still along the walk. The villagers rolled and roared in their count—one, two, three, and then another crunching run against the door. In its echo rose the sound of a new voice, coming from the highest turret of the tower.

"Do you hear that?" Tom grabbed John's sleeve to get his attention. "Master Marshal, do you hear it?" He cocked an ear— it was a woman's voice, raised to a chant from somewhere high up in the tower. The noises of the villagers obscured what she said, but she spoke in strong rhythm, full of fury and empty of fear.

John strained to listen. His face lost its color. "Oh, no. No!" He shoved Tom. "Run! To the back wall, to the postern gate. Run for your life!"

Tom's heart thumped and bounced in his chest. He crossed the courtyard at a flying dash, making for the place where he thought he saw the outline of a door. The voice of the woman rang out triumphant, chanting in a fierce, resounding ecstasy.

Something fell from the top of the tower. It struck the earth beside the village men and broke open, letting out a pallid glow and then a keening wail.

Chapter 4

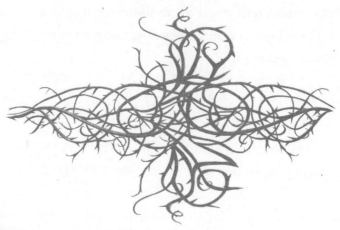

Edmund Bale did not sing like a bird. His voice rolled deep, lovely but not delicate, and seeming far larger than what his slender frame should produce. It never failed to surprise those who had only heard him speak, so different was it both in tone and shape of word, and so strangely matched with a boy who was somewhat under average height for fourteen, with sunless skin and soft golden hair. It was the duty of every village in the barony to entertain their lord on Harvestide night, and though Edmund was only halfway finished with his song, he already knew that he was not going to let his home village of Moorvale down.

The grand hall of Aelfric, Lord of Elverain, seemed built to receive such arts. The strains of Edmund's song filled its vaults to the ceiling, and the tapestries, while woven with stern and noble scenes, yet enfolded the echoes before they could turn harsh. Trestle tables ran the length of the hall, whereupon sat the folk from all the villages of the barony—Moorvale and Longsettle, Roughy and Dorham and Quail. Candles stood impaled on stands every few feet along, casting as much light as Edmund could remember ever seeing in a room at night. A fire blazed high in the grand hearth set in the western wall, though with so many folk pressed in together no one needed its heat.

Edmund knew just where to stand for best effect. He sang the *Deeds of Tristan*, a long chain of verses with couplet refrains that changed and interlocked, each telling of a brave exploit or noble act in the life of its hero. He raised his arms, faced outward from the fire. Beasts reared up in shadow and in song, but one by one Tristan defeated them: *Tristan saves a tiny village from a grute while the lord of the land cowers in his hall; Tristan rides alone to the marshy lair of the Buddleboggan, and wins a contest of riddles, forcing it back underwater for a thousand years and more; Tristan leads the villagers of Upenough to safety in the very teeth of the Nethergrim.*

Edmund scaled the heights of the refrain, rising to each note with neither trill nor glide. He had the place in his grip— mugs sat forgotten at elbows and chins lay pressed on palms: *Tristan takes the fight to the mountains, leading his brave companions against the Nethergrim when no other man would dare to tread above the foothills; Tristan descends into the lair of this greatest of enemies, meets it in single combat and strikes off its head, bringing peace to the lands once again. Tristan the Good, defender of the meek. Tristan the Righteous, unstained in deed. Tristan the Brave, jewel amongst knights.*

Edmund brought the song to a reverent close, drawing out the last note to leave it wandering in echo through the hall. A hush descended, and then, just as the folk around him rose to cheer, something struck him in the face.

Edmund spluttered, wobbled and tripped. He landed in the rushes strewn across the flagstone floor, and came perilously near to flopping onto the fire. He heard a stifled chorus of gasps, but no one moved to help him up. He rolled over, dazed, and saw what had hit him—a boiled cabbage.

"Stuff and nonsense!" The shout came from the same direction as the throw, from the high table at the head of the hall where sat the folk of noble rank. "You keep your seat from now on, peasant, and you keep your mouth shut!"

Edmund rubbed at his jaw where he had been struck. The folk in the hall sat stunned, their merriment turned into confusion and fright in a heartbeat.

"Tristan is a liar and a coward, and I'll fight anyone who says otherwise." The knight who had thrown the cabbage sported a bristly black mustache that did little to soften the bitter contours of his mouth. He curled one of his hands into a fist while he pointed about the hall with the other. "Come on, any one of you, or all of you together. Just any of you clap, any of you cheer for that boy and his song, and I will take you outside and make you eat some dirt."

Edmund, like everyone in the hall, looked past the scowling knight, in the direction of Lord Aelfric and Lady Isabeau, who sat in the chairs of highest honor. Lord Aelfric gazed fixedly down into his fine silver goblet, as though he was trying to pretend he had not heard what had just passed in his own hall.

Lady Isabeau clenched her jaw and then the arms of her chair, but neither she nor her husband spoke a word. The scowling knight resumed eating, as though he sat in his own castle and had just abused one of his own peasants.

"We were on those accursed moors for nine days, and this is what I get for my trouble." The knight plucked up a stout-bladed dirk from the table. He stabbed it down, skewering a hunk of salted pork and then waving it about. "I wouldn't feed this to the dogs! Someone bring me something edible, and sharpish, or by all thunder I will—"

"That's enough, Richard."

A wide shadow blocked the light of the fire. Edmund rolled over to find a man in lord's finery looming up behind him, seeming to have somehow stepped right out through the stonework of the wall. Everyone around Edmund stood up in surprise, and then bowed. Edmund tried to scrabble up in time, but before he could, the lord reached down to help him stand.

"You must excuse my loyal knight." The lord was a man of middle age, stout and not over tall, halfway between powerfully built and running to fat. His face was broad, his thick black hair and beard were curly, and his eyes were dark and very deep. "He has his uses, but we call him Richard Redhands for a reason."

Edmund took hold of the hand and staggered to his feet. "My thanks to you, my lord."

"My lord Wolland, I will not hear it!" Richard Redhands leaned out over the high table. "Tristan is a charlatan, a faker, a knave in lord's robes, and I will not hear his praises sung by some gap-toothed yokel!"

The lord waved his hand. "Sit down, Richard. Make merry for once in your life!"

The herald of the castle rushed into the hall through the grand double doors, looking utterly flustered. "Oh, there you are, my lord! I was waiting to announce your entrance—how did you get past me?"

The lord had a ready laugh. "I've been in this castle before, my boy, many times. I know all the secret passages!" He shot a wink at Lord Aelfric—or perhaps at Lady Isabeau—but neither of them returned it.

The herald cast a discomfited glance at Lord Aelfric, then scurried into the hall and struck his staff to the floor for silence. "Ahem—make way for my lord Edgar, Baron Wolland, peer of the realm and Lord Warden of the March!" It sounded rather silly, since Lord Wolland was already in the hall, and so, with a blush on his face, the herald then retreated hurriedly through the doors.

Edmund made his bow low and solemn. "My lord." He knew—everyone knew—that Edgar, Baron Wolland was the richest man in all the north, lord of a land twice the size of Elverain and on speaking terms with the king himself.

"That is I!" Lord Wolland swept onward to the high table, and took up a goblet in toast. "Edgar of Wolland, happy lord of that happy land just down river and across the moors from here. Come, come, good folk of Elverain, do not be cast down on this Harvestide night, where we celebrate the bounty of the year and the reunion of old friends!" At this, he slapped Lord Aelfric on the shoulder. Lord Aelfric remained so still and rigid that he looked as though he had died sitting up in his chair.

MATTHEW JOBIN

Edmund slipped back to his seat on the trestle bench, sur-rounded by family and neighbors and across from his little brother, Geoffrey. He managed to fend off a flurry of fright-ened attention from his mother, Sarra Bale, telling her that he was not hurt, that it was only a cabbage, and anyway they should keep their voices down so as not to anger the nobles any further. He felt Sir Richard Redhands's scowling gaze upon him, but did his best to pretend he did not notice.

Geoffrey leaned across the table, and dropped to a whisper. "And you're sure they came in off the moors?"

Edmund wiped cabbage juice from behind his ear. "I saw it with my own eyes."

"You all right, son?" Edmund's father, Harman Bale, hob-bled along the rows of benches to stand by his seat. He winced and staggered, holding one hand to the table and the other to his side. "Not hurt, are you?"

Edmund got up. "Father, you should rest. Your wound's not even halfway healed. Here, please, take my seat."

Harman slid with a heave of breath onto the bench. "Your old dad's not what he used to be." He was dark where Edmund was fair, his brown hair thinning at the crown. His beard had grown out ragged, poorly trimmed on one side—the bandaged wound in his belly still kept him from raising his right arm above the shoulder.

Edmund grabbed a log from the stack of wood by the fire, and used it to make a seat for himself at the end of the table. "You just need time to heal, Father. It could have been a lot worse, you know—you did stand up to the greatest wizard ever born."

Harman reached out and landed a weak punch on Edmund's arm. "Like father, like sons!" He turned and did the same to Geoffrey. "Let Vithric tremble when he hears the name of Bale, that's what I say!"

As soon as sons and father shared the smile, it faded. It was true that each of them had, in his own way, thwarted Vithric's malevolent designs; but Vithric was still alive, and none of them knew when or in what form his revenge might come.

Edmund did something he had never even considered before. He let his father into his thoughts. "Father, why do you think these nobles are here?"

Harman Bale cast a dark look up to the high table. "Whatever Lord Wolland's here for, it means trouble for us." He shook his head. "He's the richest man in all the north, and cousin to the king on both sides of his family. You mark me, son, everything that man says, does and thinks is politics."

Geoffrey scrunched his freckles together. "Then why does he act like he's the village fool?"

Lord Wolland's voice boomed out from his elevated station, cutting across every conversation in the hall. "Now, your herald, there, my good Lord Aelfric, he knows not his own business!" He extended a pudgy finger to point down the central aisle, indicating a line of well-dressed folk as they entered through the grand double doors. "He's let my noble companions enter the hall unannounced, and after I gave him the slip around the side passage, even though he's a spry young lad of twenty and I'm but a fat old codger with one too many helpings of roast quail under his belt. Ha!" He patted his paunch. The

MATTHEW JOBIN

folk of the hall gave way to nervous tittering, and then, as he prattled on, honest laughter.

"That's the spirit, everyone! That's the way—happy Harvestide!" Lord Wolland drained off a gulp from his goblet, then waved it toward the entrance of the hall. "Now, I think I shall play the herald myself, and why not? Hark ye, hark ye, good folk of Elverain, for persons of great substance and rank have entered in among you! That one there with the mug in each hand is my lord Blave of Overstoke, and over there with the bald pate is my lord Sigbert of Tand. Cheer up, Tand, your wife says it makes you look manly! Ha! Now that one there in the furs and the preposterous hat is Hunwald of the Uxingham Hundreds, and up last is young Elísalon, whose title is one of those long wizardy things that no one can pronounce. Don't try, or she might grow cross with you and turn you into a goat, or something like. You *can* turn folk into goats, can you not, my dear girl? No? Father's thunder, I thought that's what wizards *did*! Well, what I am paying you for, then?"

Edmund watched the procession of nobles thread their way between the trestles on their way up to the high table, under the pouring stream of Lord Wolland's babble. The girl he had met upon the moors, the one Lord Wolland had named Elísalon, passed him by without answering the question in his look.

Geoffrey nudged Edmund once they all had ascended to their high places. "Those are half the lords of the north!"

"All the lords of the north that live east of the river," said Edmund. "Everyone who dwells in Lord Wolland's shadow."

"It makes no sense." Geoffrey was two years Edmund's junior, and his voice had just begun to break, which made attempts at hushed conversations rather pointless. "They could have crossed the river down in Rushmeet, like folk always do!"

Edmund leaned out across his table, looking past his neighbors at the row of noble personages at the high table. Though she sat amongst the lords, Elísalon did not seem to share in their company. She spread a parchment chapter book flat upon the table, dipped a quill and started writing. Whenever she glanced up, she seemed to look everywhere in the room except at Edmund.

"We should find Katherine," said Geoffrey. "Where is she, anyway?

Lord Wolland banged his goblet on the high table. "Now harken to me again, one and all! It is time for me to play the gracious guest, and announce that on the fourth day hence, we shall host a grand tournament of arms, right here on Northend green before this very castle. There shall be jousting by the men of noble blood, contests of archery and quarterstaff for the common folk, feasts to burst your belly, and various entertainments of unsurpassed quality. I should know—I paid for them!"

The hurrah Lord Wolland's announcement drew forth from the assembled folk of the hall was not at all forced, for everyone loved a grand tournament of arms. Their good cheer restored, everyone returned to their holiday babble, the cabbage forgotten by everyone save for the dogs who fought over it in the aisles.

"An archery tourney!" Geoffrey's many freckles drew apart when he smiled. "What's the prize for first place, do you think?"

Lord Aelfric stood and, after a moment's chilly silence,

commanded the attention of the crowd. "My people. Your oaths of service are honored, your labors accomplished, and so with glad heart do I welcome you to our feast. Take of our plenty this night and remain within the bounds of my castle until morning if you wish. A happy Harvestide to you all."

The cheer this raised was not quite so loud as the one Wolland received at his announcement of the tourney, though it was bolstered by the arrival of the kitchen servants, carrying between them tray after tray piled high with the next delicious-smelling course of the Harvestide feast.

Geoffrey rubbed his hands. "Oho, smell that? Is that mutton? I'll bet we're getting mutton!"

Edmund tried for a little longer to draw Elli's gaze, then gave up. He looked about him, and could not help but feel a touch of the delight that lit the faces of his family and neighbors. The strangeness of his meeting on the moors the night before, the oppressive weight of the Nethergrim's voice, the nightmares that kept him from sleeping—all of it fell away, for just a while, amongst the celebrations of the feast. The harvest was in, every field reaped and gleaned, and the larders were as well stocked as they would be all year. Of all the holidays that dotted the calendar, Harvestide was Edmund's particular favorite, for it was the one day out of the year when he could sit down while someone else served him dinner.

"Mutton with the trimmings." The food had hardly touched the table in front of Edmund before the person who had served it moved on down the aisles—but there was no mistaking the voice.

Edmund whirled around in surprise. "Katherine?"

Chapter 5

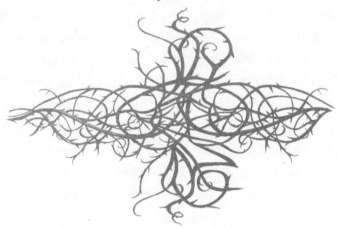

Voices resounded off the walls of Tristan's castle: "Run! All of you, run for your lives!"

Tom found the postern gate, but found it barred from the other side. He gave up trying to shove it open and turned back into the courtyard, passing through a crowd of panicking men searching frantically about them for some way, any way out.

"Help, help me, please, someone—" Whatever the villager in the grass nearby had meant to say next, Tom never heard, for his voice dissolved into a babbled scream. Tom threw himself down beneath a cart overgrown with weeds up to its axles. He crept to the other side and glanced out upon the courtyard, and wished very much that he had not.

Something drifted near, something that was there and yet not there—the blinking, melting image of a fire impressed on the eyes after they have shut, a nightmare that would not resolve into a shape and give up the awful secret of its form.

A dozen jointless limbs waved and whipped in double rows. There was nothing for a head, just a tuft of fringed, grasping feelers.

"If someone gets away, if someone makes it home . . ." A young man in a sheepskin vest backed up to the wall, then cowered down. "Tell Rahilda—"

The glowing thing lunged for the man, its many arms rippling out in a doubled wave that crackled and insulted the air. The rows of flailing feelers wrapped around the weeping, cringing form of the man before it, and a mouth opened up between them, a tiny point of toothy darkness.

Tom felt a wrenching in his belly.

The man stopped screaming. He stood up, seeming somehow to occupy the very same space as the thing that had seized him, the solid flesh of his body interwoven with its insubstantial form. He looked out upon his fleeing, panicking comrades with a face that spoke of no emotion at all, his muscles twitching without purpose—then he turned to advance on them, the wooden cudgel in his hands raised high. More waving, rippling creatures emerged from the carved and decorated box that had fallen from the top of the tower. The men of Tristan's village screamed and ran, but there was nowhere to run. All the gates of the castle were closed, and the creatures pursued them into every corner of the courtyard.

"Tib! Tibalt Hackwood! It's us, Tib—it's your friends!"

Tom turned to look out from the other side of the cart. He caught sight of another man enveloped by the glowing creature that had taken him, advancing through the grass and driving three panicked villagers before him.

"Come, now, Tib." A short young man backed away into the dark, lit by the sickly radiance of the thing before him. "It's just your friends, your old friends, Elmer and Kenferth. It's me, Tib, it's Elmer Byley—and here, here's your own uncle Osbert!"

The man trapped within the ghostly, ghastly arms did not seem to hear. The glow caressed and enfolded him, leaving ripples in the air as he advanced upon the men.

"Is he alive or dead?" A beak-nosed, lanky man held out a pruning hook at the approaching creature. "Is Tib alive or dead in there?"

"Tib, can you hear us?" The eldest of the three men around the creature held a club braced sideways to defend. "It's your uncle, your uncle Osbert."

The man they had called Tib gripped his axe, though he seemed to flail it about without knowing it was in his hands. He stared upward and leftward, at nothing Tom could see.

"Get 'round him." Osbert approached along his nephew's side, motioning the other men to do the same. "'Round him, hurry. Ell Byley, get that spear up!"

The spearman took the opposite flank. "What would you have us do, Osbert? He's your nephew, your own sister's son!"

Tib halted his march. He turned back and forth at the men surrounding him, seeming to squirm in the embrace of ghostly arms. Tom could not tell if it was hesitation, or simply twitching, like the spasms of a man who has just been hanged.

Osbert turned his walking stick to grip down at one end, readying for a strike. "It's him or us. You saw what he did to Bill Kettles. You ask me, he's already dead in there. Bring him down!"

All three men pressed forward with their weapons at the ready. Tib curled to the earth, and for one hopeful instant Tom thought the spell was wearing off, but he was only gathering for a leap. With a speed that slashed trails of light through the air, he jumped over the pruning hook to bring his axe down on the head of the man holding it. The pruning hook tumbled through the air, while its wielder crumpled onto the grass.

Tib rounded on Osbert with his axe raised high. Tom turned away in horror.

"Tib! Tib, it's me! It's your own uncle—no, please—" A thud followed the words, then a choking cry and another thud—and then approaching footsteps, and an eerie, spreading glow.

"No. No!" Tom scrabbled back from under the cart, then leapt up and fled as fast as his feet would carry him. He had been told many times that he was a good runner—in fact he had never met anyone to match him at a sprint—but Tib kept pace with seeming ease, giving him not an instant's rest as he searched for a way out of the courtyard. Their chase wound back and forth across the straggled grass, into and out of the wooden smithy and stables and over to the dark expanse of the great hall. There was no hope, no help, no safe place anywhere within the walls, and when at last he tripped over a discarded spear, it almost felt like relief. He lowered his head and covered his face with his arms. The glow grew brighter and nearer.

There sounded the clang of metal on metal, of hard breath and quick-stepping feet. The blow Tom waited to feel never landed.

"Up, Tom! On your feet!"

Tom dared a look to find John Marshal circling the creature, sword in hand. He leapt aside from an overhand swing, bringing up his blade to deflect the attack, then reversing and very nearly impaling his opponent. "You must help me. Up!"

Tom rolled up with the spear in his hands and rushed to help. Even in the midst of his terror, he felt a twinge of awe at the fluid dance of John's swordplay. He had always understood that John knew how to fight, but until that moment he had never truly grasped what that meant.

"Stay behind it." John turned his blade, twisting aside a lunge made by the creature. "When you see your chance, strike to kill."

Tom, on the other hand, did not know how to fight, and even the desperate strength of his terror could not replace skill and training. Time and again, he missed his chance to strike at the creature, and time and again, John Marshal saved his life, leaping about with a speed that belied his years.

"Rightward, Tom." John sidestepped, blocking an overhand chop by bracing the flat of his blade across his forearm. "Step rightward—and attack! Now!"

Tom did as he was asked. His thrust came slow, but he made it with such force that the creature had no choice but to turn and block it.

That gave John Marshal the opening he needed. He drove his sword through the glowing, grasping feelers, and into the chest of the man within. "Whoever you are in there, I am sorry."

The creature stopped and dropped its weapon to the grass. Inside the glow, the man's mouth filled with blood, but his eyes seemed to fix upon the world for the first time.

MATTHEW JOBIN

"John Marshal?" Tibalt Hackwood blinked in surprise. "Why . . ."

He died standing up, collapsing through the rippling, ghostly arms to drop into the grass, dragging the point of John's sword down with him. The creature flailed and whipped up high, shimmering the air, and the dark-toothed mouth puckered in.

Tom felt horror, pity, remorse—then sickness, dizziness. "He was still alive." He fell to one knee. "He was still alive in there."

"I know." John Marshal gasped for breath, bent over double, his sword stuck deep in Tib's chest. "Now, Tom, we really must get clear of this place while we still—"

He never got to finish. The jointless, waving limbs reached out along his blade, up his arms—and into his eyes. His shout barely got past a gargle. His face froze, a grimace of pain on one side but drooling slack on the other. The glow took him and turned him, wrenching his head aside with such speed that Tom saw the muscles pop and bulge. He withdrew his blooded sword and advanced on Tom, step by relentless step.

Tom stumbled backward through the grass. "Stay away!" He held up his spear against John's approach, but trembled so badly that the point wobbled back and forth. "I warn you, stay away!"

There was not a trace of understanding on John Marshal's face, not a hint of the man who had done all he could to ease the many burdens of Tom's life. He did not even look at Tom. He stared at the sky, his mouth hanging open. He raised his sword, readying a killing blow.

A horn sounded from the gatehouse of the castle, dark and deep, in a hideous harmony that hurt Tom's ears.

The glowing thing that had once been John Marshal turned and lumbered away. Other deathly lights converged with his, a swarm of creatures coming together in a bunch in front of the gatehouse, where stood a woman somewhat advanced in years, her silver hair bound in a simple queue down her back over a dark-hued dress trimmed in fur.

"You must wait until moonset to leave this valley, sir knight." The woman had her back to the creatures, looking up instead at the two dozen men ranged about atop the castle walls. "Should you happen upon the Skeleth without warning, I may not be able to protect you."

Tom recognized the woman's voice from the odd, rounded drawl of her accent—she was the one who had chanted the spell from atop the tower. He dried his tears on his shoulder, his sorrow frozen by new fear.

"Your eminence." Sir Wulfric of Olingham bowed from the roof of the gatehouse. "Honor compels me to inform you of your peril, should all not go to plan."

"I care nothing for your compulsions, nor for your honor, sir knight," said the woman. "Attend to your business, as I shall to mine."

"Gives me the crawlies, she does." The whiny-voiced man had the sort of whisper that carried on the wind. "Reminds me of my old gran. I ever tell you about—"

"Shut your noise, Tanchus." The burly crossbowman cut him off. "Maybe your old gran was deaf, but I'll wager this one ain't. You want to end up inside one of them glowing things?"

Tom looked around him. The glow cast by the creatures lit

up a field of slaughter, bodies lying crumpled in the grass as though tossed there by a giant. He crawled off, hiding himself in the shadows under the stables, and tried his best not to give himself away by weeping too loudly.

Sir Wulfric leaned down from the battlements. "What of my lord Tristan, your eminence?"

"He is not your concern, sir knight." The wizard woman turned away, moving through the assembled creatures without the slightest show of fear.

"Your eminence." Wulfric seemed to hesitate. "There was no honor in our deeds here."

"Your father wants his victory and is prepared to do what is needful to achieve it. You would do well to learn from his example. Good night to you." The wizard woman put a double-mouthed horn to her lips. The harmony shook and shattered, it leapt and lurched. The creatures followed her at a shambling march eastward and away down the road, John Marshal among them.

Wulfric turned to address the brigands in the castle. "Men of the Rutters, hear me. You have your orders—follow them and you will earn my noble father's gratitude."

"It ain't his gratitude we're wanting, sir knight." Aldred Shakesby came up into view from the gatehouse. "We want his coin."

"S'right!" More than one man chimed in. "We've done our bit. Where's our pay?"

"That will come," said Wulfric. "Until then, you will secure this castle and hold for my return. Raise the gates and prepare my horse." He turned away and descended out of Tom's view.

"You heard him!" Aldred turned to his fellows. "To the winch! Hop to it!"

Tom picked himself up from the grass and slunk over to the gatehouse, cursing himself for having lain still so long. He waited for the inner gates to rise, then crept along the tunnel, hoping to slip out before anyone could come down to count the slain, but the side door opened just as he passed it.

"On your knees, boy." The crossbowman leveled a bolt at Tom's gut. "On your knees, and tell me why I should let you live."

Tom fell to his knees. He could not think of anything.

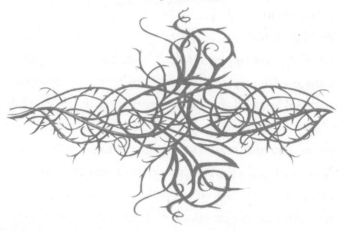

Chapter 6

Edmund leapt from his seat. "Katherine? Wait—Katherine, come back!"

Katherine picked up her skirts and tried to dash away. Edmund would usually have had little chance of catching her long-legged strides, but the hem of her dress tripped her up before she could get clear of him.

Edmund caught up to her between the aisles. "Katherine, why are you serving supper in the castle?"

Katherine wore a rough, drab housedress that did not quite seem to fit, from the way she pulled and picked at it. "I work here now." A thick cloth wimple wrapped her hair, hiding it completely and framing her face in a way that did not flatter it, as though it had been made for someone with a smaller head. "Papa's not the marshal of the stables anymore. I have nowhere else to go."

Edmund blinked. Of course—Katherine was a girl and not

yet of age. Without a father to speak for her, she had no place in the world. "I can help. Let me help you!"

Katherine coughed, and wiped her runny nose. "You can't help me, Edmund."

"Katherine, please, let me try." Edmund had often dreamed of helping Katherine. "I'll think of something, I'm sure of it." In his dreams, she needed him, and only him. In his dreams, she could find no one else to turn to, no one else to rely upon. In his dreams, she did not have to stoop to kiss him.

"Hark ye, hark ye!" The herald bellowed louder than was really needed, perhaps to compensate for his earlier mistakes. "Silence, one and all! Your lord will speak!"

Lord Aelfric rose from his carved and cushioned chair. "As you all know, it is our custom every year to choose from amongst the peasantry a king and queen of Harvestide. By the oldest of traditions, the king and queen are granted a place of honor for the night, and will sit in my own chair and that of my lady Isabeau for the remainder of the feast."

"Father's thunder! Do you say so?" Lord Wolland slapped the table. "What fun—how quaint are you folk here in Elverain! But my lord Aelfric, whatever will I do without your sparkling conversation? Do send up a witty pig-farmer or the like!"

Lord Aelfric did not acknowledge Lord Wolland's interruption, instead merely waiting for it to stop before he carried on. "It is also tradition for the couple to be young, a boy on the cusp of manhood and a girl in the first flower of her youth. I see that there are young folk here about the hall who stand ready for your approval, sons and daughters of the merchants and craftsmen of your own villages."

MATTHEW JOBIN

Edmund looked about him and saw a collection of perhaps a dozen boys and girls standing up about the hall, all of them very obviously dressed to get attention. The boys were mostly the sons of rich merchants from Northend, and the girls were either the prettiest in their villages, or at least thought themselves so. They all lined up by the wings of the high tables, trying to crowd past one another while at the same time trying not to look too obvious about it.

"I'll bet Tom and Papa are at Lord Tristan's castle by now," said Katherine. "And I'll bet they're having more fun than we are."

Lord Aelfric held up his hand. "By tradition, the king and queen are chosen by the acclaim of the folk of the land." He stretched out a hand to Luilda Twintree, who had contrived to push herself up closest to his view. "Let us hear from our first—"

A roar, a chorus, a double thunder cut him off. "Edmund Bale!" It came from the tables where sat the folk of Moorvale, and just as loudly from across the hall where sat the miners of Roughy. "Katherine Marshal!"

Edmund turned to Katherine in shock. He found her going pale, and trying to sidle out of the hall.

"Silence!" Lord Aelfric was met with nothing like silence, but he tried to shout over the roaring crowd. "It is tradition that—"

"Edmund Bale! Katherine Marshal!" Once the shout began, it took on a momentum that could not be contained, as though the idea, once proposed, suited just about everyone. The boys and girls lined up for their chance to be king and queen looked like they had all drunk from the same vat of vinegar. Two children came forward from the opposite end of the hall. After a moment Edmund recognized them—Sedmey and Harbert, the kids from Roughy who had been among the Nethergrim's intended victims.

"My lord." Sedmey made a peasant's curtsy before the high table. "If it pleases you, Edmund Bale and Katherine Marshal are the reason me and my brother are here tonight. They went into the mountains, my lord, into the Girth, and they fought the Nethergrim to bring us home safe again. There's no one in this hall who should be our Harvestide king and queen but them."

"What's this?" Lord Wolland stood from his table. "The Nethergrim, you say? Where are these two heroes?"

There was nowhere to hide. Folk drew back from Edmund and Katherine, leaving them alone together in the middle of the hall.

"Then it's settled!" Lord Wolland clapped his hands. "Those two there, king and queen of Harvestide! Who would dare to pick another?"

Lord Aelfric looked at a loss for words. He turned to Lady Isabeau, then back to the crowd, but all he could utter was something else about tradition that no one bothered to hear.

"Edmund and Katherine, king and queen of Harvestide!" The folk of Moorvale—save perhaps for Luilda's family— raised their voices all at once. "Three cheers for them!" The other claimants to the crowns looked upset, but could not withstand the sustained applause, and soon returned rather glumly to their seats.

"Well, come on then." Katherine undid her wimple, letting free her long dark hair. "Take my hand."

Edmund trembled. He held forth his hand, and she slipped it into hers. Lord Aelfric came down from his high table with a crown in his hands woven from stalks of golden wheat. He wore the same impassive, icy look Edmund had always seen on him, though perhaps just a little icier than usual. Lady Isabeau followed him with a crown woven from flowers, but she wore an oddly sly and satisfied smile on her face.

Lord Aelfric held Edmund in a long, cryptic stare and then, with sudden decision, stepped forward to crown him. "Well, well—not wholly undeserved, I suppose."

"Thank you, my lord." Edmund was not sure whether, under the circumstances, he was supposed to bow, so he contented himself with a nod of the head.

Lady Isabeau held forth the flower crown. Katherine curtsied and lowered herself down, only to find the crown jerked back before it touched her head.

"We will accept the boy, but not the girl." Lady Isabeau turned back to the crowd. "Choose another."

"What?" Surprise forced sharp questions from Edmund. "Why not Katherine? What's wrong?"

"By ancient custom, the king and queen of Harvestide must be chosen from the folk of our villages." Lady Isabeau stepped away from Katherine. "This girl has no parents residing in the villages of Elverain, and since she is unmarried, that means she is without standing among you. She is a maid of this castle, and ward of my husband. She is no longer one of you. Choose another."

The folk of the barony muttered to one another, and even Lord Aelfric shot a bemused glance at his wife. Edmund felt sick, but there was nothing he could do.

"That's better." Lady Isabeau's face broadened into a smile once the votes were called and Luilda had won. "What a goodly girl, this one. A fine wife and mother she will make to some townsman, a good example for the younger girls."

Luilda fairly skipped up to Katherine's place. "Ooh, isn't this fun?" She took Edmund's hand. "Too bad you're so short, but we'll make it work!"

Lady Isabeau crowned Luilda, then rounded on Katherine. "What are you doing still standing here? There are pots to wash—back to the scullery with you!"

Edmund wanted to shout at the injustice, to cast a mighty spell, to walk right up to Lady Isabeau and clout her on the ear. Instead he stood helpless in his stupid, scratchy crown and watched Katherine hang her head low and scurry away.

Lord Aelfric took the arm of his wife, and raised his wispy voice as loud as it would go. "My people, we shall now retire for the evening. Enjoy the plenty of our feast. Hail to the king and queen of Harvestide."

The lord and lady exited to the left, while the Harvestide king and queen ascended to the right. Edmund wanted to take off his crown and throw it at whichever snooty Northend boy thought his father had bought it for him. Luilda Twintree giggled and simpered on his arm, throwing winks across the hall at Lefric Green and blowing kisses to her family.

"Now, sit here, right here, my boy." Lord Wolland patted

the seat of Lord Aelfric's chair. "I want to hear all about your exploits. Beats talking about pigs all night!"

Edmund led Luilda to Lady Isabeau's chair. He drew it back, and bowed. "My queen." He took Lord Aelfric's seat and shot a furtive look along the table at Ellí, who continued to scribble in her books as though he were not present. Servants came and bowed before them and set out the next course of the feast, more sumptuous than anything Edmund had ever seen in his life—roast venison, goose in almond milk, and jellied eels sliced out in strips.

"Now then, Your Grace, attend me over here." Lord Wolland snapped his fingers. "You must tell me your tale! Is it indeed true that you traveled to the lair of the fabled Nethergrim?"

Edmund felt the heat of many gazes from up and down the length of the high table. "It is true, my lord."

"Ha!" said Lord Wolland. "And look at you! A nine days' wonder. And what did you find there?"

"The Nethergrim, my lord."

"Not dead after all, eh?" Lord Wolland shot a knowing wink at his companions.

Richard Redhands made sure his snort was heard by one and all. "You see, my lord? I have always said that old Tristan was a charlatan."

Lord Wolland scanned the crowd seated at the tables before them. "And that tall girl, the serving maid, she came with you?"

"Katherine saved my life, my lord, more than once," said Edmund. "We would all have been overrun by bolgugs, but she took up her sword, and—"

"A sword? Pah!" Richard Redhands waved his spoon. "What utter twaddle! How could some peasant wench—"

"She saved my life, sir knight." Edmund cut across Richard's words and ignored his vicious glare. "She did everything folk say of her, and more, if you want truth."

Lord Wolland roared and thunked his goblet on the table. "By the cloven crown, even the maidens are a danger here! How old is this girl?"

"Fourteen, my lord," said Edmund. "Like me."

"And her last name is Marshal." Lord Wolland took up Richard's dirk to carve himself some venison. "By chance, is she related to a *John Marshal*?"

Edmund hesitated, unable to read Lord Wolland's deep-set eyes. "She is his daughter, my lord."

Lord Wolland's smile broke wide upon his face. "Then I do not find this girl's deeds such a wonder, my lords, for I knew her father well, and it seems that the apple has fallen near the tree." He popped a bite of the venison into his mouth. "Indeed, I had hoped to look in on John Marshal as I passed through Elverain, so that we might talk over old times together."

Edmund could not guess the meaning of the looks exchanged between the lords and knights at the table. "Oh—I'm afraid you can't meet with John Marshal, my lord. He is gone away."

Lord Wolland took a sip of wine. "Is he indeed? That is most unfortunate. Tell me, my boy—do you know where he was bound?"

"To Tristan, my lord. To his castle at Harthingdale." As soon as the words were out of Edmund's mouth, he wished that he had thought instead to lie.

All trace of jollity vanished from Lord Wolland's eyes, though the smile remained fixed upon his face. "To Tristan." He set down the dirk, but turned it over and over on the table. "And why is that?"

"They are old friends, my lord." Edmund tried not to stammer. "Perhaps they wished only to see each other again."

"See each other." Lord Wolland let forth with a laugh, softer and more barren than before.

A servant approached with a jug of wine, made a bow and poured it out for the nobles. It gave Edmund the pause he needed to duck out of the conversation before he caused any more trouble. He tried to get Ellí's attention, acting as though they had never met. "Elísalon." He could not quite say it the way that she had, but he still liked the sound of it. "That's a Mitiláni name, isn't it? From away south?"

"So it is, and so am I," said Ellí, with only the faintest trace of an accent.

Edmund leaned past an annoyed Luilda to get a closer look at what Ellí was doing. "What are you writing about?"

Ellí stoppered her inkwell. "I'm working on a translation. This is in the Dhanic language, of the most ancient form. Not one in a thousand can read this, but if you really are some sort of wizard, perhaps you might be able to assist me."

Edmund read the words on the page in front of Ellí. *Tsalamemyu. Idhak tsaluri* . . . He resolved their meaning into his own language, then tried not to gasp aloud.

"No." He shook his head and made sure that his lie carried along the table. "I'm afraid I can't understand that at all."

He sat back in Lord Aelfric's chair, staring down at his feast without hunger. He turned over the words again and again in his mind: *I am being watched. Meet me in the cellar, tomorrow night at sunset. Come alone.*

Chapter 7

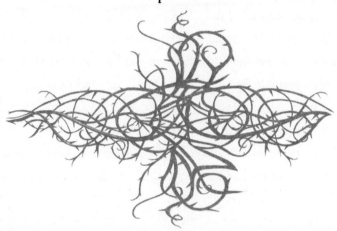

Katherine crept along the cold, swept passage. "Indigo?" She looked about her and kept her voice to a whisper. "Indigo, where are you?"

An enormous gray head stuck out over the door of a stall at the far end of the stable. Indigo fixed Katherine in one dark eye. He snuffed at the air and twitched his ears, then drew back from view.

Katherine took a careful glance behind her. The stable stood half again as high as the one on the farm back home, a single row of stalls graced by decoration that far surpassed what she would find within the dwelling of a prosperous merchant. Boys shouted and heaved outside, hauling up a whole morning's worth of dung and carting it away in barrows, their voices ringing flat against the sides of the castle walls.

Remnants of Katherine's old life greeted her no matter where she chose to look—Soot, Yarrow, Bluebell, all the mares from Papa's farm, squashed with their foals into stalls meant for one. It set her teeth on edge; any fool could see that the foals should be kept out in pasture, a stony hillside in the lee of the wind where they could find their stride and strength. They should be outside, eating grass grown on limestone, learning the scents of the meadows and the sights of field and wood. Someone should be checking them for sickness, someone should be watching them grow and waiting for just the right moment to wean them from their mothers.

Anger gave way to sorrow. "Forget me." Katherine picked up her rags, her wash bucket and her bundle of ash-and-soda soap, then turned her back on them. "You're not mine. You never really were." She hurried past heads thrust out in greeting, ignoring the whinnies and snorts and invitations to play. It felt like a millstone pressing down upon her back—everything her papa had trained her to do, everything she had wanted to become, all wasted, all useless, all for nothing.

The next stalls she passed bore the marks of long residence. Spare bridles sized just so hung from the posts, and blankets of matching colors lay folded with care upon the trunks. Here and there leaned a lance, as much the steed's weapon as the rider's. Many of the stalls bore the names of their occupants carved into the beams above: Firebrand, Sword-of-Glories, Dauntless. Katherine knew them all, remembered every warhorse as a spindle-shanked colt who followed his mother everywhere. She had birthed them, trained them, coaxed in them a fire, a love of the charge and the clash of arms. Though they were all grown up into fierce, proud stallions, they still nosed out to snuffle for the touch of her hand. She forced herself to

MATTHEW JOBIN

hurry past. She could spare little time, and so could enter at only one door.

"Indigo." She raised the leather loop from the door to his stall. Indigo nudged aside to let her in. He put his nose to her in greeting; she gave him half the carrot she had saved from breakfast.

"Are you well?" She lingered at his side, stroking his neck though she knew how he hated to be bothered at his food. "How are they treating you?" He had not grown up the same color as his mother—white hairs amongst the black made him look like a thundercloud, a deep slate that in some casts of light really did hint at blue. He had grown up perfect, the finest horse of war she could ever hope to train. He had the stride, the strength and the proven fire. They had proven it together.

"We should be training with the lance right now, out on the pastures back home." Katherine ran her hand over his withers. "We should be practicing the turn and charge—but look at me. What am I, now?"

She set her rags and bucket by the door, and tried to drag her ill-fitting workdress into shape. Indigo took his chance to shove his face into her belt, looking for the other half of the carrot.

"Get off, you great silly!" Katherine nudged him away, then reached for the brush that lay in the corner of the stall. "I can't stay long." She swished it along his muscled neck and down each of his forelegs. He blinked and stretched his lips, enjoying the attention as he always did, but that only made her feel worse.

Indigo was not hers anymore, not even to raise and train. Her papa was marshal of the stables no longer. None of them were ever going back to the farm. Home was home no more.

"Papa, come home safe." It was not the swirling chaff that made her eyes water so. "Come home soon."

She felt a prodding at her arm. "You must think me a fool." She stroked the whorl of fur between Indigo's eyes. "I fear for things that have already happened, and for things that may never happen at all."

Indigo tossed his head up and down. He bent to drink from his trough.

Katherine whistled, then warbled a song to hold the misery at bay, her voice always weaker than she thought it should be, breaking and trailing to a lisp over the ends of the notes. Papa would come back. All would be well, even if they had to live somewhere else, even if they had to make their living a different way and never trained horses again. She could wallow deeper into the mire of her worry, or rest upon all that had proven good.

"Tom is free." She swished the brush along Indigo's broad, straight back, then down his muscled hock. "Did you know that? His stupid old master will never find him now. Lord Tristan will take him in and take good care of him, I'm sure of it. Maybe he'll make a man-at-arms of him, somehow. Wouldn't that be grand?"

Indigo turned an eye on her, big and brown, full of what she would always say was sympathy.

"Papa won't be long." She reached for the curry comb and

swept it in tight circles through his coat. "He'll have a talk with his old friend Tristan, and together they'll set everything right. You'll see."

She spun out her tale of dreams come true for her own hearing. "And Harry, too—I'm sure he'll return before long." She whisked bits of chaff from Indigo's withers. "You're promised to be his, but he'll still let me train you, so in a way, you'll still be mine."

Indigo whickered, then blew out a snort. Katherine spoke no more of Harry, or of where her thoughts of him always led. There were some dreams she dared not speak into anyone's ear, not even Indigo's.

She bent down and took one raised hoof in her hands. "I've no right to ask for an easy life just because of what we did up in the mountains." She scraped the mud from the insides of his metal shoes. "It doesn't work like that, does it?"

Indigo nuzzled at her side. Dust drifted in the sunbeam.

"We faced the Nethergrim itself." She rubbed a hand under his chin, just the way he liked best. "We might have made all the north safe for years to come—*that's* our reward, *that's* our thanks."

Indigo pushed his head against her. She stroked his black mane. She felt like herself again.

"Papa will be home soon, and all will be well in the end." She took up his tail to comb it straight. "I really shouldn't worry so much."

A voice broke loud over the silence of the stable. "No, no, run along, now. We'll see to his horse ourselves." The hinges of the stable door creaked, and autumn wind raced down the passage. "What, does your lord not attend to his own steeds, at times? Ha! You surprise me not a bit."

Footsteps approached—soft shoes, then hard boots, then the plodding clop of hooves. Katherine looked left and right for a place to hide. She considered simply leaping out, babbling an excuse and scurrying past with rags and bucket, but then the men started talking again, and what they said froze her to the spot.

"I believe we are alone, Father." The second voice sounded young, with a highborn accent to match the first. "What news of his grace, our king?"

"You leave the king to me, Wulfric my boy." Lord Wolland's voice seemed to roll with the easy rhythm of his tread. "Keep your wits on the task before us. Winter seeps across the world; we have time for one lunge, one throw of the dice, then all must wait for spring."

Katherine dared to peek into the passage. Two men approached, Lord Wolland and a young knight who was broad of shoulder almost to bursting from his armor. Flecks of spittle clung to the mouth of the horse led by the young knight, a warhorse of masterful size whose stumbling gait spoke of the last heaving lunges of exhaustion.

"The folk of Rushmeet have shut their gates, barring all passage on the bridges." Wulfric steered his hard-breathing mount into the stall right next to Indigo's. "I was received in Quentara with ill humor and much suspicion."

"Good! I am most glad to hear it." Lord Wolland sauntered in behind them, and shut the half-height door. "A lesson for you, my son: It is good to have an enemy who suspects nothing, but it is better still to have an enemy who suspects the wrong thing."

Katherine kept her breaths slow and soft. She pressed herself into the corner of the stall. Indigo twitched his nose, then pinned back his ears. He fixed a dark eye in the direction of the nobles, as though he could see right through the wall and despised what he saw.

Lord Wolland leaned on the rail of the stall, so near to the corner that Katherine could see his elbow protruding into the passage. "I sent you with orders, my boy—have you fulfilled them?"

Wulfric's words came at a plodding pace, as though he was weighing up each and every one. "They are fulfilled, Father, though I feel the stain upon my honor for my part in it."

"You sat too long at the feet of the bards, my boy!" There sounded the slap of hand on armored shoulder. "You are coming to manhood, and it is time to cast off the fancies of youth. Honor is a tool. You use it to bind your enemy's sword into his scabbard, while your own blade remains free to hand."

Wulfric jingled the harness as he untacked his horse. "Yes, Father. But can we not have our victory another way?"

"Another lesson, my son: Never rest on chance, when you can reach for certainty." Lord Wolland's voice sounded so incongruously plum and cheery that Katherine could hear the smile on his face. "Without the aid of Madam Drake, too much would depend upon taming our good friend Aelfric."

"Aelfric is weak, my lord and father." Wulfric heaved up the saddle and set it over the rail of the stall. "His lands are less than half the size of yours. He would be a fool to oppose us."

"But that's just what he is, my son—a fool. A stiff, stead-fast, honorable old fool." Lord Wolland spoke in indulgent tones, as though describing a dear friend. "This much I know of Aelfric—he is not easily moved, even when he thinks all hope is lost. Indeed, for such a romantic as he, lost causes are the best causes. Why do you think he held up the banner of the Stag in the old wars, right to the bitter end, though it nearly cost him everything?"

"For honor, Father."

Lord Wolland clapped his hands, as though a jester had earned himself supper with his jokes. "Ha! Never mind, my son—for all his honor, Aelfric will break, just as we wish. You see, he has acquired a great weakness in these latter days, one that I intend to exploit for all it is worth."

"What weakness is that, Father?"

Another slap on the shoulder. "He loves his son."

Katherine sidled closer to the door and cast a stealthy glance into the passage. There was no getting past the two men without being heard or seen, and now that she had stood listening for so long, she had no idea what might come of being discovered.

"Aelfric has read the letter that I wrote him and knows perfectly well what it means." Wolland pushed back the door to the stall and strode out into the passage. "When all is in readiness, I will ask what I need of him, and he will grant it to me."

Katherine leaned in as close as she dared. She pictured in her memory the elegantly scribed letter she had seen Lord Aelfric reading over and over in his chambers. If the light had been just a little stronger, she might have seen through the thin parchment to read it from behind.

Wulfric made the telltale scrapes of someone cleaning out mud from the shoes of his horse. "What did your letter say?"

"Ah, my boy," said Wolland. "Remember that you are not merely my only son and heir, but also a knight sworn into my service. If I need for you to know something, I will tell you. Mostly, I tell you to hit things, because that is what you do best."

A long pause followed, interrupted only with the swish of brushes through the coat of Wulfric's horse. "I am not stupid, Father."

Lord Wolland roared with ready mirth. "And who said that you were? Oh, very well, my son. I do not wish to leave you wholly in the dark. Here is how it stands: Wolland and Quentara are the two great powers of the north, each on one side of the wide river Tamber that forms the spine of our kingdom. We in Wolland now hold sway over the neighboring baronies of Tand and Overstoke, and of late our will has carried amongst the Uxingham Hundreds. The Earl of Quentara has counted Lord Aelfric a firm friend since their childhood, and if it comes to it could likely rely also on what force Tristan could muster. We are thus divided east and west of the river, with the city of Rushmeet straddling the gap, content to play both sides and take their tax on the trade that crosses on their bridges. Something of a deadlock, you see, especially with such a wide river and so few bridges to span it."

Another long pause. "And that is why we are in Elverain."

"Very good, my boy! You have it exactly." Wolland sounded

like a teacher congratulating a student for finally working out two plus two. "This little place is nowhere, and yet it is the gate to all that we desire. And with the aid of Madam Drake, and the somewhat-less-willing help of good Lord Aelfric, we shall *have* what we desire."

"Father . . . my lord—" When Wulfric hesitated, he drew out his words even longer. "What will men think of us, claiming victory so?"

"They will think, my son, that we are their masters, and that is all I need for them to think," said Wolland. "Now, let us come to it before Aelfric's stable boys find their way back in here. My weapon—it is ready? It is moving?"

Wulfric heaved a heavy sigh. "Your weapon moves, Father."

"Good, good." Wolland drummed out the beat of a march upon the rail. "And what of Madam Drake?"

Wulfric made a cough of disgust. "Her eminence barters like a common merchant. She demands to be made your Lord High Mystical, when all is done."

Katherine put a hand to her forehead. When all *what* was done?

"Good." Lord Wolland clapped his hands. "Excellent!"

Wulfric tossed the brushes and tools in the corner of the stall. "I do not understand, Father."

"Another truth of politics, my son: You can trust someone only once you understand what she wants from you." Lord Wolland leaned with careless ease against the stable wall, his rotund frame filling most of the passage. "Madam Drake craves the dignity of high office. She can only achieve such an end by binding her cause to mine. I am well content with that."

"Very well, Father. What then is your next command for me?"

"To wait upon my word, and in the meantime enjoy the tournament and knock a few of Aelfric's knights into the dirt." Lord Wolland opened the shutters to the window that looked out into the courtyard, letting in the light of the first autumn day when the sun's main strength seems not quite enough. "Not such hard asking, I hope?"

"No, Father." Wulfric followed Wolland out into the passage. To Katherine's surprise, they turned to come her way, and she only just had time to squash herself into the straw beneath the half-height door.

Wulfric took but a few steps before he came to a halt at Indigo's stall. "Now, there." He leaned in to look over the door. "There stands a handsome creature."

Katherine crouched but a few feet from Wulfric, so close that she could have touched him just by reaching up her arm. She stole a glance—Wulfric might have been eighteen at the most, but with the bulk of someone fed on good meat every day of his life. The hand he put to the door bore calluses and cuts whose pattern Katherine knew well, for she had ones to match on her own right hand from training with a sword.

Wulfric gazed on Indigo in open awe. "Such a stride, Father, such form and fire. I have never seen his equal."

Indigo raised his head and flattened back his ears. Katherine feared that he might step right up to the door and take a nip at Wulfric's hand, but he contented himself with ignoring him and turning instead back to his hay.

Lord Wolland paused only long enough to throw a glance into the stall. "You know the custom of the joust, my son. Defeat the man who rides this horse, and he is yours."

Wulfric lingered a moment longer, staring at Indigo in astonished reverence. "That is the finest horse I have ever seen." He turned to follow Wolland from the stable. "I will have him, Father."

Chapter 8

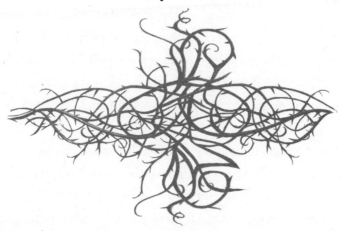

Clouds slipped past above in silent shrouds. The sun hid his face from the world; Tom wished that he could do the same. He tugged the lead, coaxing the donkey onward past the killing place. The wind played chilly tricks with the corpses of the men strewn about him in the courtyard, rustling their clothes and making it look as though some of them were only just stirring from their slumbers in the grass.

Tanchus leaned against the gatehouse wall, trimming his fingernails with a wicked-looking knife. "Now, you tell me, Hamon. Why didn't you just kill this here boy last night?"

"You can go on and kill him right now, if you like." The crossbowman busied himself with inspecting the action of his weapon, cocking it back and firing it without a bolt. "When you're done, toss him on the cart with the rest of the corpses, and then take 'em all down for burying, and when you're done with that, go clean out the dung chutes, since that was what the boy was going to do next."

"Oho! I see now." Tanchus stepped forward to poke Tom in the belly. "So, how's it feel to be a slave? Eh? How's it feel?"

Tom knew better than to answer. He twitched the lead and walked on beneath the raised inner gates of the castle, leading the struggling, straining donkey and the cart loaded down to bent axles with the piled dead.

The clops of the donkey's hooves hollowed out into echoed taps on the cobblestones that paved the tunnel. Tom found that there was no need to ask the men to raise the outer gate, for it cranked up as he crossed through the tunnel, with grunts and jerks and shouts from above of "Heave, boys, heave!" Another cart trundled in off the drawbridge, smaller and in even worse repair than the one he drove. A troop of four peasant women pulled it by hand, their heads low, their forms huddled, flanked by a pair of Rutters bearing swords and wearing thoroughly ugly smiles.

The heavy, recessed door drew back in the side of the tunnel. "About time, you hags!" Aldred Shakesby stuck out his head. The scar on his face twisted one side of his mouth into a smile that the other side did not match. "What took you so long? Did you have to grow that barley from the seed?" His laughter made his speaking voice sound almost musical by comparison.

One of the women stepped out before the others, heavy of hip and clothed in a housedress dyed a rusty-red. "Where are our men? Where are our husbands, our brothers and sons?"

"Shut your noise." Aldred wore a jack of heavy leather,

studded with iron knobs set two fingers apart. He turned to call down the tunnel. "Tanchus Vidler, Hamon Ruddy, get over here! Search 'em for weapons, then lead 'em in."

"Now then, my lovelies, now then!" Tanchus rubbed his hands as he approached the women. "Arms out, let's make sure this ain't no trick!" He took to his task of patting them up and down with great relish.

Tom stopped his cart on finding that one of the corpses had slid partway off the back and lay dangling with his arm dragging on the ground. He laid the man out straight again, sickness churning at his stomach, then took a deep breath and led the donkey onward.

Aldred leaned in to sniff at the contents of the villagers' cart. "Now, that's the stuff! There ain't two handfuls of decent food in this whole castle. You there, what's your name?"

"Rahilda Redfield."

"Redfield, right—wasn't your husband beadle of the harvest this year? How much barley have you got in stock down in the village?"

"Why don't you come down to the village and count it yourself?" The big young woman restored a sack of barley that had fallen from the cart, placing it amongst baskets of parsnips, field beans and sourcress. Spatters of blood dribbled off the back of the cart from the severed throat of a slaughtered pig.

Tom nudged the donkey forward, drawing up before the brigands and the village women, and, finding no space to pass by, stopped in front of them with his head hung low. The women turned to look at him; the shriek that came next doubled and redoubled in the confines of the tunnel. One of the women, her hair half gone to gray, shoved her way past the brigands and threw herself down beside Tom's cart.

"Ell. Elmer! My sweet boy." The old woman trembled. She caressed the broken head of one of the corpses. "He was my son, my son, my only son."

Tom stared down at the cobblestones. He wanted more than anything in the world to kneel with the woman and speak some word of comfort in her ear, but he knew that he could not, that he had no friend amongst anyone there. No one in the castle there cared a thing for him—the women because they thought he was one of the brigands, and the brigands because they knew that he was not.

"Mum." A bony young woman put her arms around the old one, using the embrace to drag her up again. "I know it's hard, I know it is, but we've got living folk to look after. That's for us to do. Come now, Mum, come now, come away."

The old woman leapt up, then leapt to the attack. "Murderers!" She sprang at the brigands, trying to wriggle out of her daughter's grip. "Monsters! Murderers! What have you done?"

"You stay your hand, Diota Byley." Rahilda stepped forth to block her way. "We're in deep enough trouble as it is, so don't dig us in any deeper. Brithwen, you hold your mother back, now."

"Mum!" The thin young woman grabbed her mother by the back of the dress. "Hold, Mum, please!"

Diota Byley wrenched and wrestled, but could do no more than swing a fist an arm's length away from Aldred's amused face. "Murderers!" She collapsed on the flagstones of the tunnel.

Tom kept his face turned away, hoping to escape both the

wrath of the women and the notice of the brigands. In amongst the loud and angry echoes, a voice whispered in his ear. "How? How can you do such things? You're just a boy."

Tom glanced aside. The youngest of the village women stood at his shoulder—in truth but a girl on the edge of womanhood, with free-flowing auburn hair and a heart-shaped face anyone would call pretty, even through the redness and the tears.

"I'm not one of them." Tom dropped his voice as low as it would go, hoping that his words would be lost in the tumult. "My name is Tom. I'm from Elverain. I came here with John Marshal."

The girl's thin brows went up. "John Marshal? You mean Lord Tristan's old friend? Is he here?"

Tom had no chance to answer. Rahilda knocked him out of the way, then fell to searching through the bodies on the cart. She rounded back on the brigands. "Where is my Donston? Where is my husband? Where is he?"

"If he ain't on that cart, and he ain't lying dead in the courtyard, then let's just say our employer's found a use for him." Aldred scratched his nose. "Aye, best leave off thinking of him altogether."

"Some of you might find yourselves new men for marrying, and sooner than you'd think!" Tanchus seemed to find himself the height of wit. He scratched his chin, sizing up the women before him. "Let's see, let's see, who'll I choose? Hmm, you there, with the curls. How old are you?"

The auburn-haired girl went white and tried to hide behind Tom's cart.

"You keep away from my sister!" Rahilda seemed to forget

her talk of caution. She sprang up and charged, and might have made it all the way to Tanchus had the crossbowman not been ready.

Hamon Ruddy pointed his loaded crossbow at Rahilda's chest. "Just you stop right there, if you don't want this boy to cart you down to the graveyard with the menfolk."

The women let their anger give way to despair. Diota Byley sat on the cobbles, weeping with such force that it sounded as though she would choke, while Rahilda collapsed against the tunnel wall, striking at it in hopeless fury.

"Come now, all the talking's done. I'm not going to stand here listening to your wailing." Aldred Shakesby made a show of turning away. "Get to the kitchen, and get our dinner started."

"But here, give us that first." Between them, Tanchus and Hamon got the ale barrel out of the cart. They staggered off together, crab-walking the barrel through the tunnel.

Aldred flicked a hand. "Kitchen's along the far side, behind the hall at the back." He opened the side door up to the gatehouse. "Get in there and get to work. And you there—boy! You think those bodies are just going to get up and walk to their graves all by themselves? Get on with you, or I'll have you hanging from the walls by your innards. Move!"

Tom led the donkey onward, clopping over the drawbridge and out onto the castle green. The sun threw off its cloak of cloud and shot its fire off the mountains that ringed the vale around him. Streams traced down through stands of spruce and fir, touching and flowing one into the next until they gave rise to the river that rushed through the meadows behind the castle, filling all the valley with a whispered lullaby. Had the circumstances of the day been any different, the beauty of the place would have made him stare about in happy awe.

"Jumble!" Tom whistled on the castle green, and then again once in the encircling trees. "Jumble, it's me. You can come out now. Come back. It's me."

No answer came. Birch and alder leaned this way and that down the course of Tom's travel, on a road that nearly bogged out time and again around the skirt of the castle hill. Fields spread out into the forests surrounding, inroads of axe and plow into a carpet of elm, ash and oak gone bare for the winter soon to come. Women and children stared at him from field and garden, but none of them approached.

The road rose out of crackgrass and bog, up by turns through meadows and then copses of trees standing naked in the chill. Huts ringed the bulging end of the road, their gardens seeming to edge right up to the banks of the river. The graveyard stood on high ground, in sight of water but not so close as to risk a flood. The shallow pit opened up by the brigands was not nearly wide enough.

Tom let the donkey off the harness to graze. He took up a shovel abandoned near the pit and got to work. Every now and again, someone from the village crept from the trees to watch him, but when he turned their way, they always slipped back out of view.

"Jumble!" Tom tried whistling again, in between digs of his shovel into the earth. "Jumble, it's me! Come on, boy, come on out."

The whistle came back down alone from the mountains. The donkey shot a look at him, chewing on a mouthful of long grass, then snuffled farther on toward the trees.

Tom took a long look at the faces of the dead as one by one he laid them out in the grave. He found Tibalt Hackwood's hat lying in the gory bottom of the cart and replaced it on his head before he arranged him next to his uncle Osbert. He made sure that all the men lay on their backs, faced up in a row toward the boundless sky.

A question came to him then. He would not have been able to say from where, if anyone had been there to ask.

"I will." He spoke his answer to the dead, down on one knee with the butt of his shovel to the earth. "I swear to you all that I will." He stood and started throwing in the dirt over the row of blank and staring faces.

It felt as though the chilly wind blew against the sun, slowing its progress through the sky and drawing out the pain of the day. Tom's arms ached to numbness from hauling the bodies of the village men up onto the cart, most of whom weighed more than he did. It took three trips up and back from the castle to bring them all down to their common grave. By the time he had laid out the last of the dead, he could hardly see where he swung his shovel in the falling dark.

"The dung chutes are over there, boy!" Tanchus leaned forth to shout as Tom passed by the entrance of the great hall. Bawdy songs and torchlight filtered through a crack in the door behind him. "Hop to it!"

Tom turned in the direction of his next task, but before he had gotten far, he stopped before something he had not noticed the night before, the one thing in the courtyard that looked like it was well made. A statue stood moonlit on a cleared spot of ground, fashioned in the likeness of a stallion rearing up on its hind hooves, the most handsome and noble horse Tom had ever seen, carved from the stone of the mountains with skill, long patience and love. The great forehooves were raised to give a thunderous blow, the shapely head thrown back in proud fury. Letters ringed the pedestal on which the statue stood. Tom bent to look at them, wishing—and not for the first time in his life—that he could read.

"It says 'Juniper.'"

Tom turned to find Rahilda standing behind him, a sack of barley balanced on her shoulders.

"It used to be one of those standing stones you see about, but Lord Tristan had it carved to look like his old horse," said Rahilda. "Just like Tristan to spend a fortune on that, and make a mess of the work on his walls."

Tom touched the cold stone flanks. "It's beautiful."

"My sister tells me you're not with that bunch." Rahilda nodded up at the brigands on the walls around them. "But if you're not, why didn't you run when you had the chance?"

Tom stood up. "I could ask you the same thing."

Rahilda shrugged. "There are folk here—children, elders—who could never get away. I won't leave them."

Tom let that be his answer, too.

Rahilda started walking. "My sister says you know John Marshal." She glanced over her shoulder, seeming to expect Tom to follow.

Tom caught up with her in two long strides. "I grew up on

the farm next to his. He's the closest thing to a father I ever had."

"Where is he now?"

Tom held out his hands and let them drop. "Gone."

Lord Tristan's great hall stood more than twice as high as a house, its sharp slate roof coming to a peak within a few feet of the battlements. Windows ran its length, cut back into the timber, all of them shuttered. The kitchen stood at its north end, in shadow from roof and wall.

Rahilda went inside, then emerged a moment later with a bowl of porridge, barley and field beans all in a glop. "Here. Take this down to Lord Tristan. They're holding him in a cell beneath the watchtower."

Tom took it and turned to go. He looked back. "Is there anything you want me to tell him?"

Rahilda thought it over, then sighed. "Tell him he should have kept a better lookout on the world."

Tom hurried off across the courtyard, one hand over the bowl to preserve its warmth. He mounted the steps to the thick wooden door of the tower, found it barred, and so banged on it.

A slot drew back in the door, and a pair of eyes glinted. The door opened, and a man with big arms and a bigger belly leaned out. He was dressed in a shirt of chain armor that clanked against the keys at his belt. "That slop had better not be for me. I saw them carting that pig in here, and I want some fresh pork."

Tom ducked his head, almost bowing to the man. "This is for the prisoner."

The jailer picked up a lantern from the room's lone table and held it out. He jutted his double chin at the stairs. "He's down there."

Tom took the lantern and descended. The lancet top of the arched stone staircase brushed through his hair, even though he crouched as he walked. He felt out each of the dank stone steps before he committed his weight. He dared to hope, just a little. He had not sat listening to the tales of Tristan all his life as had Edmund and Katherine, but he still knew that he was approaching the presence of the greatest hero the world had ever known.

"Who is there?" A voice called from beyond the last stair, past the iron bars of a cell and out of the darkness beyond.

Tom reached the door of the cell at the bottom of the stairs. "I've brought you some food, my lord." He held up the lantern to see within—the cell was rather large, a room of the same size and shape as the guardroom above it. A pair of raised stone slabs stood in the center, each of them large enough that someone could lie down on it. Funny paintings ran the circuit of the walls, surrounded by the sort of squiggly symbols Edmund liked to read. Piled sacks littered the floor, beside a fold of carpet on an old table and a chair painted red and blue with two broken legs.

"My thanks to you, then." Someone stood up in the shadows, a man taller than Tom and twice as wide at the shoulders. "I do not recognize your voice."

Tom darted a wary look up the stairs, then dropped to a whisper. "My name is Tom. I am not with the brigands. I came here from Moorvale, with John, the Marshal of Elverain."

"John has come? He is here?" The man felt for the pillar and stepped closer, coming into the light of the lantern.

Tom let out a gasp, and almost dropped the stew. Hope guttered and died within him.

The man was old. Lines cut deep into the skin of his face, and though his shoulders were indeed grand, they were also stooped. His hair gleamed white, save for two dark streaks in his beard, one on each side of his mouth. Tom took all of this in afterward, for it was the man's eyes that transfixed him in shock and understanding. They were set and shaped in ideal proportion, spaced exactly wide enough and perfectly even, but a thick, milky film covered the whole of their surface.

The prisoner raised a hand while seeming to gaze into the empty space above Tom's shoulder. "I am Tristan."

Chapter 9

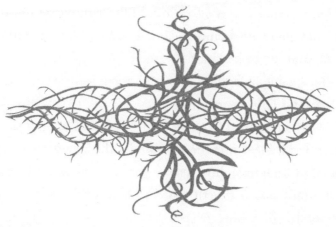

Ellí held a finger to her mouth. "Quiet. Stand right there, Edmund. Don't move. Watch my eyes."

Edmund could find himself looking nowhere else. Ellí's blue eye dilated, until the iris was a tiny strip of clouded sky encircling night. Her brown eye contracted to a pinpoint, a shaded forest where he might wander and lose himself forever.

Ellí reached into the sack slung at her belt. She drew forth dust—it glittered as she threw it high into the air. "ALL FLOWS, NOTHING STAYS. I PUT MY HAND INTO THE STREAM."

Edmund looked up. The dust arced and began to fall.

"BY MY WILL I TURN THE CURRENT." Ellí's voice took on a vibration that Edmund felt in his belly. "BY MY WILL THE FERMENT CURLS. ALL FLOWS, NOTHING STAYS. I PUT MY HAND INTO THE STREAM."

Edmund shuddered. He gaped. The bits of dust hung in the air. At first they seemed utterly still—but they descended, ever so slowly, their turning edges glinting, reflecting a light whose source he could not see.

"We can speak freely now," said Ellí. "No one can hear us here." The glittering dust turned and turned, stars winking on and off around her head.

Edmund felt as though a whisper and a shout would sound just the same. "Where are we?"

Ellí's voice seemed to come from behind him, even though she stood in front of him. "We are under the Sign of Obscurity."

Shadows—voices, presences—moved through the edges of Edmund's world. He felt a thrum beneath his feet. "I don't understand."

"Edmund, listen to me." Ellí's hair slipped free from the net that bound it. It cascaded around her face as though it had a will to move and flow, every strand of it a different shade, blown by a wind that Edmund could not feel. "Lord Wolland means to start a war. Indeed, he has already started it."

Edmund hissed. "A war? Then what is he doing in Elverain?"

"Every war needs allies."

The hairs on Edmund's arms stood up and stayed raised.

"Lord Wolland means to make war and he means to win." Ellí held a hand to her forehead, the palm over her blue eye, her face contorted as though in pain. "He has made a bargain to secure the aid of creatures that once came near to exterminating every man, woman and child in the north. He is in the service of the Nethergrim, and he does not even know it."

A trembling dread filled Edmund at the mention of the Nethergrim's name. He tensed and came to understand that he was waiting for the Voice to intrude upon his thoughts, even there under the Sign of Obscurity. "Why are you telling me all this?" he said. "What do you need me for, and how did you even know my name when we first met?"

"I'm telling you because I hope that you will help me." Ellí drew in a long breath through pursed lips and took her hand away from her face. "I need you because you thwarted the Nethergrim once already, and no wizard in centuries has been able to do that, no matter how well trained. I know your name because the wizard who taught me everything I know whispered it when she thought I was not listening." The blue in her eye had dilated to nothing, leaving a glassy void.

Edmund turned his head. He was nearly sure that he had heard the sound of his own voice in the distance, shouting or maybe screaming. He shuddered but tried not to let his fear show.

"The creatures whose power Wolland seeks are called the Skeleth, in the language that is mother to the tongue we are speaking now." Ellí picked up her skirts and turned to leave, and Edmund found himself following her, out through what might have been the doorway through which they had entered. "From what my teacher found in the archives of the Chancery down in the Tithe, the Skeleth threw down whole kingdoms into ruins in ages past. They serve the Nethergrim, killing and ravaging without remorse and without end, and if the legends are right, they cannot be defeated in battle."

A heavy tread broke the silence of the passage outside. "I swear I heard something! Ulf—hey, Ulf, get over here!"

Edmund leapt back from the threshold in fright. He looked wildly about him, but the low cellar chamber had only one door.

A young, tall castle guard poked his head into the cramped cellar chamber where Edmund and Ellí had hid themselves. Excuses for what they were doing down there raced through Edmund's mind.

"Be calm." Ellí put her hand on Edmund's arm. "Calm, now. Stay with me. They won't be able to see us."

An older guard, sallow-cheeked and balding, stepped in behind the first. He raised a torch, flooding the room with light. "What are you talking about, Gammel? There's no one here."

Edmund recoiled. He stood within arm's reach of the two guards, so close to the torch that he could feel the heat of its flame upon his face. The tall one turned to look right at him— his face took on hollow, frightening shapes—and turned away again, poking through the sacks and stores along the wall.

"The guard is nothing. He does not matter." Ellí did not even try to whisper. "Stay calm, and feel nothing."

Edmund fought down his fear. He glanced at Ellí. "Why can't they see us?"

"Their eyes see, but their minds ignore the sight." Ellí stepped out of the way of the path of the tall guard's search. "Their ears hear, but the sound means nothing to them."

Gammel pawed through barrels and sacks, walking right past Edmund again and again. "I heard something before, I swear I did! It's one of those Wollanders, I'll bet, snooping about the place."

"To do what, report to their lord on the state of our cheese supplies?" Ulf turned and left, bringing the torch with him. "I've had just about enough of you for one night."

Gammel shook his head, looking right at Edmund, then shrugged and followed his companion out.

"I've seen a spell like this before, but from the other side." Edmund caught up to Ellí on her way out of the cellar behind the guards. "I don't remember the dust, though."

"Every wizard makes her spells in her own way," said Ellí. "She finds her own balance and pays her own cost."

"What's the cost of your spell?"

"You have much to learn of our ways." Ellí winked at Edmund with the brown eye. "It's not polite to ask that sort of thing."

Edmund emerged behind Ellí into the courtyard of the castle. Echoes fled wide of him, and the night sky above seemed to ring and shake with the meter of his steps. He felt a shiver, fear and delight run together. "Can you teach me how to do it?"

Ellí smiled at him, though the ever-shifting visions of her spell smeared it out into toothy trails. "I'm just an apprentice myself, but if you would like to learn from me, I would be happy to teach you what I know."

Edmund had dreamed almost as many dreams about learning magic as he had about kissing Katherine. In most of those dreams, though, the teacher was a stern old master whose grudging respect was only slowly earned, not a friendly, lively girl scarcely older than he was himself. He could hardly believe his luck.

The browning remains of Lady Isabeau's garden seemed to curl and twist into the sky. A guard walked the parapet above the courtyard, and another coughed from atop the turrets of the keep, but they seemed to walk on empty trails into another world, and showed no sign that they had noticed Edmund and Ellí passing beneath their gaze.

The longer Edmund stayed within the spell, the easier it became to distinguish between the sights of his own world and the fragmented visions that trailed around them. He hurried himself to walk abreast with Ellí. "So where are we going?"

"Your lord Aelfric comes from an ancient family, older than the kingdom itself, in fact." Ellí ascended the narrow stairs that led up to the raised, narrow door of the keep. "All the legends tell me that when the Skeleth were last summoned, they ravaged someplace nearby to here. Lord Aelfric keeps a library, books he has inherited from his forefathers down through countless generations. If there are records left of what happened the last time the Skeleth were raised, they will be there."

"But that's in Lord Aelfric's private chambers!" Edmund recoiled from the empty sound of his own voice, and dropped to a whisper. "We can't just go in there!"

"We must," said Ellí. "The fate of all the north might depend on it." She did not pause at the door of the keep, and the guard posted there spared neither her nor Edmund a glance. Edmund felt a nagging tug of conscience, but Ellí swept on inside without an instant's hesitation, and he was not about to lose his new teacher so quickly.

The great hall roared with another night of noisy feasting. Edmund followed Ellí on tiptoes around the benches and past the hearth, taking care to avoid tripping over anyone on his way behind the tapestries at the back of the room. The narrow passage beyond led to a set of stairs that he took two at

MATTHEW JOBIN

a time. When he reached the top, he pushed the door wide to enter the hallway above. Servants slept on rush mats in alcoves along the passage, huddled in pairs for warmth outside the bedrooms of the great folk they served.

Edmund turned back to Ellí and found a gleam in her blue eye that matched the thrill he felt. "I must admit—this is fun."

Ellí gave him a wink; he found her prettier on the brown-eyed side, somehow. "This is where I will need your help the most. I can't keep up this spell for much longer, so we should find what we need as quickly as we can. Start with the oldest stuff first."

"Right." Edmund guessed at which door to try and got it right the second time. "In here." He ushered Ellí into Lord Aelfric's private study and closed the door behind them.

"Look at all of this!" Ellí grabbed a pile of scrolls from the shelves and started flipping through the dirty, half-ruined pages. "There are scholars down in the Tithe who would kill for half of what's on this shelf alone. Would you light those candles for me?"

Edmund reached for the flint and tinder, lit the candles impaled upon the pewter holder, and dragged them close. He knelt at the bottom shelf and started searching. The words, glyphs and drawings under his fingers tempted and teased at him, seeming to crawl back and forth across the page beneath the swirling shadows of the spell. Ancient legends passed before his eyes, tales of the deaths of kings he had never even heard about, accounts of travels to places he had never known existed.

"Many centuries ago, after the fall of the Gatherers and the collapse of the great Dhanic empire, a wandering tribe crossed over the mountains from the west." Ellí spoke softly as she searched the highest shelf, her skirts swaying and dangling by Edmund's hands. "They found the remains of the old empire easy pickings, so they marched here in ever greater numbers, looking first for plunder, then for conquest."

Edmund picked up a book, then placed it aside—tax records. "Who were they?"

Ellí reached down to poke at Edmund's hair. "From all I have read, they looked a lot like you do. They were the old Pael, and we are speaking the child of their language."

Edmund pulled out a rather torn and tatty book from the shelf. He had to turn it facedown to hold it, for the stiff leather binding only remained on the front. The back side of the book was nothing but a ragged, ruined page, the ancient stitching along the edges coming out in fraying loops.

Edmund set the book on the thick oaken council table and turned through a few pages. "Ellí. Here."

Ellí bent to look. "This is it! Oh, well done, Edmund!" She read along in breathless fascination: "There came three kings, three brothers, three kinsmen of the Pael: Ricimer, Thodimund and Childeric the Fair; an axe-king, a sword-king and a king of tall spear. The brothers marched for mastery across the north, each taking for his queen a maiden sister of the Dhanu. Each king built a tower for his queen, a Pael tower by a Dhanu stone."

Edmund leaned in over the table. "Wait, go back. Read that last part again." He listened, then wanted to jump into the air from excitement. "There's a broken-down old castle on a hill beside my village. One of its towers is older and taller than the others, and it's next to a standing stone that looks older still."

Ellí's brown eye twinkled in delight. "And you wondered why I might need your help."

Edmund felt a blush creep up around his ears.

Ellí placed her hands on the book with an air of reverence. "This is the *Paelandabok*, the work of unknown hands in the dark years before the making of your kingdom. Bits and pieces of it survived as quotations in the works of other authors, but I don't think anyone outside Lord Aelfric's family has seen the original in centuries." She followed the closely scrawled text onto the other page: "A tower by the riverbend for the Queen of the Wheels, one within the mountain vale for the Queen of the Heart, and one in the fairest of the lands between water and wood for the Queen of the Thrice-Opened Eye."

Edmund leaned in to look at the words as Ellí read them. "No one remembers any of this, anymore. It's our own history, and we don't even remember it."

"Forgotten history is often repeated." Ellí picked up the *Paelandabok* and handed it to Edmund. "Go to the tower near your village. Find out what you can."

"Me?" said Edmund. "Just me?"

"Once my spell ends, I'll be under watch again." Ellí gave Edmund a pleading look, just as she had done out on the moors. "Edmund, it's up to you."

Edmund looked at the *Paelandabok*, then at Ellí. A sinking feeling came over him. "And we're taking the book. We're stealing a precious, irreplaceable book."

Ellí nodded her head. "I'm afraid we must."

"Come on, then." Edmund sighed. "It's not as though I've

never done it before." He reached for the handle to the door—
then leapt away again.

Ellí rose from her chair. "Edmund, what is it?"

"Hear that?" Edmund pushed Ellí back into the corner of
the chamber. "Someone's coming!"

Stealthy footsteps shuffled to the threshold. Even though
Ellí's spell still held, Edmund found himself pressing back toward the wall. The door swung slowly wide without a creak,
and someone stepped into the room.

Edmund nearly dropped the book in his hands.

"Isn't that your friend?" Ellí stepped wide to let the new-
comer pass on by. "The serving maid?"

Katherine wore her ill-fitting workdress, and the candlelight showed her dark around the eyes, the hollowness swollen
by the shadowed whirl of Ellí's spell. She peered about her in
wary confusion at the burning candles on the table, coiled and
ready to bolt. She went back to the door and listened, and then
with a look of tight fear on her face that made Edmund want
to pop from the shadows and announce himself, she crept to
the other end of the table and sat down in Lord Aelfric's carved
and cushioned chair.

Ellí nudged Edmund. "Has that girl lost her mind? What is
she doing here?"

The fire lit along the curve of Katherine's chin and sparked
in the depths of her eyes. She pawed through the pile of parchments set in front of Lord Aelfric's place at the table, then
pulled one out and set it before her. She leaned on one arm,
staring down at it, then tucked back a strand of hair behind

her ear, and Edmund saw the look of rising horror on her face.

Edmund came near to Katherine, passing around behind the backs of the chairs. She held a single scroll of parchment, elegantly scribed and fixed with a waxen seal. Her dark eyes scanned the words, once and then again.

Ellí nudged her way up beside Edmund. "What is that she's got? What does it say?"

Katherine put down the scroll, pale to her lips. She picked it up again, turning it to the light of the candle. Edmund read it over her shoulder:

From Edgar, Baron Wolland, to his most noble and excellent peer Aelfric, Baron Elverain, greetings, health and honor,

The Stag has been flushed from cover. The Duke of Westry sits in chains beneath the Spire at Paladon. Your name is whispered in council, amongst others whom His Grace the King has long suspected of treachery. Your rigid loyalties have cost you, as I have always told you that they would.

In the name of our long friendship, I extend one chance to you, one hope before the stroke that will fell not just you, but your legacy. I shall soon depart to visit your lands, traveling by an unexpected route. We will use the distraction of a tourney as a reason for my visit. When the time is right, I will ask you for something. You will give me what I want.

I offer you one chance only. Seize my hand—or fall, and young Harold shall fall with you. The king will not be merciful to traitors this time.

Do not think too long on this. I do not have the luxury of patience.

Given under my signet, from my castle at Norn, upon the quarter day of Woodmoon, in the fifteenth year of the reign of His Grace our glorious King,

Edgar

By the way, if there is anyone who knows what you have been plotting these last few years, I would keep a close eye on him.

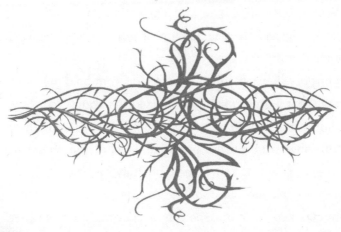

Chapter 10

Tom's shock fell away, leaving a blank hollow in his gut. The great hero he had sought was a blind old man, his best hope no hope at all.

Tristan shuffled closer, feeling out until he touched the bars of his cell. "There is no light." Sounds grew edges—Tom breathing, Tristan breathing. A sweet and floral scent hung ill at ease in the lifeless air.

"No." Tom remembered the noble rank of the old man before him. He bowed. "No, my lord."

"My eyes retain one power." Tristan's voice was a worn keepsake, an old and long-loved robe. "I can still tell night from day, and torchlight between. I fear that my welcome is an empty thing, yet you may have it gladly."

Tom leaned against the bars. Fright and confusion met and danced in him. He hung his head.

"You have suffered." Tristan felt out with his fingers. Tom had never known someone wholly blind, but guessed that for such a man, touching was something like seeing. He held forth a hand for Tristan to grip through the bars.

"Young, but tall." Aged and worn though it was, Tristan's hand still carried the impression of matchless strength. "And somewhat underfed, I fear."

"I forgot—here, my lord, your food." Tom held out the bowl. "It's not what a great lord will be used to eating."

"I am an old campaigner." Tristan dug the wooden spoon into the bowl and ate the porridge without the slightest hint of complaint in voice or face. "You may lay trust that I have survived on shorter commons than this."

Tom looked over his shoulder, listening for the jailer. He reached out and rattled the door of Tristan's cell, then stuck his finger in the lock.

"I did try that myself—a few times." Tristan hummed in mirth. "Alas, this door was one of the only things in the castle I was able to build as sturdily as I had planned."

"Forgive me for asking, my lord, but why does everything look so broken-down in here?" Tom succeeded in doing nothing but pinching his finger in the tumblers. "The whole castle, I mean."

"I have been told many times that I made a better hero than I do a lord," said Tristan. "I trust too easily and see the good in everyone."

Tom gave up on the lock. "I cannot think that is much of a flaw, my lord."

"That is what I always said, but Vithric never missed a chance to mock me when my trust proved misplaced." Tristan did not truly seem to be reproaching himself. "I am about to do the very same thing again, right now. You tell me that you came here with my old friend John, and though he is not here to speak for you, I am going to take you at your word. It is an old habit, and one that has gotten me into the worst sort of trouble."

Tom made a furtive, futile search of the bars, hoping against hope to find some flaw, some way to get Tristan out. He found them all to be perfectly sound, built from hard iron and set with skill into the stone. "Was there a prisoner here, my lord? Before you, I mean."

"No, no." Tristan's joints crackled as he lowered himself down to sit on a stool by the door. "This was meant for a storeroom, a treasury of sorts, a place to guard a thing, not a person."

"The box." Tom remembered the pallid glow, the keening wail, the rows of glowing, waving, jointless limbs. "The thing that held those creatures."

"Indeed so," said Tristan. "Vithric told me that they are called the Skeleth. We found their casket right here, between these two slabs that must once have been places to lay out the honored dead, and when Vithric made me understand how dangerous were the creatures held within it, I made sure to keep it locked away as best I could. Only three ever knew of its existence—Vithric, John and myself."

Tom peered into Tristan's cell. The two raised slabs were solid, but empty, and the broken-down furnishings scattered about on the floor would not have looked out of place in the humble dwelling of a peasant. A burst-open sack of dried lavender was the source of the floral scent. It had leaked out half its contents by the central pillar, spilling onto the iron ingots, pink over rust.

"We two have one comfort," said Tristan. "I know every brick and plank of this castle, and I never bothered with listening holes or things of the like. If we keep our voices low, we may speak without fear of being overheard."

Tom did not know where to begin. He opened his mouth to speak, but his thoughts tumbled over one another—the horrible, flickering creatures; the jerking bodies of the men; the wizard-woman chanting; the screams; John Marshal's face, dead but moving. Then he remembered why John had come to Tristan in the first place. The Nethergrim had returned, and Tristan's old friend Vithric was its servant. It was too much, all too much. The words did not come.

A rat skittered out across the floor of the cell. Tom watched it make a few darting forays near Tristan's feet to lap up gobbets of fallen porridge. He did not know what use it was to conceal the sound of his weeping, but he tried.

"Courage, Tom," said Tristan. "All is not lost."

Tom trembled. "How do you know that?"

Tristan stood again. "We are here speaking, are we not? Who knows what may yet come of that? Tell me what you know, and let us see what we can make of it."

Tom started where the pain was fresh. "A wizard-woman turned the men of your valley into monsters." His voice wavered and broke. "Two dozen hired brigands hold your castle, the women and children cower in fear down in the village, and you're—you're—"

"Stone blind?" Tristan's laughter had yet more power than

his grip—soft and simple, joyful and unconquered. "So are you, down here, or near enough to it. Perhaps you will come to understand. Let us be silent for a moment. Do not try to think of anything. It may help you to close your eyes, despite the darkness."

Tom shut his eyes.

"Do not hide from your fear," said Tristan. "Do not flinch from it. Let it find you. Let it show you what it wants you to see."

Tom beheld the faces of his friends, Katherine brave and Edmund quick. Thinking of them made him think of all the other folk in the north with friends, with family. He stopped grieving over John Marshal and the other monster-men, and remembered the direction they were going when last he had seen them—eastward, back into settled country, back toward the towns and villages of the north, toward his home. He clenched the bars.

Lord Tristan touched Tom's fingers. "I will not lie to you. I felt horror as my sight began to fail me, I pitied myself and wept bitter tears for what I was about to lose, but I remembered that I had led three hundred people in to settle this valley, and while I lived I would be an aid to them. Let us now put aside our despair, for it serves no cause."

Tom could hold it in no longer. "My lord, Vithric is alive."

He hesitated then, unwilling to speak further, for at his words Tristan's face lit up with a joy that stunned him with its strength, and felt like an act of murder to crush.

"He faked his death many years ago." Tom forced the words out. "He is a servant of the Nethergrim. Two weeks ago, he tried to kill me and six other children."

Tristan's face froze. "That cannot be." He stared at nothing, slack and befuddled, like an old man who had lost his grip on the world. "It cannot be so."

Tom grieved for the world in which he lived, where telling a simple truth could be an act of cruelty. "It is so, my lord."

Tristan put his head in his hands. He blinked and blinked. "Of course. Yes, of course. That is how Warbur Drake knew that the Skeleth were here."

He looked up to the mold-rimed ceiling of his cell. His milky eyes strained and failed to fix. "And now at last I see a darkness."

Tom felt his fingerhold on hope slipping once again. "My lord, your people—you said that while you lived, you would be an aid to them."

Slowly, and with every sign of pain and struggle, Tristan roused himself again. "So I did."

Tom spoke from his heart and hoped it would not sound like an insult. "Courage, my lord. All is not lost."

Tristan took his own words back without the slightest show of anger. "Indeed so. Truly so. We are here, Tom, living now, so let us do what we can here and now."

Tom rubbed his tear-pricked eyes. "I will help, my lord, any way I can."

"Our enemy's greatest advantage is their position here within these walls." Tristan's voice regained its calm power. "We must gather all we know of their numbers, their habits and weaknesses. It may give us a chance to overthrow them."

Tom raced through everything he had seen on his way inside. "I counted two dozen brigands, my lord, give or take a few.

Some of them guard the walls, but they already look restless and bored."

"Good. It is as I hoped—they lack discipline." Tristan stroked his beard. "Warbur Drake is gone? The woman you saw, the wizard."

"She left with the creatures."

"Our situation improves yet more," said Tristan. "Who is in command? The young knight?"

Tom shook his head. "No, a man called Aldred Shakesby. Old, with a bald head and a scar that runs from eye to lip."

"Ah." Tristan raised his brows. "That is also good. Very good."

"Why?"

"I know the man," said Tristan. "He was the steward of this castle, the man I hired to ensure all ran smoothly here in the valley."

Tom drew in a breath. "Then you have been betrayed from within!"

"Thoroughly." Tristan paused to laugh softly at himself. "Vithric once told me that my great weakness was that since I never lied myself, I had little skill for detecting falsehoods in others. He told me that many times—how I wish I had listened!"

A voice from up the stairs cut across what Tom was going to say in answer. "Boy—you down there!" The jailer's chair creaked, and his keys jingled. "How long does it take to give the prisoner his slop?"

"I'll be right up!" Tom called back, then whispered to Tristan: "My lord, I'm afraid of what will happen to your people under the thumb of these brigands. Help me find a way to free them."

The jailer stepped onto the stairs above. "Boy!" Lantern light swelled out through the mouth of the staircase.

Tom seized Lord Tristan's scar-horned hand between the bars. "Help me, my lord. Please. What do I do?"

Tristan's sightless eyes searched in darkness—then widened. "The food." He turned to Tom. "My steward was late with the harvest. How much food is there in the castle?"

"Almost none, my lord."

Tristan dropped his voice at the approach of the jailer. "Tom, a well-defended castle has dominion over all the land around it, but only if the men who guard it have enough to eat." He felt out for his bowl of pottage, but bobbled it and knocked it over in the putrid straw.

An idea came to Tom with such speed and force that he could hardly believe he had thought it on his own. "Yes, my lord. I understand."

The jailer bent down his head to emerge in front of the cell. "Come to have a look at the great hero, have you?" He raised the lantern to show Tristan groping about him, more than a foot away from the place where he had dropped his meal. "Ha! Get your fill of this old buzzard while you can, boy. I doubt he'll have much time left to squawk." He mimed the act of hanging, sticking out his tongue over his jowls.

Tom knelt by the bars and felt his long arms through. He scooped up the bowl before the last gooey dregs could leak out. "Here, my lord."

Lord Tristan turned at the sound. "I thank you again." He had splashed some of the porridge in his long white hair, so that it hung down in a clump over his ear.

Tom placed the bowl in Lord Tristan's blind grip. He dropped his voice low, so low that he was not sure Tristan's old ears would hear. "I think I have a plan."

"I put my trust in you." Lord Tristan turned away, shuffling off into the dark.

"Come, boy, don't test my patience." The jailer turned away, lantern in hand. "Don't think anyone will care an Anster farthing if you disappear, so you'll want to keep me happy, and hop when I say hop. Come to think of it, I'm going to send you over to the hall for my share of that ale I saw them hauling in."

Tom followed the jailer over to the stairs. He could not help looking back one last time. Lord Tristan crouched by the pillar, doing his best to shoo the rats away from what remained of his porridge—and eating it with a finger, for the spoon was lost somewhere in the straw.

The jailer turned around and snorted. "Sorry sight, hey? All them fancy stories, and then you see him. He should have died back in the old days, in his glory. Hanging him would be a mercy, you ask me."

Chapter 11

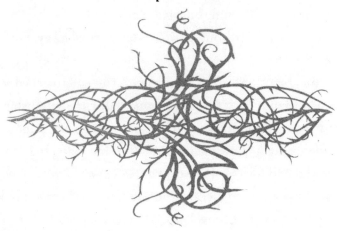

A shadow crossed Katherine's back: "Girl! Quit that mooning!"

Katherine blinked. She reacted, but too late. A laundry-stick smacked hard across her knuckles, causing her to drop the tunic she was washing with a splash into the tub.

"You look what you're about, you hear me?" Goody Bycross, head laundress of Castle Northend, loomed in at Katherine's shoulder. "You make a mess of my lord's good shirt and I will make you wish you were never born."

Katherine rubbed her hand. The cut that ran from finger to finger had healed almost clean, two weeks after she had gotten it by cracking a bolgug on the mouth with the pommel of her sword beneath the mountain of the Nethergrim. The strike of the laundry-stick had opened it again, and gotten lye soap under the skin. She looked down at the angry, itching slash, then balled up her hand into a fist and rounded on the head laundress.

"You mind your place, you great thick strumpet." Goody

Bycross set her teeth—not an old woman yet, though she already walked with her shoulders hunched. She waggled the laundry-stick at Katherine. "Don't you dare face up to me!"

"I'm not," said Katherine. "I'm facing down to you."

Everyone in the laundry shed stopped what they were doing, runner-boys and pot-girls, the row of washerwomen beating at the linen and the withered old crone stacking wood for the fire.

Katherine remembered where she was, and what had become of her. She remembered that she had no home, and that all the toughness in the world would not provide her with supper. "Forgive me. Please. I'm new."

Goody Bycross pushed past her. "You're no man's daughter now, girl, and don't you forget it. You heed your betters or I'll have you out on your ear."

Katherine stared at the hard dirt floor of the laundry shed. "Yes, mistress."

"I want fresh linens up in the ladies' day chamber, and new tablecloths for the hall." Goody Bycross pointed at a bundled load that would stagger a mule. "Get moving."

Katherine cast a glance through the shed at the other laundresses, then back at Goody. "Just me?"

"You're built for hauling a load, and so far as I can see, you're good for naught else." Goody Bycross had already moved on down the line, inspecting the work of the girls and women under her command. "When you're done, go scrub the floor of the great hall. Yes, the whole thing—I'll let you know when to stop."

Katherine stooped to heave up the linens. She could just manage to get her arms around them, but the first two times she gained her feet, their unwieldy weight nearly made her trip and fall down again.

"Serves her right," one of the laundry-girls whispered, loud enough for absolutely everyone to hear.

Katherine tried to peer over her bundle to mark who had spoken. It did not matter; a giggle spread up and down the rows of girls soaking dirty washing in the tubs. Whispers grew to become mutters, and then brazen talk:

"Doesn't know her place in the world, that's her problem."

"Oh, she'll learn it here, soon enough."

"Her father raised her wrong, that's the truth, and now see what's come of it." They kept at it, sticking barbed words into Katherine's back on her way out the door. "She'll grow old alone, you mark me."

The sun stood high enough to flood between the walls of the castle's inner ward, casting its wan autumn smile over a frantic swarm of activity. Smoke curled in great black puffs from the wooden kitchen by the keep, bakers hauled in carts stacked with fresh-cooked cakes of bread, and a dozen men worked double-time, cleaning barracks and smithy down to the last speck of dust. Katherine dodged from the path of boys hauling plates and serving-ware out of storage, then nearly tripped over a bard who sat rehearsing his music on the grass. A ringing fanfare sounded, and guardsmen stepped in march-time along the battlements toward the inner gates. The castle shook and bustled with preparations for the tourney, and could hardly have looked more chaotic if it was under attack.

"Katherine!" Footsteps sounded behind Katherine on the path through the garden. "Katherine, wait—it's me!"

MATTHEW JOBIN

Katherine looked over her shoulder. "I was hoping you'd come find me." She could not set down her bundle of linen anywhere nearby without getting it dirty, so she wobbled back and forth with it clutched in her arms. "I'm glad you're here, Edmund. We need to talk."

"I know." Edmund waited for the procession of servants to pass by toward the great hall with the nobles' noontide feast carried between them, then took a careful look around. "Lord Wolland's here to start a war."

Katherine stared at him. "How do you know that?"

"Never mind that right now." Edmund tried to make himself look as though he were discussing something of no consequence, faking a smile and gesturing to the bright pennants and happy folk in the courtyard while at the same time muttering under his breath. "Remember the wizard girl at Harvestide? The southerner, Elli—she's fighting a secret war against the Nethergrim. There are creatures called the Skeleth who once laid waste to all the north, and Elli's afraid they're coming back."

"What are you talking about? What does this have to do with Wolland?" Katherine stumbled back and forth, straining to hold on to her unbalanced load.

"Here." Edmund held out his arms. "Here, Katherine, let me help you."

"If you like." Katherine shifted her bundle onto Edmund, who staggered under its weight and promptly dropped it.

"Sorry!" Edmund reached down to gather up the linen, red to the ears, and somehow managed to scuff more dirt all over it with his silly-looking shoes.

Katherine stooped to beat the linen clean. "Edmund, how

can you be sure that some old monsters from ages ago are coming back?"

Edmund gave up trying to help her. "I read it in a book."

Katherine sighed. "Another book? Where did you get this one?"

Edmund cast a nervous glance about him. He dropped his voice to a whisper. "From Lord Aelfric's study."

Pins and needles prickled up Katherine's neck. "What?"

"It was Ellí's idea." Edmund spoke so fast that his words smeared together in a nervous babble. "She said we had to find true knowledge of the past to understand what's about to happen, and she was right! There were these three kings, you see, and three queens, and if the book's right about them, they were—"

"So," said Katherine. "Some wizard girl in Wolland's service tells you she's fighting the Nethergrim, and without asking a single question about why she wants you to do her bidding, you just run off with her to plunder Lord Aelfric's private library."

"It's not like that!" Edmund spluttered. "Ellí's wise, and good. And very nice."

Katherine crossed her arms. "I'm sure she is."

"No, no, that's not what I mean." Edmund shook his head. "There are creatures coming, horrible things that serve the Nethergrim, and—"

"How can you be so sure?" said Katherine. "How do you know you're not just running errands for a greedy wizard—or worse, doing something Wolland wants?"

"Girl!" A screeching voice interrupted Katherine's retort. Goody Bycross poked her coiffed head through the low

MATTHEW JOBIN

entrance of the laundry shed, and brandished her stick at Katherine. "Get a move on, you great ox! Did I give you leave to flibbet about with a boy? You mind your work, curse you!"

Katherine heaved up her linens. "We'll talk about this later." She turned her back on Edmund and mounted the narrow stairs into the keep. "I have work to do."

The arched fireplace in the corner of the great hall burned low, and the tiny arrow-loop windows did little to relieve the gloom. A girl made a round of the walls, snuffing every other candle and oil light. Two dozen castle servants were ranged throughout upon the benches, some working at crafts and mending while others wolfed down a hasty meal of porridge and leeks before returning to their duties. Sir Richard Redhands sat with Lord Overstoke at the high table, speaking of hawks and boars, spears and hounds, meat and blood. Katherine had only been in the castle for a day, but already knew better than to try taking the grand stairs behind the nobles. She turned instead to go the long way around, up the spiral stairs toward the sentry-walk, only to find Lady Isabeau standing in her path.

"Katherine." Lady Isabeau backed Katherine out of the way with a glare. "I have heard ill reports of your efforts in our service so far. Is even laundry too complicated a task for one such as you?"

"No, my lady." Katherine put a foot behind her to steady herself and succeeded only in ripping the hem of her workdress.

Another, larger figure followed Isabeau down the stairs. "Ah yes, John Marshal's daughter!" Lord Wolland ambled into the passage. "Your young friend told me of your many deeds of valor at the feast last night. How splendid to meet you at last!"

Katherine made a deliberately clumsy curtsy in reply, feeling Lady Isabeau's hard glare on her. "I'm just a maidservant. No one in particular, if it please you, my lord." She fumbled for a better grip on her linens and made to hurry past.

"Nonsense, nonsense!" Lord Wolland put out a hand to bar Katherine's passage. "Our meeting is truly a fortunate one, my girl, because my lady Isabeau and I were just discussing a matter of the highest importance, and we do humbly beseech your wisdom on the subject."

Katherine had not the faintest idea of what to do. Lady Isabeau shook with rage, cold and small, in Lord Wolland's round shadow. The smile at Wolland's lips never seemed to quite match the look in his deep-set eyes.

Katherine chose simple obedience as her best course. "What subject is that, my lord?"

"War," said Wolland. "My lady Isabeau maintains that war is a monstrosity, a blight and stain upon our world, while I argue that it is both good and necessary, a wholesome enterprise that destroys that which is weak and sets on high that which is strong. What is your judgment on the matter?"

"You take nothing seriously, my lord Wolland, and you never have." Lady Isabeau looked like she would shove Lord Wolland off the nearest battlement, if only she dared. "You treat matters of high statecraft as fit for discussion with the lowly slattern who washes your bedsheets!"

"And when war comes, my lady, who dies—only those who draw up the plans in the grand councils?" Lord Wolland held out his hand to Katherine. "Say on, my girl. Of what worth is war?"

Katherine braced her bundle of laundry against her knee. "Most folk just want peace, my lord. They have nothing to gain and everything to fear from war."

"Ah, but, my girl, the making of peace is the very object of war!" Lord Wolland clapped his hands, as though Katherine had said just what he expected her to say. "There is never a man born who does not desire peace; even he who plots to start a war does it to achieve a peace, a new and more pleasant peace full of bounty and ease for the victor. The world, alas, does not allow such a life to simply happen to most of us, a fact that you must know full well. Peace, like plenty, must be taken, it must be seized. All peace, all good and gentle peace, is nothing but a prize won in war."

Katherine had never heard such nonsense in her life. "Someone is always the loser in your scheme of the world, my lord. Victory in war breeds cruelty, and cruelty breeds revenge. War only makes more war."

Lord Wolland put his arm around Katherine. "My dear girl, look about you." He gestured to the various people in the hall. "You see before you men and women of various ranks, of different fortunes and stations in life. Some think that these differences are fixed by the stars, or written in the blood. Not so. That fixing—this man the lord, that one the servant, that one the slave—that is peace. In days of peace things carry on as they are, but in war all things are possible."

Lady Isabeau stormed over to an elderly man setting out

the decorations on the high table. "You halfwit! Did you not listen?" She picked up a silver tankard carved into the likeness of a prancing stag, and shoved it into his trembling hands. "Take that away at once!"

Katherine dropped her voice. "My lord, should you achieve what you desire by making war, what will you do then? If you set your life by rising, what happens at the summit?"

"Ah, my foolish girl. This world is large enough that a man may strive and strive, and he may dwell all his life on the upward path." Lord Wolland let Katherine go, but with a careless ease that said that he could seize her again, any time he liked.

Fear and revulsion propelled Katherine up the spiral stairs. She crossed the sentry-walk and found the ladies' day chamber empty. She set down the fresh linens, folding them to make it look as though they had not been dropped, then picked up a bundle of firewood set beside the hearth and hopped up the next flight of stairs to the garret room where the Lady Elísalon had been given lodgings. She listened at the door and caught a faint, familiar sound, something that reminded her of Edmund.

"My lady? I've come to tend your fire." Katherine prised back the door. The sound she had heard was the frantic scratching of pen on parchment. The fire in the hearth burned a bright purple-blue, fueled by a pile of veined, bone-white things that did not look at all like wood. Ellí sat hunched in a chair beside it with a book laid out across her lap, next to a spinning wheel and spools of carded wool. She scrawled across it with a fine quill pen, but did not seem to be looking at her work. Instead, she was shivering, rocking back and forth in a swaying loop, staring into the strangely colored fire.

Katherine entered and shut the door behind her. Ellí breathed in and out with a hissing shudder, like someone slowly freezing to death. A whimper escaped her lips—she came to the end of the page and turned it, then dipped her quill into an inkwell with a trembling hand.

Katherine stole up to the girl's shoulder. She leaned over to look, and could not help but consider the charms of her face. Ellí was neither plain nor pretty, but her brown eye flickered with a fragile warmth. She had a small mouth, set in a trembling bow, her teeth clenched over her lip.

—*seek to rule his mind.* Ellí scrawled in broad strokes across the page, as though racing to catch up with her thoughts: *Tempt him, bring him, draw him in with every lure.*

Ellí paused. She moved her hand down a line and wrote again, slower than before and with a rounded, handsome script: *Yes, your eminence. I hear and obey.*

Katherine felt her guts churn and tighten.

All else flows apace. Ellí scribbled fast again. *Your Sisters and Brothers keep to their tasks. Do not fall behind.*

Ellí paused a moment. Her lips twitched—half a smile— then she scribbled onward:

And good day to you, Katherine, daughter of John, the former Marshal of Elverain.

Ellí turned her face to Katherine. The effect made Katherine jump—Ellí's other eye, an icy blue, seemed lit up by a completely different intelligence than the brown. The expression on Ellí's face, which had looked like a desperate fragility, seemed revealed as a mask, a ruse—come closer, my dear, so that I might seize you by the neck.

Katherine's vision misted over in rage. She reached back a hand and smacked Ellí across the blue-eyed side of her face, hard enough that the noble young lady spun from her chair and dropped to the floor. Then Katherine raised the skirts of her workdress and kicked at the fire, scattering the strange white sticks. Embers whined, crying out like babies abandoned in the cold.

Ellí rubbed at her cheek. She sat up. "Who . . . what are you doing in here? The servants were told not to—"

Katherine grabbed Ellí by the loose folds of her dress. "Who was that? Who were you speaking to?"

Ellí hissed and struggled. "Unhand me. Let me go, you low-born wench!"

"Hurt Edmund and I will kill you." Katherine leaned in close. "I will spill your guts on the ground. Do not think for one moment that I won't."

Ellí reached into her belt. "ALL FLOWS, NOTHING—"

"Enough of that." Katherine wrenched the girl around and shoved her up against the wall, scattering the dust in her hand across the floor. "Now, you will tell me exactly what you were doing, what Lord Wolland is planning, and who you really serve."

Ellí's blue eye contracted, the pupil disappearing under inward-crawling veins. "COME INSIDE, CHILD, COME INSIDE." Her voice took on a thousand ringing tones. "STEP WITHIN AND FIND ME."

Katherine froze. A vision blotted her sight, shapes forming from the swirl of blue—eyes within eyes, snaking tails entwined and knotting, a mouth of cruel beauty, a spiral turning ever inward to a point it never reached. A falling, flailing fear clutched at her, the feeling that had pursued her in her dreams every night since her escape from the mountain of the Nethergrim. She fell back shuddering, lost and alone.

She felt a blow to her leg, then another to her face. She staggered and lost her footing, tripped up by her workdress. She only just got out of the way of a flashing thrust; Ellí had a knife out. Katherine sprang back, planting her back foot, her father's lessons at swordplay drawing themselves out so clearly in her mind that she could hear his voice—*when your enemy has a blade but you do not, use everything around you for your defense. Never lose your footing, and wait for the overconfident strike.* She kicked the spinning wheel into Ellí's path, giving herself space to maneuver and a moment to get her bearings. Ellí came at her again, but this time she was ready. She twisted inward with the thrust, rolling out of the way and bringing down her fist on Ellí's forearm.

Ellí dropped the knife and broke away, making a desperate lunge for the door, but Katherine blocked her path. She made a clumsy feint that did not fool Katherine in the least, then backed into the opposite corner of the room, from which the only exit was the stairs that led up onto the roof of the tower. "No one will believe what you saw up here."

"Edmund will believe me." Katherine circled the girl, keeping her moving, waiting for her to step the wrong way. She kept watch on the movements of Ellí's body, averting her gaze from the spiraling blue eye.

Ellí grabbed for a skein of wool that lay beside the spinning wheel, then dodged backward and onto the stairs. She threw it upward while holding on to the loose end. "I MAKE MY FLIGHT FROM A THOUSAND FALLS." The thread in her hand drew taut, jerking her with sudden force into the air.

Katherine charged up the stairs, but just missed grabbing hold of the fluttering hem of Ellí's dress. Ellí flew high and away out of reach, off the roof of the tower and into the autumn clouds above. It happened so quickly that the lone guard on the turret, who stood watching the other way, did not even see her go, turning instead to blink in surprise at Katherine.

"You're not supposed to be up here," he said. "What do you think you're—"

Something fell to strike the roof of the tower between them with a thump. The guard gaped at it, as did Katherine. A goose lay broken and dead upon the stones, and then another fell nearby, bouncing off the battlements and then tumbling down into the courtyard below.

"Father's thunder! What is this?" A voice rose from the courtyard, distracting the guard long enough for Katherine to duck back down the stairs.

"Edmund? Edmund Bale, are you still here?" She hunted around the inner ward of the castle, past servants and grooms standing in awed bunches around every fallen bird. Many of them stared up into the sky, but by then Ellí was long gone amidst the clouds.

Chapter 12

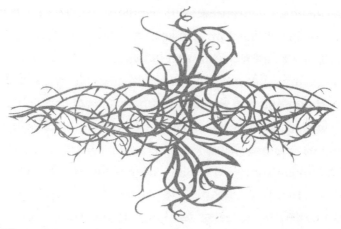

Geoffrey nocked his arrow. "Who's there?" He drew to the ear, staring out at the mossy scatter of stones that were all that remained of the gates. "Who's there?"

After a breathless moment, an answer came. "Who." A winged shape glided past on the wind above the walls. "Who, who."

Edmund dropped his guard and shot his brother a wry look as the owl flew past overhead. "You didn't have to come up here, if you're scared."

"Shut your face." Geoffrey relaxed his draw. "You're scared, too."

Edmund sat down amongst the rubble of the gates. "Hold that torch a bit closer, will you? I can't make out the words." He used a leaf to brush a caterpillar off the page and found his place in the crawling text: *Each king built a tower for his queen, a Pael tower by a Dhanu stone.*

"It's here." He looked out over the broad valley that sheltered his village, the curve in the great river Tamber, the moon-touched pastures and fields of home. "It's here, it has to be." He turned back to examine the Wishing Stone, then the jagged towers of the broken-down old keep around it, hoping to notice something he had never noticed before.

"There's the fire pit, just as we left it." Geoffrey handed the torch to Edmund and walked over to an ashy depression a few feet from the Wishing Stone. He knelt to pick something up—a girl's shoe. "This is Emma Russet's."

Edmund scanned the walls. "Has anyone ever been in that tall tower, that you've heard?" He pointed. "That one there, with the funny angles and those markings up the side."

"I never wanted to see this stupid place again." Geoffrey let the shoe drop into the grass. "Where's Katherine? Is she going to meet us?"

"Don't be such a baby." Edmund brought the spitting flame of the torch as close as he dared to the parchment of the *Paelandabok:—the covenant was made, the king through his queen, thrice-sighted, thrice-blind. Horse by horse and hero by hero did armies fall before the Skeleth, They Who Crawl Below, they who are seen and yet unseen, form without substance, man and monster both.*

"Geoffrey, have you ever heard of something called a Skeleth?" Edmund took up the tattered book and crossed through the overgrown grass beneath the crumbled walls of the old keep. "In the old stories, maybe, or from travelers at the inn?"

"You can't tell me you feel all right up here." Geoffrey sat with folded arms beside the fire pit. "This is where the bolgugs

MATTHEW JOBIN

caught me and Tilly, and dragged us away to the Nethergrim. Peter Overbourne died just down the hillside, over there."

"You are not helping me think, Geoffrey." Edmund raised his torch as he approached the tallest tower. "If all you're going to do is moan and cry about—"

"You cry more than I do, so shut up about it!" Geoffrey leapt up with his fists balled tight.

Edmund recoiled. "I do not!"

"Yes, you do." Geoffrey jutted out his chin. "You cry in your sleep all the time."

"Liar! You take that back!" Edmund advanced on his brother, brandishing his torch—and tripped over something in the straggled grass.

"What's this?" He reached down and unwrapped the flappy thing from his foot. He held it up—a wide square of double-stitched cloth, embroidered in a simple peasant pattern and knotted at two corners.

Geoffrey blinked at it—and blinked, then turned away. "Tilly's shawl." His voice broke. "That was Tilly Miller's."

Edmund let the shawl flutter to the ground. The last time he had stood within the tumbled walls of the old keep, he had watched a pack of bolgugs drag Geoffrey and Tilly away to the lair of the Nethergrim. He had pursued and persevered and brought Geoffrey home safe again, but Tilly lay withered and dead, unburied in the mountains.

He turned to his brother. "Do I cry that often?"

"Every night." Geoffrey kept his back to him. "I think you talk to it, in your dreams."

Edmund's skin prickled and crawled. "Talk to what?"

Geoffrey turned a tear-marked, bitter look on him, then stomped away across the grass.

Edmund set the *Paelandabok* atop his folded cloak and drove his torch into the ground beside the Wishing Stone. He sat down and read on: *Childeric the Fair, king over men, reached his hand for kingship over that which men cannot rule. The iron-hearted king, golden-browed, he raised the most glorious standard ever seen beneath the grand tent of the sun, and yet was he brought low by That which dies and yet lives, That which reigns over all things hateful to men. He was betrayed by That Which Waits Within the Mountain—*

A cold, horrible, familiar feeling crept over him. *That Which Waits Within the Mountain*—the Nethergrim, the Voice, the eyes within the smoke.

"I don't see how you can be so sure it's here." Geoffrey startled Edmund from his unhappy trance. "No one really knows what the ancients were like, or why they did what they did."

Edmund looked about him at the ragged, ruined walls. "The Pael tower by the Dhanu stone." He ran his hand over the surface of the Wishing Stone, feeling out the carven symbols weathered nearly smooth by centuries of wind and rain.

Geoffrey's voice echoed from the far corner of the keep. "Here's the bolgugs, just where Katherine dragged them."

Edmund glanced up to see his brother prodding at what was left of the bolgugs he had blinded with the very first spell he had ever cast, on that night two weeks before—only two weeks? It felt like a lifetime. The bolgugs lay sprawled beside their crude, ugly weapons. Rain had come to wash their blue-black blood away. Something else had come to pick the flesh from their corpses down to the bones.

"Not so scary now, are you?" Geoffrey stood over the skull of a bolgug. His lip quivered, he trembled—then he seized the heavy, spiked club lying near and started smashing the skull to powder. "*Are you?*"

Edmund turned the *Paelandabok* to better catch the torch-light. "Geoffrey, come over here." The symbols inked on the next of its pages seemed to match the faded designs on the surface of the stone. He traced out the symbols one by one upon the stone with his finger, while following along with the inscription in the book.

"Folk used to make wishes on that thing." Geoffrey flopped on the grass next to Edmund. "I wouldn't touch that stupid rock now if you paid me ten gold marks."

"Listen." Edmund read the symbols aloud: "One, one, two, three, five, eight, thirteen. Mind-trust-truth, eyes-trust-lies. After that there is one of the Signs of magic, the Sign of Perception."

Geoffrey wrinkled his snub nose. "Is that some sort of riddle?"

"I think so," said Edmund. "The folk who lived here must have wanted to keep their knowledge hidden from the unworthy."

Geoffrey rummaged through the bundle at Edmund's side. "People have been coming up here for years and years." He pulled out another torch and lit it from the flame of the first. "I'll bet the oldest folk in Moorvale used to play around these walls when they were kids, and their parents before them, back to who knows when. If there was anything to find, someone would have found it by now."

"Don't be so sure." Edmund read the symbols again: "One, one, two, three, five, eight, thirteen. The rest of it means something like 'Trust your thoughts, not your eyes.'"

Geoffrey shrugged off the coil of rope he carried on his shoulder. "All the doors and windows of that tower look like they were bricked up ages ago, which is why no one's ever been inside it that we've ever heard about. How are you going to get in?"

Edmund stared at the blank-faced bricks of the tower. "One, one, two, three, five, eight, thirteen . . ."

Aha.

Edmund got to his feet. He shut the book—it puffed must into the air. "Here, hold this."

"Ugh." Geoffrey scrunched up his freckled face, but he took the *Paelandabok* from Edmund's hands. He beat bits of rot from the pages, then held it as though it could poison him by touch. "What is this thing, anyway?"

"It's a book." Edmund paced out the distance from stone to tower. "I suppose it's too late to teach you how to read one."

"I can read, you twit! I mean what sort of book? Where did you get it?"

Edmund returned to his brother. "Ellí helped me find it."

"Who?"

Edmund looked up at the tower, guessing at the height of his mark. "Didn't you see her? Lady Elísalon—she's traveling with Lord Wolland."

"Oh, her." Geoffrey nodded. "Is she a friend?"

"She helped me get that book, didn't she?"

Geoffrey waited, though with little show of patience. "Aren't you going to do a spell, or something?"

"Learning how to be a wizard is more than just making a fire burst. It's thinking, it's figuring things out." Edmund licked a finger and held it out to gauge the wind. "Didn't Nicky Bird try to climb that tower, back when he was our age?"

"He almost died in the fall," said Geoffrey. "It's why he limps. He's always said that there was something wrong about that tower, that he should have had a good grip between the bricks, but then, all of a sudden, he didn't."

Edmund felt a surge of excitement. "Did he ever say how high up he got?"

Geoffrey scratched his head—then pulled out a leaf that had gotten stuck in his mass of curly hair. "He's told the story so many times at the inn, I can almost recite it by heart. Right under that ring of funny carvings, there, just past halfway up."

Edmund hopped into the air—Geoffrey was pointing exactly where he had hoped he would. He stretched out his hand. "Here, give me your bow."

Geoffrey held his bow in close to his chest. "What for?"

"Just give it," said Edmund. "It used to be mine, anyway."

Geoffrey took a step away, then relented and slapped the bow in Edmund's hands. "Suit yourself, though I can't see what use you'll make of it."

"Oh, you'll see." Edmund drew back, took aim and let his arrow fly. It sailed up toward the mark—but then it veered sideways and disappeared into the night.

Geoffrey followed an infuriating pause with an even more infuriating look. "Were you maybe trying to hit the tower?"

Edmund snapped out with his drawing hand. "Shut it. Give me another arrow."

"Why, so you can throw that one away, too? I've only got so many."

"I said give me an arrow!"

Geoffrey put another arrow in Edmund's hand. "Then mind the wind—it's blowing sharp above the walls. You've got your feet too wide apart, by the way, and you're shanking the arrow with your thumb."

"Don't tell me how to shoot." Edmund planted his feet. He tensed up, drew back and let fly. The arrow whistled high into the air, never getting near the tower. Geoffrey had to hop aside to make sure it did not come down on his head.

"You're hopeless," said Geoffrey. "You couldn't hit the broad side of a mountain."

Edmund snarled and grabbed an arrow from the quiver on Geoffrey's back. He narrowed in his stance, aimed and let fly. His third arrow sped on an arc that looked as though it would strike right on target—but then it spun sideways and tumbled end over end out of sight.

Geoffrey held out a hand. "Just tell me what you want to hit."

Edmund sighed and gave his brother back the bow. "The twenty-first brick, counting from the bottom."

Geoffrey felt behind him for an arrow. "Why the twenty-first?"

"What's one plus one?"

Geoffrey crossed his arms. "Is this some sort of trick?"

"Just answer me," said Edmund. "What's one plus one?"

"Two, of course."

"And what's one plus two?"

"Three."

"Two plus three?"

"Five!" Geoffrey scowled, but then his eyebrows raised. "Oh."

"And five plus three is eight, and eight plus thirteen is twenty-one." Edmund pointed up the wall.

"Right, right." Geoffrey raised his head slowly, counting under his breath: ". . . eighteen, nineteen . . ." He nocked an arrow, drew back and shot, hardly even seeming to take the time to aim. The wind veered the arrow hard, but either by luck or design the gust pushed it right on target. The arrow sped to the spot on the wall that Edmund had marked—and went straight through.

Geoffrey gaped, then let out a *whoop*. "That stone, it's not even there! It's a spell! You knew it was just a spell!"

Edmund turned to him. "Good shot. Really."

"That was brilliant!" Geoffrey thumped Edmund's shoulder. "You're brilliant! How did you know—"

It occurred to Edmund an instant too late that nothing in the riddle had told him exactly where the door was. The grass split, and the earth gave way beneath him. Geoffrey reached out and seized his collar, but then scrabbled at the yawning edge and fell in behind him. Torches and book, arrows, bow and brothers, all tumbled down and down together.

Chapter 13

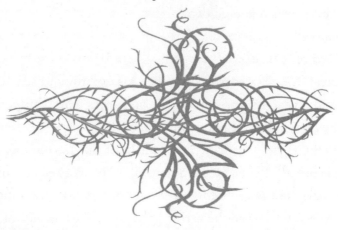

Tom lay awake, just inside the door of Tristan's great hall. He found himself in no danger of nodding asleep—instead it felt as though the watches of the night had stretched out forever, and that ten sunrises should already have come and gone. He tried not to think of all the folk who would likely be dead by the time the sun truly did return, should any part of his plan go amiss.

He turned onto his back. A roof of braced and pillared hardwood arched high above him, over a floor of patterned stone strewn with moldering rushes. Trestle tables ran the length of the chamber, all at odd angles, all covered in dust. Tapestries hung between the pillars that braced the walls, each depicting a man at life size beneath a coating of soot. A knight stood square and grim within the first on the left, his gray beard flowing out over his chain cowl and the point of his sword driven down through the head of the twisted creature at his feet. A very tall man stood bent as though to squeeze himself into the frame of the first tapestry opposite. He wore huntsman's green and cradled a great boar-spear in the crook of a lanky arm. Tom remembered the stories well enough—he looked upon Tristan's old companions, the Ten Men of Elverain, the great heroes who had ridden with him against the Nethergrim long ago. He found himself wishing that they could somehow come alive, that some unknown magic would bring them leaping from their tapestries for one last daring rescue, but instead they stood frozen in the warp and weft of their cloth, looking down upon the scene of their old friend's ruin.

Tom crossed his hands on his belly. He shut his eyes and opened them—then shut and opened them again. How long could it possibly take Rahilda to get the word out to her neighbors? How long to move what needed to be moved? Were they arguing about the merits of his plan? Would they try it? Would someone betray them? He rolled onto his side, pressed to the flagstone floor by his doubts.

When the moment long awaited arrived at last, it shouldered anticipation aside without the slightest courtesy. "Fire!" Tanchus burst through the front door of the hall. "Fire in the village!"

Tom sat bolt upright. The men in the hall had helped themselves to no small portion of the ale, but even so, the cry of "Fire!" had them up and scrambling in a heartbeat.

Hamon Ruddy snorted awake. "What's that? Fire? Where?"

"Fire in the—" From the grunt and thud that came next, Tanchus tripped over a bench in the dark.

Tom got up onto the balls of his feet. He peered about him, and in the glow of the embers from the hearth spied the brigands rising from their stupor to a quick-spreading panic.

"Ow!" Tanchus kicked the bench he had fallen over and let out a stream of truly vile curses. "Fire in the village! In the barns, the grain sheds, the food stores! Fire!"

Amidst the chaotic shouts that greeted the news, Tom heard the crossbowman rounding on Aldred Shakesby. "You jack-in-the-dirt! I told you we should have hauled the food inside the walls. You've ruined the whole caper!"

"Shut your mouth! Move!" Aldred clattered about for his sword. "All of you, up! Move!"

Tom slipped out into the courtyard, stealing through the shadows by the wall and through the rubble of the unfinished keep. He watched the brigands charge outside in a mob and thought he had completely escaped notice—but then he walked right into the path of the jailer rushing forth from his post in the tower.

"Hoy!" The jailer grabbed Tom by the shirt. "Where are you going? What are you sneaking about for?" He held his sword, a thick, saw-bladed thing that looked better suited to torture than to open battle.

Tom made a face of horror, which was not so hard to do given the circumstances. "Fire, fire in the village!"

The jailer blanched to his stubbly jowls. "The food. All the food!" He let go of Tom and turned to yell. "Raise the gates! Raise the gates, we've got to get that fire out or we'll all starve!"

Tom slipped back into the shadows and ran crouching to the smithy, an open structure built without a north-facing wall. Shadows grew into shapes as he crept farther in: a stack of wood, a barrel, tongs, and then an anvil. He leaned around the anvil to peer into the courtyard, where a swelling mass of brigands collected by the raising gates.

"Half of you, stay behind to watch the walls!" Aldred barked himself hoarse beneath the gatehouse. "D'you hear me? No, don't all of you just—curse you all, listen to me! Get back here!" No one seemed to heed him. As soon as the inner gate had been winched above the height of a man's head, the brigands charged off in a mass through the gatehouse tunnel. The fat jailer was not at all the fastest of their number, but once he threw off his mail shirt, he managed to keep up with the pack, following his fellows through the gates and out of view.

Tom poked his head out of the smithy, then darted off the other way, across the open middle of the courtyard. He cast wary looks all about him at the walls, and seeing no one, he doubled his pace toward the foundations of the keep and the postern gate behind it. It was no longer blocked from the other side, as he knew since he had been tasked with carrying loads of refuse through it and down to the river that day. He pulled up the heavy iron bar from its hooks, let it drop in the weeds, and shoved the door wide. Clammy air greeted his face from the narrow, descending tunnel beyond.

"Rahilda?" Tom called out down the steep stone steps. "Rahilda, it's Tom. Are you there?" He waited for as long as he dared, but instead of Rahilda, he heard a very different voice from the other direction.

"All the more reason to do it now, that's what I says." A voice cut whining through the night, coming back from the walls in ugly echoes. "I'm telling you, that old goat's holding out, and this is our chance to take what we can get from him. You got the key?"

Tom turned back, his heart in his mouth, and peeked out over the unfinished foundations of the keep. Two figures passed him by on their way toward the tower, one of them holding a lantern whose flame juddered and shook in the swirl of the wind.

"I don't know about this." The burly, bearded crossbowman passed but a yard from Tom's hiding place. "The boss finds out and we're both cooked."

"He ain't going to find out—not in time, that is." Tanchus cackled from behind the light. "You ask me, this whole business is like to go up in smoke, now, so I'm taking what I can and getting clear of it." He bore a sword in his other hand, a massive, wide-guarded blade he could barely hold up with one arm.

Tom's heart thumped in his chest. He crept out from cover and followed the brigands into the watchtower, his mind wheeling wild and his plan in shattered pieces.

The voice of Tanchus echoed up from the cellar where Tristan sat prisoner: "Here's how it's to go, old man. We've got a crossbow fixed on you. We're going to open your door, you're going to come out, and you're going to show us where your treasure is, or we start killing your villagers, one by one, right here in front of you, and not quickly, if you follow."

Tom crouched at the top of the cellar stairs. He peered out and caught the glow of the lantern, the only light in the tower. Tanchus held it aloft, while Hamon kept his weapon trained on Tristan.

The pieces of Tom's plan tumbled and fell—and then assembled in a new shape. The danger of it took his breath away, but he could think of nothing better. He tensed to spring, waiting for the sound that would trigger his move and hoping with all he had that Tristan would understand and react in time.

Tanchus moved out of Tom's view, up to the door of the cell. "You'll play nice, then?"

"I have nothing that such men as you would want." Tristan felt his way to the door of his cell.

Tom stared hard at the lantern. He would only have one chance. He got up onto the balls of his feet and licked the palm of his hand.

"Hah, and I thought folk said old Lord Tristan never lied." Tanchus leaned on the heavy-bladed sword. "So you're telling me you stomped about up in the Girth thirty years ago, plundering one ruin after the next, and all you got for your trouble was your old sword here and a box full of them Skelly-whatsits? Start talking, or we start killing."

Tristan's voice lowered in defeat. "I will lead you to everything of value in this vale and can only hope that it will satisfy your greed."

"Good enough for me," said Tanchus. "Out you get, then." There was a snick, then a clank as the lock turned.

Tom pushed off with his right foot, taking the cellar stairs in two strides. His third stride became a lunge, a flying leap down the staircase. "Tristan!" He snatched the lantern from Tanchus's hand and tumbled with it to the floor. "Lights out!" He snuffed the wick and felt the flame burn his palm as it died.

A whiny voice rose in confusion. "What in all—?"

Tanchus had little time to exclaim. Even as Tom squirmed aside on the floor, hoping to get clear of the two Rutters, a large shape moved past him in the dark. The crossbow twanged, then thuds and grunts of pain resounded in the gloom.

"I have them." Tristan spoke from the floor in front of Tom. "Find the key."

Tom rolled onto his front and crawled over to the captured men. The one nearest let out a groan—it was Tanchus—then he tried to shift.

Tristan slammed Tanchus back to the floor. "Lie still, and you may yet have the mercy of being tried fairly for your crimes."

Tom scooped up the key, then reached for the crossbow. He found it broken, the string snapped and the bolt stuck in a bale of straw in the corner of the room.

Tristan kicked his sword out of reach across the floor. "This is indeed fine work, Tom, but you took a terrible risk."

"You put your trust in me, my lord, and I did the same for you." Tom tossed the crossbow aside. "With light in the room, you might be just a blind man, but if everyone else is blind, too, then you're the greatest of all warriors again."

Lord Tristan's milky eyes could still sparkle. "I thank you—but it would seem to me that we are in the deepest danger still. Are there not twenty brigands in the castle upstairs?"

"Not just at the moment, my lord." Tom reached for a coil of rope along the wall and bent to tie the crossbowman's hands behind his back. "There—we can make use of this one. We can keep the other in the cell for now."

Tristan stood, turned and heaved Tanchus through the

doorway as though he had weighed no more than an empty shirt and breeches. Tom fumbled down, found the lock and turned the key, then coaxed the flame of the lantern back to life.

"I'll kill you!" Tanchus's voice rose to a scream. He threw himself at the door of the cell. "I'll kill the pair of you! I'll boil you alive! I'll cut you open and pull out your guts!"

Tom felt along the floor and picked up Tristan's sword. "My lord, this is yours." He turned Tristan's palms upward and placed the sword across them. "Will you come with me? There is much to do, and little time."

Tristan smiled and gave the sword back to Tom. "I am in your hands." He took a grip on Hamon Ruddy's back, and another on Tom's shoulder. "Lead on."

There followed a strange procession, first a man walking with his hands bound behind him, then a blind old nobleman of strikingly muscular frame, and then Tom, arms shaking from the effort of holding up a great sword-of-war. They mounted the circular stairs of the tower, and emerged through the narrow door that led onto the walls. Tom cast a glance over the battlements and spied torches to the south, coming up the road from village to castle.

"You'd best start running now." Hamon Ruddy had regained some pretense of sneering calm. "If the boss catches you, he'll have you flayed alive."

"Knave, be silent and walk faster." Tristan kept a hard grip on the collar of Hamon Ruddy's padded jack and walked him out through the narrow door that led onto the walls. He wore the rest of the rope coiled over his shoulder, keeping the man on a tight rein. By the time they reached the open door to the guardroom over the gates, the brigands had reached the edge of the castle green, their torches growing ever nearer.

"Inside, hurry." Tom went in last and shut the door behind him. The guardroom beyond lay still and dark, lit only by the moon through its arrow-slit windows, but that was enough to see that it was furnished with a table, trunks and beds, and hangings on the walls to break the draft. The smell of doused ashes permeated the place. A pair of winches had been mounted by the walls, one east, one west, each connected to one of the gates in the tunnel below. A series of holes pierced the floor in a line, all covered by flaps of leather.

Tristan maneuvered Hamon Ruddy over by the hearth. "Tom, I must warn you that I do not think my former steward will bargain for a hostage."

"That's not my plan, my lord. Hold him there, for just a moment." Tom leapt down the set of narrow stairs by the wall and found the door that led out into the entrance tunnel firmly locked and barred.

He raced back up to the gatehouse. "My lord, will you please raise the inner gate?" He put the sword to the brigand's back. "You, go up to the arrow slit. Say exactly the words I give you, and nothing else."

Lord Tristan's bushy brows rose with his smile. "Aha! I think I understand." He pushed the crossbowman across the room. "The stories speak truth—I do indeed keep my word. Hear me now. You will have my mercy if you obey this boy in all he says, but that is your only hope for clemency. I trust you understand me." He turned without help and stepped over to the inner winch.

Hamon Ruddy shot Tristan and Tom a look of venomous hate. Tom felt some surprise that it did not make him flinch. Perhaps it was because he knew that too many people would die if he failed in his plan. Perhaps he was simply too angry to be afraid.

He tapped Hamon with the flat of the sword. "Move." He nudged him over to the nearest arrow slit.

Tristan heaved at the winch, doing the work of two men with ease. The rope drew taut, the drum turned, and the inner portcullis rose up. He set the ratchet in the winch so that it would not fall, then felt his way back to rejoin Tom by the windows that overlooked the approach to the castle.

Tom peered out through the arrow slit and spied the party on the road coming to a halt in front of the lowered drawbridge. They were roughly twenty in number, the same size as the party that had left the castle not long before. From the sacks on their shoulders, most looked to have partaken in some hasty plundering, and at least three of them dragged stolen horses along on rope leads. Torchlight glinted on the points of their spears and on the blades of their naked swords.

Aldred Shakesby stepped out in front. "Those accursed harpies tricked us! They've emptied the food stores, set their grain shed afire and run off into the woods somewhere!"

Hamon Ruddy turned to stare at Tom—under his rage there was just a hint of admiration. Tom leaned in to Hamon's ear and whispered.

"About time you got here!" Hamon shouted it through the arrow slit. "That boy sprang the old man from his cell! They've killed Tanchus, and now they're running riot in the courtyard!"

"Well, we'll fix that right enough!" Aldred threw down his plunder. "Raise the gates!"

Tom turned to Tristan. "Outer gate, my lord. Raise it, but don't lock it."

Tristan hauled on the winch connected to the outer portcullis. From outside came the sound of men forming up and getting a fighting hold on their weapons.

Aldred leaned back to shout. "Where are they now?"

"By the stables," said Hamon at Tom's prompting. The outer portcullis cranked up, just over the height of a man.

The steward's voice rose to a shout. "Kill the boy. Leave the old man alive if you can, but don't try too hard." He raised his sword. "Right, ready, boys? Charge!"

The men gave forth a vicious cheer and rushed the gatehouse. Tom pushed Hamon aside and looked down as the last man passed out of view below. "Now, my lord! Let go!"

Tristan took his hands from the winch, and the outer portcullis slammed to the ground. Tom leapt across the room to the inner winch and yanked the ratchet free. The wheel spun, the chain clanked faster and faster—and then it stopped with a crash that resounded from below.

"What in all thunder?" The gates rattled in their tracks. Tom grabbed the wedge of wood beside the winch and jammed it over the portcullis to prevent it from being raised. Tristan did the same on his side.

A chorus of shouts rose up from the tunnel—confused,

then enraged, then fearful. Tom peered down through one of the holes in the floor to find Aldred Shakesby staring up at him from twenty feet below, surrounded by his men, all of them trapped between the gates.

"We got them all." Tom stood and bowed to Tristan. "Your castle, my lord."

Tristan broke into a belly laugh, so loud and so cheery that it silenced the brigands below. "Oho! Oh, ho-ho-ho! My dear boy, my dear boy, this is a feat worthy of every bard and minstrel from here to the golden domes of Üvhakkat! Come, let us see what we have caught in our nets!"

Chapter 14

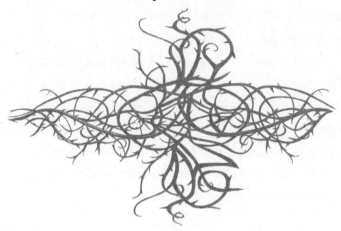

Edmund rolled over, seething in pain. He had landed hard, but on something soft. "Geoffrey?" Fear flared in him. "Geoffrey, where are you?" He heard no answer. The trapdoor through which he had fallen levered back into place above him, sealing him in darkness.

"Geoffrey!" Edmund heaved himself up, felt frantically beneath him, then breathed in relief. He had fallen on a pile of heavy earth from above, and not on his brother, as he had feared.

A groan rose from a few feet away. "You donkey-brains." Geoffrey coughed. "You dunderhead! Why don't you ever *think*?"

"You're all right, then?" Edmund reached out blind. "Nothing broken?"

"Get off me." Geoffrey stiff-armed him. "You could have gotten us both killed!"

Edmund sat back again; his brother sounded well enough to be his usual irritating self. "Find the torches, then, and strike a light."

Geoffrey rummaged, then scraped, causing sparks to spit lurid trails through the darkness. Edmund retrieved the *Paelandabok* and found it not much more damaged than it had been already. He gathered up the arrows that had spilled from Geoffrey's quiver and found the bow lying beside him in the dirt.

Geoffrey lit a torch and held it out. "Now what?"

"Now we see what we can find." Edmund offered the bow and arrows in exchange. "Follow me."

The low, rough tunnel might have been an ancient ruin, like the ruins Edmund had seen up in the Girth, but there all similarity ended. The stones looked uneven, set with thick, crumbling mortar, quite unlike the grand blocky dwellings of the folk who had once lived around the mountain of the Nethergrim. The faded paintings that covered them spoke of warrior kings with swords and lances held aloft in defiance against ranks of twisted creatures, creatures that Edmund would not have believed existed, had he not already seen a few with his own eyes.

"Just think." Edmund tapped the ceiling. "Folk have been climbing and playing about in the old broken keep for years and years, never knowing this was right below their feet."

"I liked the world better when old castles were just old castles." Geoffrey lit a second torch for himself and drew his shiny new fighting dagger in his other hand.

Edmund knelt beside a scene that showed two women

standing with joined hands above an ornately decorated box. "Look at this." He burned away some cobwebs, then translated what he found written below: *"The Skeleth are seen and yet unseen. Trust your thoughts, not your eyes."*

"That's like what we just did up in the courtyard," said Geoffrey. "We put an arrow through that brick because of what we knew, not because of what we saw."

The passage turned at the footings of the tower to meet a set of spiral stairs around a massive central pillar. Little remained within the circular chamber beyond to tell of its former use. An age-squashed litter of leaves, mud and twigs choked the landing. Edmund guessed that the rain must come pouring through from the broken roof of the tower far above and found himself amazed that the structure had remained standing for so long.

"Look—flowers." Geoffrey stepped into the room and felt out the round wall in the torchlight, tracing the twining designs painted there. "Lilies, I think."

Edmund opened the *Paelandabok* and checked to make sure. "The flower of death. One of their symbols for the Nethergrim. And there, a pair of raised hands, just like we saw beneath the mountain."

"And look at this." Geoffrey scratched away some ancient mud to show a pattern that ran at the height of his knee, an undulating band that might once have been painted green, from the few flecks remaining.

"Follow that all the way around the room." Edmund pointed. "See? It's a snake, eating its own tail. The Nethergrim again."

"Ugh." Geoffrey stood up. "Did these people serve it, too?"

"I think they fought against her, as best they could." Edmund paused before the painted design of an inward-turning spiral. "The Nethergrim has come back into the world many times, and in many different shapes. She has used both men and monsters to serve her ends, but in every age of the world there have been folk who have stood in her way."

He followed the images in a slow circle around the chamber. "Every time we destroy one of the Nethergrim's forms, we send her out of the world, and she has to convince someone to let her back in again."

Geoffrey peered over Edmund's shoulder. "Why would someone do that?"

Edmund glanced at him. "Ask Vithric."

Geoffrey turned in disgust from the wall and nearly tripped over the remains of a table that had lost a leg and spilled its collection of jugs and vials to the floor in centuries long past. Edmund followed him up around the circular stairs, to find another round room on the floor above.

"This one looks just like the one below." Geoffrey took a brief glance into the room, then continued upward. "I doubt we could learn much in there."

Edmund held his torch out into the room that Geoffrey had just passed. Prickles ran up the back of his neck.

Geoffrey stopped on the stairs above him, peering into the room on the next floor farther up. "Edmund." His voice came out breathless. "What is happening?"

Edmund turned to look up the spiraling stairs and saw Geoffrey before and above him. He whirled around, toward the warmth of flame and flood of light. He found Geoffrey on the stairs below, holding his torch aloft, confusion turning rapidly to fright upon his face.

"This room isn't just similar to the one below." Edmund stepped out into the circular chamber and found the ruined table just where he expected it to be. "It's the same room."

"That can't be." Geoffrey ran onward up the stairs—and emerged from below.

Edmund's prickles turned to chills. "You stay here. Let me try it." He went downstairs this time. As soon as he emerged below the level of the next floor down, he found Geoffrey looking up at him.

Edmund joined his brother on the landing. "You go upstairs, and I go downstairs. Ready? Go!"

The brothers ran away from each other, Edmund down and Geoffrey up—and crashed into each other on the landing of the stairs.

"Ow!" Geoffrey staggered back from Edmund. "What are we going to do? We're stuck in here!"

Edmund stepped into the room. "Help me look around." He scanned the whole surface of the wall. "Maybe there's something we can learn in here to help us."

"Here." Geoffrey knocked a rotting pile of tapestries aside. "Here, Edmund. There's writing."

Edmund rushed over and waved away a whole colony of skittering bugs. "*The Skeleth are shapes without substance. Right is left, up is down.*"

"Sounds like what's happening to us," said Geoffrey.

Edmund paced around the chamber again, passing by the

spiral, then the head of the snake, then the raised hands upon the wall. He stopped. "Geoffrey, look. The snake has two heads."

Geoffrey looked at Edmund, then around the room. "No it doesn't."

"Follow me." Edmund walked around the room one more time, with Geoffrey following close at his heels. This time he felt it, the shift and subtle warp of a spell. He passed the spiral again, then the raised hands—and he was sure. "Stop. Stop here. Feel it?"

"Feel what?" said Geoffrey.

Edmund grabbed his brother by the arm. He followed the feeling outward, from the room to the edge of the stairs. "The missing brick outside, and this chamber—they aren't really tests or traps, they're lessons. They're teaching us what the Skeleth are, and teaching us how to defeat them."

Geoffrey shuffled behind him. "Defeat them how?"

"By a spell, one with multiple parts." Edmund kept the doubled sight of the heads of the snake fixed in his vision, one in the corner of each eye. "Follow right behind me. It's here."

"What's here?" said Geoffrey. "What are you doing? You're just waving your hand in the—oh!"

Edmund found the rift, the very slight imperfection in the folded space of the chamber. "Here." He got his hand into it and felt the change of air. "Here, come through." He forced the gap wider, first with his hand, then his shoulder, then he jerked Geoffrey through behind him, and dropped to his knees on a set of stairs that he had never seen before.

"Ha!" Edmund descended through a half circle of stairs,

then waved his torch across a pair of stone doors that barred his path. "Give me a hand with this." He set his shoulder to one of the doors, and with Geoffrey's help it gave way with a grinding squeal.

Geoffrey poked his torch through the gap, then let out a hiss of awe. Two corpses, one a man, the other a woman, lay rotted to bones in the chamber beyond, each upon a slab of stone.

Edmund pushed in first. "I knew it!"

Geoffrey ducked through behind him. The crypt barely gave the brothers the space to stand together, and the ceiling arched in just above their heads. He held out his torch over the corpses—the glow of his flame awakened glints of gold. "A king and a queen."

"But which king and queen? That's the question." Edmund set his torch in a hole in the wall that seemed made for the purpose. Skeletal though she was, the queen lay in a repose that suggested peace. The king, on the other hand, looked to have died by some great violence, for though his corpse had been arranged with care, most of his bones looked badly damaged, and one side of his skull had been shorn clear off.

Geoffrey burned away some cobwebs from the wall with his torch. "What are these?"

Edmund set down his sack and drew from it his wax-covered writing tablet and stylus. "Those are just what I was hoping to find." He started sketching the outlines of the spell painted on the wall, the curled and spiky symbols that recorded the thoughts of a long-dead wizard.

"The Sign of Perception, and then the Sign of Closing." He brushed away some cobwebs, then traced out a long passage about the sealing of boundaries and something to do with a casket, or a prison. "The Pillar of Inversion, yes, good . . ."

"Ugh!" said Geoffrey. "And what are *those*?"

Edmund followed Geoffrey's light—depicted on the stone were long lines of funny squiggles that he took at first to be the letters of an unfamiliar language, until he looked more closely. The painted creatures were nothing but rows of jointless arms undulating around maws of jagged darkness. "There's something written under them. Aha! Yes, these are the Skeleth."

Geoffrey drew back in disgust, taking his torch with him. "I think I found something I hate worse than bolgugs."

"I need that light!" Edmund set the book on the slab of the queen. "Look, there's a row of warriors above the creatures, and—Geoffrey, get back here. You should see this."

He drew his knife, a double-edged dagger that was a twin to Geoffrey's, and scraped away some of the filth from the wall. Shadowed by the ceiling, covered in the drippings of centuries, stood a third line of figures.

Geoffrey peered at them. "It's like the squiggly monsters from the bottom row are standing with the men from the middle." He raised his torch to bring the flame nearer. "Or in front of them."

Edmund stared. "Not in front, inside. They're together, each monster bound to a man." He traced out a figure—the squiggled rows of arms seemed to wrap around the man's body. "And here, see? There are the two women standing beside each other, with the opened box just like we saw before, and—look, look there—the men and the monsters have been pulled apart again."

He followed the wall to the next scene. The squiggly creatures were being drawn into the box, leaving the men untouched. Geoffrey wandered away again, forcing Edmund to retrieve his own torch from the wall.

"The Skeleth are man and monster both." Edmund read aloud from the words painted under the scene. "The man can be freed if he awakens to what the monster cannot know."

"Oho, look at this!" Geoffrey shifted aside some ragged cloth from the breast of the king to expose an axe clutched in bony hands. "Give this thing a polish and I'll bet it could chop a shield right in half."

Edmund turned to look. The meaning of it struck him—an axe. He turned back through the pages of the book. *There came three kings, three brothers, three kinsmen of the Pael—Ricimer, Thodimund and Childeric the Fair; an axe-king, a sword-king and a king of tall spear.*

"Of course." He returned to the symbols painted on the wall. "This is not the tomb of Childeric, the king who summoned up the Skeleth. This is the tomb of his brother, Ricimer, one of the kings who fought against him."

"Then I'll bet he's the one who killed all those Skeleth things." Geoffrey wiggled the axe, then tried to ease it from the grip of the dead king. "Anyone who could swing this thing around must have been a real terror in a fight." He heaved and grunted, levering the axe with a crash onto the floor.

Edmund turned to stand over the queen. The remnants of a red silk gown clung in tatters to her bones, covering what might once have been a linen shift or tunic. The gown had wide sleeves, and was bound with a golden, star-shaped brooch.

"The image of the sun." Edmund answered Geoffrey's questioning look. "The return of hope and life."

He ran his fingers over the words incised around the rim of the brooch, translating them in as simple a form as he could: "I am the weapon that wounds the wielder. I am the defense that is no defense at all. I am triumph in surrender. I am that which, by being given, is gained."

"Another riddle," said Geoffrey. "These folk seemed to love them."

Edmund flipped the brooch over. "For my beloved sister." He sidled along the wall of the tomb, passing by the corpse of the queen. Crossed strips of decayed leather held the remnants of long stockings to the bones of her legs, while on her head there remained the shreds of what would once have been a veil. A pair of heavy pendant earrings lay on either side of the skull, with no ears left to hold them.

Geoffrey held his torch over the queen, the flame too near the corpse for Edmund's liking. "I wonder if she was pretty."

Edmund looked into the empty eye sockets of the queen, then reached down and took up the brooch. "I am the weapon that wounds the wielder . . ." He felt a twinge of guilt, but placed it into his sack.

"Here, help me." He seized the head of the axe and waited for Geoffrey to get hold of the handle. He strained and hauled the axe up off the ground, and then, to Geoffrey's disappointment, maneuvered it back onto the breast of the king.

"Out." Edmund nudged his brother through the door of the tomb. "Go on, outside. We're finished here." He turned at the threshold of the door to the tomb.

Geoffrey's freckles scrunched inward in the torchlight. "What are you doing?"

Edmund went down on one knee before the corpses of the king and queen. "Thank you. Both of you." He stood and left, closing the doors behind him.

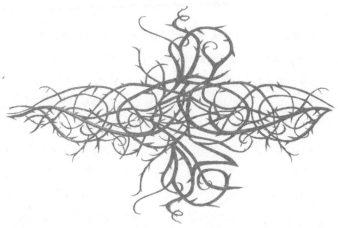

Chapter 15

What songs there were to sing had been sung. What cheer there was to shout had been shouted. Another night's noisy feasting had come and gone, leaving silence the victor once more. Katherine kept one hand to the grand curtain walls, following the side in shadow from the moon. Gray-silver starlight touched the slanted roof of the long wooden stable, painted thick the blacks of gap and grain and hung night in shrouds beneath.

A stable boy slumbered at his post, curled in a sheepskin blanket on his bench by the door and hugging a half-eaten piece of Harvestide cake. Katherine felt a sudden urge to kneel down and tuck him in, but resisted it, slipping around him instead and down the straw-littered passage. The sounds of sleeping horses soothed her, as they always had, the chorus of their breathing making her feel that, somehow, all would be well.

"Oh, look at this." She slipped into Indigo's stall and reached for the brushes by the door. "What have they done to you?"

Indigo stamped a hoof. The grooms had made a proper mess of his mane, braiding it in silly knots against the lay of the hair.

"I'll see to it, don't you worry." Katherine picked at the knots of the braid, working them loose one by one. Indigo watched her as she groomed him, one dark eye roving to fix on her hands, then her face. From outside came the sound of the inner gates trundling up, then falling shut again.

Katherine reached up to free Indigo's forelock from its tangles. "When I close my eyes and lie down to sleep, sleep won't come." She spoke into his long gray ear, telling him her troubles as she had done since he was a foal. No one but Tom would believe that he understood her, but he nudged her when she sighed, and nuzzled against her when she felt her fears rising up to smite her hopes.

"I know just enough to be afraid, but not enough to know what to do." She brushed the knots from his tail. "Who can I trust?"

Indigo raised his head. For an instant it seemed to Katherine almost as though he had an answer, that if she could only read his movements well enough, she would know it, but then he blew out a snort and turned toward the door.

"Good squire!" The stable boy startled awake down the passage, let out a *whooph* and rolled onto the floor. "Ow. Good squire, you're back! I was just resting my eyes—not asleep, I swear it. Do you need—"

"Hush, now." The answering voice sent a thrill through Katherine. "Go back to sleep. I'll see to my horse myself."

"Yes, good squire. I'm glad you're home. Please don't tell on me."

"I would never. Sleep well."

Katherine felt a tingle at the sound of soft approaching steps. She tugged at and smoothed down her homespun dress, even though it was homespun, and even though she stood in darkness.

Indigo seemed taken by an entirely different mood. He twitched his ears again at the footsteps in the passage and stomped a heavy hoof in the straw. He made for the door with an air of irritation.

Harold of Elverain, Lord Aelfric's only son and heir, led his dun-colored stallion down the passage. "Katherine?" He stopped at Indigo's stall. "Is that you?" He leaned around Indigo's gray bulk, looking over the half-height door. Katherine's heart leapt at the sight of him, lit from behind by moonlight from the window. The sensation stunned her with its power—and frightened her with how helpless it made her feel.

"You've been gone so long." Katherine pushed Indigo aside to let Harry in. "Where have you been for so long?"

"Away south, with the king." Harry stood just her height, though he was two years the elder. "Learning to connive and deceive. Watching our kingdom shudder and shake itself apart." He wore an ornate sword in a silver-chased scabbard at his belt and a shirt of mail under his surcoat. If there was a more perfect image of a handsome young squire, Katherine could not picture it.

"Papa's gone to Tristan, and that's made your father

suspicious of him though I don't know why. Your father says Papa's not marshal of the stables anymore—he's thrown me off the farm and set me to work here." Once the words started, they poured forth from Katherine in a torrent, and the tears came with them. "Lord Wolland rode in off the moors with half the nobles of the north—he wants something from your father and he thinks he can get it. There's a letter, and some sort of weapon, and a wizard girl in Wolland's service who was talking to . . ."

She found herself shaking. "I'm afraid, Harry—for my papa, for you, for Elverain and all the north. I've been alone, all alone." Edmund's face bubbled up into her thoughts, but she pushed it away.

"You are not alone anymore." Harry drew near, though he had to dodge around Indigo's attempt to block him. "Don't you worry about any of that, now. Let me speak to my father on your behalf. Let me help you." Even his whispers were somehow handsome, touched with grace in form and tone.

Katherine did something that she thought she would never dare to do. She collapsed onto his shoulder and threw her arms around him. "I don't understand what is happening."

"You don't need to understand, anymore." Harry put a finger under her chin, lifting her face to his. "For my part, I'm glad that I found you alone."

"Why?"

He seized her. He kissed her. She fell and she flew.

After a while, Katherine began to worry that she was kissing too hard, or too soft, or drooling on him, or making a fool of herself, somehow. She pulled away. "Am I doing it right?"

"How should I know?" Harry seized her close again.

"You've never kissed anyone?"

"Not really." He paused for breaths at intervals. "Not like this."

Indigo whickered and shook out his mane. He stepped away from them and bent down for some hay.

Katherine reeled. The bliss blinded her, seeming to blank out all the world. It took all her strength not to fall into it, to let the thrill of it drown all else. "Wait. Just a moment."

Harry let go. "What's wrong?"

"Shouldn't you be telling me what's wrong?" Katherine drew back from him. "You said that the kingdom was shaking itself apart. What is happening in the south? Why is Wolland here? What does he want with your father?"

Harry sighed and leaned against the door. "Do you really want to talk about all that right now?"

Katherine wavered. She did want to talk, wanted desperately to know what was going on—but then Harry looked at her again, a flash of gold in the moonlight. It made her dizzy.

"You truly care for me?" She let him come near again. "Please don't say yes if you don't mean it."

Harry took her hand. "While I was down at court, there were folk who tried to charm me." He even smelled perfect, clean and pure. "I sat down to feast with ladies and lords of the highest blood. They talked their grand intrigues all around me, flirted and whispered behind one another's backs. Some of them seemed to care what I thought, asked my counsel on matters I barely understood, started sounding me out for the sort of lord I would become one day. There were even a few offers of marriage, some of which might not have been jokes."

"Of course they weren't jokes." Katherine smiled, but her belly lurched. She had seen just enough of hall and castle to imagine the grand courts away south in the core of the kingdom. A thousand painted ladies in silk and brocade danced through her thoughts, each of them making eyes at Harry, all of them skilled in arts that she would never learn.

Harry laced her fingers into his. "But every single night, when I lay down to sleep, the same thoughts spun in my mind: 'How is Katherine? Is she well? Is she thinking of me?' And so my single week at court seemed to last an age, and I fear the great lords and ladies of the realm found me something of a bore."

What strength of will Katherine had ran to water. She touched his sleeve, then traced her fingers up his arm.

Harry shifted closer. "And then, on my way home, I learned that you had gone up into the Girth, gone to seek the Nethergrim." He kissed her fingers, one after the next. "I heard that you had marched off into the deadliest danger, and that you had come home safe again, all at once. That one instant was enough for me to know what it would feel like to lose you, enough for me to know my own heart."

"Why?" Katherine shook her head; it all seemed too good to believe. "Why, though? I'm not—"

"Everything is a thrill with you." Harry pulled her in and placed her arm around his waist. "Every other girl is playing a game, sizing me up, weighing me against her other prospects.

You just . . . are. When you look at me, I look inside myself, and wonder how to make myself worthy of you."

Katherine melted. Indigo got bored and turned away.

Harry broke the kiss after what felt like several lifetimes. "I brought you something, from a whitesmith down in Rushmeet." He reached into his belt. "I hope you like it."

He held out something that glittered in the moonlight. "I was going to buy something gold, but I really thought silver would look better."

Katherine let him put the necklace on her. She leaned against him. "This cannot be real. This cannot possibly be happening."

"Why not?" He put his hands on her hips, then his lips to hers again.

Katherine's world spun and reeled. Time both rushed and froze. Pigeons scattered from the rafters above.

"My lady!" The stable boy spluttered from his post down the passage. "May I—yes, of course, as you wish. I'll stay right here."

Footsteps grew in volume, along with the swish of skirts. Katherine and Harry jumped apart just in time.

A figure stepped into view, blocking the light from the window. "Harold."

Harry blanched. "Mother."

Katherine retreated from the door, as though there was somewhere she could hide within the narrow confines of the stall. She willed the hay-strewn floor to rise and swallow her.

Lady Isabeau kept her hands folded in her embroidered sleeves. "The captain of the guard had orders to find me when you arrived." She kept the majestic calm of one who has the power to choose between mercy and justice. "It is fitting for a man of noble blood to let the servants attend to his steed, and more fitting still that a son should come without delay to greet his parents when he enters their home."

Harry flicked a furtive glance at Katherine, then molded his face into a look of bland, empty charm. "Of course, Mother. I was merely looking in on Indigo, here. He is to be my horse, after all." The speed of the change made Katherine even more dizzy than before, and a little sick.

"That might explain your presence here." Lady Isabeau flicked a stinging look at Katherine. "Not hers."

Katherine could feel the flush on her face. She stood helpless in her frumpy workdress, pinned in her lady's gaze.

Harry drew himself to his full height. "Mother, Katherine should not be made into some lowly serving girl." He stepped out from the wall, and came face-to-face with Lady Isabeau. "She is a trainer of horses, and her talents should be respected and used."

Lady Isabeau stood a full head shorter than her son, but did not back away a single inch from him. "And are you a lord who has need of such a servant?"

Harry deflated. "No, Mother. Father has not seen fit to grant me any land of my own."

Lady Isabeau held out her arm for her son to take. "He will do so, when he thinks you have matured enough to deserve it. Come, we will awaken him together. We have much of importance to discuss."

"Yes, Mother." Harry stepped away from Katherine as though she were not there. He led his mother and his horse off down the passage, leaving Katherine alone again.

Indigo snuffled at Katherine's arm. She turned and buried her face in his mane—not alone, after all.

Chapter 16

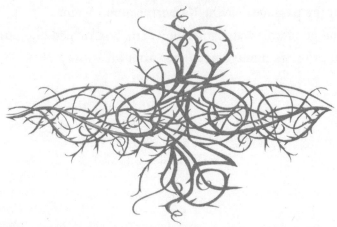

Tom felt his way down the narrow stairs that led under the foundations of the keep. His lantern burned cobwebs from his path. His feet slid on the moldy grunge that covered each high and shallow step. He tried to avoid bracing his elbows on the casing stones around him, for things skittered up and down the walls, things he had no wish to look at any closer, let alone to touch.

"Tom!" Two dozen voices shouted in chorus. "Tom, it's us!"

The humid pall of the tunnel gave way to a piney breeze. Tom emerged over the steep-walled cove he had seen on his first assault upon the castle. The outer door hung wide before him, above the descent to the dock and river's edge.

"Everything all right?" Rahilda called out from the first of four little boats steering into the cove. "I heard shouting." Each boat held a half-dozen figures, black against black water, pulling hard with their oars to turn out of the current.

"We've got the brigands trapped in the gatehouse." Tom

clambered down the stone steps. He hung his lantern on one of the posts that held up the dock. "Lord Tristan is alive and free."

"I am sorry, Tom. We should have been here sooner." Rahilda seized his hand and stepped out of the boat. "Like herding cats, this bunch." Her weight added to Tom's sank the dock to the waterline.

"The brigands still have their weapons." Tom reached out to lash Rahilda's boat to the dock. "They've started taking their axes to the door in the side of the tunnel. It's only a matter of time before they get through."

"Well, we'll see to them. Step quickly, everyone!" Rahilda started climbing. "One at a time on the dock. Quickly, now!"

Tom helped every woman and girl in each of the next three boats up onto land. Some clutched makeshift weapons and trembled timid white, while others seized his arm and stomped up the stone stairs at a furious march. A pair of threshing flails passed Tom by, a half-dozen sickles and other tools of the garden, clubs made from distaffs meant for gathering spools of wool and a few long knives from the kitchen.

"Everyone remember your jobs when we reach the top." Rahilda propped the outer door wide with a noisy squeak. "Those of you tasked to the gatehouse, take your positions in the courtyard or up in the watchroom. The rest of you, search about for bows—check the tower and the barracks first. We can't rest easy until we've got these men disarmed."

"Don't you worry on that score." Brithwen Byley clambered up the stone steps behind her. "We know perfectly well what they'll do if we give them the chance."

Her mother, Diota, thumped her stick upon the stairs. "Ask

me, we should just pour some boiling oil on them and be done with it."

More boats came in, two fishing skiffs and a barge. Tom helped a stream of folk onto the dock, then sent them on their way up the stairs into the castle. A young woman propped her aged mother with one arm and bore her infant in the other. Two more children followed close behind, gripped to her trailing skirts. Chickens squawked, pressed tight in coops on the barge. A little girl led a line of goats up the stairs, helped by a boy who wore a sword he could not lift.

Rahilda's sister seized Tom's hand on her way out of her boat, and held it tight. "You are the cleverest boy I've ever heard about. The cleverest boy in all the world."

Tom did not know what to do with such an obvious untruth. "I'm glad I could help."

"My name's Melicent, by the way." The auburn-haired girl drew in until her feet touched Tom's. She took hold of his other hand. "We were never properly introduced."

Tom wriggled free of Melicent's grip. "We must be quick. Those brigands are still armed."

Melicent kissed Tom on the cheek. "That's for saving us." She lingered a moment, as though waiting for Tom to say or do something, then flitted away up the stairs.

Somewhere in the act of raising woman, child and elder onto land, Tom lost the joy of victory. Faces came to him, first the men he had buried, then the others, dead in the eyes and yet moving with vicious speed, wrapped within the ghastly, reaching shimmer of the creatures. Last and largest loomed John Marshal.

"Is it true, young man?" The last woman in the last boat reached for Tom's hand. "Does my lord yet live?"

"He does, but don't take my word for it. Go on up and see for yourself." Tom brought her onto the dock, then guided the empty skiff out on its line to rest downstream. He left a few women in charge of loading in the grain and ascended the steps into the castle.

Torches spread and spun out through the dark of the courtyard beyond. A dozen people spoke at once: "Mama?" and "Everyone gather, gather here!" and "Where's your sister? I told you to watch your sister!" The courtyard around him had turned into a half-lit maze of villagers and livestock. Bawling children marked islands of huddled kin. Dogs chased one another through flitting pools of torchlight scattered thin across the space, but none of them was Jumble.

"Welcome, one and all." Tristan stood with one hand upon the hilt of his sword and the other raised in greeting to the villagers. "Be not afraid. We shall put a wall between ourselves and the world tonight, and then take thought for the days to come."

Tom threaded through the crowd to join him. "My lord, we have all the folk inside, and we've started loading the food."

"Well done, Tom." Tristan nodded his snowy head. "Come and stand before me. I have something for you."

"Tristan!" Aldred Shakesby's voice rasped out in the dark from the gatehouse tunnel. "Tristan, come over here and let us parley! You don't have the men to hold us for long—come to a deal while you have a deal to make!"

"Keep at it, boys!" Younger voices boomed in echo behind

him. "Three swings apiece, then hand off your axe." Two men at a time took turns at the side door set into the tunnel, hacking at it high and low. The door, like much of the castle, had not been made as well as it should, and though Tom had done his best to brace it up from the other side, it was only a matter of time before it gave through and let the brigands loose.

Pangs of dread struck Tom in the belly. "Forgive me, my lord, but all we have done is trap twenty men, just twenty brigands. Lords plot a war with the help of evil wizards, the women of your valley have lost their sons and brothers, and those creatures . . ." He could think only of John Marshal's twisted face, trapped within the deathly glow. "What do we do now?"

"Hold out your arms," said Tristan.

"My lord?" Tom did not understand, but he did as he was asked.

"You have things confused, Tom." Tristan took off his sword-belt and threaded it around Tom's waist. "You are the hero of this story, not the bard who tells it. It is for you to win the victory, not to rate its importance to the world."

Tom shook his head. He was no hero—what a thought! "But, my lord—"

"Hush, now. Did I say this gift was one you could refuse? I am a lord of the realm, after all, and I must get my way at least some of the time." Tristan snugged the sword-belt tight. "There. Let it ride at your hip, just like that. After a while, you'll feel naked without it."

Tom's hand fell to cradle the hilt. "It's very heavy, my lord."

Tristan took his shoulder. "You are still growing, Tom." He

turned him to face in the direction of the gatehouse. "Come, there is a hard task that needs doing."

Tom walked Tristan across the grass, falling in with a group of village women converging on the gatehouse. A pack of brigands clustered at the inner gate, blocking Tom's view of their fellows who chopped away at the side door behind them.

"Oh, now, what's all this?" Aldred Shakesby pushed up to the bars. The scar on his face made his snarl all the uglier. "You must be joking."

Lord Tristan stepped in front of the villagers. "Men of the Free Company of Rutters, you have committed great wrongs against me and my people. You have made this war. Your only hope for the milder justice of peace is to renounce it here and now."

Diota Byley raised her stick. "You heard him. If you men want mercy, pass your weapons through the bars and surrender."

"Mercy? From you?" Aldred passed a vicious look around at the women. "Do you have any idea what we will do to you hags when we get out?"

A murmur ran through the crowd. Melicent flinched back from the circle, and a few others followed, their weapons dragging low.

The steward sneered and waved a hand. "Back to it, boys! That door will give way soon enough. Pay these shrews no mind."

Rahilda joined the circle with Hamon Ruddy's crossbow and a case of bolts. "I found these." She placed them both in Tom's hands.

"I'll give you all one chance, and one chance only." Aldred curled his lip back to his scar. "Put down those sticks and whatnot and let us out, and we'll go easy on you."

"Liar," said Brithwen. "You'll act just the same whether we surrender or not."

Aldred peered out between the bars. "Most of you have children, don't you? Little ones over there on the grass? You want to see them grow up? You want to see your sons be men one day? Then you'll do as you're told. You have no business making war."

"Don't you tell us who has business!" Diota struck the bars and drove the men back. "You think you can come in here, turn our lives up and over, kill my only son and then tell me I have no business in it? It's you who have no business here! It's you who have no right!" She smacked the bars again and again—they rang and shuddered.

"Oh, come now." Aldred snorted. He turned to his men. "Look at them! What will they do, weep at us? Shriek and lament until we surrender?"

Tom cranked back the crossbow. He set a bolt in the channel and pointed it through the bars. "Whatever we might do tonight, we won't be weeping over it."

Aldred spluttered. "Tristan, be reasonable!" He turned to plead over the heads of the women. "We'll be through that door soon enough, so you can play nice with us and make a deal, or—"

"You have heard my judgment, Aldred Shakesby." Tristan turned to the women beside him. "Young Melicent, are you here among us? Perhaps you should not be around such hard business. Would you care to lead me to the hall?"

Aldred shook the bars. "Curse it all—Tristan, get back here!"

"We have nothing further to discuss." Tristan let Melicent turn him toward the great hall. "I leave my orders in the hands of the captain of my guard."

Aldred stared at him in confusion. "Your captain?"

Tristan touched Tom's shoulder as he passed. "See to it. When you have these men subdued, come take counsel with me in the hall."

Tom took a step toward the gates. He fixed the face of John Marshal in his mind, then the other men bound with him in the torment of a living death, and then the men freshly buried by the edge of the village. He pointed the loaded crossbow at Aldred Shakesby. "Surrender your weapon."

Aldred backed away. "What? Now, come—you don't even know how to use that thing!" He tried to hide behind the other brigands, but they dispersed, leaving him exposed in the tunnel.

Tom took careful aim. "I point it at you and I pull this trigger. If I miss the first time, I've got twenty more bolts."

A brigand slid his sword hilt-first through the bars. "I'm done. I'll take my chances with Tristan."

Aldred foamed. "You cowards! What's the matter with you? Are you afraid of a half-starved boy, a blind old man and a pack of housewives?"

Rahilda wept from fury and rage. "Tell me this—when that

wizard woman's done with the man I love, what will be left of him? I just want to know if I'll get a chance to bury him proper."

"That wasn't us." Another man put his weapon through. "That was Drake. I had no idea that was her plan, I swear it." Another followed in surrender, and another.

Tom held his aim on Aldred. "Last chance."

Aldred spat a curse and threw down his sword.

The women stepped up to the gate to pull the weapons out of reach. They set down sickle and kitchen knife to take up sword and axe. The brigands sat against the tunnel wall, resigned to their defeat.

Tom let the crossbow drop down, then fired the bolt into the earth. He looked about him and spied amongst the ragged courtyard grass the box from which the ghostly creatures had sprung the night before. He approached and bent to inspect it—perhaps *box* was not the right word, but he did not know what to call such things. It was a good deal smaller than a clothing trunk and had been fashioned entirely out of metal, dull of gleam but so old that, for all he knew, it might once have shone like the moon. Three women had been sculpted on the lid, their arms held out to clasp one another in a line, making a pair of handles between them.

Tom ran his hand along the carven rim. He tried to do justice to the sword he wore, tried to be martial and stern, but failed and wept, his hands across his face. All he could think of was what he was going to tell Katherine about her papa.

Rahilda found him there, knelt in darkness in the grass. "I bless the day you came to us." She grabbed him around his skinny shoulders and kissed his forehead. "You are always one of ours, now, forever one of our own. Don't you forget it."

"I won't." Tom picked up the box and turned for the hall. When he had lain awake at night, back home in Elverain, he had dreamed of one day being something other than a slave, but he had never dreamed of being a leader, or a hero. He had not dreamed, not even once, of how burdened he would feel once he was free.

"My lord?" He ascended the wooden steps. Two torches sat in sconces within, one close and one far. "My lord, it's me."

"I am here, Tom." Tristan sat alone by the cold hearth.

Tom set the sculpted box on the floor by Tristan's feet. He took a torch from the wall and used it to wake the fire. The flickering light cast the tapestries on the walls in warm reverence, two rows of men standing brave and battle-sure.

"Do you like them?" The lines of a smile crinkled around Tristan's eyes. "I always did."

Tom set the torch back in its sconce. "I wish they were alive, my lord. I wish they were here." The man in the nearest tapestry wore his hair in long braids beneath a simple pot helm. The weaver had set him ferocious, forever charging forth with hatchet and sword in hand. Beside him stood a pair of blond boys, each carrying a longbow taller than himself. The men in the tapestries looked as though they could do anything, fight anything, conquer all before them. The Ten Men of Elverain, Tristan's old friends and companions, looked down upon Tom from either wall, and he felt like a fool for wearing a sword at his waist.

Tristan broke into Tom's thoughts as though he could hear

them. "Finely made as these are, Tom, they fail to tell the whole of the tale."

"I don't understand," said Tom. "Weren't they brave?"

"Brave indeed, brave beyond measure," said Tristan. "Resourceful, openhearted, live of wit—yet still there is a deception here, the fond myth that shrouds the honorable tomb. You see these men with all accomplished, their lives at an end and their glory secured. The past is a safe country, for there all the chances have already been taken, the hard things already done."

Tom turned the other way. Across from the twin boys stood a man who seemed to burst the edges of his tapestry. He bestrode the whole of its width, legs akimbo, holding an enormous mattock butt down to the earth.

"Which are you looking at?" said Tristan. "Owain? Thoderic?"

"It looks just like someone from my village," said Tom. "Katherine's cousin, Martin Upfield."

"Then that would be his father, Hubert Upfield," said Tristan. "I have never known a man as worthy of the name *hero*."

"What does it matter, my lord?" Tom wanted more than anything to hold on to his victory, but it felt like trying to remember a dream. "The Nethergrim is alive, but the men who once fought it are gone. Hubert might have been a hero, but his son is just a farmer."

"Hubert was a farmer, too, just a four-acre cottar working his little plot of land around your village," said Tristan. "He hated the whole idea of war—he was the most peaceful man I have ever known. He learned the arts of battle from need, not from desire. He fought only because he had reason to fight."

Tom stepped along to the last tapestry on the right side of the wall. The man depicted there was beardless and young, with dark hair that fringed his brow. He clasped the fingers of one hand over the hilt of the sword that hung at his belt, while his other hand held the reins of a horse that peeked in from the edge of the tapestry. The face was a masterwork of the weaver's art, the line of the graceful jaw meeting the chin in a faint cleft, the nose shaded in with expert craft between two large and handsome eyes. Tom found letters stitched at the bottom. He could not read them—he did not need to read them. He knew from the face that the name beneath it read JOHN.

Tristan held out his scarred and callused hands to the fire. "The tales of my old companions leave out much, perhaps too much. There is no hint woven here of the doubts we felt, the fears, the arguments over what to do. We felt helpless, Tom, many times—and, yes, sometimes we despaired. In any task worth memory there are moments when it seems too hard to accomplish."

Tom looked across to the tapestry opposite John Marshal's. He had seen the man woven within it before—a middle-sized man with a strong jaw and thick, short hair, faced directly out, one hand tracing a sign of strange power and the other ringed in flame. He did not need to read that name, either, for he knew that it said VITHRIC.

The chair by the hearth squeaked back. "And now, hero,

for so I name you, I summon your aid to rid our world of the Skeleth." Tristan got to his feet. "There will be no rest for you, Tom, no days of ease and triumph, no time to feel the relief you give to others."

Tom bowed his head. He turned to Tristan, and in doing so bumped the scabbard of his sword against the wall. "But I don't know how to do it. I don't know how I can possibly do what you ask of me."

"Such is the path of the hero," said Tristan.

Tom returned to the hearth. He picked up the box and took Tristan's hand to lead him from the hall. "It's not the path I expected to walk."

Tristan smiled. "That is what John used to say."

Chapter 17

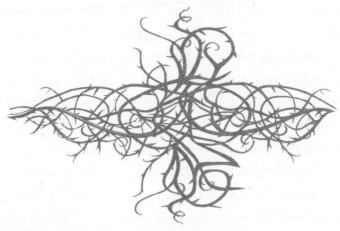

Edmund did not know how best to sit on ground he could not feel. "I don't like it here."

"Neither do I." Ellí hunched with him beneath the Sign of Obscurity, the hem of her long dress draped so that it spilled across his shoes. "But it's the only way for us to safely meet. I am still being watched." The glittering dust she had thrown into the air drifted slowly down, seeming to crown her with a halo of stars.

Edmund kept his gaze fixed on Ellí's face, dizzied by the churn of light and shade, ecstasy and terror, death and life around him. "Who is it that is watching you?"

Ellí's blue eye glittered cold and bright. "Edmund, there is something I must tell you. Your friend Katherine attacked me in the castle, while I was in the middle of a spell."

Edmund sat back, then forward again, since the trunk of the walnut tree he had been leaning against no longer seemed to be there. "Katherine attacked you?"

"I don't quite remember how it happened," said Ellí. "I was deep under the Sign of Communion, and then, all of a sudden, your friend Katherine was knocking me about the room."

Edmund felt a shiver. "I don't understand." He blinked up at the pale and lonely sun. The daytime sky around it looked like a place for warmth to rise and die, empty without limit, and for one sickening instant he thought that up was down, and that if he did not seize onto Elli's hand he would fall into it, up and away, falling forever and forever into the blue.

Ellí took Edmund's reaching hand as though she understood exactly why he had flailed out for her. "Edmund, you might as well learn this now." Her sweet, soft voice seemed to come from everywhere. "Ordinary folk don't really understand people like you and me, and because they don't understand, they suspect the worst of us."

Edmund shook his head. "But, it's Katherine. She saved my life, under the mountain of the Nethergrim. She's my"—the next word stuck in his throat—"friend. My good friend."

"Wizards don't get to keep their friends from the world outside." Ellí gestured outward from the grove where she and Edmund sat, across the open green of Moorvale to the place where Edmund's neighbors stood all in a clump. "Most of us come to find early on that only others of our own kind can truly understand us. It's not simply what we can do, it's what we know. People like us, Edmund, have thought things that people like Katherine will never think. We know things she could never understand."

Edmund turned to look at the folk on the green, but through the smearing effect of the spell they all looked the same to him. Indeed, the longer he looked, the less they looked like people at all.

"Everything you learn changes who you are," said Ellí. "Everything you learn makes some things that you once held to be true seem untrue, and things that once seemed solid feel like the whispers of a fading dream."

Edmund hesitated, unwilling to say what he thought. "That frightens me."

Ellí turned a smile upon Edmund that seemed to have nothing in it save for loneliness and loss. "The saddest stories I have ever heard are those of wizards who tried to stay married to some merchant, or noble lady, or the like. It never ends well."

Edmund reeled, his senses spinning from the warping visions of the spell all around him. "But I know Katherine. We've been friends for years. She would never attack someone for no good reason."

"I'm sure she simply misunderstood what she saw." Ellí's smiled turned wry. "Still, I wish she wasn't quite so violent. Does she always think with her fists like that?"

Edmund felt a looming presence behind him and shifted out of the way just in time. He looked up to see his brother, Geoffrey, walking nearby with his bow and quiver of arrows, calling his name, looking all around for him but unable to see that he was right beside him.

"This is our sorrow, Edmund, this is our burden." Ellí shifted closer to Edmund to give Geoffrey a clear path to pass on by. "To help them, we must become unlike them. To save them, we must become something that they will not trust. Every time I cast this spell, I see that truth more clearly. That is its cost, by the way. This spell shows me how different I am from other people."

A sick, strange feeling ran through Edmund. He saw his little brother and knew who he was, knew the face he had been looking at for as long as he could remember, but at the same time he saw a stranger, just a snub-nosed, freckled kid wandering at the edge of the woods. Geoffrey called his name again, then passed by toward the green, and he felt for a moment as though he could watch him walk on out of sight and not care one bit if he ever saw him again.

"I am sorry." Ellí drew her long hair behind her ears. "Not everyone with the talent for magic keeps on the path. There are many reasons to leave it. Are you and Katherine . . . very good friends?"

Edmund sighed. "Not as good as I wanted us to be." He turned to Ellí. "Do you get lonely?"

"Sometimes." Ellí picked up Edmund's wax tablet, on which he had recorded what he had found in the tomb under Wishing Hill. "But what we do is worth doing, don't you think?"

Edmund felt as though the sun were growing warmer again. "We're fighting to keep the world safe from harm." He looked to Ellí. "Even if people don't understand or like us, it's still right to help them."

Ellí's smile lost its tinge of sorrow. "When I think about it like that, I feel less lonely."

"So do I," said Edmund. "And at least folk like you and me can understand each other."

"As no one else could." Ellí set the tablet in her lap. She read what was written there, and brightened. "Edmund, this is wonderful! This is it—the spell that stopped the Skeleth all those centuries ago. You've set it all down here as clear as day."

Edmund felt a glow spreading out from within.

"The Sign of Perception, yes, yes, of course." Ellí traced her finger on the tablet. "The Pillar of Inversion, the Sign of Closing . . . yes. Edmund, it's perfect."

"Something about it still bothers me, though." Edmund dug the brooch from his sack. "I found this on the dead queen in the tomb. See those words around the rim?"

Ellí read the words inscribed upon the brooch. "I am the weapon that wounds the wielder. I am the defense that is no defense at all. I am triumph in surrender. I am that which, by being given, is gained."

She flipped the brooch over and read the back. "For my beloved sister." She stared at it awhile, then shook her head. "No, that's nonsense, just some *Ahidhan* claptrap." She put it back in Edmund's hands.

Edmund felt across the brooch with his finger. "If it didn't matter, then why was it there?"

"Edmund, you have come far with magic on your own, but now you should learn something of its nature," said Ellí. "What we call magic is divided into three paths, *Dhrakal*, *Eredh*, and *Ahidhan*."

Edmund raised his eyebrows. "There are different kinds of magic?"

"Three kinds," said Ellí. "Three paths of magic, each one founded by one of three sister queens—but you must understand, Edmund, that the three paths are not equal. As my teacher used to say: one path is true, one is false, and the third path is useless."

Edmund leaned closer. Such was his excitement at his first proper lesson, that even the dizzying visions of Ellí's spell fell away beneath his notice.

"The first path is the one we walk," said Ellí. "That path is called *Dhrakal* in the old Dhanic tongue, and it is the one that not only allows its students to see into the true nature of the world, but gives them the power to alter its rules to suit their desires. That is what ordinary folk mean when they say we cast a spell. We can do it because we understand the laws that govern the world, the first and most important being the Law of Balance."

"Everything has a cost." Edmund leapt ahead of Ellí's words, trying to show that he knew at least a little. "You can have what you want, but you must always pay for it."

Ellí nodded. "Yes, very good. You have already met the founder of *Dhrakal*, in a manner of speaking. In fact, you are the first person to see her in centuries."

Edmund felt a thrill. "The queen under the tower!"

"The tower you found was called the Tower of the Queen of the Wheels, and as you might guess, the Wheels are the five Wheels of magic—Substance, Essence, Thought, Change and Form." The dust had descended far enough that it now glittered all about Ellí's shoulders. "So it is written, that queen preserved the truest and most powerful of the ancient arts, and when a wizard today casts a spell, he follows down the road she made."

"Then what about the other two?" said Edmund. "The *Paelandabok* talks about three kings and three queens."

"The other two founded the other paths, the false one and the useless one," said Ellí. "The false one is called *Eredh*. They are seers, stargazers and makers of pacts, those who say they can pronounce the doom of fate. That was the queen who made the great mistake, the queen who brought the Skeleth into the world to serve her husband, King Childeric, in his war. If that's not proof that their way is false and dangerous, I don't know what is."

Edmund looked down at the brooch in his lap. "You said this had to do with *Ahidhan*, the third path."

"The useless one," said Ellí. "We true wizards understand that everything is in balance, that light needs darkness, that order and chaos are two sides of a single coin. The followers of the third path, the witches of *Ahidhan*, believe that there are things for which there is no cost, changes you can make without paying for them."

"What sort of things?"

Ellí shrugged. "I don't know, since I've never met one. My teacher says that all they do is go around pouring smelly potions down the throats of sick people, and nursing sheep, and things like that. She says that they're deluded and their magic is useless, and that the sick people were either going to get well or die on their own."

Edmund read the riddle once again. *I am that which, by being given, is gained.* A meaning teased his mind, then danced away uncaught.

"Come, then." Ellí nudged him. "When you asked me to

teach you, I doubt you only wanted lessons on history and theory."

Edmund looked up at Ellí. "What do you mean?"

"I mean that I would like to teach you a real spell." Ellí set down the tablet between them, turning it facedown. "That's what you want, isn't it?"

Edmund clasped his hands and had to resist rubbing them together. "Yes!"

"Good. I'm going to teach you how to do what I did to you out on the moors," said Ellí. "I'm going to show you how we wizards defend ourselves against people who raise weapons against us."

Chapter 18

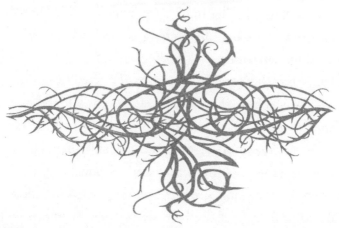

The jousting field bloomed in patterned color, a summer garden of tent and pennant set up in defiance of the dying year. Katherine paused to catch her breath, resting her heavy wicker basket on the road that led down from the castle hill.

"Now that one there, that's a bad rider." A few folk from Northend town had climbed the hill to watch the jousting practice, with an eye toward where to place their bets once the tourney started in earnest. Katherine straightened up to look and spied a knight in red riding Indigo along the jousting lists, a long track with a fence down the middle to keep the two combatants apart. There was no joust just then, though—the knight charged alone, his lance lowered at the cross-shaped quintain set up at the opposite end. Indigo cantered, but veering, stepping high, his every motion speaking of a rising rage. The knight jammed his spurs hard into Indigo's flanks, jerking back and forth at the bit to keep on target.

Katherine hauled up her basket. "A very bad rider." Even as she spoke, Indigo swerved against the jousting fence and scraped the man off. The red knight landed on his back in the dirt, in front of a gang of watching squires who knew better than to laugh out loud.

Clouds bunched and menaced in the sky. Katherine hurried her pace as best she could, lest the rain fall and ruin her meal before she could deliver it. She cast a look of longing across the field toward the knights at boasting play upon their great horses of war, at the young squires polishing the armor of their masters and the grooms cleaning tack and saddle. She would rather be any of the men before her, highborn or low, than what she had become. She pushed sweaty locks of hair up beneath her wimple, steeled herself and ducked under the side flap of the grand reviewing tent.

"My lord. My lady." She knew that she had to announce herself, much as she would have wished to simply sneak in and out. "I bring your noontime meal." She glanced warily around, uncertain of whether she would find Ellí there with them, but saw no sign of her. She curtsied on her way to the rear of the tent, to the trestle bench spread with the tablecloth she had washed and laid out that morning.

"You again?" Lady Isabeau sat in prim splendor on a padded chair next to Lord Aelfric. She eyed Katherine up and down. "What on earth possessed Master Cook to send you down here? Where are our page boys?"

"I do not know, my lady." Katherine craned to look through the open front of the tent toward the jousting field. The red knight grabbed for his fallen lance, and for an instant it looked as though he was about to attack Indigo, right there on the field with everyone watching. Then Harry came out onto the lists and got between them, and after a few tries caught hold of Indigo's reins and led him away.

Katherine breathed a sigh of relief and turned to open the basket. She pulled out wrapped slices of beef, cheese and river trout, then some ceramic jars of sauces and jellies, and started arranging them on the table.

"You stupid girl! What are you doing?" Lady Isabeau made Katherine jump. "Is that how you set table at your father's house?"

Katherine looked down at the food, then over at the nobles. She had no idea what was wrong. "We did not often have beef at home, my lady. I am sorry—I don't know what to do."

Lady Isabeau snapped her fingers at Katherine. "You dullard!" She drew her lips tight. "You utter—"

"Ah, Katherine Marshal. There you are!"

Katherine turned—and so did Aelfric and Isabeau—for Lord Wolland had a voice of born command.

"Come, come." Wolland beckoned from the open front of the tent. "We have a small dispute regarding horses to settle, and I espied you on your way down from the castle."

Katherine waited, unsure of whom to obey. She looked to Lord Aelfric.

Lord Wolland smiled upon the seated lord and lady. "That is, if you could spare this girl from her services?"

Lord Aelfric flicked his fingers. "Take her."

"And keep her," muttered Lady Isabeau.

"Good!" Lord Wolland stepped in and took Katherine by

the arm. Lady Isabeau grimaced at the sight, so Katherine let herself enjoy it, just a little.

Lord Wolland led Katherine out through the front of the tent. "It is but a small matter." He was a lord of the realm, but he stumped along at Katherine's side like a prattling, jovial uncle. "But a matter for which none are better suited than you, my dear girl. Here we are, here we are—have you settled it, my good lords and knights?"

He stopped by the horse-tents at the far end of the field, where grooms and smiths worked in preparation for the tourney soon to come. A crowd of noblemen, Harry among them, stood in a circle around a familiar blue-gray shape. Indigo raised his head and stamped at Katherine's approach, pushing a few of them out of his way to come and greet her.

"We have settled nothing, my lord." Dirt caked and dusted up the back of the red knight's surcoat. "And see? This stupid brute simply wanders off whenever the mood strikes him."

"He sees the one who trained him, Richard—and, I'll hazard, the one who birthed him." Lord Wolland beckoned to Katherine. "Come, my girl, step over here."

Katherine dropped a curtsy and followed, feeling all eyes on her. She held forth a hand; Indigo nuzzled it.

Lord Wolland nodded to the red knight. "My loyal vassal here—Richard Redhands, by name and by fame—tells me this horse is ill-trained."

Katherine patted under Indigo's chin. "He is not, my lord." She nodded to Richard Redhands. "Saving your pardon, sir knight."

MATTHEW JOBIN

"Yes he is!" Sir Richard fumed. "He's a bilious, bad-tempered beast. He cannot be ridden!" He raised his hand as though he meant to strike Indigo's rump. Katherine almost hoped that he would try it.

Harry wore his father's colors. They suited him—but then, so did everything. "I'm afraid that Indigo here threw Sir Richard, while they tilted at the quintain."

Sir Richard Redhands screwed up his face, so that his mustache looked about to rise up into his flaring nostrils. He muttered something foul.

"And before that, he threw Sir Galien." Wulfric slapped the back of one of the knights. "Tossed him hither and yon like a straw dummy, and—"

"And so, Katherine." Lord Wolland held up a hand for silence. "I would like to put Sir Richard's claim to the test."

He took Indigo's reins and held them out. Katherine knew what he wanted. She glanced around her—exposed, alone, a peasant girl in a humble, sweaty workdress, surrounded by the richest and most powerful men in the north. She felt like a pawn, a plaything, the butt of a joke.

She looked at Indigo. He raised his head, cocking his nose toward the jousting field.

She might never have the chance again.

Richard Redhands clenched a fist. "My lord, how can you defer to some peasant wench in a matter of—"

Katherine sprang up onto Indigo's back. She hiked the skirts of her dress to sit astride. Indigo shifted, twitching his ears toward the jousting field, but waited for her signal to begin.

"The horse does not seem quite so ill of temper as you say, Richard." Wulfric exchanged a smile with his father. "Perhaps you were too free with the spurs?"

"Good. Yes, good." Lord Wolland waved his hand. "Finish the show. Let us have you ride him down the lists."

Katherine looked down. "My lord?"

Lord Wolland took the lance from Sir Richard's hand. He offered it to Katherine. "Show us. Charge at the quintain."

Katherine hesitated, glancing toward the grand reviewing tent. She was in enough trouble already.

"A girl charge at the quintain, you say?" Lord Overstoke drained his goblet. "Ha! This I'd like to see!"

"So you shall, my lord." Katherine touched her heel to Indigo's flank. Indigo trotted to the end of the jousting lists and sprang to a flying charge.

Wind threw Katherine's hair behind her. Indigo's hooves drummed upon the turf, shifting to a headlong gallop. Katherine nudged in her knee to correct their course over the bare grass of the lists. The quintain stood at mid-field, a tall cross with a battered old shield on one arm and a sack full of sand dangling from the other. The sight of the target roused her and made her forget her fluttering skirts. She steadied up her lance and passed within sight of the open front of the reviewing tent.

"What on earth—?" Lady Isabeau stood from her chair, gaping as Katherine hurtled past. The peasant folk of Northend hollered and cheered from the rope that marked the boundary of the lists.

Katherine lowered the lance to point at the target painted red on the boss of the shield. Exhilaration sharpened her, brought her forward in the crouch. She matched the pull of her arm to the rise and fall of Indigo's pace, keeping the wobbling lance point on target. Twelve yards, six yards, two yards—yes. The lance struck square on the dot, sending a shudder back down her arm. The weight swung wide, shoved hard by the strike, spinning out high enough for her to duck under its whirling return. Indigo followed through at a canter, his strides the perfect coupling of power and grace, ready for his rider to draw her sword and fall in amongst the panicked enemy.

"Girl! How dare you?" Lady Isabeau's shrill exclamation was nearly drowned in the cheers from the peasants across the field. "How dare you!"

Katherine wheeled Indigo around. She trotted him back in front of the reviewing stand, as was custom. She dipped her lance in salute to lord and lady, and rode off the field. The noblemen assembled at the horse-tents might have thought her an oddity, perhaps even a joke, but they cheered for her all the same.

"Well struck, well struck!" Wulfric of Olingham bellowed and clapped. "By the cloven crown! That was straight on the dot."

"My lord Aelfric!" Lord Overstoke leaned out to look at the reviewing tent. "My lord, why do you have this girl slaving in your scullery? She's worth three of my marshals, at the least!"

Lord Wolland held out his hand for Katherine's lance, acting for all the world as though he were her faithful squire. "I think our little dispute has been settled, then, yes?" He looked around him at the other lords and knights. "Good sir Richard, I fear that you owe my son Wulfric here an apology, and—what was the wager?"

"Two gold marks, Father," said Wulfric. "But there is no hurry to collect on a man of honor."

Richard Redhands turned to storm away. The other nobles hailed Katherine in a laughing roar, but she cared for their applause not a bit. She touched a hand down Indigo's flank, then stroked her fingers through his mane. He snuffled at her side. Riding him once more reminded her that she would never ride him again.

"He will be yours."

Katherine looked up. Harry slipped around to her side of Indigo's great bulk. He glanced back at the nobles, then dared a step nearer. "I will find a way. He will be yours someday, somehow. This I swear."

A groom came in between the horse-tents with a flask of wine. He bowed and started serving the noblemen assembled there. Katherine seized on the distraction to touch Harry's hand, squeeze his fingers once in thanks, then let go.

"So this is Elverain's great secret." Lord Wolland took some wine, then stepped over by Indigo's proud head. "Old John Marshal and his maiden daughter, off on their little farm, turning out better steeds than anything I can acquire by coin or by craft."

Harry winked at Katherine, then moved to join Wolland. "I regret to say, my lord, that they are not for sale."

"I thought not." Lord Wolland chuckled. "So, my boy, will we see you astride this fine beast in the tourney? You are well of age now."

Harry stiffened. He hesitated. "No, my lord, I do not think so."

"What? Why ever not?" Lord Wolland stared at him, the

very picture of honest surprise. He held forth a goblet full of rich red wine. "You are young and hale, Harry—drink from the cup of chivalry while you may!"

"It is not—" Harry stole an embarrassed glance at Katherine. "I can't."

The lords and knights assembled by the tent smirked at one another and shook their heads. Lord Wolland exchanged a glance with Wulfric, one that Katherine did not like at all. She felt the urge to leave and to pull Harry away with her, but knew she had no power to do so.

"Oh, come now, come now." Wolland placed the goblet in Harry's hands. "Only child you may be, but you cannot stay at your mother's skirts all your life. Do you wish to earn your spurs, or simply have them handed to you by right of your title?"

Lord Overstoke laughed, and the other nobles took it up in a burst of derision. "I have always said he was rather too pretty." He nudged one of the knights, pointing at Harry, then Katherine. "You tell me, my lord—which one of them's the maiden?"

"An old man's child," muttered Lord Overstoke. "His mother's son."

Harry opened his mouth in angry shock, then looked down at his boots. Katherine struggled for something to say, even something that might get her into deeper trouble herself, if it could save Harry from what she feared was coming.

"A pity, truly." Wulfric lowered his thick brows. "The spurs of a knight are the mark of his manhood. It shames us all when they are ill given."

Harry found his voice. "I am my lord Aelfric's faithful vassal, as well as his son. I obey his wishes."

"And he wishes to preserve you to carry on his line." Lord Wolland seemed full of kindly good humor. "But he should consider not only whether you survive to inherit, but what sort of man you will be when you do."

Harry looked about him, surrounded by men who seemed to be weighing him in the balance and finding him wanting. He held the goblet in close at his chest, but did not drink. "Just . . . just what do you mean by that, my lord?"

"My boy, my boy." Lord Wolland put a hand to Harry's shoulder. "I told your father many times not to raise you by the hearthside. He should have sent you off south to squire—you might have learned something of the world. More to the point, the world might have learned something of you."

Harry spluttered. His features darkened, but he made no reply.

"It is for a knight to make war." Wulfric crossed his tree-trunk arms. "It is his right and proper craft. A girl may make sport of it, if she so chooses, but for a man of noble blood it is duty. To spurn it is to spurn his honor, to spurn his manhood and his high birth."

He nodded to Katherine. "Your pardon for my saying so."

Desperation led Katherine in amongst the men. "We are proud of our lords here in Elverain. They have ruled long in wisdom, making war when war was needed, but seeking always for a fair and gentle peace." She did not quite dare look straight at Harry. "We love them for it."

Wolland waved a hand. "Our world has no room for such fine sentiment." He turned full on Harry. "The lord who is content with his lot stands to lose it. We are wolves, Harry, the captains of wolves. The fate of thousands can shift at a glance between men at the high table, the world turns on the whim of he who dares all. That which you stand to inherit was carved from the flesh of other men in ages past. What will you do with it? That is the first question I ask all young men of substance, for their answer will either make their dynasty, or break it."

The contents of Wolland's letter to Aelfric flashed through Katherine's mind. She glanced at him—and found him watching her in return, his deep-set eyes glittering dark.

Harry wavered. "I can ride, my lord." His voice lost its firmness. "I can fight. I do not need to prove it to a crowd."

"I see," said Lord Wolland. "Perhaps then you should choose a champion to carry your honor where it is needed." He smiled at Katherine. "This young maiden, perhaps, could lift a lance in your stead."

Harry went red to the ears. Katherine tried to catch his eye, to shake her head, beg him no.

"I need no one to fight my battles for me!" Harry drew himself to his full height. "I will joust in the tourney, my lord, against any man you choose."

As soon as he said it, his color drained—but the error had been made with too many to hear it. A silence fell. The lords and knights around him nodded to one another.

Lord Wolland's smile widened to his ears. He turned to his son.

Sir Wulfric bowed to Harry, stooping down to let his shadow cross him. "It will be an honor, good squire. We shall meet upon the field tomorrow."

Chapter 19

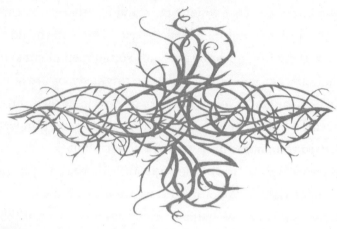

The thrice-opened eye went blind with the heart's blindness. The thrice-beloved king cast his love upon the pyre with his honor and his truth. In his anger, in his fear, in betrayal of his kin, King Childeric called upon the Skeleth, They Who Crawl Below, they who shape as one with men, but are not men. In his lust for lordship without limit, Childeric asked for that which could be halted not by sword, nor by axe, nor by spear. He had asked for that which could kill without end and, screaming to the last, he received his gift.

Edmund balanced a pebble on the rat-eared corner of the page to weigh it down. He drew up his cloak against the wind that blew in sudden gusts across the village green of Moorvale. It was a warm wind for autumn, southerly and kind, but even so its pulsing breath did not please him in the least, or anyone out on the green behind him, from the sudden shouts of disappointment it evoked:

"Oh, a pox on it! Did you see that? That was a bull's-eye, dead to the middle, and then that accursed breeze—"

"You always blame the breeze, Nicky Bird. You're not fooling anyone."

Edmund followed the scrawling text onto the facing page: *The land where the Skeleth walk is now waste. It is ruin, given up to death, a land under the sway of That Which Waits Within the Mountain. We have tasted the bitter fruits of King Childeric's greed. Upon the banks of the river we have made our redoubt, and there we fight an enemy that knows neither mercy nor fear.*

The hairs on Edmund's arms went up and stayed raised. He looked behind him, up and west to Wishing Hill, then over through the square, past the mill to the turn of the broad river Tamber. The statue of the old stone knight that stood in the center of the square faced eastward, toward the bridge over the river and the empty moors beyond. No one in the village knew who the knight was or what he had done to deserve a statue in his honor. His head and right arm had broken off long ago, so that no one even knew if he was meant to be raising a hand in welcome or shaking a sword in defiance.

Edmund raised the pebble and turned the page—parchment flaked in his hand, and a whiff of wind nearly sheared the page clean off. *They are seen and yet unseen, they are form without substance, they are man and monster both. They serve only their master, only That Which Waits Within the Mountain—*

"It's your turn."

Edmund startled. A thin, curved shadow hung suspended over the pages of the book—a horn-handled bow of springy yew. Geoffrey held it out, the quiver of arrows in his other hand.

"Come on, Edmund!" Martin Upfield called from the other side of the walnut tree Edmund had been using to block the wind. Martin stood with a crowd of peasant folk at one end of the common green, a place used for grazing livestock most days, but on that morning the sheep and cattle had been moved across the road and replaced with a line of ragged old archery butts. Almost every man Edmund knew stood in clumps at the near end of the green, and a goodly handful of women, besides. Even as he looked across, Missa Dyer loosed and struck firm into her target, bringing a cheer from her brother Jordan and half the Twintree clan.

"I've been looking for you all morning." Geoffrey dropped the quiver in his lap. "The practice is half over already."

Edmund grabbed the feathered flights of the arrows before they could spill forth from the quiver. "I don't want to take a turn."

"You've got to shoot, Edmund." Geoffrey held forth the bow. "You're over thirteen; it's the law. Every able-bodied man in the village is here, and there's a clerk walking about with the tax rolls making sure we all showed up."

"I'm busy!" Edmund struck the open page before him. "Do you think that figuring this stuff out is easy? I'm trying to find a way to defend us from the Skeleth!"

Geoffrey shook his head. "I don't see those Skeleth things anywhere. Why are you so sure they're coming back, anyway? Just because that wizard girl told you?"

Edmund closed the *Paelandabok* and slid it into the sack at his feet. "What do you think we were doing in that tomb?"

"Stomping around like fools and nearly getting ourselves killed, so that you could pull up some dusty old spell, and—let me guess—you showed it to the wizard girl, didn't you?" Geoffrey shot Edmund a sour smirk on their way over to the targets. "You think you know everything, but you're really stupid, sometimes."

One of the villagers stood aside from his place at the mark to let Edmund step up. "So, then, Edmund, tell us another story from your books, there." Short, shaggy-bearded Nicky Bird flipped an arrow end over end, catching it in one hand, then the other. "Come on, a good one with some great fancy wizard throwing his spells about."

"I told you before, spells don't work the way you think they do." Edmund set his left foot at the mark. "True magic is a way to see the laws that rule the world, to find the balance of things, the opposite natures of which all is made, and then—"

Geoffrey snorted. "What did I tell you? He doesn't make a lick of sense anymore."

Edmund sighed. "All right, then, a great fancy wizard." He sighted down to the target. "There's Mad Mull of Millthwart— it's said he worked out a spell that could scythe a whole field of wheat with a wave of his hand."

"Now, that one can't be true—aim up a bit, Edmund. Here." Martin Upfield loomed in—head and shoulders taller than Edmund and more than twice his weight. He shifted Edmund's arms and turned his shoulders. "There, try like that."

"Seems to me that any man who could do a spell like that could just give out all the bread he likes—set himself up for a king, somewhere." Nicky drank deep from a cowhide waterskin. "That's just an old wives' tale, it has to be."

"No, it's true." Edmund held the shaft of his arrow with his thumb, just as he had been taught. "I've read about it in too many different places."

"Hunh." Nicky Bird scratched at his curling beard. "So what happened to him?"

Edmund released—the arrow skipped off the top of the target. "There's more than one version of the story."

"Let's hear 'em all, then! The one I like best will be the true one."

Edmund plucked up another arrow. "Well, the first is that one day he stood on the wrong side of the field."

"Ha!" Nicky nudged Martin. "Hear that? What's the other?"

"It's a bit more complicated." Edmund did not like the look of the arrow in his hands, an old broadhead with a crooked shaft. He drew up another. "So the story goes, the spell worked perfectly, made him as much wheat as he wanted, any time of the year. He was able to balance the cost on the Wheel of Substance by—well, never mind that part. He started bundling up bushel after bushel and bringing it in to the cities by the wagonload."

Nicky shrugged. "And?"

"The bottom fell right out of the grain market. Not a farmer in the land could sell his crop for so much as a brass farthing. Riots in the streets—death by pitchfork."

"Ha!" Nicky turned to Martin and nearly stabbed him with the arrow in his hands. "Ha! You hear that?"

Martin swatted the arrow away. "I heard it. Stop poking me."

Edmund drew back another arrow. He considered trying to explain the third version of the story, the one that sounded as though it might be true. He gave it up for too tangled to tell—how could he explain what magic really cost if the wizard abused its power? He would rather not be cut in half by an invisible scythe, but by the same token he would not like to die by inches inside, consumed from within by bread that was no longer really food.

"I don't know, Edmund." Gilbert Wainwright stepped in above the end-nock of his bow to fit a new string at the next mark over—nearer to thirty than Martin and Nicky, but by all accounts the follower of the three, ever since they had been boys together. "I hear your tales about these wizards working marvel after marvel, and yet here we are, still plowing our fields by muscle and sweat. Our king's no wizard, our lord's no wizard—don't see how those stories can be true and the world still be the way it is."

"That's because you don't know how magic works." Edmund waited for a lull in the wind. "You don't know what it costs, and you don't know what the world is really like."

"Hey, now, Edmund, no harm meant." On a face like Gilbert's even a look of reproach seemed mild. "Not trying to tell you your business." He turned to aim his shot, seeming to take but an instant to gauge arc and wind before he loosed and struck square in the middle of his target.

"No one's going to argue with you about what wizards can do, Edmund—not anymore." Nicky turned to watch Edmund's following shot. He tutted and shook his head. "You shanked it a bit. Are you keeping your fingers wide on the string?"

"Of course I am!" Edmund grabbed another arrow. He nocked it, taking care to space his fingers around the flights. He drew to the ear, sized up the target, and let fly.

A familiar sinking feeling followed. Geoffrey started snickering behind his back well before the arrow landed—in the grass beside the target.

"Well, the wind took that one. Nothing you could do." Martin Upfield raised his hand, looking up and down the row. Gilbert did the same, then Aydon Smith, Jarvis Miller and old Robert Windlee, who must have been five times Edmund's age but could still hit the target without fail. The shooting stopped, and then Gilbert walked out with a few others to gather up the arrows.

"Never mind it, Edmund." Martin gave Edmund an encouraging smile. "We all know you've got other things you do well."

"The Wizard of Moorvale. Hey? There's our lad." Nicky prodded Edmund's side. "Why don't you work on that scything spell? Be a big help at harvest next year. It'll be our secret!"

A voice piped up shrill from along the row. "You there, with the hat. What's your name? Speak up—Hugh Jocelyn, Jocelyn, yes—let's see your arrows."

Edmund looked up to see a small and well-dressed party passing crossways behind the archers. He felt a thrill of sudden fright and stuffed the *Paelandabok* into his sack. Lord Aelfric rode his horse beside a black-haired young clerk who recorded the name of every man at the practice. Lord Wolland followed with Wulfric and Richard Redhands, who were both armed as though they were about to ride to war.

"Ah, the fabled archers of Moorvale." Lord Wolland signaled for his knights to dismount with him, then walked along behind the row of men lined up at the marks. "Let us see if the legend bears any truth."

"You shall indeed, my lord." Aelfric stepped to the ground and put his reins in the hands of the page. He walked right up behind Edmund, coming so near that he nearly trod on the sack that held the book Edmund had stolen from his private chambers.

Edmund felt a bead of sweat roll down from the line of his hair. He kept his gaze away from the nobles behind him, waiting to fire on the signal. He tried to think only about the wind, and not about what Lord Aelfric did to thieves.

"You there, churl!"

Edmund jumped. He whirled around, wild excuses at his lips, but Sir Wulfric was talking to Martin Upfield.

Wulfric clapped Martin on his broad shoulder. "You are made for war. There is need of such men as you."

"Sir knight." Martin turned and bowed. "I have no love for war."

Wulfric let out a short, hard laugh. "Come and seek me, or remain forever a fool." He stepped back from the line of archers and stood in a tight clump with the other knights and lords.

Henry Twintree called out from down the line. "Ready, all? Draw and aim!"

Edmund nocked an arrow to his string, drew it back and waited for the signal to fire. Of all the torments of archery drills, the massed volleys were the least painful to him, since no one could ever quite be sure if the arrow that missed the target was his.

Henry Twintree bellowed. "Fire!"

Edmund loosed his arrow with the volley. Dozens of arrows whipped in an arc through the sky, shuddering into their targets in a deadly swarm.

"Ha!" Lord Wolland clapped his pudgy hands together. "Well done!"

Edmund stared about him at the green. Not one of the arrows had missed the target. Not even one—and that meant that he had hit. He had actually hit!

"Very good indeed." Lord Wolland nodded to Lord Aelfric. "I have always taken an interest in archery. It is of great use on the battlefield, if properly deployed. I seem to recall that your grandfather used a company of archers to good effect in a battle not far from here, when my great-uncle Adalbert thought to invade."

"You remember rightly, my lord." Lord Aelfric faced south and pointed out with all the fingers of his gloved hand. "The battle took place in that direction, in a field just east of Longsettle. My grandfather concealed a troop of archers from Moorvale in a copse of trees by the road. They passed unnoticed by Adalbert's scouts as they took the field, then fired on the flank of his army once the battle was joined, causing great damage."

Lord Wolland turned to Wulfric. "What do you think of such a ploy, my son?"

Wulfric's face turned sour. "I do not like it, Father. It was unmanly. There was no honor in such a victory."

"It was war, sir knight." Aelfric shot a hard look at Wulfric. "Honor lies with the innocent. Those men fought and died to keep their homeland free of pillage and ruin."

Lord Wolland laughed. "Oh, now, that is unfair, my lord!" He swept out a hand to the line of Moorvale men. "My great-uncle would have used these people well enough. Indeed, by now they would think themselves Wollanders, and all would be well with the north after all. But for my part, I call it well played, one for the histories. You have inherited quite an asset in these levies of peasant archers, and you are wise to keep with the tradition."

"I thank you," said Aelfric. "Your great-uncle did not live to know of it, but his campaign had pushed my grandfather to his last strength. Those archers swung the battle and the war, and their children's children practice at the targets once a week because I know it full well."

"You see, Wulfric?" said Wolland. "Useful stuff, archery. We must train up a company or two. Oh, don't pull a face, I won't make you do it. Perhaps good Lord Aelfric would be so kind as to lend us a troop of his best peasant bowmen to help us get things under way."

He turned his smile back on Aelfric. Hatred crackled between the two lords, in silence but with such force that Edmund felt the urge to slip away out of sword distance.

"My lord, I fear that I must deny your request." Lord Aelfric did not sound as though he regretted refusing Wolland in the least. "The men of Elverain train at the targets to defend their homes and families. That is the only right use of war."

"I would have thought you above such a trite and commonplace idea, my lord." Wolland's deep eyes glittered. "In all my years of life, I have discovered but one useful truth: Bold action in war sets a new order for the ages. In battle, in war, in daring attempt, is the life of a man exalted. Fortune, yes, but moreover fame, glory, a hand in the shaping of the world. Through deeds in war a man lays the path on which the future wanders. His children rule, while the children of other men bow and serve. The king upon his golden throne: What is he but the echo of a better man who drew up his plans at a rough-hewn table? Through deeds in war, a man carves himself into the memory of the world."

"It is not for us to decide who is to be remembered and why, my lord," said Aelfric. "My archers will defend their homes as their forefathers have done, against any who come to challenge them."

Lord Wolland's smile only grew. He took a small but deliberate step toward Aelfric. "There are forces against which a storm of arrows are but a gently falling rain."

Lord Aelfric was the taller man; he drew himself up into the image of what he must have been like in his youth. He loomed over Wolland. "Show them to us, my lord, and we shall put that to the test."

The hands of knights and men-at-arms drifted toward the hilts of their swords. Edmund glanced along the row of archers.

MATTHEW JOBIN

Not a few of the village men had nocked an arrow to the string and stood tensed, ready for anything.

A muffled groan from along the row broke the silent tension. Edmund turned to find his father stumbling up to the mark beside him with his bow and quiver.

Harman Bale puffed, red at the cheeks, one hand held over his side. "Am I late?" He dumped his bow and quiver on the grass, spilling out his arrows. "Not late, am I?"

"Here, Harman, have a sit down for a while." Martin Upfield took Edmund's father by the elbow and tried to guide him away from the archery range and over to a seat in the grass. "You look half done in."

Edmund's father pushed Martin away with his free hand. "Curse it all, I'm not an old man yet!" He stumbled and seized his side again.

"Not yet, Harman Bale." Old Robert Windlee eyed him up and down. "And maybe not ever if you prance about with a half-healed belly wound."

"Father?" Edmund moved to brace up Harman's other side. "Are you sure you should be out here?"

Harman grabbed for his longbow. "Don't you start with me, boy." He lowered his voice. "Those are nobles over there, Edmund, almost every man of substance from here to Paladon, and our lord Aelfric's showing off our skill for them. I'll be tied and tossed in the river if I let that Henry Twintree hog all the credit for every bull's-eye we hit."

He stepped into his bow, straining to bring the string up to the nock—then he groaned and let go.

"Look out!" Edmund leapt from the path of the whippy

bowshaft as it sprang across the grass, striking Sir Richard Redhands square in the face.

"Ow!" Richard Redhands grabbed for his nose. "By all thunder—ow!"

Lord Wolland stared at his knight, then burst out laughing long and loud, slapping his thigh in noisy mirth. Wulfric took it up in his father's echo, and then a few chuckles sounded up and down along the line of archers. Richard Redhands turned in a fury and charged straight for Harman Bale.

Edmund had time for a single thought—if a blow should land, it must not strike his father. He threw down his bow and arrows and stepped out in front Richard Redhands. "Please, sir knight, my father's wound is still fresh. He received it defending my mother's life from a cowardly attack. Surely a gallant and honorable knight such as yourself would understand, and forgive."

"Boy—out of my way." Richard Redhands stepped sideways, making to go around Edmund and get to his father.

Edmund blocked his path. "You must not strike him, sir knight. His wound has not yet healed."

The knight set his teeth. "I said *out of my way!*"

Edmund braced himself. "No."

The force of the blow sent him spinning, then falling. He landed hard upon the earth.

"Son." Edmund's father shook his shoulder. "Edmund?"

Edmund rubbed at his jaw. His vision blurred and doubled. He reached out his other hand to push himself up; Richard Redhands trod on it, his hand on the hilt of his sword.

Lord Wolland stepped between Richard and Edmund. "Not

now." His smile remained fixed, but his eyes bored deep. He dropped his voice low, low enough that Edmund, who lay at his feet, could only barely catch the words: "Not yet." He turned his back on Aelfric, leading his knights away across the green. It was only after his party had gone out of bowshot that Edmund felt safe enough to get to his feet.

Chapter 20

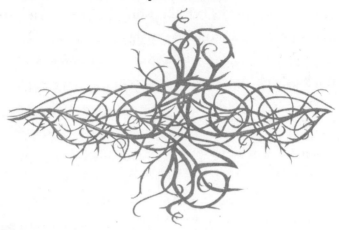

Tom put his hands on the chill stone of the battlements. The sun stood high over the pass, casting white-gold in the valley. The many chances he had taken came back to him in twinges, in bursts of belated fear at all that he had risked, and images of all the ways things could have gone so very wrong. They seized at him but found no purchase. Nothing had gone wrong—not yet, at least.

"Here, my lord." He reached back for Tristan's arm and led him to the edge of the wall. He leaned out to look down—the drop fell sheer into the dry scrub of the moat far below. The horses abandoned by the brigands wandered in a pack, grazing on the green outside the castle with their leads trailing behind them.

"You must travel with the greatest caution." Tristan felt out for the top of the wall before him. "You will be riding down the very road the Skeleth took out of this valley, and there is no telling where they will strike first."

Tom reached back to haul the carven box up onto the battlements. He fumbled it and dropped it onto the flagstones of the walk behind the wall. It swung open, revealing the plain smoothness of its interior, a box like any other, save for what it had once held.

"It's all so very dark to me still, my lord." Tom righted the box and latched it shut. "I don't understand war, or politics, or anything lords and wizards might plot or do."

Tristan drew in a long breath, then puffed it out white into the chilly air. "Whenever we felt lost, in the old days, John would give me this advice. Number the points of your confusion—it will at least show you that they are not numberless."

"What little I know, my lord, amounts to a bundle of sticks without the twine to bind them." Tom joined Tristan at the battlements. He looked off amongst the trees that ringed the green, as though he might find his answers lurking in between the trunks. "I know that the brigands who seized your castle were hired by the lord of Wolland. I know that Lord Wolland is working with the wizard woman who opened this box, letting out creatures who took over the bodies of John Marshal and the men from your village. Those creatures can't be killed, for if you stab one, you only slay the man inside, and then the creature takes you, instead. The wizard woman led the creatures east, back up the road to settled country, but for what purpose? And why would a man, a mortal lord, want to loose such an evil on the world?"

"Here I can be of some help," said Tristan. "When old king Bregisel won the war to claim the kingdom thirty years ago, he saw fit to create me a lord of the realm. He granted me dominion over Harthingdale—but Harthingdale had long fallen into disuse, its castle abandoned and its people fled. When I arrived, I found that casket you hold buried deep within the dungeons below. It was Vithric who explained to me what I had found, and the terrible danger it portended."

Tom flinched. To him, the name of Vithric had taken on the meaning of a curse. "But, my lord, what makes you so sure Vithric was telling you the truth? He drained the life out of two children, right before my eyes, and he would have done that same to me if Edmund had not stopped him. Why would you trust what he said?"

Tristan's sword hand clenched in, then released, settling back onto the battlement. "I do not doubt what you told me about Vithric, even though it wounds me to the heart." He turned back to Tom. "But even if my old friend has fallen into evil, he was not always so. You must believe me, Tom, Vithric was once my most trusted companion and adviser. He had a hundred chances to bring the whole world to ruin in the old days, but he fought with all he had to save it instead. How he turned from that into the man who wished to murder you is a riddle I have yet to solve."

Tom hitched his belt, making sure that the gear he carried would not get in his way on the descent. "Yes, my lord." He could hear the pain in Tristan's voice and did not press the matter further.

Tristan shrugged the heavy coil of rope from his shoulder. "Vithric told me that the tall tower of this castle was once known, in the tongue of the ancient people who threw off the yoke of the Nethergrim, as the Tower of the Queen of the Heart. Those folk had done a great service to the world by overthrowing the Nethergrim and her servants, but in the chaos that followed they were too weak to resist invasion from a vigorous folk coming over the mountains from the west, the people from whom we take our name and language—the Pael."

He looped one end of the rope around his waist. "This queen had two sisters, and each of the three practiced a different form of the secret art that folk call magic—*Ahidhan*, *Eredh*, and *Dhrakal*, to use their words. Each sister married herself to a conquering king of the Pael, so that the two peoples might share the land without strife. The brother kings, though, could not keep peace between themselves—ever did two turn upon one, only for their alliance to weaken and break, an endless turn and turn of feud and retribution. At last, one of the kings, pressed to the last throw by his brothers, forced his queen to do what all of her people had sworn never to do—make contact with the Nethergrim once more.

"She was of the *Eredh*—a seer, a speaker of dooms and a maker of pacts." Tristan tied his end of the rope into a knot. "It was said that she alone of all the queens truly loved her husband, and perhaps that is meant to excuse her part in what followed. She brought the voice of the Nethergrim back into the north, and into the thought of her king. A price was paid, a bargain struck, and the creatures named the Skeleth came forth into the world. What folk had sought to build upon the ruins of the Nethergrim's dominion washed away like sand at a riverbend. Conqueror and conquered became one people in shared suffering, as the Skeleth ravaged, ruined and despoiled their homes."

"Then—how?" said Tom. "How are we even here to speak of it? The Skeleth must have been stopped, somehow."

"It fell to the other two sisters," said Tristan. "Here my knowledge fails, for I am no wizard, and Vithric told me that this part of the account is out of all record. Somehow, though, the two surviving queens trapped the Skeleth with a spell, sealing them within the very casket you hold. They feared to hide or bury it anywhere, lest someone find and open it, so instead they chose to keep it safe within this stronghold. Here it sat, undisturbed for centuries, until I found it. I swore to keep it safe and told only those I trusted most with the secret of its existence—John Marshal, of course, and also Vithric."

Tom shouldered up a pack stuffed to bursting with all the food and supplies Rahilda and the village women could cram into it. "And now those creatures are loose again upon the world, a force that can kill without end."

"A mighty spell was once cast to seal these creatures away," said Tristan. "To trap them, to save the north, it must be done again. We need both *Dhrakal* and *Ahidhan*, both the paths of magic that trapped the Skeleth. With the help of one of each kind, we might learn how the Skeleth were sealed away and find a way to repeat the deed."

"My friend Edmund won't be hard to find," said Tom. "He broke the spell of the Nethergrim. I'm sure he can help us."

"From all you that have told me, your friend follows the path of *Dhrakal*." Tristan held out the free end of the rope. "You remember how to find the other, the Revered Elder of the *Ahidhan*?"

"South at the junction on the other side of the pass, then

two bridges and east to the Harrowell." Tom wrapped the rope around his waist and legs, then tied a knot at his middle. "If I get lost, ask a farmer or a boatsman."

Tristan took up the slack. "I wish that I could be of more aid to you than serving as an adviser and a lowering winch."

"Lowering me here will get me on my way much faster than using the postern gate and rowing around the castle." Tom looped the dangling end of the rope through the handles of the carven box and tied it tight. "For my part, I wish I understood what Lord Wolland wanted out of all of this."

"That is no great mystery," said Tristan. "Wolland is a lord, and lords want land. If he and Warbur Drake are indeed in alliance, all that he must do is move his own army across the river to claim what Drake has cleared. It is a monstrous thought, a betrayal of everything right and noble, and yet I can believe him guilty of the act. By treachery he struck in the old wars, changing sides without warning and taking our former king hostage. For his service, he was scorned as a faithless scoundrel and given nothing in reward—and ever since, a dark fire has blazed behind those deep eyes of his."

Tom shook his head. "But if anyone makes war, will not the king punish him? Lords and knights all swear oaths to serve the king, so they cannot fight one another."

Tristan sighed, then almost laughed. "How I wish it were that simple. Oaths bind only those who think them sacred. It is a sorrowful truth that many men have spoken oaths they do not mean to keep."

Tom liked the world of lords and kings less and less, the more he knew of it. "It seems foolish for men to make war upon one another, when there are things in the world that threaten them all in common."

A wistful smile worked the corners of Tristan's mouth. "Why those who think as you do never seem to sit on thrones is a question that grieves me more and more as I get older."

Tom stepped to the battlements. "Thank you, my lord. At least I know enough to tell friend from foe."

Tristan followed him to the edge. "I do not suppose I can prevail upon you to take my sword."

"It's too heavy, my lord." Tom lowered the box to dangle it over the edge.

"Very well." Tristan looped the rope in his hand. "Take a good grip, now."

"I'll ride one of the horses those brigands left behind out there." Tom hooked a heel over the wall. "I promise I'll turn and run if I see trouble." His hands met Tristan's on the rope.

"Often have I wished for children of my own." Tristan braced his feet on the wall. "But never so much as today. Return to us safe, Tom, and soon."

"I will."

Tristan took up the weight on the rope without the slightest strain. "Over you go, now. Set your feet on the wall so that you do not spin."

Tom scrabbled out under the overhang and braced his feet on the wall. The rope played out in sure and steady measures from above, lowering Tom to the earth as though he were as light as a dandelion seed.

"I'm down, my lord!" Tom let go in the scrub at the bottom of the moat.

Tristan leaned out from far above. "The wind grant you speed, Tom." He waved a hand. "We will hold for your return."

Tom untied the rope and picked up the box, then climbed onto the rise across the moat. The brigands clustered at the gate, their hands at the iron bars holding them inside. Aldred Shakesby stood among them, his hood thrown back from his bald pate. The scar on his face made his snarl all the uglier. He raised a finger and pointed; Tom could not catch his words but had no trouble understanding what he meant by them.

Sacks of hasty plunder lay in piles on the road. Tom could still smell the ashes from the burned-out barn—no one had told him if only that building had gone up in flames, as he had planned and hoped, or if some of the women were now home-less, amongst their other sorrows. He could not see the village through the trees, and that was not the way he was going, so he stopped wondering. He had too many things to mourn for already, and too much to fear.

"Here, now." He found what he had hoped to find, half a mile up the road toward the pass out of the valley. One of the horses stolen by the brigands, a bay gelding with the gait of a draft horse, ran skittish through the scrub along the road, trailing his lead out behind him and nearly stepping on it in his wanderings.

Tom set down the box and held forth an open palm. "Is the rope bothering you? Here, I can help." He got the horse in hand with much less trouble than he had feared. The horse was big, a bulky giant, but like many massive beasts had a gentle eye and a trusting nature. He doubted that Katherine would have approved of his wild leap onto the horse's back with the box under one arm, but what mattered was that after some scrambling he sat astride.

"Come on, then." Tom tried to remember what Katherine did to speed horses up. "Let's try a trot." He squeezed his knees, then tapped his ankles in. The horse raised his head, turned an eye on Tom, then trudged on at the same speed as before. Tom decided to take his gift just as it was offered.

The road leveled out before him and began to rise toward the pass. Tom let one more wave of relief come and go—if nothing else, there were people safe in a castle who had felt no safety at all the day before. Whatever else might be so, there was that. He cast a look back at the castle, then the tower, and urged the horse to greater speed, again without success. He let his guard relax—and if not for the utter silence of the valley, he might never have heard it.

He did hear it, though, and when he did, his heart felt as though it had frozen. It was a whine, lost and weak, coming from the trees that bounded the road between castle and village. He had already passed well by the spot—it was a last, despairing call, almost a goodbye.

"Jumble!" Tom sprang from the back of the horse. He dove through needled branches, down a hummock and into an open grove. He dropped to his knees before the form amongst the fallen leaves, patches of black-and-white fur and two odd-colored ears drooped low.

Jumble tried to raise his head. He lacked the strength; it fell back to the earth.

Chapter 21

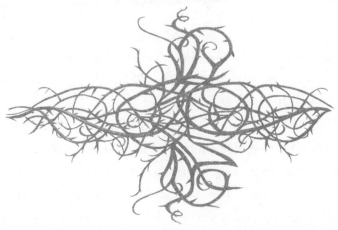

So tell me, Edmund Bale. When will it be your turn to drive the cart?"

Edmund jolted up. "What?" He sat on the edge of Gilbert Wainwright's best wagon, his legs dangled down so that his heels nearly brushed the turning wheel below. He held the *Paelandabok* on his lap, arms braced along the pages to hold them flat in the wind.

"The cart, Edmund, the wagon." Mercy Wainwright sat beside her husband at the front, bouncing their infant son on her knee. "When will you drive one of your own, and who will sit beside you when you do?"

The words of the book swirled in Edmund's mind . . . *for his loyal men came death within life, for his enemies an end without a grave. He gained dominion over kin and kine, and set up his throne over all things on two feet and on four, but it did not last, it could not last . . .* He tried and failed to understand what Mercy was getting at. "I don't know what you mean."

"Don't play dense, Edmund." Mercy loosened her baby's hold on a hanging lock of her hair. "You stand to inherit the inn one day, and you're not even all that ugly. So, who will be sitting on your wagon when you do?"

"Oh, let him be, love." Gilbert drove the wagon with one hand upon the reins and an arm around Mercy's waist. "Edmund's got plenty of time to find a wife."

"Tourney days are lovers' days, man of mine." Mercy kissed Gilbert on his stubbled cheek. "Or have you forgotten?"

Their daughter, Celia, looked up at Edmund from her game of dolls on the floor of the wagon. Emma Russet nudged Miles Twintree and turned to smirk at Edmund from her seat on the back. Of all the passengers on the cart, only Geoffrey seemed to find Mercy's inquest into Edmund's marriage prospects as uninteresting as Edmund did himself. Edmund let his eyes slide back down to the lead-ruled line of words: *As there is no alliance between water and fire, nor is there concord between the wolf and the lamb, so is there no faith to keep between living men and That Which Waits Within the Mountain.*

"Very well, Edmund, you force me to guess." Mercy tapped her angular chin. "Molly Atbridge?"

Edmund looked up from the book again. "What—who? No."

"Ah. Then—Siffy Twintree?"

"No." Edmund spoke over a chorus of retching sounds from Miles and Emma.

"Anna Maybell?"

Edmund sat up rigid. "No!"

Mercy's smile sharpened. "Someone else, then." She exchanged a look with her husband. "Thought so."

"Who?" said Emma, and then to Edmund: "Who?"

Edmund looked away, flushing hot to the roots of his hair.

"Let him read his books, Mercy." Gilbert twitched the reins to steer them over the bridge across the Swanborne stream. "Edmund Bale goes his own way in the world; no one doubts that anymore."

"Reading some dusty old book on his way to a joust, though." Mercy tutted, and winked at Edmund. "Don't you know how hard girls try to pretty themselves up on days like this? Don't let it go to waste!"

Edmund shook his head and returned to the open page before him. Gilbert's wagon bore him south out of Moorvale, down the Longsettle road toward the castle and the jousting field. The sun shone white, warm and kindly for an autumn afternoon. The folk of Moorvale were ranged along the road in carts, on horseback and on foot, chattering in clumps at a holiday volume as though their world could never fail and fall apart.

"What are you reading?" Miles Twintree thrust his shadow between Edmund and the page. He was Geoffrey's age but looked younger, a mousy-haired boy burned berry-brown from his labors in orchard and field. "Come on, what is it? Some kind of magic spell?"

Edmund shrugged Miles aside. "If I told you what I was reading, you wouldn't understand a word of it, so I'm not going to bother."

"You don't tell me anything, anymore." Miles turned away sulking. "Just because I didn't go to that stupid mountain."

Geoffrey looked up from the floor of the wagon, where he

sat sorting his arrows for the archery tourney. He cast a glance at Miles. "What's wrong with him?"

"He wishes he had gone to see the Nethergrim." Edmund shook his head and returned to his studies.

Gilbert leaned back from his seat. "Now, what are you kids whispering about back there?"

"Nothing, Master Wainwright." Edmund nodded to him with a fake smile. "Just talking about the joust. We're all excited about it."

"Especially for Harry's turn!" said Emma. It occurred to Edmund that her hand-embroidered dress and carefully arranged hair were quite possibly done in hopes that somehow Harry might notice her in the crowd.

"Ha!" Gilbert shook his head. "Just don't go making wagers on our lad Harry."

"Oh—no, Master Wainwright." Edmund laughed. "Very bad bet, so I hear."

Gilbert leaned back to the reins. "I just hope he falls quick and easy, and doesn't get too badly hurt. Last thing I want is to lose Elverain's only heir."

"It's just a joust, though." Emma started to look genuinely worried. "Blunt lances. It's all for show, isn't it?"

Gilbert shook his head. "Men die jousting from time to time, Emma, blunt lances and all. It's a sport for rich fools, you ask me."

"Gilbert!" Mercy swatted his shoulder. "Don't scare my little sister like that!"

"Why, what's the trouble?"

Mercy leaned to whisper in his ear.

"Father's thunder!" Gilbert laughed and whipped the reins to speed them. "Is there a girl in Elverain who is *not* in love with Harry?"

The road descended gentle and sure, turning past cottages, byres and fields on the way down to Longsettle, then through it and up again toward Northend and the castle. Bright banners and pennants had been hung about the square in the colors of Elverain, dark green and silver-white, above a milling crowd. Pavilion tents stood on the field at the foot of the hill before the castle, each flying its own colors and devices.

"Who's that coming up the road, there?" said Gilbert. "That's Katherine, isn't it?"

Edmund stood up to look. Katherine wore her best blue dress, and her hair had been worked into an elaborate, ribboned braid that matched its color. She wore a closed and inward expression, the way her father always looked when someone asked him to tell a brave old war story.

"I'll walk from here, Master Wainwright." Edmund hopped off the back of the wagon.

"Thanks for the ride." He joined Katherine at the verge, avoiding the knowing, smiling gazes of the Wainwrights. The wagon pulled away along the road, Emma giggling and whispering into Miles's ear on the back.

"I came to find you as soon as I could." Katherine turned back south again, following the disappearing wagon down toward the jousting field. "Some things have happened."

"I know they have." Edmund wanted to give Katherine a compliment, but it came out all wrong: "Why are you dressed like that?"

Katherine would not look at him. "Even maidservants get holidays sometimes." She walked a few more paces with her brows drawn low. "Edmund, I have come to warn you of the danger you're in."

"*I'm* in danger? The whole of the north is in danger!" Edmund hesitated, then plunged on. If he could not trust Katherine, he could not trust anyone. "I found out some more things about the Skeleth, in a place you'd never expect in a thousand years. There's a tomb of an ancient king and queen, right beneath the old keep on Wishing Hill!"

He looked about him to make sure there was no one nearby on the road. He dug into his sack and held out the wax tablet. "This is a powerful sealing spell, one that can trap a creature even if that creature can't be touched. And here, have a look at this!" He flashed the dead queen's brooch in front of Katherine. "There's a riddle on here that I'm sure has something to do with the spell, but I can't figure out what it means."

Katherine stared at the brooch. "Where did you get that?"

"I told you," said Edmund. "The tomb, right under Wishing Hill."

"So stealing another book was not enough." Katherine turned away. "Now you've started robbing graves."

Edmund shook his head. "No, no, it's not like that! I'm going to bring the book back, just as soon as I'm done with it, and I needed this brooch to help figure it all out. The Skeleth are servants of the Nethergrim, you see, and long ago this old king called Childeric—"

"I don't care about what old kings did long ago," said Katherine. "There's a war coming, Edmund, here and now, and we have to make ready for it."

"That's what I'm trying to tell you! The Skeleth are coming, and Ellí told me—"

"Edmund, everything that girl has told you is a lie." Katherine crossed her arms. "She's drawing you in, playing you for a fool. She's not on our side."

"Is that why you attacked her with a knife?" Edmund had never faced himself to Katherine in anger before. "She told me about that, too."

"I caught her in the middle of a spell." Katherine kept walking, forcing Edmund to follow. "She was in contact with—I don't know—something or someone very bad. I think they were talking about you."

"That's ridiculous." Edmund forgot to keep his voice down, even though by then they had passed in amongst the shops and stalls of Northend. "If it wasn't for Ellí, I wouldn't even know that the Skeleth were coming!"

"And how do you know that they are?" Katherine matched his angry voice. "You keep talking about these Skeleth things, but I've never seen one. All I know is that Lord Wolland is planning to start a war, and you're running about looting and stealing because some wizard girl in his service is telling you to do it! Why do you like her so much, anyway?"

"Until two weeks ago you'd never seen the Nethergrim before, either, but you can't deny what we found up in the mountains," said Edmund. "Why are you so suspicious of Ellí? She told me you just leapt on her without warning, that you attacked her for no reason at all!"

"Who are you going to trust, Edmund?" Katherine swept away. "Her or me?"

Elli's words of warning returned to Edmund: *Ordinary folk don't really understand people like you and me, and because they don't understand, they suspect the worst of us.* He struggled for an answer to Katherine's question, following her all the way up the lane that led from town to castle. He passed by Geoffrey drawing back for his first shot in the archery tourney, but did not care to linger long enough to find out how well he did.

The jousting lists consisted of a hundred-yard track, bounded by a simple rope barrier to keep out the crowd. On its far side stood a reviewing stand where the wealthy and noble sat under the shade of a brightly colored canopy. Harry stood beside a nearby pavilion, his arms held out at his sides to allow a servant to buckle a coat of plates over his chain armor. He glanced over at Katherine, then away.

Katherine let out a curse. "They've started early. Hurry, Edmund—we're going to miss it!" She paced onward as quickly as her skirts would allow, seeming either to have forgotten all about her argument with Edmund, or to assume that she had won.

Harry picked up his shield and walked off with his servants in train behind. Katherine watched him go, her hands clasped tightly together, then turned and pushed her way into the swelling crowd of peasants at the side of the lists.

"Katherine?" Edmund shoved in behind her. "Wait a moment. I want to watch, too!"

Folk jostled and pushed in around the barrier, looking for a good view. Trumpets sounded from the reviewing stand, calling the crowd to something like quiet. Edmund forgot his anger for a while, for like most peasants, he loved a good joust.

"In the name of Aelfric, Lord of Elverain." A powerful voice intoned across the field. "And in honor of those noble persons who are our guests, I declare this tourney open!"

A cheer went up from all around. Rowdy men broke out into local fighting songs. Edmund struggled to keep in sight of Katherine as she shouldered folk aside on a straight line to the edge of the jousting lists.

The herald raised a hand for silence. "And if it please my lords, we begin the day's engagements with a contest of the highest importance."

Katherine shoved her way to the barrier and leaned out over the rope. Edmund slid in beside her and swept his gaze up and down the field. Two of the knights sat astride their chargers, one at either end.

"To your left, my lords, we have an honored guest from the barony of Wolland, eager to do battle for his liege and father who sits among you this day. Sir Wulfric of Olingham earned his spurs this very year, and he rides before you to prove his skills with the lance. Sir Wulfric, are you prepared?"

The herald gestured down the field. Wulfric wore an azure surcoat over his armor, emblazoned with the head of a ram.

The edges of his shield caught the sunlight. He raised his lance in salute.

"Look at what he's riding!" Edmund pointed at the chestnut behemoth under Wulfric. "Mother's grace—that's got to be the biggest horse I've ever seen!"

Katherine bit her lip. "Eighteen hands and two." She looked back in the other direction, toward Harry's tent.

"Oho, I would not want to be Harry right now." Edmund waved down the rope at a few of the folk from Moorvale he saw in the crowd. Wulfric's horse whinnied with impatience.

The herald stretched out his other arm. "To your right, my lords, is a young man familiar to all of you. My lord Aelfric's own son, Harold, a squire clean of limb and bright of eye, seeks to prove his mettle before you today. Harold, are you prepared?"

Harry raised his lance to the sky, seated astride Indigo's broad gray back. The trumpets blew a clear and ringing note, and a cheer went up from the crowd.

Katherine let out a breath. "Indigo."

"Silence!" The herald threw up both hands. "Your lord will speak!"

Lord Aelfric stood to give his blessing. He was too quiet to hear.

Edmund let the pressure of the crowd push him up against Katherine's side. "Isn't this great? Best tourney I've ever seen! Nothing like a grudge match to light everybody up."

Katherine leaned as far out as she could over the rope. "Do you think he looks ready? I think he's ready."

Something glinted at her neck. Edmund stared at it—a necklace, silver set with precious stones.

Edmund stepped back from Katherine. He looked at her beribboned hair, her feminine dress, her anxious face. He turned to look at Harry riding out onto the jousting field and found his gaze locked with Katherine's.

Harry set his lance under his arm. The scarf tied around the end matched the color of Katherine's dress. She mouthed three words at him and touched her fingers to her lips.

Edmund awoke to sickened understanding. He stumbled back from Katherine, wanting nothing in the world but to run away from her. She gripped the rope white, staring out at the contest before her as though he were not even there.

The trumpets sounded, hooves thundered and the crowd rose roaring. The horses bore down upon each other as though it were they and not their riders who were about to exchange blows. Both men leaned forward in their saddles, feet dug hard into their stirrups. They lowered their blunted tourney lances and prepared to strike. The crowd whooped ever louder.

The horror that had risen in Edmund turned to rage. Hatred dripped its poison in his veins. He fixed a glare on Harry's braced and charging form.

"You won't be winning anything today." It was a simple thing, changing the Signs so that he could break wood instead of metal. In amongst the roar of the crowd, no one heard him cast his spell. He made the spell his own and made his own cost to pay for it.

He raised his right hand and held out his new knife on the

palm. He raised his left hand and splayed out the fingers in the Sign of Sundering. "I GRANT THE CURSE OF PEACE."

Edmund's knife snapped at the hilt.

Wulfric struck Harry's shield square in the center. Harry made equal contact with Wulfric's shield, but his lance broke apart with a resounding snap, shattering into dozens of long, sharp splinters. The force of Wulfric's thrust drove Harry from his horse, one broken stirrup dangling from his foot and a long splinter of his lance stuck in his chest. His arms flew outward, then swung back to his sides as he fell, lying as though sleeping in the air.

The crowd choked in mid-cheer. Edmund's hatred froze and cracked.

Harry hit the ground.

Katherine let out a scream. People all along the rope cried foul and called for someone to help the fallen man. Squires and grooms rushed out from the tents. Wulfric dropped his lance and drew off. Lady Isabeau stood up from her high seat across the field, then fainted down into the benches below.

Edmund reeled away from the crowd in guilty shock, hands grasping at his stomach as though he was the one who had been wounded. Katherine clutched the rope and sank to her knees, soiling her dress in the trampled earth. The men raised Harry on their shoulders and bore him from the field. Edmund could see nothing but an arm hanging limp and running with blood.

He felt a hand on his shoulder. "Follow me. Hurry."

Edmund turned in surprise and was met by the gaze of one brown eye and one blue. He reached out his hands and was pulled into a cloud of gently falling golden dust.

Chapter 22

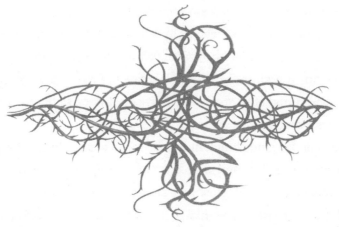

On top of all else, on top of the cold, the weariness and the desperate fear, Tom was lost. He peered out from the rushes by the banks of yet another stream. A boat glided past, long and low, turning with slow grace in the current. It dragged ropes and fishing lines in a tangle from the stern. Tom leaned out to call for help, but found the boat empty. It bumped and spun around the bend of the stream, and was gone.

Tom turned south, following the banks through rushes and rocks. It seemed as though every time he went around one little lake, he found another. He had fallen in amongst a maze of brooks and rivulets sometime before dawn, and there seemed no pattern to the narrow wooden bridges he had found in his wanderings. The farms he passed along the way looked thoroughly odd to him, stretched along the strips of land between the waters, islands of cottage and field bound by trees, dotted with docks where more boats bobbed in the stream.

The draft horse had a bad gait for riding. Like Tom, he had spent his life plowing fields, and just like Tom, he did not quite know how to move as a team of horse and rider. Tom could not seem to match the graceless rhythm of the horse's steps, and as the day had worn by, he had felt an ache creeping up his back from the effort of staying astride. Worse yet, there was no saddle—and worse yet still, Tom could not use his hands to grip the horse's mane.

Jumble lay senseless, cradled in Tom's arms. He had hardly even stirred when Tom dug out the crossbow bolt from his side, but he breathed, slow and shallow. Tom had made a cold poultice from pieces of his shirt, water from a stream and some strifemallow he had found by luck along the banks. He had cupped a little water into Jumble's mouth, wrapped him up in his cloak and held him close, hoping for the warmth of his body to stand in for the campfire he could not afford the time to build. The wound had begun to heal—that was not the worry. The worry was that it had started to fester before Tom could tend to it, and that the cold shivers running through Jumble's body were a sign of something worse to come.

The pale autumn sun sparkled on the water, casting up reflected twins of hanging branches spreading leaves of red and gold, of rock-bounded gardens and little cottages on islands. It seemed like a place where bad things could not happen, but Tom knew that there were no such places.

The wind shot cold beneath his collar. Jumble shuddered, then fell limp again. Every time it happened, Tom curled down to check on him, fearing the very worst, but every time he saw the furry walls of Jumble's chest still rising and falling. He had

MATTHEW JOBIN

spent most of the day cursing himself for not turning back and bringing Jumble to the castle, but it was too late.

"I'm here. Jumble, I'm here. You're safe, you're with me." Tom hoped for even the faintest woof, but did not get so much as the flutter of an eyelid.

The height and girth of the trees surprised him, as well as their broad claims upon what dry land he saw. Most of the cottages retained a guard of them thick enough to obscure his view—he had to pass through a few joined islands before he learned that the place was more densely settled than he had guessed at first, and yet there was no one to be seen, not in garden, boat or field. There was no hint of decay or disuse, no holes in roofs or crops gone to seed. It was as though everyone around had just gone off for a walk, all at once, the moment before Tom arrived.

The banks rose before him, up to a bridge that crossed his view over a rushing, rocky run of stream. Over the scents of tree and foaming water came the powerful tang of fish. Tom got off the horse to let him drink. He looked out from the verge and got his bearings from the curve of the grand Girth mountains to his west. He turned east, looking across the bridge and down the road, and felt his hopes rise again. The sight before him looked just as Tristan had described it, the tall stone chapterhouse in the dell beside the spring, surrounded by paddocks for livestock and gardens gleaned and turned down with care for the winter. He was not lost, after all. There were even distant figures moving about the place, through the vineyard and in between the barns and cattle byres.

Tom led the horse across the bridge, the reins in one hand

and Jumble in his arms. The road seemed to drop into trees on either side, back into the land of twisting lake and stream. The figures at the farm moved all in a clump along the rows of orchard trees and disappeared from view behind a roll of land.

"Hello?" Tom moved down the road as quickly as he could without jarring Jumble. "My dog is hurt. He needs help." The trees drew in along one side of the road, by a culvert over a hedge where stood a hut used for drying and smoking fish, from the look and the smell of it. He hurried past the door, only for it to burst open beside him. Hands reached out to seize him and drag him inside.

"Ow!" Tom tumbled down onto the hard dirt floor, banging his elbows in an attempt to brace Jumble's fall. He squinted about him in the sudden, smoky dark and saw a dozen folk crouched in hiding amongst the piles of coiled nets and rows of gutted fish dangling from the rafters.

"Quiet." A fat young man holding a fish-boning knife pressed a finger to his lips. "Keep your voice low, now. No shouts."

Tom stared about him, his mind a-spin. He let his hand trail through Jumble's fur. "Please. I need help and I bring a warning. I'm looking for the Revered Elder of the *Ahidhan*."

An old woman spoke from behind a hanging fall of fishnet. "Is that a stranger?"

"I've never seen him, not in all my days," said a young woman with a mallet for her only weapon. Tom slid a closer look at her. Under her tattered overcloak, she wore a kind of loose, heavy robe, dark blue edged with silvered white.

"I've just come from Harthingdale." Tom glanced around

the hut. It seemed wrong to hold back any longer. "I am very sorry to say it, but I think you are all in the most terrible danger."

The man with the knife cracked a bitter smile. "I'm afraid your warning comes too late." He pushed the door open and pointed outward. "Have a look."

Tom followed the man's gesture east toward the farm. He caught sight of the figures again, in vineyard and field. At less of a distance than before, even the late afternoon sun could not hide the glow they gave off, and the work they were doing around the great stone chapterhouse was the work of methodical destruction.

Tom felt the grip of fright. "I've got to go back to my horse. There's something on the saddle that I need, and I then must find the Elder as quickly as I can. Please, if you know, tell me where she is."

The old woman nodded to Jumble. "Your dog is not well."

"He's been shot," said Tom. "The wound's going bad."

The old woman leaned upon her walking stick. She groaned and grabbed at her hip as she gained her feet. "Let's have a look at him, then."

Tom brought Jumble over to the old woman. His eyes opened to the dark inside the hut—and he froze, his heart in his mouth. For an awful instant he thought he stood before the wizard woman he had seen at the gates of Tristan's castle, but then he came to understand that the old woman merely resembled her: the same silver hair, though in a messier style; a similar frame of body, though somewhat heavier; a similar face, though soft and round. The woman before him looked older than the one who he had heard chanting in wild fury at the castle, stooped into the last of her years.

The old woman touched her wizened fingers through Jumble's sweaty fur. "This is a very fine dog." Under the rags she wore blue and white, like the young woman with the mallet, but also a strange buckle, a disc of beaten brass edged with silver. Letters ringed the rim—Tom could not read them but knew just by looking that the disc stood for the sun.

Jumble opened his eyes. He looked at the old woman. His ragged tail twitched, then dangled down again.

"What a sweet one." The old woman scratched between Jumble's off-colored ears. "Yes. Yes, you are."

She sat down with a creaky groan and opened a leather sack at her side. "Put him in my care. I will do all that I can for him." She stretched forth her arms. "What is your name?"

"Tom." He handed Jumble across to her. "Lord Tristan sent me."

"I am Thulina Drake, Elder of the *Ahidhan*." She nodded around her. "These folk you see around you are the last of my students. We are running for our lives. Would you like to come with us?"

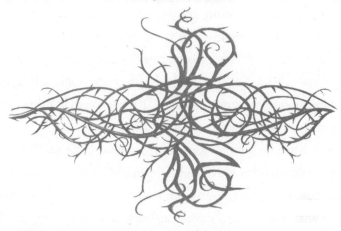

Chapter 23

"How long has she been up here?"

The voice came from above, lonely in the dead night sky. Katherine looked up to see a guardsman ascending to take his place atop the small turret that projected from the castle's keep.

"She was there when I took my watch at sunset." The guard on duty in the turret yawned, then bent to collect his things.

The first guard, a young, rangy sort, leaned out to look down at Katherine, who sat huddled in a corner behind the battlements. "That's the marshal's daughter, isn't it? Doesn't she know she can sleep in the hall?"

"I don't care where she sleeps." The other guard slung his crossbow on his back. "What news of Harry?"

"No news." The young guard poured oil into the basin of the watchlight. "If he dies, do you think there will be war?"

"I doubt it," said the other guard. "Wolland's twice our

size, at least, to say nothing of Tand and Overstoke. We'd be crushed."

"What about the king, though? Surely, for the death of a lord's only son and heir—"

"Pfah. The king. Weak as a kitten."

"The way I hear it, the Earl of Quentara doesn't like Wolland much," said the young guard. "They've been enemies since who knows when. This could be his chance."

"Let's hope for our own sakes he doesn't take it." The other guard turned to climb down. "Good night."

"Good night." The young guard unbuckled his sword and set it down. He lifted a drinking horn and took a gulp while waving to the distant figures of the guards who walked the tops of the outer walls.

Katherine shut her eyes for a while, then opened them, staring up. The stars wheeled overhead—silent, their patterns suggestive of everything, and then nothing.

The watches of the evening passed. Every so often, the young guardsman would poke his head over the side of the tower and glance down at Katherine. The moonlight caught his face from time to time and seemed to show him watching her more than anything else he had been charged with protecting.

"Are you hungry?" His voice came after such long silence that it made Katherine jump. She looked up at him.

"You must be hungry," he said. "Or thirsty. You've been up here all night."

"I'm not hungry."

The guard rummaged through something on the turret and

spoke with his mouth full. "Well, let me know if you change your mind, and I'll toss something down to you."

Constellations rose; others set. The young guard's helmeted head appeared again. "What are you asking the sky?"

Katherine ran a hand down her cheek, though she had done with crying long before. "I'm asking it please, please no. Please not him, please not now."

The guard glanced up, then down again. "Worth asking, I suppose."

He left her to her silence, watching around into the dark distance and signaling his fellow guards with an all-clear from time to time. His yawns came louder after a while—closer and closer together—then Katherine heard the sound of the trapdoor being raised on the roof of the keep below.

"About time, Ulf." The young guard bent to pick up his things. "I nearly fell asleep. Any news?"

A narrow, balding head stuck up from below. "Is the old marshal's daughter up here?" A third guard climbed up onto the roof of the keep, wrapped in a heavy cloak.

The young guard pointed. "She's over in the corner. Why? What's the trouble?"

Katherine stood up, slow and stiff and in a clutch of fear.

Ulf reached for the ladder to the turret. "Harry's awake—he's past the worst. They say that he'll live, more than likely."

Katherine let out a cry. She put her hands to her face, then hugged herself.

Ulf turned to look from halfway up the ladder. "Oh, I see her now." He took the young guard's offered hand. "Anyway, I was down in the barracks when the news came in—Harry's awake, and he's calling out for Katherine—Katherine Marshal, over and over again."

Katherine leapt up and raced for the trapdoor down into the keep.

"I wouldn't bother." Ulf shook his head at her. "Not a chance my lady Isabeau will let you in there."

Katherine threw back the door. She cast a last glance up at the silent sky and at the guards changing places on the turret above. Ulf looked down at her, shaking his head, while the young guard stared at the stars with a more thoughtful look on his face than any she might have guessed he could wear.

"I'll tell you this." Ulf's voice faded from Katherine's hearing as she hurried down the stairs. "Whatever happens, I feel sorry for that girl."

Chapter 24

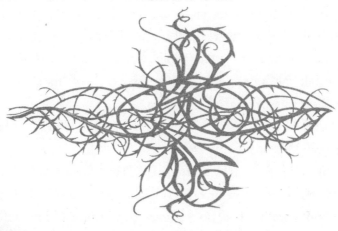

This place." Edmund looked about him, shivering. "Horrible."

They had marched three rises out, across the old stone bridge over the Tamber and up onto the moors. Behind them stood the posts of the bridge, the span across the water and the thatched roofs of home. Before them stretched a land both wild and dead, a heartless claim on the horizon, gray beneath a pall of black.

"It doesn't get any prettier, I'm afraid." Ellí stopped at the crest of the rise. She knelt to search through the moorspike grass, and pulled out what looked to be a beaded, woven bag concealed amongst the bladed leaves.

Edmund glanced behind him, gazing down at the mill and the hall, the homes and gardens huddled beneath the distant Girth. Against foreground of moor and backdrop of mountain, his village looked terribly lonely and small. "Why did you bring me out here, and why did we have to wait for night?"

"Think about it, Edmund," said Ellí. "Why does the land look this way?"

The words of the book came back to Edmund. *The land where the Skeleth walk is now waste. It is ruin, a land given up to death, a land under the sway of That Which Waits Within the Mountain.*

He felt the hairs stand up on the backs of his arms. "It's here. This was Childeric's kingdom."

"The fairest of the lands between water and wood," said Ellí. "And now look at it."

Edmund set his sack on the road. "How far are we going?"

"It's ten miles, give or take." Ellí dumped out a loaf of hard old bread from her bag, then packed in a bundle of her clothes, along with an iron lantern and a flask of oil. "The sooner we start, the sooner we'll be there." She hauled up her bag and turned east.

"Wait." Edmund took Ellí by the sleeve. "If someone did something bad, but did it in a moment of weakness and now regrets it, how should that person be judged?"

Ellí turned to look at him. "There is no reason to hide it, Edmund." The moonlight at her back left her face a shadowed blank, a blank on which his fears drew a dozen awful visions. "I know what you did."

Edmund's hands trembled, so badly that he had trouble getting a grip on the drawstring of his sack. "If he was really, truly sorry, does that make what he did less wrong?"

"You are asking where good and evil truly dwell," said Ellí. "Are they in what you mean to do, or only in your actions?"

"I didn't want to hurt him." Edmund hugged himself. "I just didn't want him to win."

"It's a harder question for us wizards than it is for other folk." Ellí started eastward down the road. "What we wish for and what actually happens are often much closer together."

Not a tree broke the horizon, nor a cloud to dim the stars. A hard wind rippled the heath, working its way under Edmund's shirt no matter how he turned himself. He paused at a ridgetop, then set down his sack to adjust its contents, hoping to find some way for them to lie that would stop their points and edges jabbing at his back.

Ellí waited for him. "Have you had a chance to study the spell?"

"Yes." Edmund did not want to add that he barely understood what he had read. "I'm sure there's something missing from it, though. That riddle I found still bothers me. When I look away from it and think about something else, an answer almost comes."

"I hope you figure it out soon," said Ellí.

"Me?" said Edmund. "But you're my teacher."

Ellí shook her head—the twining locks of her hair bounced outward and back. "Edmund, I don't know how to do spells like that."

Edmund stared at her.

"I could not possibly hope to break a spell cast by Vithric and the Nethergrim itself, the way you did up in the mountains," said Ellí. "I told you that I would try to teach you everything I know, but you must understand that if anyone can defeat the Skeleth, it's you."

The tingle that ran up Edmund's arms came from many sources at once—cold and fear, excitement and pride, and something else, something that happened when Ellí's forearm brushed against his.

A half smile turned Ellí's lips. "I won't be your teacher for long."

They ascended the shoulder of a hill that had somehow passed down as legend in the village, though no one Edmund knew had ever seen it. Beyond it, so said everyone, the land forgave no trespass. Humps of rock stuck out on the ridges ahead, bare and formless, raised wounds on battered earth.

"I don't know how scared I'm supposed to feel out here." Edmund shifted his belt, so that the fighting dagger he had stolen from his brother rode close to hand. "I can't see anything dangerous, but I know I'm in danger. It's like when I was up in the Girth—I know I don't belong here, somehow."

"You're right," said Ellí. "You don't. Come on, we're more than halfway there."

"Halfway to where?" Edmund hurried after her. "You came with Lord Wolland over these moors, on a stretch of road that no one has walked in the memory of the oldest folk alive. You took this way when you could easily have crossed the river down in Rushmeet and come up the Kingsway, like everyone always does. Why?"

Ellí heaved a long breath. "I am not like you, Edmund. All I ever wanted was a comfortable room at court and enough coin to pay for food and parchment. I came with Wolland because that was what I was told to do, and I never had the courage to ask him about his plans."

The West Road ran on and on, straight as a lance into

nothing. Save for the stars, there was no telling land from sky at the horizon.

Edmund waited on Ellí, and waited. "Will you tell me where we're going, or at least what we're hoping to find when we get there?"

Ellí spent a long time thinking over her reply. "Yes. I'm sorry, I've gotten too well used to keeping secrets. I think I've figured out where the Skeleth were first brought into the world. I must have walked right past it on the way here without understanding what it was. If we go there, we might learn more about how they were summoned up, and that might give us the key to how to put them down again."

Edmund was nearly sure he saw something move, something flitting between the bald humps of rock ahead. He tensed, watching for movement left and right as he ascended the rise.

Ellí gripped his hand in hers, then let go. "I'm sorry. I'm getting scared."

Edmund shrugged and turned to lead them onward—but then Ellí took his hand again and held it firm.

"I don't quite know how to say this, but I feel much braver when I'm with you." Ellí matched Edmund's pace, walking close at his side.

Edmund looked around him, at the moorspike crowding up beside the road, at the flat old horizon and the gibbous moon. He did not feel brave at all, just then, though somehow he could not stop trying to pretend, if only for Ellí's sake.

The land around them seemed to widen ever more as they walked on, stretching back to the horizons all around as though it would fold itself away into an endless void. Edmund found himself clinging as tightly to Ellí as she did to him, holding on to her hand as though letting go would mean wandering forever, lost in the dark.

When he noticed it, the first thing he thought was that he must have lost track of time. "Do you see that glow up ahead?" He looked around to get his bearings and make sure he was still going eastward. "That can't be sunrise yet."

Ellí seemed to rouse herself from some inward sorrow. "You are not the only one who has done things he regrets."

"Those are voices!" Edmund strained to listen to the murmur, then the distant laughter, then the metallic clatter and bang. "Ellí, wait, don't you hear that?"

"There are some things I should have told you before we left." Ellí kept a few feet ahead of him. "I feared that you would take them wrong, though, and I had to make sure you would come with me."

Edmund hurried after her, following her up between the humps of rock to a broken ridge. "What things?"

They crested the rise together.

"Edmund, I am sorry." Ellí tried to take his hand again. "I want to make amends. I do."

A sick, hot feeling took Edmund, pricking up from his fingertips. "No. Oh, no."

Chapter 25

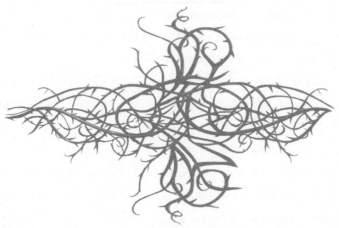

The water slapped at the ox-skin sides of the boat, threatening to come over and wash into the bottom. Tom knelt at the front and tried to work out why everything he did with his paddle seemed to make things worse. Through the hanging limbs of the trees on the banks he thought he could see a jut of land to his left. Perhaps the little lake he was on had joined another, and that was what was making all the waves. He tried to turn by jamming his paddle into the stream, but had not the least idea if he should be turning left or right.

He felt a tap on his back. "Just paddle straight, Tom." The Elder knelt up behind him. "You're making things harder for the sternsman."

"Oh." Tom returned to the one thing he had been taught, drawing simple strokes on his right with the paddle. Soon after, the boat hauled around so that it crested straight over the waves. The rocking motion stopped, and with it the feeling that they might tip over and fall into the water.

"There." The Elder reached out to guide his arm. "Straight back—good, and slide it sideways from the water, and return. Much better—now continue just like that."

A second boat drew level with Tom's. "Revered One!" The young woman who had held the mallet back in the hut stood up in the middle. "I beg you not to stir yourself, to consider your venerable age and leave the boy to—"

"Curse you for a ninny, Oriel—I was paddling boats before your mother could walk!" The Elder's retort bounced off the water, off the humped hills and island fields. "Now sit down before you flop into the river and make me swim after you!"

The sternsman of Tom's boat raised his voice just enough to let it carry. "Revered One, begging your pardon and all, but we pass a goodly number of places in the dark. Places to be ambushed, like. Mayhap we'll want to keep our silence."

"Fairly spoken." The Elder arranged herself on the wooden frame in the middle of the boat. She returned to her task, crouched over Jumble with her walking stick laid out alongside and her leather sack opened between her feet. Scents poured from the sack into the air, most of them smells Tom knew: rosemary and mugwort, lavender and feverfew. Every time Tom spared a glance over his shoulder, it looked as though the Elder was doing something different. Sometimes she murmured words he could not catch. Sometimes she prodded at Jumble's wound, cutting at the bad flesh with a small knife. Still other times, she simply ran her hands along his fur with a look of care upon her face that Tom might have expected if Jumble was her own dog, or even her child.

After a while of waiting, the question simply burst from him. "What is it that you are doing?"

She touched Jumble's forehead. "Do all things in life have a balance, child?"

Tom found himself wishing to answer, wishing very much to be as clever as Edmund. "I don't understand what you mean."

The Elder drew something from her sack. "If I eat this apple, you do not." She demonstrated her point with a bite down to its core. "Are all things so in the world?"

Tom thought hard about it—too hard, perhaps. He had the feeling that the answer to her question was something he already knew.

"The folk who call themselves wizards hold that all things are in balance." The Elder kissed Jumble on the nose three times. "If a wizard heals a body, he must balance that change in the world with another change. The easiest way is simply to wound another body. There are those of us who think such a thing is not worth doing."

She wrapped the wound with expert care. "There. Time must mend him now."

The currents merged and mellowed, and after a while of staring about him, Tom got some idea of how the land was laid. They were no longer on a lake—they had joined a river, not nearly as big as the Tamber back in Moorvale, but steep of channel, with a rapid flow that belied its glassy face. Shapes glided past, moonlit on the banks: a fishing cottage set on poles over the water; a daub-and-wattle barn upon a bare slope; a stand of leafless trees perched as though about to fall into the river at any moment.

The answer seemed to come to Tom out of the silver-topped water. "Is wisdom such a thing? Is it one of those things without a balance?"

He heard no answer, so he turned around. He found the Elder sitting as a girl would sit, arms clasped under bent knees, Jumble lying crosswise on her lap. The breeze rippled her long gray hair against her chin. He failed at first to read her face, and for an awful instant he thought she was going to tell him that Jumble had just died.

"It is indeed," she said. "When you give someone wisdom, you still have it yourself."

She stretched out a hand under Jumble's nose, and to Tom's delight Jumble raised his head to sniff at it. His tail quivered—not quite wagging, but neither was it just a twitch.

Tom shipped his paddle across the bow at a whispered signal from the sternsman. He sat back on his haunches. "Are you a wizard?"

"I am not." The Elder rubbed at Jumble's belly. "Who is a good dog? You are. Yes, you are."

"Hoy there!" A figure waved in shadow from a dock at a bend in the stream. "News! I've got news!"

"That's no Skeleth," said the sternsman. "Still, let's have a care." He waved the third boat in their party of perhaps a score of fleeing folk toward the banks and bade the others in their little fleet to stop paddling but stay at the ready.

Tom knelt at his position in the bow. He watched about him, ready to spring for his paddle at the first sign of trouble, while the third boat drew in to converse with the man on shore.

The Elder picked bits of grass and nettle from Jumble's matted fur. "Do you thrill to danger, Tom?"

"I do." Tom brought up a borrowed gutting knife, putting it near to hand in the bow of the boat. "I never would have thought it, but I do."

He looked back. "Is this a flaw in me?"

The Elder trailed a wrinkled, calloused hand in the water. "What is time, child?"

Tom could not quite get used to the leaps the Elder seemed to take with her words. "It's . . . how some things happen after other things, I think."

"Is it a road?" The Elder flicked drops of water at him. "Or is it a river?"

Tom thought he halfway understood. "You are asking if the future is a thing we make, or a thing that happens anyway."

"One of the hardest questions our Order has ever considered is what to do if time is a river, after all," said the Elder. "Float, or paddle?"

"Paddle," said Tom. "Paddle and hope."

The Elder scratched Jumble's ears, pondering long in silence. She nodded, with a look of satisfaction. "Then you know why danger thrills you, and you know it is no flaw."

The third boat cast off again behind them. "Word of the danger's spreading through the eastern villages, Revered One." Their bowsman called over the water. "They've got riders on the way to Queenstown and Bale. No trouble on the roads, as of yet, no more sign of those creatures."

The Elder patted Tom's shoulder. "There, my child. Our warning goes swift and sure across the land."

Tom glanced back and found the sternsman handling their boat without trouble. The current drew them on in silence, so he took his chance for a rest. He turned to sit backward, facing the Elder, almost touching knees. "May I ask more questions?"

"You have answered mine. It is only fair."

"How do you know Lord Tristan?"

"We are dear old friends," said the Elder. "I know John Marshal, too. I suppose you would think it odd for me to call him a poor, sad boy."

Tom thought about it. "No. It wouldn't."

The Elder looked out over river and sky. "We did things together, long ago—he and I and some others—things that I believe we were right to do, though they never seemed to bear the fruit we hoped."

Tom touched the ornately carven box that lay on the bottom of the boat between them. "How were the Skeleth sealed away, all those years ago? Lord Tristan said that it took two kinds of magic, and one of them was the kind you know."

The Elder smiled sadly. "No one remembers." She shifted the sun-disc buckle at her belt, shifted it again, then took it off. "Believe me, if we still knew how to stop the Skeleth, we would have done it by now."

Tom folded in his arms, feeling the hard edge of the wind under his shirt. "Then why were you attacked first, out of all the places the Skeleth might strike?"

The Elder bundled up the oversized peasant dress that had covered her blue-and-white robe. "I don't know that either, unless it is simply that my sister Warbur hates me more than I had ever guessed. We were assembling for our supper late last night, and were struck without warning, and . . ."

She trailed off. "There are folk very dear to me who were alive yesterday." She ran her fingers over the top of Jumble's head. "My sister had them all killed."

Tom turned around. He picked up his oar and started paddling hard.

The sternsman whispered on the breeze. "Hoy up there. You can rest—current will take us."

"Not fast enough." Tom got his back into his work, and after a while felt the sternsman adjust to keep them straight. "Where are we going?"

"Garafraxa," said the Elder. "A castle on a lake. The Earl of Quentara lives there—Isembard, a good and loyal man."

Tom dug his paddle deep. "We'll get you safely there, and then I'll go north to find Edmund. Between us all, we'll find a way to stop the Skeleth. I won't give up until we do, and I won't let anyone hurt you anymore."

The Elder poked his back. "The perfect hero, you are."

"I don't want to be a hero." Tom reached back to touch Jumble between the ears. "I want to be like you."

Their boat shot ahead of the others, down a long curve of river running through a land of joining lakes. The work was not much different to Tom than threshing grain or pitching hay—there was a way to do it right, to pull the boat along with the greatest speed for the least effort, and just like the other work he had done in his life, once he found the rhythm, he let his mind drift in peace.

"Not but two miles more, Tom." The sternsman's voice murmured from behind him, just loud enough over water and wind. "We've made a good pace. You're stronger than you look."

The land curled low, then high and then low again along the banks. It bulged and shifted—tree and bridge, field and farmhouse. The Elder fell into a doze, curled up with Jumble at the bottom of the boat.

"And there." The sternsman pointed with his paddle. "Past the bridge. See it?"

The sight woke both wonder and hope in Tom—he felt the tingle of knowing that it is possible for something to exist by seeing it for the first time. He had seen castles before, but had never dreamed of one like that which he saw, standing high above the waves, its smooth dark walls plunging sheer into the water, an island of carven stone.

"Garafraxa, stronghold of Isembard, Earl of Quentara and Lord High Steward of the kingdom," said the sternsman. "We'll be safe enough in there, if we're safe anywhere, and Isembard will get you to Elverain as quick as can be done, Tom—depend on it."

"Hmm?" The Elder woke and yawned. "Are we there?"

"Almost." Tom switched sides to even out the strain on his arms. "Looks like a mile or so, once we are out on open water."

The bridge over the river loomed ahead, a haphazard span strung on rickety wooden pilings. The closer the boat got to it, the more plain it was to Tom that it marked land's end—just past it the banks fell away along a rush-lined shore, leaving open water on the run toward the castle. The lead boat steered to avoid the pilings below, gliding near to the banks. Tom felt his sternsman shift to follow. It was not until they had nearly passed under the span that the figure stepped out between the posts above, and all of Tom's growing hopes choked and died.

"Sister, I fear this is our last goodbye." Warbur Drake kept her hands folded in the sleeves of her dress, standing alone at the top of the bridge. "I wish that you had heeded me, all those years ago. We might have done much together."

Chapter 26

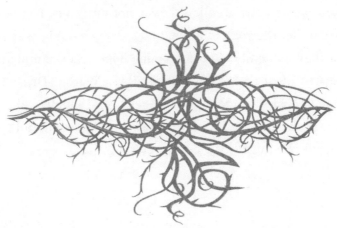

Edmund raced up behind Ellí and grabbed her by the sleeve. "An army?" He spun her around to face him. "An *army*?"

"The army's not important—they're not even meant for Elverain." Ellí shrugged him off and kept her pace down the broad slope of the vale. "They're camped in the ruins of an old fortress town. I should have understood before that this was once King Childeric's stronghold, his tower and tomb. We must get in, we must get past them, and—"

"What do you mean they're not meant for Elverain?" Edmund jabbed a finger westward. "This road leads right to Moorvale, right over the bridge to my village!"

Ellí shot a glance at him sidelong. "They're not going to Elverain, they're going through it. That's why Lord Wolland's at Northend. He's parleying with your lord Aelfric."

Edmund drew up all he knew of the world in his mind. "Quentara." He followed the path of the army, down through

Elverain and beyond into the settled lands west of the Tamber. "Rushmeet, Umberslade, the Hundredthorn. They're going south."

"A strike by surprise, from a direction no one suspects, and at the very edge of winter." Ellí nodded her head. "By the time anyone can muster a force to react, it will be too late. Lord Wolland will be king of all the north."

Edmund looked out across a bleak bowl of land that seemed like an inverted curve of starless sky. The glow rose from a ring of fires spread across the hollow. Within the rough circle they bounded moved a swarm of shadows, men and horses in restless camp. A pair of smiths beat their hammers out of time. A laugh sounded, loud and harsh, while someone else played a tune upon a flute.

"Do you see it?" Ellí pointed. "On the hill, there, right in the middle of the fires."

Edmund peered ahead. The flat expanse of the vale confused his senses, making him think at first that the shape on the hill ringed by the fires was just another hump of rock, but it was too regular in form to be a work of nature.

"It looks like the big tower of the old keep back on Wishing Hill, the one where I found the tomb." Edmund followed the stonework upward to the jagged line where it gave way to starry black. "But it's broken off halfway up, and all tumbled over."

"Three brothers, three kinsmen, three kings of the Pael— just like the book said." Ellí threw back her cloak and quickened her pace. "If only I'd understood the first time I was here."

Edmund followed at a horrified stumble over treeless

heath, toward the ring of fires around the broken tower. "But if Lord Wolland's got an army already, why does he also need the Skeleth?"

Ellí walked a few paces onward, deep in thought. "King Childeric believed that the Skeleth could make his army invincible." She turned to Edmund. "Lord Wolland believes the very same thing. He's made a deal, a bargain with a wizard who told him that the Skeleth could bring him certain victory."

"Which wizard?" said Edmund. "Vithric?"

"No, my teacher." Ellí trembled. "Her name is Warbur Drake."

Edmund watched her in silence, trying not to simply fall back into mushy-headed sympathy. He started to wonder whether Katherine might have seen something in her that he could not.

"Come closer." Ellí reached into her belt. "We'll need to get past the sentries without being noticed."

She threw the dust, spoke the words of her spell, and the night warped around Edmund. He fell with Ellí under the Sign of Obscurity, and it seemed to him that the moon hung above him without giving light.

"There." Ellí beckoned Edmund onward. The spell left trails of her smile in the night air. "Come with me."

Men and boys crossed the road in front of Edmund, and behind, trampling down the heavy grass around the sentry fires. Many wore livery, the crests of ram, rook or boar upon their chests, and in the dizzying churn of the spell it looked as though they had sprung to life on the chests of their wearers. Someone barked an order, and a rough circle of torches drew in like a swarm around an oddly shaped structure by the verge. The swelling light revealed it for a tent spread out over the ancient stone foundations of a house—around the tower such dwellings grew more dense, making it look like an odd, half-ruined village. Dozens of horses raised their heads as Edmund passed their makeshift paddocks, and a chorus of whinnies resounded through the camp.

Edmund did his best to focus his mind past the confusion of Ellí's spell. He shot glances left and right along the road, and marked a horse for every man, many of them fine stallion chargers worth more than most peasants made in a year. The fires burning in the hollow around him bounded a circle wide enough for hundreds, but not thousands. He could only guess that he stood amidst an army of knights, second sons of noble birth who owned no land, and so hoped to make their ways in the world by conquest.

He nudged Ellí's side. "Do they have any archers?"

"Forget the army. They don't matter." Ellí turned off the road toward the ruined tower, which stood on a hill just to the north, surrounded by more tents and paddocks.

Edmund could not quite bring himself to forget a camp full of hundreds of armed and hungry-looking men not ten miles from his home, but he followed all the same. He let his hearing widen out, trying to grasp the meaning of all that reached his ears. Men led horses to and fro along the road, while squires— many of them boys his own age—carried hauberks of chain armor big enough to weigh them double. An old man sharpened swords in another ancient, ruined house on the apron slope around the tower. A warhorse reared and thundered, but a squire got him down again with the offer of a turnip. Harness jingled in the hands of men brushing past on either side, the metal polished to a gleam that caught the moon.

"Richard!" A man in rough river furs stepped out from behind the tented ruin, surrounded by the torches—a guard of men dressed in like fashion to their leader. "Richard Redhands, say that we must wait no longer! Say that soon we ride!"

One of the men passing next to Edmund turned around. "We await the word of our lord and commander, Hunwald, just as we have these past days."

Edmund froze in fear. Sir Richard Redhands strode onward, passing Edmund by without paying him the slightest notice, so near that some of the slowly falling dust from Elli's spell landed on his sleeve.

"You ask me, sir knight, we've no need of waiting." The furred man spoke with a guttural drawl that forced Edmund to listen very closely to make out the words. "Once we're across the bridge, there's nothing Aelfric can do to stop us. We could be in Quentara by tomorrow night!"

"We do not ask your counsel, Hunwald of the Uxingham Hundreds." The spell made the scowl on Richard's face look all the worse. "You have been promised a great deal for your aid—do not presume that the banner of command was part of the bargain. Await your summons to battle, just as we do."

Hunwald turned away, grumbling with his men. "We're going to starve to death out here," said one. "Where's that accursed grain they promised?"

Richard Redhands strode off in the opposite direction. "It

sickens me to bring such men along." He muttered it under his breath to the young knight at his side. "I can hardly stand the smell of them."

Ellí tugged Edmund's arm. "Hurry, now. My spell won't last much longer, and if we get caught out here, we're both in deep trouble."

Edmund stepped over the wind-shot bones of what must once have been a castle wall. The foundations of the tower ahead stood intact to just beyond twice his own height, in front of a standing stone that looked just like the Wishing Stone back home. The double doors lay smashed inward, leaving a gap just wide enough for a man to crawl between them.

Edmund looked at Ellí. "You passed right by this place, and you didn't go in?"

"I was just trying to stay out of trouble." Ellí would not meet his gaze.

Edmund approached the tower. "There's something scratched into the walls here." He traced his fingers on letters that seemed chiseled into the stone with little care and even less craft, scrawling larger and then smaller across the door. "It's Old Paelic. Stranger beware, it says. Open not this door."

The letters crawled and twisted under the false light of the spell. Edmund thought he heard his own voice screaming again, just as he had the first time Ellí had cast the spell on him. This time, though, he thought he could almost make out words.

"Can you fit through?" Ellí stood a few paces back of him. "We should go through."

Edmund gave the broken doors a tentative push—they did not move, but there was more than enough space to squeeze between them and into the dusty blankness beyond.

"If someone sees us up here, we'll be caught." Ellí hovered over him, her voice hushed and urgent. "We should go inside before my spell fails."

More chiseled letters drew Edmund's eye. "Look—there it is again: Open not this door." He felt along the cracks of the letters, pulling dust and blown weeds aside to trace their shapes. "This place is defiled. It is poison. Open not this door. And that: *Ahibanas dhuguni . . . Mek dhiti ghav.* That's Dhanic, again—another warning."

"Hurry," said Ellí. "Please."

"And these here—Gatherer symbols." Edmund touched them. "They're done wrong, but I think I can read them: *Death-Below-Crawling, Away-Flee-Always.*"

Edmund stood and looked back, around him at the ring of fires and the shadowed army. "A warning, in three languages."

Ellí came up to his shoulder. "I can light the lantern once we're inside." She took his hand again—she quaked, but when he held her firm, she stopped. "I'm not so scared when you're with me." She ran her thumb up his palm.

Everything tumbled in Edmund. He started to wonder if maybe, just maybe, the way he had always felt about Katherine was a childish thing, something that would wear off as he grew up. He opened his mouth to speak, though he did not know what he was going to say.

Ellí did not let him speak. She pressed her lips to his.

MATTHEW JOBIN

Amidst the rapture of it came a thought. His first kiss was not Katherine. His dreams had not come true.

"All right, then." He turned to the door. "In we go."

She squeezed his arm. "I knew I could count on you."

Edmund turned back to the staved-in doors. He climbed up their splintered faces and felt out into the gap with one booted foot. He thought he touched solid ground beyond, but when he set his weight, his footing gave way with a snap, and with nothing to brace against he tumbled inside, into the darkness of the chamber beyond.

"Edmund?" Ellí hopped into the chamber after him. "Did you hurt yourself?"

"No, no. I'm fine." Edmund flailed out a hand and grabbed what he had broken, an old wooden stool that had survived the centuries intact, only to be splintered by his misplaced foot. "If this place is anything like the one in Moorvale—"

"Yes, it should be down from here." Ellí was already across the round chamber. She scuffled in shadow. "Stairs, yes, down. I'm letting go of my spell now, so don't raise your voice too loud."

Edmund picked himself up from the floor. "Should we light the lantern?" His skin began to crawl, but he could not tell why.

Ellí shook her head. "Let's wait until we're well out of sight."

"I don't think anyone down the hill will see a light from here." The feeling came to Edmund that something about Ellí was different—the way she spoke, and something about the way she looked—but it was too dark to see her clearly.

"Very well." Ellí knelt down in shadow—from the sounds

of it, just by the top of the stairs. She set down her woven bag and riffled through it.

Edmund felt his way over to her side. "I liked what we did, outside."

"So did I." She drew out an iron lantern.

He set down his own sack on the floor. "I've never done that, before. Kissed someone." He knelt to help her, feeling through her woven bag for the tinder and flint. "Was I . . . um . . . was I any good at it?"

"What?" Her voice sounded breathless. "Oh, yes, wonderful. Give me space to light this."

Edmund looked around him. "It's just like the southeast tower back in Moorvale." His eyes grew accustomed to the deeper dark within the tower. "Lilies, the serpent, even the double spirals."

Ellí turned her back to him. "Just a moment." She sparked the tinder—yellow light flickered under her. "Will you please go down first? I'm scared."

"Of course." Edmund stepped onto the first stair, the *Paelandabok* under one arm and his other hand on the hilt of his brother's dagger. "I've done this sort of thing before. It's all right to be scared."

She raised the lit lantern behind him. He turned his head and looked up at her with an encouraging smile.

His smile died. All at once, he knew what was wrong—too late, too late.

"I am sorry about this." Both of her eyes were blue. "At least, I think I am."

She kicked him hard. He tumbled down into the dark.

Chapter 27

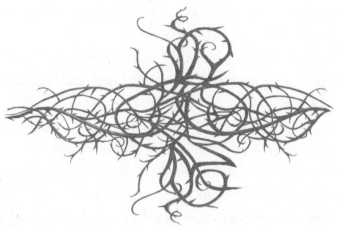

The Elder gasped in fright. Tom's heart leapt into his
throat. He started paddling furiously, driving the nose
of his boat in between the pilings of the bridge.

The sternsman goggled. "What's—?"

"Ambush!" Tom hissed. "We're under attack!"

The Elder called upward as their boat slipped under the
span of the bridge. "Warbur—sister, if it is me you want, I
will come quietly! These folk are innocent of all that might be
between the two of us."

The answer came muffled from above: "Oh, sister, if only
you had read a little more and spent fewer of your days nursing injured sheep. How many times have I told you, through
the years? There is no such thing as innocence."

The Skeleth awaited the boats on the other side of the
bridge, standing in two lines along the banks. They sprang to
the attack in utter silence, flinging themselves onto the boats
without the slightest care for themselves. Blades flashed, coils

writhed, and screams did not last long. Tom was nearly sure that the one busily slaying people left and right in the boat nearest the bank was a mild, kindly faced man he had last seen in the castle at Harthingdale.

"To the banks, to the banks!" The sternsman of Tom's boat whispered it in fright. "We've got to beach and run, it's our only chance!"

"No, into the middle." Tom looked back. "We must get through—and the Elder could never outrun one of those things."

The sternsman nodded once. He jammed his paddle in to turn them, steering them to the very center of the current. The other boats passed on toward the ambush, helpless to stop themselves before they drew level with the rushes.

Tom paddled as hard as he could, watching the Skeleth leap onto the other boats. He had one hope—that the man inside the monster still had to breathe, and that there was a limit to how far they could jump.

"We cannot leave them!" The Elder grabbed his shoulder. "No, Tom, we can't leave them!"

Tom did no more than glance back at the sternsman. They did not slow their pace. Their boat shot out under the bridge, right in the middle of the river. They braced themselves, but none of the Skeleth seemed able to reach them from the banks, though no few of them tried. They failed, though, flopping into the water yards from Tom's boat. The rushes fell back to either side. Waves struck the bow as river gave way to lake.

Then a thump rocked the boat, nearly turning it over. Something landed heavily right behind Tom, nearly throwing him out into the water. He turned around, his paddle held up

MATTHEW JOBIN

to block the blow that he knew must be coming—and looked into the face of the Skeleth standing over him.

"Master Marshal."

John Marshal's face loomed dead above him, mindless and unfeeling within the reaching, grasping glow. He kicked the Elder down beneath him, then raised his sword.

Tom did not know where the thought came from, but it seemed to him that, if he was about to die, he did not want to die trying to kill the nearest thing to a father he had ever had. He lowered his paddle.

"It's me." He stared up. "It's Tom. I will not fight you, Master Marshal."

John froze at the apex of his swing. His face twitched, and then his eyes fixed and focused.

A surge of wild hope ran through Tom. He thought of every time that John had ever been kind to him, everything John had ever done to ease the burdens of his life. "Master Marshal, it's Tom." He thought of the evenings he had spent, once a month, eating at John and Katherine's table. He remembered how he had stored those evenings up inside himself, doling out their joys over the hard days in between. An image formed in his memory, John Marshal feeding him and Katherine a stew so bad that they could hardly choke it down—and all of them laughing at it, all of them smiling, one instant when it felt as though he had had a family. "I won't fight you."

The face came alive. "T . . . Tom." John Marshal lowered his sword. "Tom." The waving limbs around him shuddered, pulling away from his body. Pain crossed his face—effort. He shook himself, like a man trying to wake from a nightmare.

The sternsman leapt from the back of the boat and swung his paddle hard across John's back. All trace of recognition vanished from John's face. He turned, leaping over the Elder with his sword held high.

"No, wait, please!" Tom reached out, but too late. The sternsman died without making a sound, tumbling backward into the water. The creature that was John Marshal turned, stepping lightly in the stern to come back around, blade at the ready—but then he stumbled and tripped.

"Paddle, Tom!" The Elder jammed her walking stick between John's legs and twisted it—the glowing limbs flowed around it, but not the flesh beneath. John Marshal flipped into the river with a loud splash.

Tom had no time to grieve or fear. He took up his paddle and jammed it into the water, on one side, and then the other, to keep them going straight. The boat leapt forward, from the river out onto the lake.

"Kill them! Kill all of them!" Warbur Drake shouted from atop the bridge behind them. "That boat, there! Kill!"

The Elder scrambled to the stern of the boat and grabbed the sternsman's fallen oar. Tom took the opposite side and drew water with all his might. More of the creatures leapt from the rushes, stretching themselves to the very limits of what sinew could bear, but none of them reached the boat.

Tom lunged out and drew hard, through water that was much less forgiving than the river had been. Currents crossed and roiled under the boat, slowing their progress out onto the lake. He dared not glance back. Castle Garafraxa loomed ahead, across a stretch of choppy black. Helmeted men moved along its battlements, and a murmur of alarm sounded over the water.

"Isembard!" The Elder raised her voice to a scratchy scream. "Isembard, it's Thulina Drake! It's Thulina! We are under attack!"

Tom spared a glance up at the walls of Garafraxa. The men atop them knew that something was wrong, that was plain enough. They shouted and moved along the battlements in ever greater numbers. A gate winched up ahead—if only Tom could keep them on course, they could paddle right through to safety.

"The dock's just past the gate." The Elder spoke between huffing hauls of breath. "Go right in, right in and we're safe." She had skill, but little strength, forcing Tom to double-paddle. They were not half so fast as they had been with the sternsman at the paddle, but they were moving.

Tom spied men rushing out onto the landing, hauling boats along a dock and leaping into them. One man seemed to direct them, an old man dressed in green, with a shiny bald head fringed by short white hair.

"Into your boats, men, hurry!" The bald man waved his sword from the gate of the castle. "Bring them in safe. Cast off, cast off!" As soon as the first boat had been loaded, he leapt into it and cut the line that held it to the dock.

Tom's bangs fell damp with sweat across his eyes. His shoulders screamed with every pull, and the castle ahead grew closer slowly, so slowly. It already felt as though he had been rowing all his life, but they were almost there.

"WATER SHALL BE DEATH IN THE VEINS." Warbur Drake's voice took on a terrifying resonance, seeming to hiss and leap along the surface of the lake. It came in bursts, an awful cadence: "BETWEEN EARTH AND METAL I SHAPE WATER INTO DEATH. WATER CHOKES YOU, WATER WILL HAVE YOU, WATER SHALL BE DEATH IN THE VEINS."

Tom gaped and froze. A snake rose from the lake before him, a snake made of nothing but water.

"Goodbye, sister," Warbur Drake called out across the waves, ragged and breathless from the exertion of her spell. "Your kind cannot be permitted to exist. You are not part of our plans."

The snake twisted upward in a fume of white water and lunged for the Elder.

"Leave her alone!" Tom leapt backward over the Elder's cowering form, swinging his paddle out in a wild arc at the snake. The paddle splashed through the coiled column of water without effect—and the snake bit him instead of the Elder, sinking its fangs into his side where his shirt had ridden up from his hip.

Pain ripped through Tom, ice in his veins, spikes in his mind. He let the paddle slip. His vision twisted until he saw only sky. Everything in him was agony, everything his body did—breathing, heartbeat, thought.

Jumble leapt up and started barking from the middle of the boat, each sharp noise a molten torture to Tom. He felt the boat begin to slew around, rocking sideways on the waves. Everything in him ached to slip into the water, to drown and end the pain.

Warbur Drake cursed, her voice shrill with anger and exhaustion. She began the chant of another spell.

Tom heaved himself up again, though it felt as though his flesh were coming off his bones. He found the paddle—such utter torment even to touch it—and drove it back into the water. He did not know whether the Elder was helping their course across the waves. He did not really know anything anymore, save for the pain, and what he meant to do before he died.

"Oh, Tom." The Elder sounded very far away. "It's not far. Hold on."

The chanting rose in rage, and then there sounded a chorus of hissing splashes. Tom could not tell if he had been hit by another spell. Jumble's barking seemed to get farther and farther away, growing dim, as though he had jumped inside a sack. What a funny thought . . .

Tom remembered that he was supposed to be paddling the boat. Shapes bobbed over the waves before him, men in boats up and down, up and down. The pain in him seemed to turn to sleepiness.

"We are almost there, Tom. Keep going."

Tom kept moving his arms, but could not quite remember why. It seemed much better to go to sleep.

"It's not far, Tom."

The shapes ahead drew closer. Tom saw the face of the old, bald man—then it smeared and melded with the clouds in the sky.

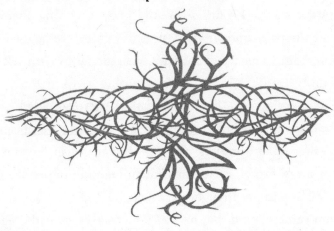

Chapter 28

P apa," murmured Katherine, hunted through the shadowed forests of sleep. *A hand reached out for her,
blooded and trembling.* She tossed and turned onto her
back. "Papa."

She woke. The cloak she used for bedding lay crumpled
down around her ankles. Sweat chilled in beads on her skin.
She sat up, shivering, trying to hold on to the substance of her
dream—why Papa, and not Harry?

More than a hundred people huddled close in slumber on
the floor of the great hall, whole families rolled under blankets
all together in the only decent shelter they would ever know.
The fire in the great stone hearth had gone to embers—it cast
just enough light for Katherine to pick her way amongst the
sleeping forms at her feet. Men and women, young and old,
lay entwined all around her, piled over with their children,
dogs and cats, all at peace, all breathing out into the frigid
air in their separate meters and registers. Katherine stopped

in the middle of the room and listened, entranced for a time, then picked her way between them and slipped out into the courtyard.

Silence was everywhere. The dark walls of the inner ward held it cupped. A lone watchfire shone atop the keep, its feeble light drowning in the sky. Katherine crossed the courtyard, shoes rustling in the tended grass, her eyes on the stars framed four-square above her. She shot a glance up the walls, to where candlelight shone through the arrow-slit window of Harry's room. She spared herself time for one more pleading wish, then opened the door on the long day's work ahead.

Goody Bycross turned from the washpots with a scowl. "Girl, you begone." She waggled her laundry-stick in Katherine's face. "You're wanted in the stables today."

Katherine stopped at the threshold of the laundry shed. "What? Why?"

"Request from Lord Wolland." Goody Bycross looked a good deal less than pleased to be bearing such news. "The lords go a-hunting today, and they want you to come along with them. Well, don't stand here with your jaw as wide as the door, shut them both and get on with you!"

Katherine closed the door on the row of women washing clothes and breakfast linens. She turned and raced back to the hall to change into a tunic and breeches. She would have skipped through the grass on her way to the stables, but for the light in the arrow-slit window above.

A boy slept on a bed of straw by the door of the stable. He awoke as Katherine approached and challenged her in a whisper: "Who goes there?"

"They say I'm wanted here today." Katherine peeled the melted stump of a candle from the shelf by the boy's bed and took up flint and steel to light it. "Do you know why?"

"Not a clue." The boy rubbed his eyes and let out an apple-wide yawn. "You're the old marshal's daughter, aren't you? You might as well do some work, while you're here."

"I'd like that." Katherine carried the candle down the passage, holding it to the wick of each lantern hanging on the wall. Boys uncurled from the straw and stood blinking, dogs gained their feet and shook themselves out, and the horses woke one by one as she passed.

"Here." Katherine held the apple she had brought along under Indigo's nose and stroked his mane as she fed him. Sorrow returned—Indigo was Wulfric's now, won by the custom of the joust. He would soon be gone, taken away to Wolland, never to be seen again. She could bear to stay with him no longer, though she would have wanted to linger until someone came to throw her out. She snuffed the candle and left.

The stables warmed with the heat of activity. Boys drew water, poured oats and mucked out stalls. They danced past one another in the narrow passage with tack and saddle in hand. The faint rumor of the sun's rising seeped in around the shutters, and with it the first of the knights and ladies coming for their horses. Katherine kept in the thick of the work, moving swiftly from one noble personage to the next, ensuring that they all left with steeds well fed and prepared. She cleaned out the shoes of a visiting stallion, then ran her hands through his tack, checking it for frays. She walked over to the storage stall and hauled up a sack of grain with her back to the door.

　　　　　　　　　　MATTHEW JOBIN

A voice spoke from behind her: "My son does not love you."

Katherine felt her insides give a squeeze. She dropped the sack and turned to curtsy. "My lady."

Lady Isabeau had not slept, and no amount of careful arrangement of her hair, veil and dress could disguise it. "He thinks he does, but he cannot. I do not say it to wound you."

A stablehand brought Lady Isabeau her riding mare, then bowed and backed away. Lady Isabeau led the mare off down the passage, causing everyone to stop and make their reverences. Katherine followed her outside, then bent to make a step from her hands.

"Men of his station in life do not have the luxury of those feelings." Isabeau gained the saddle with Katherine's help. "Be thankful it is not your lot."

"He called for me, my lady." Katherine handed her the reins, but kept her gaze averted. "He sent for me. Why would you not let me see him?"

"You know the reason. I'm sure you will be pleased to know that he is expected to live." Lady Isabeau arranged her skirts over the side of her mare and rode away toward the gates.

Katherine blinked back tears, for she had no time to cry them. A herald called out from the courtyard, and the door of the keep swung wide. Through it stepped Lord Wolland and Lord Aelfric, walking as far from each other as good manners would allow. Sir Wulfric followed behind, seeming not to notice the hateful looks shot his way by every groom, smith and washerwoman in the castle.

Katherine took the reins of Lord Aelfric's own courser and

led him from the stables, followed by two stable boys with steeds for Wulfric and Wolland.

"Katherine Marshal." Lord Wolland favored Katherine with a smile that made her want to punch him right in the mouth. "Your second name rings true once again."

"She is no marshal, my lord." Lord Aelfric looked as though he had aged into his final years overnight. "She is a ward of this castle, a girl without parents to speak for her."

"It is custom, my lord, for a marshal to attend to the horses of the lords on the hunt." said Wolland. "More than that, it is simple good sense. Shall our steeds wander off into the woods while we stalk our prey with the longbow?"

Lord Aelfric made a weary wave of his hand. "Do as you will."

Sir Wulfric stepped out before the other men. "I beg you again, my lord, to accept my apologies." He bowed to Lord Aelfric. "I would rather cut off my own hand than do injury to young Harold. It cheers me to learn that he will survive."

"Those are the chances of life, sir knight." Lord Aelfric's creaky old voice seemed to have lost what remained of its strength. "Every father learns in time that he cannot shield his child from the wandering cruelties of this world forever." He flicked a glance at Katherine, making her insides squeeze again.

A page boy in Wolland's colors stepped before them and bowed. He offered out a handful of arrows, all very straight and well crafted, each with identical fletching, black feathers from a bird that Katherine did not recognize.

"A gift," said the page. "From my lord Wolland."

Lord Aelfric took an arrow and turned it over in his hands. Two other pages made the rounds of the nobles, offering similar arrows to all present.

"What think you, my lord?" said Wolland. "Have my men made shafts to rival the storied arrows of Elverain?"

"They are of excellent quality." Lord Aelfric looked up at the boys distributing dozens of arrows to the hunting party. "This is a lordly gift to be given so widely."

"Consider them tokens of my esteem." Wolland waved a hand. "Emblems of my wish for a more harmonious union between our lands."

Lord Aelfric shot him an icy look. "I will gladly take them, my lord."

"Good." Wolland climbed into his saddle and rode away with Wulfric to join the hunters.

Katherine held out the reins of Lord Aelfric's courser. He did not seem to see her, so she pressed them into his hands.

"What is the proper course for an honorable man?" Lord Aelfric did not look at Katherine, but no one else was near enough to hear him. "The lessons of my youth come back to me across the long years. I feel the sting of it; the face of my own father gazes down on me, questions me. Have I failed?"

Katherine's dream returned. She saw her papa in chains, bound and wrapped in them up and down his arms—somewhere dark, somewhere cold. He reached for her, blooded and trembling.

"You see before you an old fool—the very pattern of the oldest of fools." Lord Aelfric put a hand to the pommel of his saddle. "The fool seeks to purchase safety at the cost of honor.

The fool pays in coin for his life, but then finds himself paying again, and yet again, in things more dear to him than life."

Katherine glanced around her. She stood alone with her lord in the center of the courtyard. The hunters waited by the outer gates. The commoners went about their business in stable, smithy and garden, all of them out of hearing.

"My lord, it is right to fear the strife of war." Katherine stepped up beside Lord Aelfric and knelt with her hands laced together. "But there are times when we must do that which we fear."

When the stern cast of his face relaxed, Lord Aelfric looked a good deal more like Harry. "Spoken as your father would speak." He stepped into Katherine's hands. "How I wish that I had heeded him, while yet I could."

Katherine raised him into his saddle. "My lord, what is happening?"

"Too many things. I wish these dangers had not come so late in life." Aelfric slipped his feet into the stirrups. "Lord Wolland is quite right; it is custom to have a marshal to attend our horses on the hunt. We will follow that custom as closely as we may."

Katherine curtsied. "I will gladly serve, my lord."

Lord Aelfric took his reins. "You seem to like the horse my son rode at the joust. I do not think Wulfric will take it ill if you ride him one last time." He spurred his mount and cantered off through the gates. The hunters turned and followed him.

Katherine spent as long as she could in Indigo's stall, feeding him and brushing him down as though it were not the last time she would ever do it. At last, when she could no longer ignore the ever more urgent summons to her duties, she saddled him and rode from the castle, following the nobles through Northend and up the Longsettle road. She turned at Thrawnthrup, passing through the humble cluster of cottages under old shade oaks and following an ox-trail through wide, flat fields harvested down to stubble. She found the hunting party gathered on a grassy slope by the eaves of the wood. The horn sounded just as she reached them, and she found herself riding in amongst the lords at a gallop down the trail that ran between forest and field.

Half a mile along they turned onto a track that wound up the side of the ridge and led into the trees. Katherine found Wulfric keeping pace at her side, a few lengths back of Lord Aelfric and Lord Wolland. Lady Isabeau's party of noble ladies rode some distance behind, while from ahead rang the shouts of the other lords and knights, singing rounds of verse best meant for the worst of taverns.

Wulfric steered in so close that his knee bumped Katherine's thigh. "I have never seen a match for that horse." He cast a satisfied look over Indigo's great and graceful back. "He will be a joy to ride."

Indigo shifted away and rode his own course along the trail. When Wulfric turned his horse to close the gap, Indigo put on just enough speed to stay clear, raising his head ever so slightly and eyeing his pursuer, until Wulfric found his horse reluctant to press the issue.

"So, my lord." Wolland rode at a comfortable pace ahead. "We are off to the usual spot?"

"We are, my lord," said Aelfric.

"Good, excellent," said Wolland. "I have never known a better place for shooting. Girl, attend us here."

Katherine nudged Indigo to the space Lord Wolland had opened up between himself and Lord Aelfric. She kept her head low in deference, even as she rode, for she could see Lord Aelfric stiffen at the impertinence of a peasant girl riding abreast with lords of the realm.

"I wish to resume our earlier conversation." Lord Wolland nodded to Katherine. "Do you recall? We spoke of the uses and purposes of war."

Katherine looked to Lord Aelfric, but when he did not move to stop her, she spoke. "I remember, my lord. I said that most folk just want peace. War brings nothing but strife and ruin. We men and women have enough trouble already in this world, and to make more of it is the mark of a fool."

Wolland smiled. "So says woman always. But she would have her sons defend her daughters."

"If everyone fought only to defend, no one would need to fight at all."

"Ah, no." Lord Wolland shook his head, his smile turned wistful. "The world is too small, my girl. It is too hard. Someone's line must fail, someone's house must crumble, someone's kingdom must disappear. A mother asks the world that her children prosper, but the children of all mothers cannot prosper. Thus, war."

"My lord, do not mistake me." Katherine clenched her reins. "It is right to make war in defense of hearth and home. It is right to root out those who threaten the common peace and put them to the sword."

Lord Wolland guffawed. "My dear girl, that sounds alarmingly like a threat!"

"She fears for her people, my lord." Lord Aelfric's voice cut sharp across Lord Wolland's boisterous noise. "Is that so hard to understand? It is no fault of hers that she knows nothing of diplomacy."

"Then let us serve as instructors for her first lesson." Wolland turned in his saddle. "My dear girl, it is often prudent for a lord to keep his anger in check, and so harness it to a larger purpose. A tricky thing indeed, diplomacy. The wise lord knows he must tread carefully to avoid giving undue offense, and yet he must also be at pains to seem like a strong man whose better nature wishes peace, and not a weak man whose survival depends on the kindness of his neighbors."

There was a very still and pregnant pause.

Aelfric turned his head to regard Lord Wolland. "You have some skill at diplomacy, my lord, by way of long and diligent study." He let the words hang. "Let us speak, then, of diplomacy, of statecraft, and of peace."

"There is only one question between us on that subject," said Wolland. "You know, my lord, what that question is. The time has come for you to give me your answer."

Lord Aelfric rode on for ten more paces. He looked at Katherine and then sat up tall in his saddle to glare across at Wolland. "My answer is no."

"You have long been praised, my lord, for the firmness of

your loyalties," said Lord Wolland. "Be that so, I yet beseech you to consider those loyalties in the light of the present day."

Lord Aelfric's owlish brows went down. "You have heard my judgment on the matter, my lord. It is final."

"The man who does not change with the times is busy carving his epitaph." said Wolland, the faintest hint of warning in his voice.

"Mine is already half carved," said Aelfric. "When it is done, I trust it will say that I was not a man who forgot his friends."

"Ah." Wolland shook his head. "As I had feared."

Their party arrived at a wide, shallow ravine in the heart of the forest. A brook wound through its center, flowing gently south, trickling and laughing over the smoothed rocks as it went. The trees grew sparse in that direction, and the canopy above very high; Katherine could see for quite a distance between the trunks. The ground rose to a ridge on either side, lined with stands of oak and maple, while beyond that, bare hilltops bumped the sky some distance off, just visible through the trees. The noble ladies took their places on the ridgeline to the right, while the knights made their way to their side of the gallery on the left.

Lord Wolland looked about him in satisfaction. "Yes. A fine spot for shooting." He shrugged off his cloak and tossed it over the back of his horse, leaving the bright red lining exposed.

"You are warm, my lord?" Aelfric turned to him in surprise, for the wind amongst the trees whispered many hints of winter.

"I am growing warmer." Wolland took up his bow and quiver. "Come, let us begin." He put the reins of his horse in

Katherine's hand and advanced a few yards to one of the last pieces of good cover before the open ravine.

Aelfric raised his hunting horn to his lips and blew three loud blasts. A flash of movement caught the corner of Katherine's eye, far off to her left behind the knights. She turned to search with her gaze through the trees, but caught no further sign of what it was.

Everything went quiet. The horses stood close, at rest but not at ease. The sun cut sharp through the barren branches above. Whispers sounded high and to the right, then a hush, then rising from the silence came the sound of the dogs. They began as muted noises, without mood or motion, then grew nearer, clearer and louder in their happy chase. Two dozen longbows creaked back. Lord Wolland's round head rose just out of cover. Arrowheads glinted from the tops of the ridges. There was a hint, then a rustle, a shake, a sudden thunder and a doe burst from cover at the head of the ravine. She was in full wild run, her black eyes bulging as she galloped out into the killing place. The horses raised their heads all together, jerking Katherine's arm back as the doe bounded down the ravine toward them, achieving a last moment of grace as she leapt into the sunlight, head high, long legs arched in the perfect form and model of flight. Then two dozen bowstrings whipped at the air. The doe lurched, stricken on all sides, and tumbled at once, her speed making a sprawling ruin of her last moments. She fell hard forward, eyes still staring wide, and as she came down, Lord Aelfric slid out from his place of cover to fall with her, one arrow deep in his left side.

Chapter 29

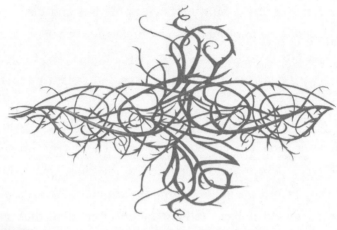

T om.

He did not know how far he had wandered, or how long. He had turned, once or twice, to look behind him, but it was no use—there was nothing against which to reckon a course. The trees stood glorious high all about him, each the image of the others, each of them the one lone tree in all the world.

Tom.

Every one of his footfalls rose into the vaulting canopy above, then returned to him in gift, in echo without the faintest ring of discord, in a hushed and reverent presentation. Each dell and rise, each glade and outcropping of mossy old stone was its own wonder, and though he put one foot before the other and walked as though still in the night of his own world, he looked on every tree as though he had never seen one before, and when he looked down, he gaped in awe at the

sight of earth, of dead leaves and crawling insects in the filtered moonlight.

Tom.

Autumn receded trunk by trunk as he wandered, backing
away through summer to the finest night of spring. The air
hung still, but not close; it smelled of leaf, moss and trunk, of
cool rock and the pollen of glade flowers.

Tom.

He roamed, lost in rapture, until he stepped without warning into the open. Before him grew a row of white birch that
ran off into the darkness left and right, each grown in its own
fashion as though they had happened to form a straight line by
chance. He turned around. Just behind him was another row of
birch running parallel to the first. They marked out a path that
bore no signs it had ever been trodden, sheltered above by a
very full growth of leaves save for an open stripe of sky along its
center. He tried to fix his direction by the stars but did not recognize them. He considered for a moment, then took the path.

Tom.

The rush of a waterfall grew louder with every step along
the trail. He emerged high at its flank, above a bowl of white
water churning far below. Rocks cut along the sides of the
fall, just past trees whose roots poked out here and there into
empty space.

Tom.

The cataract fell and fell beside him. Drops of water flew
up from the depths to prick at his face at intervals that could
never be predicted.

Tom.

Day and night as one. The moon fell crescent, then rose full. It was joy just to breathe—joy at the intake of his breath, and at the output, and at the pause between.

"Tom."

He heard footsteps. He looked back into the forest, down the path along which he had come.

"Tom." She leaned upon her walking stick, gnarled hands gripped to the sheepskin handle. He thought that perhaps he should get up to help her, but then she was beside him and sat down.

He put his hand to the earth, feeling out the edge of land and water. "Where am I?"

The Elder laid the walking stick across her lap. "What do you mean when you ask that question?"

He felt his belly—fear. "Which way is home? Which way is safe?"

"Do you want to go to the safe place?" She was an old woman. "You can, if you like. Just follow the water." She was a little girl with ringlet hair and a dusting of freckles under each of her eyes.

He held out a hand. He let the water touch his fingers. "I feel as though something I wanted to do was not done."

"That will always be so." She was a maiden in the first bloom of youth, the ringlets drawn back along her ears like a crown. "Even if you come with me now, when next you see this place, you will say the very same."

He looked at her. "If I go with you, will it hurt?"

"Yes." She was a mother-to-be, her belly big, her hair bound and veiled. "It will hurt us both."

"Why?"

Wrinkles sprouted from the sides of her eyes. "I waited for you, the whole of my life I waited, but you never came." She was an old woman again. "Not until the very end."

She wrung her hands around the walking stick. "I always knew that you would find me." Broken veins left blotches of red on her cheeks, blotting out the freckles. "But so late, so late."

Tom thought he remembered something, or at least remembered that there was something he should have thought before. It had to do with things given and received, things that stayed within you even when passed on to another.

He touched his hand to hers. "Lead me. I will follow."

She kissed his fingers—once a child, once a mother, once a woman bowed with age and dying by the breath.

Tom put his hand to the earth. He stood and helped her up. He thought he heard barking, somewhere far away.

"There is no safety, if you follow my path." The Elder leaned on her walking stick.

"There is no safety anywhere." Tom followed her out of the glade, even though each step hurt more than the last. They walked hand in hand between the birches, though the birches were not really there.

"Sit him up. Raise him, raise him sitting." The voice sounded different from before—rougher and less musical, with a hard, close echo. Pain chewed on him and swallowed him. He heard an anxious woof.

His eyes slid open. Sunlight cut in a beam through a long, slit window, right across his face.

"Give him space. Let him breathe." Someone held him by the shoulder, forcing him forward almost double. Jumble crouched whining between his feet, bandaged around the middle. He barked at Tom, making ready to leap on him, but a pair of rough hands seized him before he could move.

"It hurts." Tom gagged from it. "It hurts." He felt something digging, moving at his side.

"Quiet. Shhh." Oriel wiped his brow with something damp. "Just a moment longer. Hold to us, hold to this room. You are sitting in bed, in castle Garafraxa. It is morning, it is autumn—Tom, look at me. Hold to me."

"A bed?" Tom's vision cleared. "I'm not allowed to sleep in beds. My master would beat me black and blue."

Jumble barked loud, and then louder. "Now, then, doggy. None of that." An old, square man held a wiggling Jumble tight—the bald-headed man who had shouted orders from the castle gate. "You let him be, now. Time for licking noses later."

The pressure slackened on Tom's back, and the strange digging feeling ceased. Someone moved behind him, letting go.

"Prop some pillows for him. Keep him sitting up." The Elder hobbled off the bed, her mouth red-black in drips down her wrinkled chin. She bent and spat into a jar. "That's all of it."

"Oh, it hurts." Tom retched. His skin felt like it crawled back and forth, ribbons of fire running with every pulse of his heart.

The Elder cupped his chin. "Don't cry to me, you chose to

feel pain again." There was a twinkle behind the age-clouds of her eyes.

Oriel let her grip go slack on Tom's arms. He sank backward, but she got a bolster in behind him before he could crash down to the bed.

"We must set watches over him in turns." The Elder grabbed for her hip, then her walking stick.

"I'll be first." The old man dragged a chair beside the bed. "I've a good space of things to think about. Now, then, doggy, will you be good?"

Oriel tucked a linen sheet up to Tom's chest. "Rest now." She smoothed his sweaty bangs from his eyes.

The bald old man let Jumble hop onto the bed. Jumble padded up on the sheets, licked Tom's nose just once, then lay down at his side.

"Help me, girl." The Elder sagged over her stick. "I must rest." Oriel moved to take her arm and led her through the open doorway.

Tom watched them go. He half expected the Elder to look back at him, but instead she staggered out, her breaths coming shallow and hard. He lay back and shut his eyes.

Dream and waking thought ran together.

His eyes snapped wide-open. He knew exactly what he had to do.

He looked over at the bald old man in the chair. He raised a hand. "My name is Tom."

"Isembard's the name. Earl of Quentara." The bald old man nodded to the doorway through which the two women had gone. "I was the Revered Elder's husband, years ago, if you can believe it."

Tom hauled himself up on the bolster—weak and dizzy, but alive, awake. The sun had risen past the arrow-slit window. The pain that had wracked him was gone, leaving only a tightness on his left side, just under the ribs. He touched along it and felt the poultice set over the cut, a wet and heavy bandage filled with something that rankled his nose. He brought up his hand to sniff—he smelled bruisewort and clodderweed, crushed seeds of Gunda's-glory and other things he could not place. Beneath it lay a cut so shallow that it should have been little more than a nuisance.

Jumble slept—his bandaged, fur-fringed belly heaving in and out—but as soon as Tom shifted, he snapped awake and raised his head. His yellow eyes roved, scanning Tom up and down, and only a fool would fail to call the look within them worry.

"It's all right." Tom scratched Jumble between the ears. "I'm in no danger now—and look, I have a bandage to match yours." He swung his feet over the side of the bed and tried to stand.

"Now, now, there!" Lord Isembard caught his arm. "Didn't you hear? You nearly died last night—you're to rest."

"There is no time." Tom heaved himself to his feet. "I know that we have only just met, and it might seem very bold of me, but I must ask of you three favors."

Isembard sat back in his chair, white eyebrows raised into his creased and hairless forehead. "Well, then. Ask away."

Tom looked to Jumble. "The first favor that I ask, my lord, is that you take care of my dog."

"That's no hard asking." Isembard patted Jumble's head. "The second?"

"That you send out word to bring your people into your castles, but do not offer the Skeleth battle, whatever they try to do."

"That's harder asking, but I'll wager you have your reasons. Done. And third?"

"Passage across the lake, and then a loan of the fastest horse you have."

Chapter 30

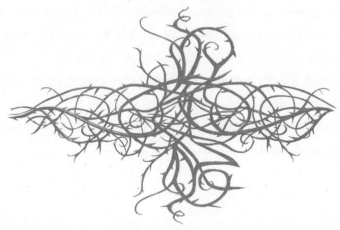

Katherine huddled in the straw next to Indigo. Some of the boys kept to their tasks in the stable around her, stripping off tack and brushing down the horses, but they moved as though lost in unhappy sleep.

Indigo chewed on the hay in his basket. He drank from his trough—but twitched his ears, one eye cocked at Katherine. He turned his head and nosed her, his muzzle dripping wet.

Katherine raised her hand to stroke his mane. "You were never really mine." She tried to stay calm but found that she could not help herself. She bowed her head and let the tears fall as quietly as she could.

A stable boy hobbled past the stall with a saddle in his hands—the saddle from Lord Aelfric's own hunting horse. "Who did it?"

Katherine got to her feet. "The shot came from up high, on the knights' side of the ravine." She stepped from the stall. "It could have been anyone—all the arrows looked exactly alike."

The stable boy trembled. "Was it . . . was it quick?"

Katherine shook her head. "Not especially."

"I didn't really know him." The stable boy hugged the saddle in his arms. "He was never kind to me. Why am I crying?"

"The world will change, now that he is gone, and maybe not for the better." Katherine put an arm around the boy's shoulders. "That's one reason—you're crying for fear."

The boy worked a nervous hand on the pommel of the saddle. "Is there really going to be a war?"

"The lady Isabeau!" The herald intoned the words from just outside the stable door. Katherine hardly had time to jump away before it opened. Lady Isabeau had yet to change out of her riding dress—the stains of her husband's lifeblood marked the sleeves up to her breast. Two of the castle guards followed close at her side, white to the jaws, hands gripped hard on the hilts of their swords.

"My lady." Katherine curtsied to Isabeau. For one tilting instant she thought she might step forward to embrace her.

"The lords of Wolland, Tand and Overstoke," cried the herald. "Make way, make way, there!" Footsteps approached the stable, men walking in hard boots.

Katherine shot a glance toward the door, then reached out. "Resist them, my lady." She clutched Isabeau's bloodied sleeve. "You must yet resist."

"Unhand me!" Isabeau wrenched her arm away. She bored a hollow, hopeless look into Katherine. "See where *resistance* has gotten us."

Lord Wolland ambled into the stable with Wulfric at his side, seeming entirely unchanged by what he had just witnessed. "My lady, we all grieve with you on this sorrowful day." His voice grew round with florid lies. "Though death is our common lot, it is yet a blow to witness a death before its time, and to know that it need not have come to pass."

The lords of Tand and Overstoke snapped their fingers. The stable boys looked to Lady Isabeau, but seeing no sign from her, they scurried off to prepare the horses once again, replacing the saddles and bridles they had only just removed.

"My lady." Wulfric cut a sweeping bow before Lady Isabeau, then strode down the passage until he reached Indigo's stall halfway along. He glanced back at Katherine; she sank against the wall.

Lord Wolland drew on thick leather riding gloves. "Though I am sure he is now wounded in spirit as well as body, I thought perhaps we might have a word with the new lord of Elverain before we depart. Young Harold is now our noble peer, and we would wish to know his mind on a few small matters."

Lady Isabeau moved toward Lord Wolland with such deliberate speed that the knights and lords around him closed ranks to block her way. "You will not see my son." She shook— the whole of her trembled. "Take what you will, my lord, do what you will, but approach the keep of this castle on peril of your life."

Lord Wolland did not flinch. He reached out, past his men, and with sudden speed cupped a hand under Lady Isabeau's chin.

"You dog!" A castle guard drew his sword, and then so did every other guard and noble in the stable, but Lady Isabeau raised a hand to stay them all.

A smile spread slowly across Lord Wolland's face. "Harm me and mine, my lady, and this castle will be stormed, your son's head will adorn a pikestaff, and not a man in Elverain will be spared." His deep-set eyes flickered dark. "Not a man."

"Take what you will, Edgar." Lady Isabeau trembled and broke. "Do what you will."

Lord Wolland leaned close—it almost looked like the beginning of a kiss. "And the river, my lady?"

"Cross it. Cross it, curse you, do what you will! Leave us in peace."

Lord Wolland let go. "Good." He tapped her cheek with gloved fingers. "Tell your son that there will be a place for him in the new order soon to come. We will welcome him in council when he is mended." He turned from her, reaching for the offered reins of his horse.

Katherine backed away from them all and bolted for the door. She raced across the courtyard, up the stairs to the keep and around the bewildered guard, then through the great hall past a solemn cobbler trying to console a sobbing charwoman. She took the stairs in a bound, knocking a page boy back onto his cot before he could shout a warning, and found the rangy young guardsman she had seen the night before standing at attention in front of the sickroom. She did not slow her pace in the slightest; she wondered what she would be forced to do if he refused to stand aside—but then he did.

"My lord." She burst in, then staggered at the sight of Harry, pale and drawn upon his bed, his sandy hair slick and wet across his brow.

"Katherine." He reached up—so weak that she had to

snatch for his hand before it dropped again. "I called for you. Many times."

"They wouldn't let me see you." She kissed his fingers. "Oh, Harry, why? Why did they kill him?"

Harry coughed—the tremors shook him. "Father. Father, forgive me." He let his arm drop back to the bed and closed his eyes. "I must save what I can."

Shouts and calls drew Katherine to the window. Through it she saw Lord Wolland's party assembled on their steeds and wagons, surrounded by knights and guards in close ranks. She turned in a blaze back to Harry. "The body of your father is not yet in the ground." She pointed outside. "There stand his murderers—avenge him! Say the word, my lord, and I will take up my sword and avenge him in your name."

"And risk open war with a land more than twice our size, on a charge of murder against its lord I cannot prove?" Harry raised himself from his sickbed, grimaced, and dropped back again. "Oh, Katherine, Katherine, you do not know of what you speak. We are beaten. We are beaten before we begin."

A clanking rose from outside, the sound of the gates winching open, then a roaring whinny that seemed to stop Katherine's heart. Before she knew what she was doing, she had leapt from the sickroom, past the guard, past a surprised Goody Bycross with a bundle of fresh linen and past a screeching, weeping Isabeau, then back through the hall and out into the courtyard.

"Indigo!" She screamed it—too late. The inner gates rose to let Lord Wolland's party pass through. Indigo tossed his head and bellowed, dragged on a thick rope lead behind a trundling wagon. The households of Wolland, Overstoke and Tand spurred their steeds to depart in haste.

"Indigo. Indigo." Katherine collapsed. Sobs rose through her in waves. She raised a trembling hand, knowing that Indigo could not see it, then lay down on her side in a ball of hopeless tears as he disappeared with all the nobles through the gates.

A single figure came through in the opposite direction, a short figure dusted by the road, his head crowned by a mass of red curls. He dodged aside from the passing horses and entered the courtyard, ignored by the bitter and distracted guards. Geoffrey Bale looked all about him in dismay, then spied Katherine from across the courtyard and came running.

"Katherine—Katherine, help!" He started his breathless plea before he reached her. "It's Edmund, Katherine. It's Edmund—he's gone!"

Chapter 31

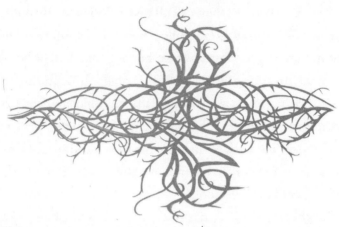

The Voice came again: **Edmund. Edmund Bale.**

Edmund plugged his ears. "Go away. Please, please go away."

What have we discussed about that word? My dear child, I will never be away. I will always be with you.

There was nowhere to go, nowhere even to look, for all was utter darkness. Edmund had scratched and scrabbled around the walls of King Childeric's tomb a dozen times and more. He had found only the door through which he had been kicked— sealed shut and barred—and a crack, a wide-split fissure in the floor between the empty slabs meant for king and queen. There was nowhere to go, nowhere to turn, nowhere to hide from the voice of the Nethergrim.

Edmund—child. Even when the Voice paused, Edmund felt it there, felt impressions on his mind that almost resolved into the features of a face. **We are going to talk for a while. We are going to talk until you understand.**

"No. No, no, no." Edmund scrabbled on the floor. Even though the Voice seemed to be speaking in his mind, without echo, without real sound, somehow it also seemed louder when he drew near the fissure in the floor. The air above it felt terribly cold.

"Katherine, Katherine." Edmund curled onto his side. "Help me. Find me." His body kept trying, by twitch and by jerk, to move him away from the torment he felt. He gripped the edge of the fissure, and for a moment he wondered whether he should just fling himself into it. Maybe that would be better, just to make it stop.

The pain you feel is of your own making. Soon you will crave my voice. Soon you will find the world empty without it.

Edmund hit up against something made of stone, a slab marked with bowl-shaped depressions in its surface. He dug his fingers into it, ripped his skin against it just to have something else to consume his thoughts for a brief moment, something other than the Voice.

Why will you not converse with me? Do you fear that when you do, you will find out how wrong you are?

It hurt less to talk back to the Voice. Edmund knew that was what it wanted, but he could not help it. "Do you get lonely?"

Do you? The Voice seemed to gather itself in the corner. **Child, have you ever met anyone who understands you as I do?**

Edmund could not find an answer—and because he could not, he knew he had answered anyway.

You are surrounded by folk who could be your

servants, your vassals, your slaves. Impressions so vivid came to Edmund that he could almost see a form sitting on the slab across from him, invisible hands folded in an invisible lap. Why do you seek to unlock the hidden powers of magic, and yet still shackle yourself with the morals of those who cannot even understand what you do, what you think, what you are?

Edmund clutched at his head. The Voice seemed to go everywhere, seemed almost to merge with his own thoughts. It took an enormous effort to distinguish what he was thinking from what the Voice was telling him to think.

It is a simple idea, Edmund, one that I know you are well able to consider. Either the knowledge and power you seek do not matter—or they do matter, and so by gaining them you increase yourself compared with others. Which is it, child?

"What I have the power to do does not make me better than other people," said Edmund. "It's how a person wields power that really matters."

What came next felt like laughter, like a landslide. Oh, child. Did Tom tell you that? He would. How tiresome.

"You've never mentioned Tom before," said Edmund. "Do you not like him?"

The lesser always has its excuses, always has its reasons why the greater should abase itself to remain equal.

"I don't think Tom is less than me." For the very first time in Edmund's life, he tried to picture Tom's face. He found that he could not quite remember it.

Do not seek to lie, Edmund. I know what you truly think of Tom. Every time Edmund had ever thought Tom a nuisance and a bumpkin came back in perfect memory. I know also what you know—that when you can call fire to your hand, when you can shape the earth and break the minds of other men, you will have no use at all for a boy who only knows how to plow a field and nurse a calf, and how to take a whipping without crying too much.

"He's my friend!"

You know that you will not need him. The Voice kept a terrible, knowing calm. You know, as I do, that you will rise in this world and he will not, that he has nothing that you want. You know, deep inside yourself, that you only pretend to be his friend because he is Katherine's friend, and that if Katherine had never been born, you would not have bothered to speak two words to him in the whole of your life.

Edmund pounded on the door—he had done it so many times, and with so much force, that he had bruised up and bloodied both his hands.

The Voice made him wait, drew out a silence until he found himself longing for its presence in his mind. You will not leave this place until I give you leave to go. He had no idea how long it had been since it last had spoken. You will not leave until we understand each other. You will not leave until you let me in.

Edmund rolled back on the floor. "Stay out!"

You hold me at the surface of your thoughts. The Voice grew closer and closer until it seemed to surround him. **Let me in. Let me in deeper, Edmund.**

"Please, no." Edmund clutched his head. "No."

You will not leave until you let me in. Even if that means you never leave.

Edmund hummed songs he knew, but such was his agony that it seemed as though the songs were false. He told himself stories he had loved all his life, but could not make himself believe that the hero would win at the end of them. He curled on his knees, head down on his crossed arms, but found that he could not even make himself cry.

I know what it is that you did. The Nethergrim thrust the image of Harry lying bleeding on the jousting field into Edmund's mind. **You used your power in anger.**

"I didn't mean it," said Edmund. "I didn't mean to hurt him."

Are you so very sure of that?

Edmund stared into the void. He found it staring back at him.

Do not feel shame at it, child. You were only following your desires where all desires lead. If something blocks your way, then that something must be removed. It is simple.

"No." Edmund shook his head. "No, that's wrong. That's evil."

Another useless word that you must learn to forget. There is no evil, Edmund, only having what you want, or not having it. You already understand this. That is why you did what you did.

Edmund tried to hide inside his favorite daydream. He let

his reverie run, turned the dirty floor into a mattress and the door into a headboard. Katherine, his love—his wife—lay in bed beside him. The day had been long, their labors hard, but they were together at the end of it.

You tire me with this girl. The Voice turned cold. **She is not what you think she is. She never was.**

"Yes, she is," said Edmund. "I love her."

Here, then. I will show you what my faithful servant has seen.

What came next was something Edmund had dreamed against his will on many nights. The Nethergrim showed it to him, put the vision in his mind and held it there—Katherine and Harry in the castle stables, entwined in each other's arms, their lips pressed together.

"I don't care." Edmund bit his lip, shaking his head, trying to dispel the vision. "I don't care, I don't care! I still love her."

Katherine snaked her hands behind Harry's neck and pulled him in. The bliss on her face was a knife in Edmund's heart, a knife that grew spines and spread in his flesh, tearing through him without leaving him even the peace of death.

Do you love her? Or do you only want there to be some such thing as the love you profess? The Voice seemed to swirl up in the cold air above the fissure, to reach for him in a kind of pity. **You cling to what you think is solid. Child, let go. If you indeed think that magic is worth learning, if that wish in you to grow in wisdom is true, then let go, and find out what this world really is.**

"What is it that you want of me?" Edmund had tried and tried not to say it, for all the unknown time he had been trapped there in the tomb. He knew that it was an admission of weakness.

What is it that you want from the world? The Voice patterned itself before him and almost seemed to be crossing its arms. **Can you answer me that?**

Edmund reached within himself. "I want to change things, to make the world a better place than it was."

So. You want power.

"I want Katherine to love me."

You lust. What man does not?

"I want to be happy."

You seek pleasure and want to avoid pain. So do cows.

"I want to know what the world is, what it's made of, what it's for."

If you truly do, then stop resisting me. If you truly love learning, then that love must eclipse all other loves. You must stop pretending that you can become Edmund Bale, the greatest wizard of this or any age, and at the same time remain Edmund Bale, peasant and innkeeper's son, good friend and honest boy.

Edmund had no defense for that. The greatest wizard—it struck too true.

Would I waste my words on you if I thought you were anything less? Know this, child—you can stand as far above Vithric as he stands above other men. You are greater yet than you know. If you turn with the current, you may travel very far indeed.

The image of Katherine and Harry in their embrace flashed

back into Edmund's mind, placed there by the Voice. He fell and fell within himself, unable to find anything to grip.

If you like, you can make the sword-girl love you. With a thousand subtle tricks, with half a moment's attention to the problem every day, over the course of several years you can turn her to you, turn her your way until she sets her life by you, needs only you, thinks of other things only as they relate to you. Then, when she trembles with longing at the very thought of you, you can make her yours.

Edmund stopped falling. He raised his head. "No. I would not like that."

Yes, child. You know you would.

"I would not." Edmund found that much in himself, and when he did, it made him strong. "I want her to love me freely, or not at all."

You must learn to rise above such thoughts. If you truly want knowledge, you must be prepared to let it change you. If you want to know, you must follow that knowing where it leads—or else remain always half knowing, bound by emotions that chain you to your smaller, former self, always in torment within, your feelings and knowledge at war—indeed, always just as you are now, writhing on the floor, afraid to let me all the way in.

"No." Edmund dug his fingers into the slab. "No. Stay out!"

It will stop hurting, once you let me in. I promise.

Edmund kept his eyes wide-open. He pretended that he stared into Katherine's face. They were so close that he could feel the flood of her breath along his ear. He opened his mouth in the darkness and formed silent words: "I love you."

But you do not.

"You are in all of my dreams." It sent a thrill through him. "I love you more than I know how to say."

These are nothing but the idle fancies of a boy.

Edmund dared to shift an inch closer, and in the dark almost made Katherine real. "I want us to have children, to watch them grow together in a happy home."

My time is your time, Edmund. The Voice grew angry. **We are meant to be together, you and I.**

"I know that I want you to be mine." Edmund reached out, as though he could touch Katherine's forehead with his fingers. "But if you cannot be mine, I still want you to be. I want you to find peace and joy, no matter what."

Images poured in a torrent through Edmund's thoughts: Harry kissing Katherine's neck, Edmund grown tall and in command of thousands, Katherine alone and yearning for him. They buffeted against him, seeking for cracks in him, seeming to get louder and louder, a flood, a roar.

Edmund lay on his back. He shut his eyes. "Stay out."

LET ME IN. If the Voice had made sound, it would have broken his ears. **We have all the time in the world. Let me in.**

Edmund could not think. He could not think. He was Edmund Bale, that was all he knew. He knew he loved Katherine, knew he wanted to know about the world—and knew that he believed it good.

You will be mine. Not hers. Mine.

"No."

LET ME IN.

"No! I won't let you!"

LET ME IN.

LET ME IN.

"Edmund. Edmund, please wake up. It's me."

Edmund took a breath, and when he did, it felt as though he had not breathed in years. He smelled something—spice and apples, mingled with a hint of horse sweat.

He opened his eyes and found that he could see.

There was light—torchlight. Long, dark hair hung down over him—a face, two eyes deep brown, endlessly deep, lit up with care for him.

"Oh, Edmund." Katherine raised him by the shoulders. "Edmund, I am sorry. I've been such a fool."

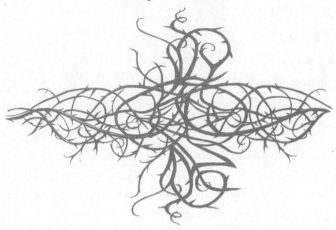

Chapter 32

Edmund braced himself against the wall of the tomb. He blinked in the light. "How did you find me?"

Katherine had never looked so perfectly lovely. "When I saw you lying there, you had your eyes closed, and I thought . . ." She could not finish.

Geoffrey held the torch on the stairs behind her. He glared at Edmund, his freckles bunched in a frown. "You really are stupid sometimes, you know that?"

"Geoffrey, don't say such a thing." Katherine propped Edmund up. "He's suffered."

"Suffered how?" Geoffrey ducked into the tomb. "By getting stuck here in the dark?"

"Can't you feel it?"

Geoffrey came near. His look of reproach faded away. He stared down at the fissure in the floor.

Edmund found himself unharmed in body, save for the

scratches on his hands. "Geoffrey's right—I have been stupid. We have much to do."

"We caught that wizard girl sneaking back through the village." Geoffrey drew away from the fissure. "She told us where you were and what she did to you—after a bit of prodding, of course."

Edmund blinked in surprise. "You found her?"

"We did, but she got away again, right up into the clouds," said Geoffrey. "I don't want to be the one to tell old Robert Windlee that all his chickens are dead."

"The sentries were too busy packing for the march to spot us sneaking in." Katherine pulled back her hair and jammed it under her collar. She drew up her hood over her head. "There—do I look like a boy?"

Edmund smiled. "No." He took in the tomb around him, seeing it in the light for the very first time. It had the same shape as the tomb under the old keep on Wishing Hill, but blank and unfinished, as though the work of preparation for the royal burials had never been completed.

"Let's go," said Katherine. "We've got to get back to the village and warn everyone that there's an army on the way."

Edmund stepped over to the corner of the tomb. "Just a moment." He knelt beside a pile of stony slabs. "There might be something to learn here."

"I can't believe it," said Geoffrey. "He's been trapped in here all this time, and now he wants to learn about the place."

"I couldn't tell what these were in the dark." Edmund blew the dust from the slabs. "Tablets, made of clay." They were covered in close, angular writing, the letters looking odd because of the surface on which they had been written, but they were still ones he knew.

Katherine slipped over to the open door. "Edmund, there's an army outside, and they're getting ready to march."

"I'll be quick." Edmund beckoned to his brother. "Bring the light over here."

Geoffrey came in again, though with an air of great reluctance. He held the torch above the tablet.

"This is written in Dhanic." Edmund traced a finger on the words. "It reads: Sisters, O my sisters, forgive me. My heart is broken, for I have broken faith with you. My king, my love, my husband is gone, taken, one of them. Sisters, O my sisters, forgive me, for I loved him. He rode with his army to join the Skeleth, and the Skeleth consumed them all."

The trumpet call, far away upstairs, seemed somehow mournful to Edmund's ears, almost as though it sounded in answer to the words he read.

"I think that's a call to arms," said Katherine. "Edmund, hurry."

Edmund shoved the first tablet aside and glanced at the one beneath. "The Skeleth are man and monster both." He squinted; Geoffrey had moved the light away. "To kill it by sword kills only the man, leaving the monster free to enslave the victor instead. O my sisters, to defeat these creatures, you must not fight them. To kill them is to die. To fight them is to fail."

"Come on, Edmund!" Geoffrey hissed from the doorway. "I hear voices up there!"

Edmund moved the tablet. The one beneath was blank.

"Edmund!"

Edmund stooped to pick up his sack and packed the *Pa-elandabok* inside. He took one look back at the fissure in the floor, then followed his brother up the stairs.

Katherine stood by the fallen tower doors, peering out and down the hill. "We'll need to get home well before the army if we're going to give a swift-enough warning. Let's steal some horses and slip out in the muddle. Follow my lead—Geoffrey, douse that torch."

Edmund slipped up beside her and looked out. The stars had spun. The cold had come down almost to a frost, colder still with the wind. "At least it's still night."

"You mean it's night again," said Katherine. "You were missing for a whole day."

They waited, knelt in the shadow of the doorway, for some clear break in the swarming mass of the army. In the hanging gloom, though, they found no way to tell whether anyone in the camps that ringed the tower hill happened to be looking their way. All they could be sure about was that none of the men around them were sleeping. Edmund had nearly come to the point of suggesting that they wait for the army to march away when a light and a shout drew everyone's attention to the place where the camp joined the road.

"Now." Katherine ducked out, stepping with balanced grace over the remains of the door. Edmund followed with Geoffrey at his heels, and before he even had time to fear an alarm, he found himself amongst a milling crowd of eager men who paid him no mind at all, for they all craned their necks to watch the small clump of riders on the road. They crowded up from the dark, trampling down the moorspike around the sentry fires. Someone barked an order, and a rough ring of torches formed to light a council of war.

"My lords, say that we wait no longer!" Hunwald of the Hundreds stepped into the light. "Say that soon we ride!"

Sir Wulfric of Olingham raised a hand for silence. "Men of Wolland, men of Tand and Overstoke, men of the Uxingham Hundreds. I ask you do not shout, do not clash your shields, but bid your squires set out tack and saddle and put oiled edges to your swords. Look you all to horse and armor, and to the days to come as the days that will bring you glory to last you lifelong." It would have been too much to ask for the army not to raise a shout at this, but they held it as low as they could.

"Prepare to march." Lord Wolland rode in amongst the crowd. "By the solstice we will be masters of the north."

As soon as Edmund saw the horse Sir Wulfric rode, he looked at Katherine. All she did was hide her face.

Indigo snorted and stamped under Wulfric's saddle. His ears shot up, and he looked about him as though straining to find something he could not see or hear. Katherine mouthed his name in silence and turned away.

"Knights." Geoffrey's eyes went wide in fear. "Knights in armor. Look at them all! No one can stop an army of charging knights! What are we going to do?"

Edmund found himself the least stunned and frightened of the three. "Let's start fretting once we're out of here." He listened for where the sounds of neighs and whinnies were loudest, and started off across the road, through the very heart of the enemy camp.

"Cold one, hey?" Someone slapped his shoulder in passing. "Don't worry, lad, we're on our way soon."

"Mm." Edmund quickened his pace, leading Katherine and Geoffrey on a wide circle through the tents, avoiding torch and firelight. They passed in between stacked bundles of supplies and a pair of grooms doing their best to get all the tack straightened out in the dark. The sentry fires stank of peat—smoke loomed everywhere.

A young knight in chain armor shouldered Edmund aside without seeming to see him, deep in argument with a horse-groom more than twice his age. "It doesn't seem a proper war to me." The knight reached for the reins of the very horse Edmund was about to steal. Edmund ducked back around the tent, his heart in his mouth.

"It never does, once you're in 'em, sir knight, saving your pardon." The groom heaved up a saddle onto the back of the horse. "War's all tricks, don't let no one tell you different. Nothing in this world worse than a stand-up fight. You could die that way!"

The young knight stood waiting, hand to the hilt of his sword. "But what glory is there in what we are about to do? What honor?"

The groom buckled the girth beneath the saddle. "Your pardon, sir knight, but is that why you came on this little trip? Glory and honor?"

The dark swallowed the long pause that followed. "I'm a third son. I want land."

"And you'll get it." The groom led the horse out of the paddock and handed the reins to the knight. "So will I, in my more humble way. Now, there's a bit of trouble there, which I hope you'll see. You seek to have a manor, sir knight, but all the manors on the west side of the Tamber already have knights to hold them. Your common servant might look for a good plot of land for his reward, but of course all the good farmland's already under another man's plow. Me, I've always wanted to be a baker, but I reckon all the villages over there already have bakers. You understand?"

Edmund felt the blood rush inward from his skin, chilling him sick. He took a wild guess at another place where he might find ready horses, and led Katherine and Geoffrey away from the two men. He felt thankful that Katherine had not brought her sword. From the look on her face, she might have been tempted to use it.

"We have to stop them." Geoffrey's skin had gone pallid white between his freckles. "We have to stop them! They're going to—"

Katherine silenced him with a hard grip on the shoulder. She mouthed two words: "We will."

A ring of tents lay struck next to the post-and-rope corral, far to the eastern edge of the camp. Edmund took a careful look around him as he approached and found much less activity on that side. The men had started bunching toward the west, eager for the signal to march, but leaving the trailing eastern side poorly guarded.

Katherine drew her hood down over her face, then crept to the edge of one of the two rope corrals. She leaned against a post and looked about her. Edmund did the same—no one seemed to be paying them any notice. They leapt the rope together.

"Here, girl." Katherine got a cart horse in hand without trouble, then found another for Edmund and Geoffrey to share. She slipped the rope on the far side of the corral and led them east, aiming for a gap in the sentry fires. Prickles ran up Edmund's neck, one after the next.

"Once we're free of the camp, we'll loop around cross-country and head for the bridge." Katherine held the leads of both horses. "It will be a dangerous run, but if we can get ahead of the army, we'll have time to prepare."

"You there—you three!" A voice shouted. "Get over here. We want some help with these tents!"

Katherine glanced at Edmund, who nearly panicked before he found a reply: "Er . . . got to help with grooming. Lord Overstoke wants us."

The man peered at them—Edmund felt Katherine tensing up at his side—but then he pointed. "Lord Overstoke's tent's over that way."

"Is it? Thanks. Lost my bearings in all the excitement." Edmund swung around, leading Katherine and Geoffrey off in the direction the man had shown, but then ducked behind a half-struck tent and resumed his original course. The hollow rose and roughened ahead; the shadowed horses thinned out around them as they walked, and so did the voices of men making their preparations. They held their breaths as they passed the remains of a sentry fire, but nothing happened. They walked on into the utter dark of the moors without a challenge.

"You must wake the village, when we reach it." Katherine helped Edmund onto one of the horses, and then raised

Geoffrey up to sit behind him. "Wake everyone, get them armed and ready, but whatever you do, don't let anyone ring the village bell."

"What are we going to do?" Geoffrey looked ready to cry. "They're an army, hundreds of knights—what are we going to do?"

Katherine grabbed her horse's mane and leapt astride. "We are going to war."

Chapter 33

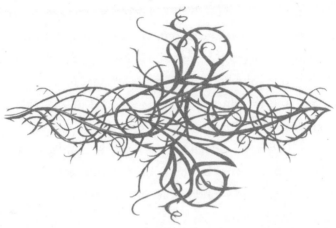

'm glad you're back." Harry still looked pale, but stronger than he had the last time Katherine had seen him. "I'd heard you'd left the castle, and I feared for you." The chamber bore reminders of his dead father everywhere Katherine looked: Lord Aelfric's store of books on the shelf; Aelfric's carved and cushioned chair at the round oak table; Aelfric's furred robe on the peg and his slippers by the hearth.

"Your people call for your aid." Katherine shut the door behind her. "My lord—Harry, I beg you please to help us."

The fire lit along the curve of Harry's chin and found gold in his sandy hair. "You must not leave the castle again, not until I tell you that it's safe."

"Is it safe for my neighbors?" said Katherine. "Is it safe for Edmund, for Geoffrey and all the folk of Moorvale? I know what armies on the march do to the villages they pass. I know what they do when they are hungry, when they are bitter from the cold and lusting after the spoils of war."

Harry threw up his hands and let them drop. "We are over-matched, Katherine. The one thing I can do is to resist Wolland no further, and trust him to keep his promised word."

Katherine crossed the room, ignoring Harry's offer of a chair. "He will not keep his word. He killed your father and he will betray you." She knelt at his side. "Harry, listen to me. We must fight, and we can win."

Harry ran a fingertip down the polished surfaces of the rings that had once adorned his father's hands. "I am not strong enough. I cannot be the man my father was."

"You can be better," said Katherine. "Stand with us, my lord. Save us. It can be done."

Harry sat up in his father's chair—then grabbed his side where the lance had wounded him. He bit his lip. "What is it that you ask of me?"

"I ask you to hear me," said Katherine. "Lord Wolland marches with three hundred knights, but no footsoldiers, no archers, no engines of siege. Once across the river, he can do just as he pleases, but if he is challenged at the bridge, he can be beaten. The power of knights lies in the massed charge, but over a bridge they will not be able to bring that power to bear. At Moorvale bridge we can stop them, but if we allow them to cross, we are all at their mercy. They will be masters of the north, my lord, to the woe of your people, and all your hopes for survival lie in a promise made by the man who had your father murdered."

Harry threw up his hands. "But what can we do? Wolland's army is twice our size, and he's got half the lords of the north at his back. He is invincible!"

"He is exposed and endangered," said Katherine. "He moves

in deception, without supplies, depending on your submission to allow him to make his move. All he ever wanted out of your father was safe passage on the Moorvale bridge—if we can hold the crossing, his plans will fall apart. He is vulnerable, Harry, but only for a moment. You can do this. You can save the north."

Harry looked away, toward the fire. His eyes took its glow.

"Put yourself in Moorvale, in my village," said Katherine. "Stand by the statue in the square. Face east, across the bridge."

Harry let his eyes fall shut.

"They will come over the moors," said Katherine. "Knights by the hundred upon their chargers."

A grimace crossed Harry's face.

"Now think of where you are," said Katherine. "You stand at the foot of a bridge over a wide, deep river, on the higher and steeper of the banks. Do not fear those knights, my lord—cavalry cannot charge on such a bridge; it's barely wide enough to let two carts pass each other. We have archers and the high ground. We can hold the bridge, and we will make them pay dearly for every step they take toward us. We will wear them down, grind at their numbers and break their will. It can be done, my lord. At the bridge it can be done."

Harry stared at Katherine. "Are you sure about this?"

Katherine smiled. "Other families talk about the weather over dinner, or gossip about their neighbors. Me and Papa, we talked military tactics."

Harry looked nowhere. He looked at Katherine, then put a hand to the table before him. His face contorted, he grabbed for his wound, but he gained his feet.

There came a knock at the door.

"Go away!" Harry brought Katherine's hand to his lips.

"Harry, I know it will be hard." Katherine tried to keep down the rising thrill. "I know what we risk, but—"

He kissed her, long and deep. All was song.

The door opened. "Harold."

Katherine felt her blood stand and curdle.

Harry let go. He turned. "Mother."

The lady Isabeau stood at the threshold. The gray light did her face no favors, nor did the double-corned headpiece that tied beneath her chin. Her ladies-in-waiting peeked into the room behind her. They jabbed each other's sides and whispered loud.

Isabeau folded her hands into the sleeves of her gown. "My lord, I wish to speak with you." She stepped beside the door, leaving a clear path out.

Harry twitched his fingers, but stopped short of taking Katherine's hand. "What you say to me, Mother, you may say in her hearing."

His mother set her lips. "Your will be done, my lord." She waved her ladies off down the hall, came to the table and stood waiting. Harry stepped around it to pull out her chair, then shut the door.

Isabeau drew up the hem of her gown and sat. "The light is poor."

Katherine found herself curtsying and kneeling to the fire. She took a handful of kindling and laid it piece by piece over the embers. A flush ran up her neck—joy aborted.

"Mother." Harry cleared his throat. "Mother, we should fight. We should stand and fight. We should avenge Father's murder, we should honor him, choose honor and duty to his grace the king. Katherine is right, we can win!"

"Sit, my son. It is seemly for a lord."

Harry paused. "Yes, Mother." He crossed behind Katherine's back and took his place in his father's chair.

"Number your forces," said Isabeau. "What strength have you?"

Harry's voice rose in pitch and dropped in age. "Mother, I am lord here!"

"Lord." Isabeau echoed it flat. "Yes, my son, you are. You bear the weight of this land and the burden of a line that joins the centuries. Your father, your grandfather and all your sires before them strove and fought to keep Elverain one, to pass it on safe when all the world around them looked about to fail. Now they wait, all in a row in their barrows. They wait in their crypts, in their rotting shrouds, their rusting swords upon their breasts. They wait, your father waits, to hear whether it was all for nothing."

"It can be done." Katherine put her hands to the table. "It must be done. My lord, there comes a moment when the wise man knows that there is no safety in surrender."

"We should have had this talk long ago, my son." Isabeau spoke across Katherine's words. "There are girls who form a hazard for men of your station. Beware such girls, Harold, for they have nothing to lose and all to gain. They will seek to trap you in their hair, to snare you in their willing arms and be granted in the madness of a moment what they could never have by right. Such a girl can afford to risk all, my son, for all that she seeks to risk is yours."

Katherine kept her gaze averted. "My lady, I seek only the defense of our people."

Isabeau looked at Katherine for the first time since she entered the room. "I see through you, Katherine Marshal. How long was it before you decided that your dear, missing father was never coming back? How long before you came aware of where your best chance in life truly lay, and what you need do to seize it?"

Her words knocked Katherine reeling. "That's not true." She looked at Harry. "You know it's not."

"See her, my son, for what she truly is." Lady Isabeau held a hand palm up at Katherine. "Faithless. Adrift. A motherless, fatherless girl with no future in this world save this one great chance. She comes to you, Harold, because she wants to rise at your side."

Katherine waited for Harry to say something—anything. He looked at Katherine, then his mother, his sandy brows drawn low.

"She is a fickle and inconstant girl, for all her strutting in the garb of a man—but she cannot help what she is." Isabeau favored Katherine with a chilly smile. "What daughter needs a father when she has a lord within her grasp?"

Katherine put her hands to the table to keep them from curling into fists. "Who was it, my lady, that you loved as a girl, and how did you come to lose him?"

Isabeau gaped—then hissed. "You will be silent! I will not match words with a lowborn, common—"

"Mother, that is enough!" Harry rose from his chair and smacked the table. "I am lord!"

"You are a boy." His mother glared him down into his seat. "You play at love and you play at war. There are consequences for the things that you do—I grieve that your father and I have failed to teach you this in time. Your father did all he could to keep the peace with Wolland, to give him a reason to spare this land."

"And they killed him anyway." Harry ground his teeth. "They killed my father because they asked for what he would not give, because he would not let Wolland use our lands to stage a massacre. And now you ask me to be a lesser man, to stoop and grovel before the men who killed him, to help them trample all the north just to preserve myself."

"Will your anger put all to rights in this world? Will Wolland lay his head upon the block because he wronged you?" Isabeau let her hands fall together in her lap. "Son, you do not know him as I know him. He is not the ordinary sort of man, and he does not mean to wage the ordinary sort of war. If you stand against him, he will butcher every man in this barony and give over their widows into the hands of his followers. I know him, Harold, I know him as you cannot. I know what he will do to anyone who turns against him. Your legacy will be the end of Elverain—the last barrow by the hill, if indeed anyone takes thought to bury you."

Harry put his head in his hands, boy and man, frightened and enraged by turns at every breath.

"My lord, forget me," said Katherine. "Forget what you think of me, think only on what I have said. We can beat Wolland at the bridge. We can."

"Then Lord Wolland will find another way," said Isabeau.

"If you thwart him at Moorvale, you will do nothing but earn his hate—hate that will rebound on you, Harold, you and all your people. I ask you to heed your father's final lesson—turn against Wolland and die."

Katherine raised her voice. "If we do not stop him—"

"—he will ride roughshod through your lands, he will put Umberslade and Quentara to the sword and he will crown himself king of the north." Isabeau checked her again. "I am not blind, I know what is to come. What remains, Harold, all that remains, is to know what will become of our family."

Katherine held Harry's gaze. "Wolland wants one thing from you, one thing only—safe passage across the Tamber. Give him that and you have nothing left to bargain. Once across, he can turn on you and deal with you whenever he likes, just like he dealt with your father."

"She bluffs, my son. She guesses." Isabeau pursed her lips. "She will have you risk your land, your birthright, just to keep you within her reach."

"I'm not doing this for myself!" Katherine came just short of screaming.

"Enough!" Harry raised his hands. "Please. Enough." He turned to the fire. Katherine watched him, rose and fell on every twitch. She felt Isabeau's glare but did not meet it.

Harry sat up. He breathed in long, then pushed back his father's chair. Katherine read the decision on his face and sank.

"Katherine." He took her hands. He ran his thumbs on the backs of her fingers. "I wish I could have been what you wanted."

Chapter 34

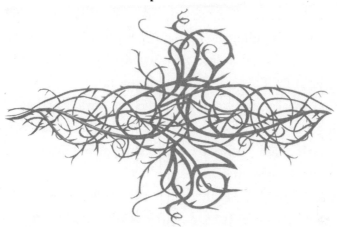

Edmund leapt from back of his horse and lost not a stride in reaching the door of the Overbournes' cottage, one of the straggle of dwellings wedged between the western bank of the Tamber and the Dorham road. Telbert Overbourne had time only to fumble open the door and utter "What in all—?" before Edmund cut him off.

"An army," said Edmund. "Get everyone up. You have to go, right now."

Telbert blinked. There was a trail of sleepy drool in his beard.

"Dear, who is it?" spoke his wife, Elsie, from the darkness behind him.

"There is an army coming." Edmund raised his voice. "Wake everyone up and get them to assemble in the square, as fast as you can."

Telbert stepped outside. He looked about him—at the moonlit

bridge downstream, then across the road at the silent doorstep of his neighbors. "But . . . what's all this about?"

"Lord Wolland." Edmund hurried back to his horse and leapt astride. "He's invading; he's bringing an army in off the moors."

Telbert woke up at last. He turned white and peered over the river at the dim gray rises to the east.

"Can you knock everyone around here awake and get them moving without raising a shout?" Edmund turned his horse to face south again. "Master Overbourne, please listen—you've got precious little time."

Elsie leaned out behind her husband. "Edmund? Is it true what they're saying? Is Lord Aelfric really dead?"

"He is." Edmund nudged his horse to a walk. "Everyone, Master Overbourne—to the square, as fast as you can go."

He rode back down the Dorham road into the square and turned at the bridge. He cast a look along the arc of stone, to the silhouette of Geoffrey standing watch on the rise and to the grim width of the moors beyond. He felt a grip of fear for his brother, then his parents and his home.

"I'll never be what you want." He spoke to the blank night sky. "I love them all too much." He half expected an answer, but none came.

The mill stood first on the left past the bridge. Edmund leapt the millrace and thundered on the door. "An army comes. Meet in the square!" He had said it and moved on before Jarvis Miller had a chance to open his mouth.

Bella Cooper was already awake next door. "Edmund? What's all this? Did you hear about—"

"There's an army coming." Edmund dashed across the street and pounded on Gerald Baker's door. He did not wait to explain, for by then Jarvis and Bella were out in the street. He slapped his horse's rump to get him walking. "Everyone meet in the square."

Bella Cooper, and then Gerald Baker, ran from house to house, waking their neighbors and spreading the alarm. By the time Edmund reached the statue in the middle of the square, he had passed Jordan Dyer, his sister Missa, and Anna Maybell shuffling past in their nightclothes. He turned and raced for home, his parents' inn just south on the Longsettle road.

Sarra Bale leapt out the front door of the inn at the sound of Edmund's knocking. "Edmund! Oh, son!" She seized him in her arms.

"Mum—Mum, let go!" Edmund wriggled free. "We've got to hurry, we've got to get everyone together."

"Where's your brother?" Harman Bale lurched out behind Sarra, still in his cloak and boots, one hand held pressed under his shirt. "Where's Geoffrey? He went off looking for you yesterday, and no one's seen him since."

"He's safe, Father, he's keeping watch just past the bridge." Edmund spied Miles Twintree peering through his window and waved him out onto the road. "Miles, bring your parents. Bring everyone."

Edmund's mother let go of his arm. "It's not another of those thorn monsters, is it?"

"It's an army." Edmund said it loud enough to put the word about to Baldwin Tailor, to the whole of the Twintree clan and all those of his neighbors still stumbling out their doors with questions. "An army from Wolland is marching in from the moors. They will reach the village before dawn."

Even as he said it, he heard a roll of hoofbeats rising up the Longsettle road, a heavy, four-beat gait—a draft horse pushed to its limits in a sprinting gallop. He stepped outside to look, his parents following. Katherine flew past the first of the houses and charged up toward the inn. She leapt from the saddle and met him at the door of the stable.

Edmund took the reins of her horse. "Where's Harry? What about his knights and men-at-arms?"

Katherine walked with him into the rickety stable beside the inn. She looked around to make sure they were alone, then shook her head.

Edmund felt fear tighten its cords around his chest.

Katherine leaned against the plain wooden rail. "If there was ever something you wanted to say about Harry, something about him not being the boy I thought he was, now would be the right time."

"Never mind that, what about the village?" Edmund yanked off saddle and bridle, and left the horse some hay. "What are we going to do?"

Katherine raised her head. "We are going to fight."

"Fight?" Edmund thought it was quite the wrong time to make jokes.

"You heard what those men said in the camp," said Katherine. "They're to be paid in land and plunder. More than that, they're hungry, and their horses will need grain to keep them on the march, our whole harvest at the least. Harry's made a deal to keep himself safe in his castle, but the rest of us don't have the luxury of stone walls to give us shelter. If that army crosses the bridge, we will be at their mercy. We must turn them back."

Edmund looked at the ground, then at Katherine. "Tell me how I can help."

"I was hoping you'd say something like that." Katherine led him back outside. She passed through the swelling crowd of her neighbors, and leapt onto the pedestal of the statue in the square. "Wat Cooper. Wat, over there, how much pitch have you got?"

Wat Cooper stared up at her, slack in the mouth.

"How much pitch have you got?" Katherine leaned over and repeated it to his wife, Bella. "For sealing barrels. How much?"

"We just got in a batch, dear," said Bella. "It'll last us till spring—but why?"

"We'll need it all. Bring it out." Katherine waved at them. "Go, both of you! Go! Now, Aydon, Aydon Smith, where are you?"

Young and brawny Aydon Smith stepped out from the crowd. "What's all this about? We've got to get running, and soon!"

Katherine grabbed him by the arm. "Aydon, do you have any chains?"

Young and brawny, and not so very quick. "What?"

"Chains." Katherine pointed east across the square. "Wide enough to stretch between those posts on the bridge."

"Er." Aydon looked. "Yes. Maybe three."

"How quickly can you forge an open link on each end?"

"What are you babbling about?" Edmund's father hobbled over from the inn. "There's an army coming! We've got to clear out of here while we can!"

"Hear me, all of you," said Katherine. "We must hold our ground. We must fight."

"Fight? Have you gone foaming mad?" Baldwin Tailor's querulous voice broke over the frightened murmur. "There's an army coming over the bridge! We have no chance!" His words drew a clamor of agreement—many went so far as to break from the swelling crowd and head for their homes to pack what they could for a desperate flight.

"Wait. Wait—listen, everyone!" Edmund sprang up to stand at Katherine's side. "If we run tonight, we might keep our lives, but we will lose our livings. Look around you. That will be another man's mill, another man's inn, and those of you who survive may find yourselves another man's servant or another man's wife. What we have here, what you have built all your lives, will be broken, and you will be hard pressed to last the winter when every single grain you have grown this year sits in another man's belly. There is an army coming, in off a march across the hard moors. They are to be paid with what they can take from their enemies. You are their enemies whether you want it or not."

He had not meant to make a speech. It just came out that way. "If I thought your best course would be to gather your possessions and run, that is what I would advise. I tell you that we must fight."

A few of the folk around them seemed to shake from their terror. Others, while still plainly frightened, were no longer frightened out of their wits. They clustered in around Katherine and Edmund, ready to listen.

Katherine nudged Edmund's side. "That was good."

Edmund turned to Katherine. "You do have a plan, don't you?"

She looked down the road, then over at the bridge. She nodded once.

"Then—what's coming?" said Hob Hollows. "What are we up against?"

"The second sons of all the gentry of Wolland," said Katherine. "Every hungry, landless boy who's grown up on horseback, wishing for a claim of his own. All of them riders, most of them knights."

"Knights? All knights?" Baldwin Tailor's voice soared high up his nose when he was frightened. "Are you mad? Nothing can stop knights on the charge!"

Katherine held up her hand again to quell the panicked murmurs. "Maybe not, on an open plain." She pointed to the bridge. "We are not going to give them one."

Baldwin spluttered. "But, they're knights—trained men of war! They've got swords, they've got armor!"

"Yes," said Katherine. "Heavy steel armor, great links of chain on their chests, and they must ride across a narrow bridge—at night, above a fast, wide river."

A few of the folk around them seemed to understand. Something like hope began to dawn on the faces of the bravest, and for others, at least the worst of their despair began to fade.

"You are farmers and tradesmen, but you are also the finest archers in all the world," said Katherine. "Lord Aelfric had us practice at the targets every week to keep us in training, and you'll kneel on his grave to thank him by tomorrow, that I promise."

The folk of the village clustered in close around Edmund and Katherine. Some of the men who had unstrung their bows bent to string them again.

"We use the darkness," said Katherine. "We use the bridge, we use panic and fire. Yes, they're knights, and they come in chain hauberks with sword and axe, but they don't come with bows or anything else that can hurl a distance. I've just scouted their camp with Geoffrey and Edmund, and I tell you we can beat them, we can send them screaming back off that bridge if you heed me and hold hard."

"But . . . what about Harry?" said Baldwin. "What about the castle, the guards and all?"

"They cannot help us tonight," said Katherine. "It falls to us to make sure that these men never cross this river, that not only Moorvale, but the rest of the north stays safe. If we hold together and follow the plan I have made, we can turn them back, here and tonight. Do you trust me?"

"I do." Mercy Wainwright stepped out from the crowd. She looked around her. "We are with you."

And they were. Edmund could see it.

"Then heed me," said Katherine. "This is what we will do."

Chapter 35

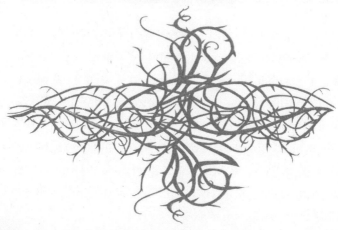

Right, open links." Aydon Smith bore a chain over each shoulder. "This is lord's iron, by the way."

"Good, thank you, Aydon." Katherine waggled the point of a militia spear in its binding—it nearly fell off the shaft. She handed it to Martin. "See if someone can fix that." She cast a glance around her at the floor of the inn and counted perhaps ten spears worth using. Some of her neighbors ripped rags, dipped them in pitch and wrapped them onto arrowheads. Others strung the longbows, testing each string with an empty draw. Knocky Turner worked at a frantic rate in the far corner, converting an old piece of fencing into a combination roadblock and shield wall. Molly Atbridge and her mother bent beside him, stretching wet ox-hides over the row of old militia shields lashed to the frame.

Aydon rattled the chains. "Lord's iron, you know—his stock. Is he paying?"

"We'll ask him later." Katherine strode to the door. "Bring what you need to make a good, hot fire. I'll come show you what to do."

More folk poured in from the roads, outlying farmers farther to the ends of the great chain of alarm. By the time the news had reached them, it had gained in detail, so most came with all that had been asked of them—torches, longbows and arrows, even a few swords. It was an effort to keep the newcomers silent once they reached the square, but by then everyone in the village knew enough of Katherine's designs to impress the need for quiet on their neighbors, with a harsh hiss and a swat for those somewhat slower of wit.

Katherine walked with Aydon onto the span of the bridge and stopped at the first set of posts. "Can you loop each end around one of these, then shut the links so that it's stretched taut across the span?"

Aydon set down the chains. "I'll need a roaring hot one." He stepped back and took note of the wind. "I've got a stack of hickory just in by my door, dry as you like."

"You might not have long," said Katherine. "Any sign of trouble, kick your fire into the river and come right back, done or not."

"Aye." Aydon set down his tools. "Don't you worry on that score."

Katherine hurried back into the square. She waved up at the roof of the mill as she passed. "All well?"

Jarvis Miller waved back to her. "We've got a lamp lit down behind the cams."

"Just give the word." Nicky Bird stuck his head out next to Jarvis. "We'll make 'em sorry they ever even heard of Moorvale."

Katherine passed on through the square and pushed back the door to the inn. "What's the arrow count?"

"Eleven score." Anna Maybell let a handful drop into a barrel. "Or a bit over."

Katherine had hoped for more. "Get a full barrel up to the mill, and half the fire arrows. Hurry—we don't know how long we've got. What about spears?"

"Fifteen," said Martin.

"Good, bring them out." Katherine turned back through the square and surveyed the field of battle before her. The mill did a fine job of blocking the south side, and its wooden roof gave a high vantage over the bridge. She let her gaze rove north. The land rose along the Bakers' croft, perfect for another company of archers.

"Come, my lords and knights." She cast a glare over the bridge at the shadowed moors. "Come take us, if you can."

Aydon's fire blazed up on the span of the bridge, and soon the tinking of his hammer sounded, spaced with muttered grunts and curses. Katherine went over to the bundle of supplies she had brought with her from the castle and took up her sword—a soldier's sword, forged from good bloomery steel but without decoration on hilt or blade. She still called it her uncle's sword, sometimes, though he had died more than ten years before she was born. Her uncle had left one mark on it, a deep score on the crossguard where he must once have turned a crushing blow from an axe. She drew the blade; the other marks were hers.

Martin bore a dozen spears out of the hall. "So who gets these?"

Katherine glanced at him. "Pick a dozen men—strong ones, some tall and some short. Tell the rest to get their longbows." She sized up the run of road through the square to the bridge. She marked out points of escape between the Coopers' and the Turners', and another up behind the smithy, then made a silent wish that she would not need to make use of them.

"Bella, Missa, over here. Grab up a bale and follow. Wat, bring some of that pitch." She took up the hay bales she had asked for and led her neighbors onto the bridge. "Mind Aydon, everyone, mind the fire. Step over the chain."

She dragged her bale up the span, to a point roughly half-way to the top. "There. Put them in a row, right across." She set it down and sighted back to the village. She risked one low shout. "Up on the mill—can you hit this?"

"Of course we can!" Nicky Bird spat off the roof. "What do you think we are, a pack of Wollanders?"

Scuffing footsteps sounded in echo from the east. Katherine turned around to find a pair of figures cresting the top of the arch at a run.

"Lights." Geoffrey Bale came in just ahead of a white-faced, trembling Miles Twintree. "Lots of them, a mile past the rise. And talking."

"Good, go on, to your places." Katherine helped Wat Cooper upend a whole barrel of thick, tarry pitch over the bales, then led her neighbors back off the bridge. "Aydon, they're coming! Toss your fire and get down here!"

The fire on the bridge slid out and fell to hiss into the river. Moments later Aydon hurried down into view. "I could only set the nearest chain." He threw his tools aside and took a spear from Martin.

"One is much better than none." Katherine turned to the cluster of folk standing in between Gerald Baker's and the mill, the last two buildings before the foot of the bridge. She counted, at best, sixty bows.

"Quiet, now, everyone! It all depends on quiet." Katherine picked out Missa Dyer from the crowd. "Missa, go back into the square. Tell everyone to keep all the lights out of view—I don't want to see so much as a candle if I look that way. You two, over there by the edge, go into the smithy, load up some coals in the brazier and bring it out. Set it by the wall, in reach of the archers."

Katherine ordered the spearmen into a rough double line, the taller men holding ready to stab over the shoulders of the shorter. "You are both our first line and our last. With luck, our enemies will never even reach you. Martin is your captain. Follow him as though he were Tristan himself."

Martin thunked the haft of his spear into the earth. "Anyone who's not in it with us to the end, just turn and run for it now. We're better off without you." He looked somewhat different from his usual self, his slow anger awakened and alight. Even his black beard seemed to bristle out.

"We won't let you down." Horsa Blackcalf took up a spear,

the oldest of Martin's picked company, old enough, in fact, to be Martin's father. The front rank of men knelt down, their feet touching the edge of the bridge.

"Good—Martin, they're all yours." Katherine passed beyond them to the folk who stood with bows and arrows in the eastern end of the square. Not all of the women had left—she counted Luilda Twintree holding hands with Lefric Green, and Elsie Overbourne standing with her husband, Telbert.

Katherine pointed into the shadows. "Someone bring up that barrel of arrows and put it in reach. Each of you take a handful and push them into the ground at your feet, then space yourselves in ranks. I need to detach one company. Who asks to lead them?"

A dozen hands rose. It was no easy choice amongst the best three. Katherine pointed. "Gilbert Wainwright, take twenty archers north, up through Gerald's croft. Put yourself along the high bend, that rocky bit—you should have a good view along the side of the bridge."

"Oh, ha-ha, good one. Good one!" The spearmen turned to laugh. "Hit them from the sides! Katherine's got it all figured, don't she?"

"Don't bother with fire arrows, and bring no light," said Katherine. "Shoot as you like once we start. All right?"

"Got it. Good luck, everyone." Gilbert turned and waved a score of folk out of the crowd. They slipped around the back of the smithy.

"Everyone else, you're mine." Katherine stepped out before the first rank of archers—Telbert Overbourne, Lefric Green, Walter Bythorn and old Robert Windlee. "I want tight volleys on my signal, arched high to drop onto the middle of the span. We'll leave the long shots to the men on the roof—and no one is to fire before I say. Same up there on the mill. Hear it? No volleys until I give the word."

"We hear." Nicky Bird sat with his legs dangling over the edge of the roof. "Bit fancier than Aelfric's old drill-and-practice runs, hey? But we'll do it, don't you worry."

"Wait, wait, up there." Knocky Turner emerged from the dark, holding up one end of his hastily built shield wall. "It's done." Molly Atbridge held the other, though rather low, and Jordan Dyer dropped his longbow to help her bring it along to the foot of the bridge.

"Now, that's good work." Martin took hold of the shield wall, and all by himself hauled it around and set it just in front of his spearmen, so that its frame braced on the far side of the huge stone posts. He banged the top of it with his hand. They now had a braced wall of shields across the foot of the bridge that came to the height of a man's chest.

"Katherine." Jarvis whispered from the roof of the inn. "I see them. They're on the ridge."

"Quiet—quiet, everyone!" Katherine got her wish at once. None of her neighbors spoke or shifted or even breathed too loud. In the silence that followed came the distant sound of metal-shod hooves on stone. The wind blew in at them from the moors, but that could not be helped.

"Take an arrow." Katherine spoke just loud enough to be heard. "Nock it, but do not draw. Listen and wait. Edmund, get ready."

Edmund clambered past her, over the shield wall and onto the span. Katherine stepped up to Martin's shoulder and peered out into the dark. She caught sight of shapes moving at the top of the bridge, a few snatches of laughter that echoed over the gentle rush of the water.

"Curse you for a pack of dogs," Telbert Overbourne snarled under his breath. "Come over here, and we'll see who's laughing by sunup."

Katherine wondered for a moment whether Lord Wolland himself rode in front. "Quiet, now. Just a moment more." She strained to listen. The approaching shapes came down the near side of the bridge, close enough to tell the strike of hoof from its echo off the water. Then they stopped.

"What's that?" Lord Wolland's voice rang out clear from atop the bridge. "Hold, what are they saying up there?"

A more distant voice rose to a shout. "They said they heard something, my lord, whispering, from north along the banks!"

Katherine raised her arm. "On the mill, there! Fire arrows, light and draw."

The words *bales of hay, right on the bridge* were cut down by a dozen shouts of "Up there! My lord, look!"

"Take aim." Katherine glanced up to the roof. A ragged bank of flames stood drawn and ready. She heard the sound of a warning shout on the bridge, and then—oh, she could kiss the clouds—the wind died suddenly to nothing.

"On the mill, fire!" Katherine tapped her cousin's shoulder. "Set your men. Archers in the square, draw high—fire!"

The fire arrows loosed. Katherine watched the burning trails arc through the air—many landed close to the target, but only one struck the center bale on the top.

"That one was mine!" Nicky Bird shouted it from the roof. "That was my shot!"

Geoffrey popped up beside him. "No, it was mine!"

"Everyone look away!" Katherine turned from the bridge. "Edmund, now!"

"BY FIRE LIGHT IS BORN. IN THE EYE OF NIGHT, A MOTE OF SUN." Edmund's voice intoned from the footing of the bridge. "AWAKE, ARISE IN LIGHT. FIRE, AWAKE!" There was a whoosh, and then a light so bright that it almost blinded Katherine, even though she had her eyes shut and her back to it. She turned eastward again, blinking hard, and through the spots in her eyes she could see the vanguard of knights straining desperately to hold their rearing horses in check as flame burst to life at their feet.

Katherine helped Edmund back over the shield wall. She found to her surprise that though her friend was breathing hard, his eyes shone brightly and he seemed otherwise well. "The spell didn't hurt you?"

"I've learned a few things since the last time I tried that." Edmund hopped lightly to the ground. As soon as he stepped near to the brazier meant for lighting fire arrows, it went out at once, without so much as a wisp of smoke.

"That's the cost of the spell." Edmund shrugged and smiled at Katherine's questioning look. "It's going to last awhile, I'm afraid."

Gilbert's voice cried out from up the banks, and Katherine caught a glimpse of a volley arcing in from the north. A few missed the bridge completely, falling under the span or looping high above it, but most must have struck home from the hoarse cries they raised. She heard the sounds of splashes—knights falling off the bridge into the river—and then louder ones, their horses falling with them.

Katherine called out for a volley, and then another, and for a moment dared to hope that she had driven off the army at a stroke. Then a voice bellowed from the dark—it was Wolland—and the sounds of panic on the bridge died away.

"Hold, everyone hold!" Katherine rushed past Martin and leaned out from the post of the bridge. The burning bales had already dwindled away to almost nothing, consumed by the power of Edmund's spell. She saw blood on the stone span, some fallen men and abandoned shields, but no one standing. One wounded knight staggered up and tried to leap over the smoldering bales, but tripped and cried out on his way down into the water.

Katherine waved back to the archers. "They're out of range; don't waste arrows."

"What's going on up there? Are they running?" Lefric Green had barely time to say it before Gilbert's shout gave the answer.

"They're charging!" Gilbert called it twice along the banks. "At the bridge, there—they're charging!"

"Boys, up and ready!" Martin got his spear high and over the shoulder of the man before him. "Lower down, Horsa. Hold hard!"

"Draw and hold! No volleys yet!" Katherine raised her hand. She could not stop Gilbert's company, though, and did not mind the havoc they caused along the thin column coming over the top of the bridge. She spared a brief moment to think that what her enemy tried was no small feat of horseman-ship—and felt a prick of grief for the horses.

"Katherine, they're coming!" Someone whispered it from amongst the archers behind her. "Do we fire? Say the word!"

"Nock and draw." Katherine held her arm high. "Wait."

She watched the bridge. A column of knights thundered in twos, spurring their foaming steeds out of the dark. The beat of their hooves came deafening. Luilda Twintree started to whimper, and someone else in the square let his bow clatter down and turned to run.

"My lord—my lord, a chain!" The voice on the bridge rose to a wild shout, but too late. The front two men ran straight into it, and the men behind them smashed over, and for long, sick-ening moments there was nothing but the sound of screams, snapping bones and plunges down into the Tamber.

"Oh." Luilda started to weep. "Oh, that's so—"

"Shut it!" Katherine flashed a hard look behind her. "Mill and square, another volley! All together, now—fire!"

Though there was no longer any light upon their targets, the archers of Moorvale had taken their gauge of the wind and had an entire column of knights amongst whom to drop their shots. The army's second advance turned all at once into a rout. Katherine hissed down her neighbors' cheers. "Not yet. Quiet! How many arrows have you got left?"

She heard some voices answer, "Just one," others, "Two or three," and then a few say, "Here, give me one, then, I'm out!"

"Keep them nocked," said Katherine. "Wait on my word."

"Men of Moorvale!" The voice boomed out from atop the bridge. "You have done nothing but rouse our anger at these tricks. You have turned but our vanguard, and now we march on you in earnest. We have hundreds of knights, and we will come across that bridge whether you fight us or not. Stand aside now and I may yet prevail upon my men to use some mercy."

Katherine stepped to the banks before his words could do their work. "You argue without force, my lord Wolland. You have tried to take this bridge twice, and been turned back twice. We will teach you a third lesson if you are in truth so thick in the head."

There was a long, long pause. "Katherine Marshal?"

"Good evening, my lord," said Katherine. "I advise you to leave the field of battle as quickly as you can."

"I will not be challenged by a peasant!"

"Why not?" Nicky Bird's voice sang out on the air. "You were just beaten by one!"

"My lord Wolland, you are defeated," said Katherine. "We have the vantage and we will keep it. It's a long march back across those moors, so I suggest you get started."

"You do not have the men to hold against us!" Lord Wolland lost his temper completely. "You do not even have the aid of your own lord!"

"Oh, do we not?" Katherine raised her voice to match him. "Look past our square, to the road, my lord, and see for yourself what is coming."

She waited, hardly daring to breathe. She stared at the bulky outline of Wolland's form atop his warhorse and could just catch his quiet talk with the men on the horses behind him.

"Come on, come on," she whispered. "Swallow it whole."

Edmund leaned to her shoulder. "If this doesn't work?"

"Then we run for our lives." Katherine cast a look back at the approaching torches. They had come far enough along that she knew Lord Wolland could see that they were roughly one hundred strong, and marching in two columns—but if they got much closer, all was lost.

Lord Wolland turned his horse and rode back off the bridge in silence. The clatter of hooves on stone dwindled away.

Katherine threw her arms around a startled, blushing Edmund, then waved her hand behind her. "Now you can cheer, if you like." Her neighbors drowned her out in the noise of it.

"Keep watch, though. They might still try something." Katherine slapped Martin's shoulder, then stepped back amongst the archers. "Who can ride? I want one for Longsettle and one for Northend. I've got a horse we can use if someone can lend us another. We want arrows—tell them we'll pay from the village purse if they balk at it."

"So Lord Harry's coming?" Hob Hollows waved out at the line of torches.

Katherine felt a smirk twitching up the corners of her lips. "He might come along eventually, but that's not him."

"Then who is it?"

"Have a look."

The torches came closer and closer, and before the nearest

had reached the square, a ripple of laughter had spread through the folk gathered there.

"Did it work?" Emma Russet led them, with Miles Twintree and a line of children, formed in two columns like soldiers on the march.

Katherine embraced her. "You sent an army running for the hills."

"Scared off by a gang of kids." Hugh Jocelyn guffawed so hard that he dropped his longbow. "So much for your battle-hardened men of war. Eh? Eh?"

The children approached in their lines toward the square two by two. As they got near to Edmund, the torches went out without so much as a hiss.

Edmund turned a sheepish smile on Katherine. "Saves having to douse them, I suppose."

Miles Twintree dropped his snuffed torch on the road. "What'd we miss?"

"The finest shot in the history of all Moorvale." Nicky Bird hopped out through the front door of the mill. "And some other things of lesser notice."

Katherine let her neighbors whoop and embrace. She returned to the bridge and leaned on one of the grand stone pillars, and watched Wolland's army pull back out of view.

Edmund followed her into the square. "You did it." His eyes sparkled with admiration. "That was the cleverest thing I've ever seen."

Katherine turned to smile at him, but then caught sight of motion on the Longsettle road. "Are those more of the kids?"

"No, we're all here." Miles turned to look back with her.

"I thought I heard noises from the south, just as we started marching."

Folk approached along the road—on foot, and walking in a clump. A man stepped out before their ranks, a ragged, frightened peasant carrying a little boy in his arms. He stared about him at the folk of Moorvale assembled in the square. "So then, you must already know."

Katherine glanced at Edmund, a hollow fear growing in her. She turned back to the man. "Know what?"

"There are monstrous creatures marching up from the south," said the man. "There's panic on the roads—villages aflame. Elverain is under attack."

Chapter **36**

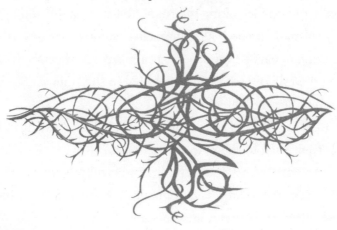

They're coming." Jordan Dyer clambered up onto the barricade that had been hastily constructed from a line of wagons to block the road between his workshop and the inn. "Not but a mile off, now—they've already reached Ernald Green's and knocked the wall of his byre right through."

Wat Cooper reached out a hand to help Jordan up over the mass of planks and spars that jutted from the wagons. "What do they look like?"

"Still like men, mostly—that's the worst part of it." Jordan turned away from a volley of frightened questions, his handsome face ashen gray. "They're coming our way; that's all that matters now."

Edmund traced out the design of the spell with one finger on his writing tablet, then glanced at the notes he had made on a loop of parchment. Every time someone looked his way, he gave an encouraging smile, but from the way they reacted, he knew that he was not convincing them of anything.

352

"I'll bet Lord Wolland's going to wait until he sees the Skeleth coming our way." Geoffrey stood at Edmund's side, bow in one hand, cudgel in the other, his paltry store of arrows at his feet. "Then when we're busy holding them back, he'll try another charge, the coward."

Edmund turned to look eastward at the shield wall. "Can Katherine stand them off again?"

"You let her do her job, and you do yours," said Geoffrey. "How long will you need?"

"Not long, once I see them." Edmund kept his gaze on the design of his spell, to avoid betraying how uncertain he felt.

"Edmund, Geoffrey, why won't you come away?" Sarra Bale tried again, for the fourth time that night, to tug her sons from their post. "Please, Edmund, if you come away, your brother will come, too. There's still time, there's still time to run!"

"Mum." Edmund plucked her fingers gently away from him. "There is nowhere for us to run. Geoffrey knows that as well as I do. We must win tonight, so let me do my part."

Harman Bale crossed over to meet them at the statue, pole in hand, though he still held the other on the wound in his gut. "There's only one reason to go to war, son—the defense of life and home." He smiled. "So here we are." He embraced both of his sons, and then did something Edmund had never seen him do out in the open before. He kissed Edmund's mother—on the mouth.

Geoffrey and Edmund stared at them, and then at each other. They kept staring, long after their father had left to man the barricades, and their mother had retreated, red in the face, to help Bella Cooper hand around the last of the supplies.

"Move those spears to the bridge, we don't need 'em here." Jordan Dyer waved Molly Atbridge away from the barricade. A tight squad of men stood just behind the jutting beams on a pair of Gilbert Wainwright's wagons. Even as Edmund watched, Knocky Turner ran back and forth, banging more pieces onto the structure with desperate speed.

"Need anything else?" Miles Twintree hauled three quivers full of arrows past the statue, leading a petrified Emma Russet on toward the bridge.

"Not just now." Edmund looked to his brother. "How many arrows have we got left?"

"You let me worry about shooting—keep your mind on your spell." Geoffrey grabbed a handful of arrows from Miles.

"Edmund, I'm scared." Emma Russet carried a bucket of water to quench the thirst of the archers, but trembled with such fright that a good amount of it had spilled onto her sleeves. "Do you think we can win?"

"We have to win." Edmund looked about him, watching the two halves of Katherine's new and hastily improvised plan take shape. The folk on the barricades carried poles—many of them just garden tools with their metal points chopped off—for shoving the Skeleth away without killing the men they held trapped within them. While they held the Skeleth back, Katherine, Martin and a troop of village men would defend the shield wall across the bridge from anything else that Lord Wolland tried, backed by every archer that could be spared from other tasks. If everything went according to design, the whole of the force on the Longsettle road could swing around to the bridge once the Skeleth were gone.

All of that, of course, depended on Edmund. He looked about him, at his brother, his mother and his neighbors, then across the square at the girl he loved more than anything in the world. If he failed, none of them would live to see the dawn. He got back to work.

The Skeleth are seen and yet unseen. Trust your thoughts, not your eyes. That seemed clear enough. The Skeleth were hard to see and impossible to touch. They could not be seized, the way the man within them could be seized. To reach them, he had to trust to what he knew of them. It was the same thing as knowing that eight plus thirteen was twenty-one. He could only seize the number twenty-one with his mind.

The Skeleth are shapes without substance. Right is left, up is down. Edmund sketched out the boxy glyph for the Sign of Closing. To trap something that had no substance, he had to make a prison with no walls. The queen beneath the tower had shown him how—make a place where space folded in on itself, where going left was the same thing as going right. He glanced at the emptied-out strongbox he had taken from the inn. If the spell worked, the creatures would never be able to escape from its confines, but he wished he had been able to find a container that would be harder to break from without.

"Edmund, do you hear that?" Geoffrey turned east, toward the shadows swarming on the opposite bank of the river. "The army, it's marching again. They're coming back!"

Edmund shut the *Paelandabok*. "Watch this for me." He strode across the square to the shield wall at the bridge. He found Katherine sitting with her arm around a boy of seven whose face he did not know.

"This is Diggory Twintree, Henry's nephew from down in Longsettle," said Katherine. "The Skeleth harrowed his whole village—there's dead folk on the road, cut down at the verge and just left there. He says his father tried to make a stand, and now he's become one of them."

Edmund turned toward the barricades facing south, then east across the river at Wolland's gathering forces. "First the Skeleth will destroy Wolland's enemies, and then they will betray him and consume his own army. History is about to repeat itself, if we don't find a way to stop it."

Martin Upfield leaned on his spear. "The Longsettle folk were going to tell us that our best hope was to run east across the bridge, and try to make it to Wolland over the moors." He pulled at his beard. "What've we done, Edmund? What've we done?"

Nicky Bird clutched his two remaining arrows, and no longer bothered to carry a quiver. "We can try running—west, into the mountains."

Edmund shook his head. "We'd starve up there, or freeze in the winter snows."

"And that's if the Nethergrim don't have more beasts up there waiting to rip us limb from limb," said Martin.

"Then . . . north." Nicky turned to look that way, toward the stands of shadowed trees that bounded the horizon. "We run north."

"And then what, swim the Tamber?" Henry Twintree picked up his nephew in his arms. "Even if we made it across somehow, we'd end up in the Dorwood, and you know what folk say about that place."

Nicky looked wildly around him. "Then . . . then, we're trapped."

"That's it." Telbert Overbourne threw down his spear. "I've got nothing to keep me here. I'm running south."

Henry snorted. "Right at the monsters, eh?"

"Around them, if I can manage it." Telbert waved to his wife. "Elsie, come on. It's all up for us. Let's go."

Katherine grabbed Telbert by the arm. "Look across the river. Those are knights, men on horseback. Their blood is up, they're humiliated and they're looking for revenge. If we turn our backs on them, they will come across and run us all down."

"Then what can we do?" Telbert clenched his hands. "What can we possibly do?"

Edmund looked across the river at the army gathered at the opposite footing of the bridge. A desperate hope seized him. He took up a militia spear someone had discarded, hopped the shield wall and raced out onto the span.

"Where are you going?" Katherine jumped up and leapt after him. "Edmund, wait, get back here! Have you gone mad?"

"Edgar of Wolland!" Edmund thumped the butt of his spear onto the stone of the bridge. "My lord Wolland, come forth! Come forth to parley!"

There was a space of silence, then laughter rolled across the river. A portly figure dressed in full armor stepped to the far edge of the bridge, flanked by guards bearing wide, heavy shields.

"You pretend to a rank far above you, boy!" Lord Wolland's voice was nearly lost in the echoes off the water. "To parley means to treat with a man worthy of command. I see no such man!"

Katherine hurried to his side near the apex of the bridge. "Edmund, this won't work. We've already made him angry and, worse yet, we've embarrassed him in front of his men. He'll never show us mercy now."

"I have to try." Edmund hauled in a full breath. "The Skeleth are not your allies, my lord! You have helped to free an ancient evil that cares nothing for the aims of men! They seek only destruction—they will betray you, as they betrayed King Childeric in ages past! You have played the fool and will earn a fool's wages!"

"You know nothing of what you speak!" came the shouted reply. "Do not think to improve your position with lies!"

"We are men and women—they are monsters!" Edmund raised his spear and waved it. "Let us cross in peace, and we will stand with you against them!"

The wind blew up along the channel of the Tamber, forcing Wolland to try three times to make his reply. "—folk of Moorvale, you have awakened my spite—run while you can—no quarter will be given—" The rest was blown away by a wind that flapped the banners stiff.

Martin joined Katherine and Edmund out on the span. "It was a game try, Edmund, but my cousin's right. Wolland's blood is up. He'll be making no peace tonight."

"Men of Wolland! Men of Overstoke and Tand!" Edmund tried one last time, turning his voice to the troops of men and horses on the banks. "Your lord and commander has made a pact with the creatures of the Nethergrim! You stand on land made waste by the Skeleth long ago—do not help them ruin the rest of the north! Lord Wolland walks into a trap, and you walk with him!" He waited, watching and listening, but could not be sure if his words had been heard.

Then came the answer. Sturdy as it was, with a sturdiness to last the centuries, the span of the bridge yet trembled with the roll of approaching hooves.

Chapter 37

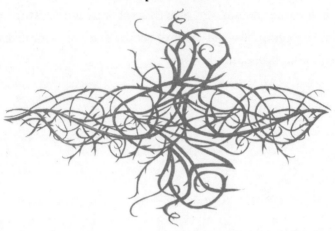

Katherine drew her sword. She glanced behind her and saw some of her neighbors leaping the shield wall with spears in hand. She looked ahead, across the river, and caught the moonlight glinting off the tips of helms, steel pauldrons over shoulders, and chain-mailed arms holding shields with metal bosses burnished to a shine.

"We can't make it back before they reach us." Katherine took up a fighting stance. "Cousin, can you swim?"

"You know I can't." Martin set the butt of his spear to the surface of the bridge.

"Don't even ask me," said Edmund in answer to Katherine's look. "I'm staying with you." He set his own spear next to Martin's.

Katherine braced her sword in two hands. "Then take your mark, both of you, and aim for the face if you can."

The knights began their charge. Horseshoes struck sparks on stone.

Katherine looked north to the darkened banks. "Gilbert!" She raised her sword. "A volley!"

A distant burst of *thwips* turned into a rain of hisses through the air. Two dozen arrows arced high over Katherine's head to fall onto the far side of the bridge. From what Katherine could see, more than half missed the span entirely and splashed harmlessly into the water, though one armored man did tumble off the side. The lead knight kept his shield braced high and took an arrow on the boss without slowing his horse.

Katherine lowered her sword, sick to her heart. "Indigo."

Sir Wulfric of Olingham reached the apex of the bridge, riding Indigo at an eager trot. Sir Richard Redhands flanked him, his heavy sword-of-war held aloft.

"They're trapped out there!" The shout rang from the shield wall. Katherine glanced behind her, and though she tried to wave them back, Horsa Blackcalf, Henry Twintree and half a dozen village men jumped out to charge up the span.

The two knights bore down upon Katherine, Edmund and Martin, leaping to a canter, and through her fear Katherine could not help but marvel at their skill. The bridge was barely wide enough to fit both horses side by side, and yet they came on at a flying charge.

"Set your spears, set 'em!" the village men shouted from behind Katherine. "Edmund, Katherine, come back to us!"

There was no time. Katherine crouched, watching the arc of Wulfric's sword at the same time that she marked the roll of Indigo's paces. There was but an instant to mourn it—by the time she finished the move she was about to make, either Indigo would be mortally wounded, or she would be dead herself.

Indigo raised up his head at the top of his stride. He lowered it, raised it—and held it there. He flared his nostrils, fixing one large brown eye on Katherine.

"This will grieve me." Wulfric brought his sword up high. "War is no place for a girl."

"Indigo." Katherine truly did not know if she could make herself do it. She knew the best move with a sword against a charging knight—duck and take the horse at the legs. A vision flashed through her thoughts: the little foal Indigo, approaching her as though a blast of trumpets had announced him. All his life, since then, she had believed that there was something that bound them together. Perhaps—she started her dodge, readying to block Wulfric's downswing and then cut at Indigo's tendons—perhaps such feelings amount to nothing, in the end.

Indigo let out a snort. He stiffened his front legs. His shoes struck a hail of sparks, and before Katherine could even think on what it meant, he had slid to a screeching halt in front of her and thrown Wulfric flying from the saddle, over her head to land with a clanging crash on the bridge.

"You stinking peasant!" The words turned out to be the last Richard Redhands would utter, for he failed to guess at Martin's strength, and in knocking the point of the spear aside thought he could charge through to the kill. Martin recovered with lightning speed, twisting the spear back to lever Richard out of his saddle and over, down off the bridge and into the Tamber.

The second rank of riders slowed their pace, for if they had not, they would have crashed headlong into the horses before them. "Wulfric. Wulfric!" Lord Wolland raised his sword, while trying to prevent his rearing stallion from throwing him. "Men, help me get to Wulfric! Help me reach my son!"

Indigo turned sideways, blocking the whole of the span. He cocked his head and threw Katherine a look.

Katherine needed no further invitation. She sprang up onto Indigo's back and wheeled him about to face Lord Wolland. "My lord, call off your attack, for if you do not, you and all who follow you will die."

"You groundling. You slatternly, ragged little milkmaid." The ready smile so common to Lord Wolland's features was at last exposed for what it was—a brittle lie. "Do you think a pack of peasants can stop me? I will have the north, all of it, and when I do, I will use no mercy on your village."

"Your deaths lie on the other side of this bridge." Katherine said it loud enough that the ranks of men behind Lord Wolland could hear her. "If we do not kill you, the Skeleth will."

"You were betrayed from the very start, my lord," said Edmund. "You seek conquest, but all the Skeleth want is destruction."

"Silence!" Lord Wolland rushed forward and clanged swords with Katherine, but could not get through her guard. Indigo reared and spooked Wolland's horse, driving him back and nearly toppling him off the bridge.

"My lord, you sought to make a deal with Lord Aelfric and then Lord Harold, promising them friendship until you had the one thing you needed of them." Katherine had to smile. "Surely you are wise enough to see that such a trick can be played on you, as well."

Lord Wolland spluttered. His answer did not make it out of his helm.

"What does she mean?" Lord Overstoke held up the ranks of knights behind him, turning his horse so that none could pass him by. "What does she mean by that, my lord?"

"You rode for days across those moors, my lords and knights," said Katherine. "You marched past ruin after ruin, through a land so bleak, it stung you to the heart. Did it not?"

The knights could not help but answer her with the truth on their faces.

"That is the legacy of the Skeleth." Katherine pointed with her sword, across the river at the crowd of creatures coming up the Longsettle road toward the square. "That is what they do to the lands of men. They are in the service of the Nether-grim—they will destroy you with as much callous speed as they use on us. They do not seek to make Lord Wolland king, they seek the end of us. All of us."

The knights hesitated, many of them staring with hard sus-picion across the river at the distant Skeleth, who by then had drawn close enough that their monstrous aspect could no lon-ger be concealed.

"Unhand me, knave!" Wulfric sprang to his feet just as Martin reached down for him. Though he had no sword, he could still fight like a cornered bear. Before Katherine could react, he had Edmund tumbling over the side of the bridge and had come to grips with Martin, wrestling back and forth with him across the span of the bridge.

"Wulfric!" Lord Wolland sprang forward, but Katherine met him sword on sword. There followed a tumult, a mad and desperate scramble over the slanted stone expanse of the bridge. Katherine could do nothing but block Lord Wolland's advance, hoping with all she had that her words would have some effect on the men who had heard them, and hoping just as much that Edmund would have the strength to swim to shore.

Lord Wolland's stabs and slashes grew desperate. "Curse you—curse you! Tand! Overstoke, help me!" His horse shied away from Indigo's furious kicks, denying him the chance to close the distance and come in for a killing strike.

"I did not come here to make war upon all men." Lord Overstoke backed his horse, forcing the knights behind him to follow suit. "I did not ride with you, my lord Wolland, to make a waste of all the north."

"She's lying!" Wolland raised his sword. "Curse you all, she's tricking us! We will have the north, all of it!"

"What I see across this river looks like a pack of misshapen beasts attacking men and women." Lord Overstoke turned his horse around. "I say back! Back, men, or come through me."

Lord Wolland's face writhed into a snarl. He pointed his sword at Katherine, his deep-set eyes flashing black. "You accursed wench!" He jammed his spurs into the flank of his horse, causing gouts of blood to pour down its legs. "I will see you dead!"

"Before you do, my lord, tell us how much you love your son."

Wolland stopped, his sword raised high. Katherine spared a glance behind her. Martin held Wulfric facedown on the bridge, hands up behind his back. Edmund had not fallen into the river after all—he hauled himself up from behind the nearest post and lay heaving for breath on the span.

"Father." Wulfric struggled, red in the face. "Forgive me, Father. I have shamed you."

"It is no great shame to lose a wrestling match to the son of Hubert Upfield, companion of Tristan himself." Katherine smiled back at Wolland. "Or don't you remember your histories?"

Wolland's face contorted, until it looked as though he might burst. "Give me back my son. Give him back, and I will go. You have my word of honor."

"Done." Katherine waved Edmund back down the bridge. "Over the shield wall, Edmund. Cousin, bring Wulfric forward."

Martin dragged Wulfric to his feet and walked him past Katherine and Indigo. Katherine nodded to Lord Wolland—he returned it.

"Come on, then, we're needed in the village." Katherine nudged Indigo around and turned away, but as she did, she saw Martin's face go white, staring past her at Lord Wolland. She swung back with her blade, knowing that she could not hope to block what was coming.

"I grant the curse of peace!"

There was a pinging sound. Katherine felt no pain, no blow. She turned to find Lord Wolland cowering, still grasping the hilt of his shattered sword. The sword in her own hand seemed strangely light. She looked at it and found it broken, the blade snapped off just past the crossguard.

Katherine stared at Edmund. An awful understanding dawned on her. The crash of the joust replayed itself in her memory, and then the sight of Harry lying bloodied in the dirt.

"I'm sorry. It was me." Edmund met her gaze, then looked away. "I didn't mean to hurt him. I'm sorry."

Katherine paced Indigo away from the column of knights. "Back to the square, hurry!" Martin needed no further cue. He seized Edmund and ran for the relative safety of the square.

Lord Wolland dropped his broken sword. He fixed a look of fulsome hatred on Katherine and raised his hand. "Men of Wolland! Forward on my—"

Wulfric caught his arm and wrenched it back down. "You will keep your word, Father, and dishonor yourself no further." He took the reins of Wolland's horse and turned him eastward, away from Moorvale.

Katherine gave Wulfric half a smile. "There is hope yet for the barony of Wolland." She wheeled Indigo around and galloped for home.

Chapter 38

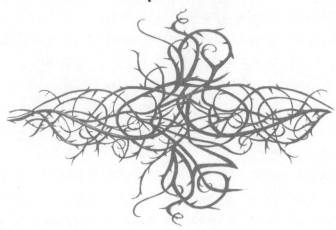

The horn sounded from the south—and resounded, two notes thrust against the very idea of harmony. The more they echoed, the worse they got.

"They're coming!" Missa Dyer clutched her head, staring openmouthed over the barricade that blocked the Longsettle road. "They're coming! Oh, they're horrible, they're—" What she said next got lost amongst the terror-stricken shouts of her neighbors.

Edmund knelt on the pedestal of the statue, crossing back and forth through all he had read. Perhaps, just perhaps, he could do it—save for one piece, the one thing that utterly baffled him. *The Skeleth are man and monster both. The man can be freed if he awakens to what the monster cannot know.* The Signs of the spell jumped and slipped in his mind, a whirl of colors, thoughts and meanings. Nothing he knew could make sense of it.

He picked up the brooch he had found on the breast of the queen and read the riddle inscribed around the rim. *I am the weapon that wounds the wielder. I am the defense that is no defense at all. I am triumph in surrender. I am that which, by being given, is gained.* He stared down at his notes, his guesses at the hole in the spell. What could it mean?

"Here they come!" Katherine leapt onto the barricade. "Hold together, everyone!"

Edmund looked up and wished that he had not. The Skeleth sprang forward in a mass. The faces of the men trapped in the ghastly rows of limbs looked worse than merely dead—more like men frozen at the moment of death, a final agony drawn out forever. The sight shook him so badly that he nearly forgot what he was doing.

"Set your poles!" Katherine shouted her command along the wagon barricade, facing south down the Longsettle road toward the approaching Skeleth. "When they come up, give them a hard shove back—but remember, don't stab them, don't kill!"

"Stupidest battle I've ever heard about." Hob Hollows took his place atop the wagons. "Got to win it without killing anybody."

Edmund touched his fingertips together and prepared to call on the Signs of Perception and Closing. The Skeleth passed by the common green in between the first of the cottages down the Longsettle road, by Nicky Bird's little shack and by Walter Bythorn's long, low byre. They moved in a rough clump, one hundred strong in the veiled gray of the hour before sunrise. Their glow seemed like a rot, the last glimmer of a dead firefly.

"Get ready—don't back away!" Harman Bale held his pole overhand, the butt of it poised to jam down over the barricade. "We've got to buy my son time!"

Edmund breathed in through his nose. The Sign of Perception rose in a spray of white and amber in his mind. He focused his thought around it until he felt no fear, felt nothing but the certainty of its power. He moved his body into the stance that matched its form.

"They have a wizard!" Jordan's shout came over a sudden chorus of cries. "Edmund, they have a wizard!"

Edmund snapped up his head. The earth of the road rumbled and split, shaking the ground under the barricade and throwing many of the defenders back from its frame into the square. Someone stood amongst the Skeleth, but was not one of them. She wore her long gray hair in a simple queue down her back, over a dark-hued dress trimmed in fur.

"Edmund Bale." It could be no one but Warbur Drake. She spoke from across the barricade, a quarter mile down a road filled with raging monsters and screaming villagers, and yet Edmund heard her as clearly as though she had stood at his side. "I pictured you somewhat taller. Go on, then. Try your little spell. It might present a salutary challenge."

"Edmund, Edmund, you've got to cast the spell!" Geoffrey grabbed his arm. "Edmund!"

Edmund ducked down, out of view of Warbur Drake and the Skeleth, and frantically studied his tablet. He jammed Sign to Sign, guessed at angle and chord, hoping to find some way to get it past a counterspell.

The first of the Skeleth to come over the barricade did so at a flying leap, knocking Missa Dyer spinning off the back of the wagon. Warbur Drake sounded her double horn once again, the notes rippling against each other brash and sour, and the rest of the creatures swarmed toward the square.

"Edmund!" Katherine swung her pole down hard, knocking a second Skeleth back before it could gain its footing on the spars and climb over. "We can't hold them off for long!"

Missa Dyer let out a cough as she hit the ground, and lay limp. The creature kept coming, dodging in between the row of villagers on the barricade, rushing out to leap on top of Missa with its sword held high.

"Get off my sister! Get off her!" Jordan Dyer jumped from his post on the barricade. He brought his pole crashing down on the man inside the twitching, reaching coils. The Skeleth staggered—blood poured from the man's nose, then his mouth. He dropped the sword in his hands, blinked, and seemed to wake up—then he collapsed and died—

—and the Skeleth took Jordan instead. It leapt and reached up the pole, and before Jordan could so much as scream, he was one of them, a dead-faced monster.

"Don't kill them!" Edmund shouted at the top of his lungs. "You must not kill or the Skeleth will take control of you!"

He took one more glance at his tablet and books—it was now or never. He brought himself into the Sign of Perception.

"YOU-WHO-CRAWL-BELOW, I NAME YOU, I GRIP YOU." It felt like it was working—an answering hum in his mind seem to vibrate with his voice. "I SHUT YOU FROM THE SUN, I—"

His mind snapped and reeled. The air around him hissed, then with a *whoomph* his breath seemed to flee from his mouth, and then from his lungs.

"AIR IS FICKLE, AIR BREAKS FAITH." The voice of the wizard woman crackled on the wind. "BREATHE OUT, AND FIND IT FLED. OUT AND NEVER IN AGAIN. THE AIR BE DRAWN FROM YOU, AND UNMADE. THE AIR BE UNMADE WITHIN YOU, AND SO BE YOU UNMADE."

Edmund pitched over, grabbing for the stone leg of the statue. He missed—he struck his head, seeing stars, white, then black.

"Edmund?" Geoffrey grabbed him by the collar. He ripped his shirt wide. "Edmund, why aren't you breathing?"

Edmund flailed out with both his arms. The pain was beyond bearing, beyond knowing. His lungs pushed out, out and out, sucked into themselves within his chest.

"AIR IS STEADY, AIR IS JUST." Another voice rose to a chant, higher in pitch than the first. "AIR ABHORS THE EMPTY, AIR FLOWS WHERE IT IS DRAWN. THE AIR RISE WITHIN YOU, MADE UPON THE TIDES OF BREATH. BE THE AIR REMADE WITHIN YOU. BREATHE. EDMUND, BREATHE."

With what felt like a pop, Edmund started breathing again. He rolled onto his side, bubbling spit from his mouth, and saw Ellí up on the barricade, her arms in the action of the Sign of Air and the Sign of Making. Between her and Warbur Drake thrummed a humming shift of wind, slices of it buffeting back and forth. The two spells canceled each other, brought the air back into balance—but the effort cost Ellí far more than her opponent. The last residues of the spell smacked Ellí left and then right, lances of air released unbalanced in the world.

"It's that wizard girl!" Geoffrey reached for an arrow. "Katherine, beside you on the barricade, it's her!"

"No!" Edmund grabbed his brother's leg. "No, she's helping us!"

Katherine stepped along the barricade toward the place where Ellí stood swaying from the cost of her spell. She turned to look at Edmund, sword in hand.

"Trust her," said Edmund. "Trust me."

Ellí staggered down. Katherine reached out to cushion her fall.

Edmund gave his brother a shove. "The old woman on the road, the one with silver hair, she's your target. Go on!"

Geoffrey raced up to the barricade. "There's a wizard down there—that one, the woman by the dye tubs. Bring her down!" He fumbled for his bow, then an arrow.

"I see her." Hob Hollows grabbed for his bow and took aim along with Geoffrey and a few others—but then, with a searing blast of words from Warbur Drake, every longbow on the barricade snapped at once. Ellí lay dazed, unable to counter the spell. In the confusion that followed, another Skeleth nearly made it over the wall, and it was only by the surprisingly quick action of Wat Cooper, knocking it back with a hard swing from his garden hoe, that it did not kill Ellí then and there.

Edmund gained his feet, though when he did, he stumbled, seeing gray. The bow-breaking spell rippled in the eye of his mind—its cost, the fact that as each bowshaft hit the ground, it took root and turned into a lovely, fragrant young yew tree from which dozens of new longbows could eventually be made, must not have bothered Warbur Drake very much. His neighbors, family and friends fought a desperate stand against the onrushing Skeleth. He could spare no thought for his own pain. He must not fail.

"Edmund, look out!" The warning came nearly too late. Edmund leapt aside from the swing of a long pole. He had forgotten all about Jordan Dyer, consumed within the luminescent coils of the Skeleth. Jordan was a young man in good health, and the Skeleth used all the strength he possessed. Edmund could do nothing but roll away from his books and off the pedestal of the statue.

Katherine jumped from the barricade, tackling Jordan to the ground—but almost at once, Jordan was up on his feet, seeming to care nothing for the bruises and cuts he had suffered. Katherine grabbed up the sword dropped by the first of the Skeleth and chopped his pole away, but that only brought him forward at a headlong run, without the slightest fear of her blade. Katherine backed and twisted, leading Jordan on. When at last he sprang, she leapt aside through the door of the mill, and he tumbled past and down the steep bank of the Tamber.

"MOTHER OF RIVERS, RISE AND FLOOD THE EARTH." Warbur Drake started up another chant. "SWELL FOR RAGE, BRING THE ENDING, DROWN ALL IN THE DEEPENING TIDE. RISE, MOTHER, RISE YOU SULLEN, RISE YOU HATEFUL, RISE—"

"SLEEP, MOTHER, SLEEP!" Ellí spoke over her, her words desperate, out of rhythm. "MOTHER OF RIVERS, COME TO

REST. THE EARTH EMBRACES YOU. BE STILL, COME TO REST."

Edmund heard the sound of crashing, rushing water from the east, as though a flash flood had started up without warning. The river rose, waves lapped up hard against the banks—then sank again, receding.

"Edmund, hurry!" Ellí trembled on her knees. She spat up a gut-full of water. "I can't hold her for long." Edmund watched her teetering from her imperfectly cast counterspell, the unbalanced Signs around her snapping and tearing at her in ways that ordinary folk could not perceive. Any doubt he had that she truly meant to make amends disappeared.

"Everyone, everyone from the bridge, to the barricade!" Katherine rushed back across the square, with Martin Upfield, Nicky Bird and a dozen more villagers. "We've got to give Edmund time." With speed born both of skill and desperation she charged at a Skeleth that had made it over the wall, a man who held a woodsman's axe and looked about to cleave Wat Cooper in half with it. She stabbed in, looking for a moment as though she meant to kill, but instead got her blade hooked under the axe-head and then jerked the weapon away, disarming the creature. Martin crashed into it a heartbeat later, bowling it backward through the dirt of the square.

Edmund gained his feet. "YOU-WHO-CRAWL-BELOW, I NAME YOU, I GRIP YOU." He made the Sign of Closing. "I SHUT YOU FROM THE SUN, I SHUT YOU FROM THE AIR, I CONFINE YOU."

One breath went by, and another.

"Oh, no." Edmund staggered. Terror rose to claim him. "No, no."

The Skeleth came on, clawing and grabbing at the barricade, as though he had not spoken a word.

"Hold them!" Katherine leapt up onto the wagons and bashed down at a Skeleth with the flat of her blade. "Edmund, hurry! Try again!"

Edmund looked out in horror from his perch atop the pedestal. The Skeleth bunched in between the inn and Jordan's workshop, clambering for holds, getting knocked down by villagers, but then getting up again without seeming to feel the pain of it. Warbur Drake looked much the worse for wear, swaying behind the Skeleth—but not half as bad as Ellí.

"Edmund." Ellí got to her feet. She met eyes with him. "I'm sorry for what I did. The true me, the real me, liked you very much."

Out of the corner of his eye, Edmund saw something move through the ruined land beyond the barricade, someone in armor galloping at full tilt up the Longsettle road. He held a sword in one hand. He rushed alone over the broken ground toward Warbur Drake, toward the Skeleth.

With a soreness in his heart, with fear in every part of him, Edmund felt once more for the Signs of Perception and Closing. He moved through the first part of the spell. Please, please work—

Nothing happened.

"My student, consider this your notice of failure." Warbur Drake's voice came as lightning. "I CALL ON DEATH—"

Ellí brought her arms in across her chest. "I AM THE HOPE OF LIFE—"

"—YOUR HEART IS STILL—"

Ellí broke; Edmund felt it happen. He felt her command of the Wheels give way, felt her terror, her despair.

Warbur Drake clenched her hand into a fist. She glowered at Ellí with focused hatred. "YOUR HEART IS STILL, IT IS STILL. STILL."

Ellí fell, pitching backward on the wagon. She looked at Edmund, then at nothing.

Warbur Drake sneered, though blood seeped from the corners of her mouth. "There were plans to make you one of us, Edmund Bale." She brought up her hands into the Sign of Unmaking. "I deem you not worth the trouble. And now—"

Whatever she had meant to say was never said. With one swift strike of sword, her head rolled to the street, a look of simple surprise frozen on her face. Her body pitched over on top of it.

Lord Harold of Elverain did not pause over his kill, for the Skeleth swarmed and surrounded him. He tried to press forward, but could make no headway against the lunging, slashing creatures on every side. He wheeled his horse and retreated along the road. "Katherine!" The rest of his words were lost amidst the clamor of the battle.

"Hold them, hold them back!" Katherine leapt and dodged from spar to spar, smacking and swinging. "Edmund, hurry!"

The Skeleth, free of the will that had guided them, seemed to rage with redoubled fury. First the poles were ripped from the hands of the villagers, then some folk were pulled off the barricades, and then, with a rending crack, the joins of the spars and beams began to give way. There was barely time for Katherine and the others to leap back from the wagons. She tried to regroup them for a stand in front of the statue—then the first of the Skeleth came through.

Katherine wavered, sword shaking in her hand. "Papa."

John Marshal leapt through the gap in the barricade. Poor Wat Cooper could not move fast enough—John's sword plunged into him before there was even time to shout a warning. Wat dropped, spouting blood, and John stepped over him, coming straight for the crowd of villagers surrounding Edmund, as though two dozen folk against him were even odds, or better.

"No! You will not have them!" Katherine leapt forward and met her father, blade on blade, but John had all the strength of his youth returned to him, with all his wits and experience, speed and skill—and none of Katherine's fear. She gave ground, inch by inch, back toward the villagers. The other Skeleth pushed through the barricade and swarmed out in a half circle, pushing in toward their shrinking, frightened knot.

"We've got to run!" Edmund's father threw down his pole. "We can't win this—run!"

Edmund would have said the same, but he knew that running would not save them. Instead he took up his father's pole and made ready to leap into the fray. He wondered whether it was worse to die by the hand of a Skeleth, or to kill and become one of their number. No matter—he would soon find out.

Katherine staggered and fell to the ground, then leapt up again, just before her father could finish her off. "You will not have them!" The Skeleth that had once been Jordan Dyer came up out of the river and joined the rest of its kind in a tightening noose around the villagers.

Edmund grabbed Geoffrey by the arm, then embraced him.

MATTHEW JOBIN

"You tried," said Geoffrey. Their mother found them and held them both.

All was lost.

Then a figure stepped out from the edge of the square—tall and rawbone thin. He placed himself in between John Marshal and Katherine.

Edmund stared, too stunned at first to understand what he saw, or how he could be seeing it.

"Put down your sword, Katherine." Tom bore no weapons. He stood before the creature that was John Marshal, without defense and without fear. The creature raised its blade to strike him down—and stopped, locked in his gaze.

"Katherine, look upon your father," said Tom. "Trust him. Put down your sword, look upon him, and tell him that you love him."

A file of peasant women leapt down from a collection of shaggy mules and draft horses and followed Tom into the open, passing out from the trail that led around the village green. They stood in a line before the Skeleth, each one seeking a particular creature. The Skeleth halted their advance and stood staring still.

"Papa." Katherine let her sword fall to the earth. She took Tom's hand and stood beside him, faced toward her father. "Papa, I love you. Wake up."

John Marshal lowered his sword. The feelers around him grasped and whipped, but inside them, a flicker of understanding crossed his face.

The words of the riddle came back as a blaze in Edmund's mind. He wanted to laugh. "Of course. It's so simple."

I am the weapon that wounds the wielder. Love sometimes injures he who loves. Edmund knew that quite well indeed, and yet he knew that love was worth it, all the same.

I am the defense that is no defense at all. The love that comes with defenses and conditions is not truly love.

I am triumph in surrender. Love cannot be taken. It can only be given.

I am that which, by being given, is gained. If you give love, you have not lost it. The one you love has received it, but you still have it within you.

"Are you Edmund Bale?"

Edmund turned. "What? Yes."

A heavy young woman in a rusty-red housedress and a tall old man carried an odd-looking metal box between them, carved with ancient glyphs and with a handle made from the joined hands of three female figures. They set it down in front of Edmund and raised the lid, showing it to be empty inside. "You'll want this."

The Skeleth advanced in silent ranks, their weapons dangling in their hands. The newcomers—peasants, all of them—flinched but did not break.

"Father," said a girl.

"Brother," said a woman.

Another: "Son."

"Master Marshal," said Tom.

"Papa." Katherine raised her hands. "Papa, it's me. I love you, Papa. I love you."

The faces of the men inside the monsters came alive. The glowing creatures ripped free of their bodies, they seethed and ran into a swirling, angry ball, and as they did so, the hateful character of the Skeleth grew plain for all to see. The Skeleth howled, all together, a coursing vomit of hate. They spat their spite for the world of the sun, the world above, the world where men held sway. Edmund knew just what the box was for.

The tall old man had blind, white eyes, but he still managed to tap Edmund's shoulder. "Now. Your spell."

"YOU-WHO-CRAWL-BELOW, I NAME YOU, I GRIP YOU." Edmund raised his hands in the Sign of Perception. "I SHUT YOU FROM THE SUN, I SHUT YOU FROM THE AIR, I CAST YOU DOWN INTO THE PRISON MADE FOR YOU." He made the Sign of Closing. "YOU ARE CONFINED."

The howl nearly popped his ears. Everyone, every living man, woman and child in the square fell to the ground at the thunderclap cry of the Skeleth. Edmund fell with them, but with a heavy effort dragged himself up again, and when the last squealing feeler fell into the box, he slammed the lid hard shut.

The sun rose over the moors.

Edmund lay heaving, draped over the top of the box. The metal felt warm beneath him for a moment—it shuddered, then fell still and cool. Voices swirled up around him, the wild and fulsome noise of mingled sorrow and relief. He felt the terrible cost of the spell take hold in the deepest part of himself. He paid it gladly.

"I am a monster." John Marshal wept slow and hard. "I saw it all. All of it. I am a monster."

"No, Papa." Katherine held him. "You're not."

The other strangers reached out for the men that once were

Skeleth, holding them through a storm of remorse, the horror of waking from a nightmare to find it had all been true. The big young woman in the rusty-red housedress only just stopped a man running out onto the bridge to leap off it and kill himself. She held him tight and let him wail until he fell into a trembling quiet.

Edmund let himself droop in rest over the top of the box. If anything else should threaten his village that day, he had nothing left with which to stop it. He fell in and out of a dream. He could feel no more joy—too much had been lost. He wished that someone would take thought to go up to Ellí and close her eyes, her beautiful brown eyes.

A shadow fell across him, a long, thin shadow from the new sun of the day. The shadow stooped, reached down, and took him up.

"I knew you could do it," said Tom. "I have always believed in you."

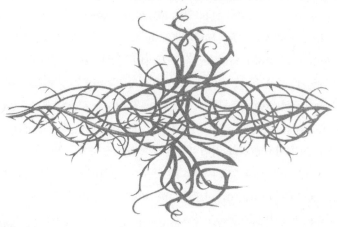

Chapter 39

The guardsman struck the butt of his spear to the ground. "The lord Tristan of Harthingdale!"

Tom placed his hand at Tristan's elbow. "By your leave, my lord."

They proceeded into the hall of Harold, Lord of Elverain. The fire in the great arched hearth blazed up tall, keeping the autumn draft outside. The tapestries on the walls displayed their ancient deeds of stern valor, but to Tom they seemed made for the moment, hung in celebration of bravery rewarded and hope renewed.

Harry stood from his great chair at the high table, surrounded by his knights, his councilors and clerks. He raised a hand bedecked with silver rings. "My lord Tristan, I welcome you to my home, to feast and council." His men gave way to allow Tristan's passage to the chair at his left hand.

Tom drew back the chair for Tristan. Harry's bright eyes fixed on him. "Ah, yes—Tom, is it? We in Elverain are very much in your debt." He shifted the heavy chain of office that he wore around his neck, and looked lost for what to say next. "Are you now my lord Tristan's servant? You may wait on him at the high table, if you wish."

Lord Tristan chuckled. "Young Tom here has other matters to which he must attend." He tapped Tom's arm. "Off you go."

Tom bowed before them both. "My lords." He stepped lightly down from the high table, slipping through ranks of attendants and servants busy setting up what looked to be the very finest of feasts. He found his place in the corner, far away from the crush, where a boy and a girl waited for him, his two dearest friends in all the world.

"So." Edmund shifted over to give Tom space on the bench. "Now what?"

"Now? Now we eat." Katherine handed Tom a trencher of bread stacked high with salt pork. Tom needed no further prompting.

"I mean what happens now?" Edmund passed Tom a bowl of lentil pottage. "What about Wolland, what about the other wizards Katherine heard about, the ones throwing kingdoms down far away? And what about . . ." He trailed away. The firelight threw shadows that seemed to tower over him, to menace him and him alone.

Worry clouded Katherine's eyes. She leaned across the table, gazing upon Edmund, but could not seem to find words. Then she glanced aside, up the hall at Harry—and then, back at Edmund. Her brows lowered, her gaze darkened, and she did not answer Tom's questioning look.

The guardsman struck his spear again. "Isembard of

Garafraxa, Earl of Quentara. Make way!" Then, after a pause: "And make way for Thulina Drake, Revered Elder of the *Ahidhan!*"

"Lookie here, Tom." Lord Isembard seemed to care little for proper form, for he veered aside from the center aisle of the hall as soon as he entered. "Got someone for you."

Jumble landed on Tom but an instant later, springing into his lap in a burst of thorough glee. After he was done snuffling Tom up and down, he started on Edmund, and after a few giggling dodges Edmund started to look like himself again.

"Dogs have much to teach us." The Elder leaned in at the table, braced upon her walking stick. "Ah—this can only be Katherine Marshal and Edmund Bale."

Edmund and Katherine stood up to bow and curtsy. The Elder waved them down again.

"Just as I pictured them." She smiled at Tom, touched his shoulder, then hobbled onward down the aisle.

"Lord Isembard—Revered One." Harry coughed from the high table. "Will you attend our feast? We have much to discuss."

"Coming, my lord Harold, coming, in our best time." Lord Isembard offered his arm to the Elder. "We are not all so young as you."

Edmund turned to watch them go. "This will be a bit thorny for Harry. He did kill her sister, after all."

The folk at the high table fell into council, while those below fell to feasting. A file of folk hailed Tom and his friends, passing in clumps and packs throughout the feast. Nicky Bird slapped Tom's side, Bella Cooper pressed his hands, and even

Edmund's father greeted him with solemn respect. Miles Twin-tree brought them a mug of sweet, spiced cider; Emma Russet brought them each a necklace she had made herself, each a different colored stone on a leather loop. Tom and Edmund took theirs at once, and each accepted a kiss on the cheek. Katherine already wore a necklace, one made of silver studded with real gems, but after a moment's hesitation she took it off and wore Emma's. Others came in their turns; Tom introduced his friends to Rahilda Redfield, then to her husband, Donston, and her sister Melicent. He found himself forced to tell the story of his retaking of Tristan's castle, with Melicent acting out the best parts in the aisles beside him. No one lingered long, though, not even Geoffrey. Everyone seemed to know that the three friends wanted themselves to themselves that night.

"Now, I think, we rest while we can." Tom poured out mugs of sweet cider for his friends, then for himself. "Now, I think, we feel sad for what we lost, but we don't let that make us forget the good that we have done."

Katherine thunked her mug against his. She looked to Edmund, who joined them after a moment's hesitation.

Edmund drank deeply. "If that was what we could do when we're apart, just think of what we can do when we're all together."

Tom felt the hackles on the back of his neck stand up. He turned around and saw his old master glaring at him from across the hall. Athelstan pointed at Tom and clenched his fist.

Katherine's eyes flashed dark. She stood up and looked ready to go right across the hall at Athelstan, but Tom held her back.

"Let it be," he said. "Let it be, for now."

Edmund flicked a disdainful glance across at Athelstan, then smirked at Tom. "You're friends with some important folk now. Let's see old Athelstan go up against Tristan, Isembard and the Elder all together."

"Never mind them," said Tom. "Let's see him try to get past Rahilda."

Lord Tristan's voice rose above the clamor in the hall. "With a glad heart will I aid you." He turned to Harry. "What wisdom I have, and what power remains to me, is yours in friendship."

Isembard clapped his hands. "Then so be it. We lords of north and west will stick as one!"

Tom lost what was said next at the high table amidst the cheers. "That sounds good."

"It is good," said Katherine. "If Harry works with Tristan, they'll have no trouble securing everything west of the Tamber until spring."

Edmund seemed to have gotten back his appetite. He plucked up the same piece of mutton as Tom, so they ripped it in half between them.

"I can't imagine Wolland staying long on the moors," said Katherine. "There's been no more sign of his army—they're likely on the way home already. All we have to do is watch the river, rebuild our strength, and wait out the winter. Come spring, I bet the king will march north, and woe to Wolland then."

There came another cheer—Nicky and Horsa started up on flute and fiddle, and even Lady Isabeau, seated at her son's side, seemed to warm at the sound of it.

"Child." John Marshal stopped at their table. "Are you enjoying the feast?"

Katherine turned at once, worry in her eyes again. "Are you, Papa?"

"I've just been in the stables." John's body bore no wounds, yet to Tom he still looked injured. "I think Indigo was pleased to see me, though it is always hard to tell with that horse." Jumble was happy to see him, though—that was not hard to tell at all.

John rubbed Jumble under the chin. "You took good care of Tom, did you not? Good lad." Jumble barked and licked his nose.

Edmund fidgeted, bit his lip, then spoke. "Master Marshal, I've been looking through everything I can find about the Skeleth, and you must know that there was nothing you could have done, nothing that—"

John held up a hand. "Let us speak of that another day." He looked at each of them in turn. "Again I have the happy duty to tell you, all three, how well you have done, how proud you have made me. Katherine—Tom, Edmund, look at me. You saved the north."

Tom had not thought of it like that. From the looks on the faces of his friends, neither had they.

"Other folk helped, but it was you three," said John. "Three children thwarted the plots of lord and wizard, of the Nethergrim itself—again. Let our enemies chew on that for a while."

Katherine reached across the table. She took Tom's hand, then Edmund's.

"Now, I'll leave you three to your feast. I have business with an old friend." John Marshal strode up through the aisles, crossed behind the high table and tapped Lord Tristan on the arm.

Evening slipped inside and found itself a welcome guest. The glow of fire and food melded and made joy. Tom looked from Edmund to Katherine. Whatever worried them, whatever they feared, John Marshal's words would not let them fall to fretting.

The guardsman's spear banged the floor again.

"Now, who can that be?" Harry looked up from a shared joke with Tristan.

"I cannot think who it might be, my lord." Lord Isembard drained his goblet. "All the good and loyal lords of the north are already here!"

Harry waved a hand, still laughing. "We want no more lords! Away, away!"

"Er, it is not a lord, saving your pardon." The guardsman bowed his way into the hall. A man followed him in, a man who looked thoroughly confused at the merriment he saw around him. He passed behind Tom's back—he smelled of horse sweat and did not look as though he had slept in some time. He wore warm clothes made for traveling, and upon his breast there shone a brooch—a hunting hound trampling the antler of a stag.

Edmund leaned across the table. "Who's that?"

"King's messenger," said Katherine. "He looks like he's been riding hard."

Harry stood, and called for silence. He gestured to the messenger. "You are welcome here. What news do you bring?"

The messenger stopped in the middle of the hall. He looked about him at the feast, frozen in suspense, waiting on his word. Tom caught a flicker of remorse on his face.

"Come, then," said Harry. "Out with it."

"My lord." The messenger turned back to the high table. He drew a breath, then coughed, then spoke:

"The king is dead."